Browse the critics' glowing praise for
USA Today **bestselling author**
Rhonda Pollero and her delightfully addictive
Finley Anderson Tanner novels

"Witty, upbeat, all-around entertaining."
—*New York Times* bestselling author Janet Evanovich

"A fun, fascinating journey you won't want to miss."
—*New York Times* bestselling author Nora Roberts

"Hilarious . . . will make readers eager for an encore."
—*Kirkus Reviews* (starred review)

"Rhonda Pollero's humor and compelling mystery will keep you turning pages."
—*New York Times* bestselling author Tess Gerritsen

"Stylishly entertaining."   —*Booklist*

FAT
Chance

Rhonda Pollero

POCKET BOOKS

New York London Toronto Sydney

Pocket Books
A Division of Simon & Schuster, Inc.
1230 Avenue of the Americas
New York, NY 10020

This book is a work of fiction. Names, characters, places, and incidents either are products of the author's imagination or are used fictitiously. Any resemblance to actual events or locales or persons, living or dead, is entirely coincidental.

This Pocket Books paperback edition December 2009

POCKET and colophon are registered trademarks of Simon & Schuster, Inc.

For information about special discounts for bulk purchases, please contact Simon & Schuster Special Sales at
1-800-456-6798 or business@simonandschuster.com.

The Simon & Schuster Speakers Bureau can bring authors to your live event. For more information or to book an event, contact the Simon & Schuster Speakers Bureau at
1-866-248-3049 or visit our website at www.simonspeakers.com.

Designed by Jamie Kerner
Cover design by Janet Perr
Photograph of glasses and woman: JupiterImages; house: Getty Images

Manufactured in the United States of America

10   9   8   7   6   5   4   3   2   1

ISBN: 978-1-4391-6028-2
ISBN: 978-1-4391-0098-1 (ebook)

To Dr. Louis Raso and Dr. David Fischman,
Thanks for keeping me glued together—
literally.

FAT
Chance

*The difference between the wrath of God and
the wrath of your mother is that eventually,
God forgives you.*

one

THE ONLY SMELL BETTER than Lulu Guinness perfume is eau d' new car. I breathed in a long, slow, steady stream of the leathery scent as I steered my brand-new BMW 330Ci off the Brauman Motorcars lot. *My* was a bit of an exaggeration. Technically, the lovely new car belonged to BMW Leasing Corporation, but that was a minor detail. One I was happy to ignore as I weaved through the late morning traffic on Okeechobee Boulevard.

The timing was perfect. The cherry red car was exactly what I needed to lift my spirits. I was in a funk after the whole Patrick breakup disaster, so when the dealer called me yesterday, I didn't waste any time arranging to take next-day delivery.

Like everything in life—a little bad came with the good. Though my previous car was totaled through no fault on my part, I still had to fork over nearly fifteen hundred of my own dollars on the new lease. Luckily,

I had cash in the bank. Less than a week ago, I deposited a big check. But not before I scanned it, saved it, and turned the image into a self-congratulatory screen saver on my home and office computers. Hey—it's not like the law firm of Dane, Lieberman, and Zarnowski cuts a check payable to me in that amount every day. No, this was a freak occurrence. A signing bonus of sorts. Or, as I like to think of it, twelve thousand ways for my boss to announce to the world that Finley Anderson Tanner is a valuable asset to the Palm Beach legal community.

The check represented the negotiated dollar amount it had cost Vain Victor Dane, Esquire and Asshole Extraordinaire, to make amends for firing me. My shoulder muscles pinched at the mere thought of my employment lord and master. Don't get me wrong, I like my job at Dane, Lieberman, and Zarnowski. Okay, so *like* might be a bit strong. As an estates and trusts paralegal, I get to do a variety of different things, which makes it mildly interesting. What makes it a great deal more enjoyable is that I have the autonomy to come and go almost as I please.

I "please" a lot.

The very nature of my job requires me to be out of the office often. Is it a crime if I happen to take the occasional detour into Nordy's on the way back? No. The real crime would be missing out on a sale for the sole reason that I was chained to my desk. It's a nice desk, by the way. At least it is now. In the last year, I've done pretty well in the struggle up the corporate ladder department. Well, if you overlook the arrested, jailed, hospitalized, almost killed, and fired—*twice*—bumps in my career path. None of those things was my fault. *Mostly* they weren't my fault. Okay. *Some* of them weren't my fault.

Turns out, I have a knack for ferreting out murderers. Okay, so *knack* might be a bit of an overstatement; it's more along the lines of . . . "there but for the grace of God I didn't end up dead." But you get the gist.

Multitasking, I eased onto I-95 north while simultaneously skipping through the newest playlist I'd created for my iPod. It *was* my iPod too, as of the fifteenth of the month, when I made the last payment. So budgeting isn't my strength, but I have found ways to cut corners. Secret ways. Hopefully they'll remain secret. Not even my closest friends know that my precarious financial situation has forced me into the underground world of outlet shopping. My wardrobe is a testament to factory damage and slightly irregular.

I tensed as I steered onto Blue Heron Boulevard in record time. I was on my way to Iron Horse Country Club. It's a small, private club nestled behind one of the hundreds of manicured entrances and manned security gates dotting Palm Beach County. Most people are *invited* to lunch with their mothers. Not me; I get *summoned*. On elegant stationery, no less. I could easily picture my mother in her penthouse, seated at her expensive French desk, gold pen in her perfectly manicured hand.

I'd dressed carefully for my command performance. I'd chosen a vintage suit in mint green that

I'd found at a church thrift store. Not any church sale, mind you, but the semiannual sale at Bethesda-by-the-Sea, the church in Palm Beach where the rich and famous worshipped. The pale color accentuated the fleck of green in my otherwise blue eyes and my pay-for-it-later tan. I'd added a white BCBG cami with mint trim. I'd slipped on a pair of white Steve Madden wedges I'd picked up at a cool 70 percent off, thanks to a small smudge on the patent leather on the side of the left shoe. Since this was lunch at a country club with my mother, I not only had to wear green—the color she prefers—but I also had to do the required hair thing. I was prepared. I had a mother-of-pearl clip at the ready.

My mother's membership at Iron Horse was part of the spoils from one of her divorces. Clicking my fingernail against the walnut-grained steering wheel, I tried to recall which husband had been the avid golfer. As I drove under a canopy of banyan branches, I inhaled the crisp, summery scent of freshly mowed grass filtering in through the vents. For some reason, the homey smell reminded me of the only man my mother had married for true love. Thinking about Jonathan Tanner caused my heart to twist inside my chest. He died almost fifteen years ago and I still miss him. I was two when he adopted me, and I couldn't have asked for a better father. I loved him and he loved me. Which probably explains why I don't have daddy issues.

Amazing considering I was a teenager when I found out the truth. Well, the half-truth. My mother had always told me that Finley and Anderson were family names. That part was true. What she'd neglected to explain was that they were the family names of the two men she'd been sleeping with when she'd gotten pregnant with me. As far as I know, neither man ever knew about me. And I have no burning desire to go on some sperm donator search.

I considered it once. I was online, killing time before swooping in on a last-minute eBay auction for some links for my build-it-from-scratch Rolex project, when a pop-up ad flashed, promising to find anyone anywhere in twenty-four hours or less. I thought about it for a nanosecond, then decided I truly didn't want to know.

I did, however, want those gold links, but I was outbid at the very end of the auction by someone with the screen name JulesJewels.

I pulled up in the horseshoe-shaped drive in front of the massive, pillared building. I grabbed my purse and my hair clip, then reluctantly handed my keys to the valet, a kid barely old enough to drive. Then I sprinted up the front steps.

Luckily for me, The Clubhouse was a completely inappropriate name for the large, lavish, two-story building. The first floor included a gym, a spa, locker rooms, steam rooms, a lap pool, showers, and twenty-four-hour a day attendants. Upstairs, there was a long polished bar and two dining rooms.

Thankfully, the ladies' room was on the way to the restaurant, giving me an opportunity to slip in and twist my hair into a subdued style that would not inspire my mother's ire. I paid a lot of money to highlight my blond hair. It seemed like a waste to hide it, but the alternative made me decide to be wasteful.

With my hair secured, I smiled briefly at the mute attendant standing in the corner. It seemed to startle her, possibly because the snobbish members treated her as if she were invisible.

My palms began to sweat as I walked on the plush carpet, past the sparsely populated bar toward the restaurant. The seven or eight men at the bar were dressed in the horrid ensembles golfers tended to fancy. Guess no one told them that no man looked good in plaid pants and an Easter-egg-colored shirt.

As I approached the maitre d' of the less formal dining room where lunch was served, I could smell the sumptuous scents of various foods. My stomach went from clenched to growling in record time. The dining room was huge, with floor-to-ceiling windows overlooking the golf course. The table settings, like the window treatments, reinforced the Iron Horse train theme. The maitre d' knew me on sight and simply said, "Welcome back, Miss Tanner. Please follow me."

My mother looked up instantly and shot me a disapproving glance. I took my seat, then a waiter appeared and flipped my napkin onto my lap.

I took the menu he handed to me, and he offered to give me a minute. "You look lovely, Mother. Is that a new dress?" I try, I really do. But cracking through the cement of my mother's emotions is like adding another face to Mount Rushmore using nothing but a dull spoon.

Thanks to good genes, regular Restylane, and minor plastic surgery, my mother was a fifty-year-old with the face of a thirty-five-year-old. To her credit, she worked out with a personal trainer when she was in town, maintaining her size 2 body. Since the average age of the other people in the dining room was somewhere between sixty and ninety, she stood out from the crowd.

She would have anyway. My mother was a striking brunette who carried herself like the budding star she'd once been. All that training hadn't gone to waste. Her regal persona had easily evolved from opera diva to country club diva. Other than eye color, my mother and I didn't share much in the looks department. Or the temperament department. Or, well, *any* department.

"You're late. As usual," she said. "I don't know why I bother to make the effort to always arrive on time when you're invariably late, Finley."

In less than five seconds, she'd fired the first shot. This did not bode well for me. "I don't know either," I replied. I wasn't being facetious. I had no idea why she didn't just show up fifteen minutes later than whatever time she told me. We'd arrive at sort of the same time, and everyone would be happy.

The hovering waiter returned at the subtle wave of my mother's hand. "What are the specials?" she demanded.

The guy rattled off the specials. Which, by the way, were always the same on Thursdays. And why she asked I have no idea. Regardless of the specials, she always ordered the same thing.

"You had me at deep fried." I smiled at the waiter and added, "I'll have the tuna egg roll, then coconut shrimp, extra mango relish, with french fries, please."

My mother snapped her menu closed, glaring at me as she ordered a small chef salad, no egg, no cheese, no ham, no dressing.

No fun.

"Finley," she whispered in that disapproving tone she considered reasonable just as soon as the waiter was out of earshot. "Keep eating like that and you'll be as big as a house. How much weight have you put on in the last two months? Ten? Fifteen pounds?"

"Four," I said, struggling not to grit my teeth. "Ninety-six more and I'll be eligible for gastric bypass."

Arching one perfectly shaped brow disapprovingly, my mother shifted against the back of the richly upholstered chair. Discreetly, she glanced around the dining room, husband-seeking radar on full alert.

Not for me, of course. In my mother's eyes, I was a lost cause, twenty-nine going on pointless. Conversely, she was on the prowl for husband number six. She'd been seeing a doctor for a couple of months, but she liked to hedge her bets.

"Don't be flippant, Finley. Your sister's wedding is just weeks away, and how will it look if you eat yourself out of your maid-of-honor dress?"

"I'm a size six, Mom. Hardly Jabba the Hut."

"Lisa is a size *two*. I'm constantly puzzled as to why a woman whose prospects of marriage are diminishing *rapidly* wouldn't make every effort to look her best. To be honest, Finley, you've let yourself go. And what's this I hear about you not bringing Patrick? You can't attend the wedding without an escort. What will the St. Johns think of us? What exactly did you do to drive him away?"

As usual when I'm with my mother, I have fascinating and quick internal comebacks. But I'm not dumb enough to say them aloud or tell my mother the real reason Patrick and I split. The facts wouldn't matter. Not with my mother. She'd simply accuse me of being at fault, commitment-phobic, irresponsible—take your pick—then send Patrick some sort of fruit basket to apologize for my poor behavior.

Absently, I flipped the butter knife back and forth against the crisp linen tablecloth. "We decided to see other people." Partially true.

When Cassidy Presley Tanner Halpern Rossi Browning Johnstone, former rising star of the Metropolitan Opera, got curious, she was like the proverbial dog with a bone. "That's ridiculous. The only time people say that is when they already have another person to see. Is that it? Did you cheat on Patrick?" She put her hand on her throat. "Oh, Finley, tell me you didn't cheat on him with that rental cop."

That "rental cop" was Liam McGarrity. Tall, dark, yummy, still-involved-with-his-ex-wife Liam

McGarrity. "He's a private detective, Mom. Not some mall security guard."

"He might as well be," she argued. "You've gotten into quite a few mishaps thanks to that man."

I really wanted to stick a fork in my eye. Thank God our lunch was arriving and I could eat instead of resorting to self-mutilation. "I solved two murder cases," I reminded her, quite proud of myself, even if she wasn't.

"Which you have no business doing," she said as she picked up her fork. "If you really wanted to do some good, you'd have gone on to law school and worked within the system. Look at your sister. You don't see Lisa getting mixed up with uneducated riffraff."

I love my sister. I really do. If only she weighed three hundred pounds, screwed up once in a while, and sat around watching TV all day while eating bon-bons. Then I'd love her even more. I couldn't compete with my sister on any level. I stopped trying when I was five. "She's a pediatric oncologist, Mom. I don't think there's a lot of riffraff in peds intensive care."

"Don't take that tone with me," she warned. "Not when I'm about to do you a generous favor."

My definition of a favor and my mother's definition of a favor were completely different animals. In fact, I had no doubt that if asked, my mother would claim that commenting on my weight was an amazing act of kindness. As were her constant taunts about my failure to measure up in comparison to my sister. Lisa is my younger sister. She is faultless to a fault—if that's even possible. She's a successful doctor who's about to marry into one of Atlanta's wealthiest families. Hell, by the time she's thirty, Lisa will have discovered a cure for cancer and donated her findings for the betterment of all mankind. Me? My life has been reduced to surfing eBay and watching *What Not to Wear* marathons.

Being an estates and trusts paralegal serves its purpose. I make enough money to pay rent, the minimum balances on my credit cards, and make my car payments. I got fired while investigating the Paolo Martinez murder, but since my involvement brought some heavy-hitting clients to the firm, Vain Victor Dane had no choice but to rehire me. I didn't go cheap, either. I negotiated a twelve-thousand-dollar bonus for myself, and, with luck, my credit application at Barton's jewelers will be approved and I'll soon be the proud owner of a ladies' pink oyster face Datejust Rolex. The watch retails for thirteen-eight, so I'll only need a two-thousand in-store credit to swing it. I'll miss the hunt for parts on eBay, but I'll have the watch of my dreams. Guess once I have it I'll have to find another hobby.

"Finley!"

"Sorry," I muttered, leaning back so the server could put my second course in front of me. "Thank you." I swallowed only one bite of my fried shrimp when I noticed my mother's fork still hovering above her untouched salad. I did a little mental calculation: napkin in lap—check. Fork in correct hand—check. Feet crossed at the ankles—check. I met her gaze. "Is something the matter?"

"Aren't you going to ask me why I invited you to lunch on a Thursday?"

If my memory served me correctly, it wasn't exactly an invitation. But I knew nothing would be gained by pointing that out. "Sure. Why did you need to see me today?"

Reaching into the large Chanel tote tucked next to her chair, my mother produced a neatly folded, multipage document with a pale blue cover. Dramatically, she laid it on the table, then slowly slid it in my direction with the tips of two manicured fingers.

Resting my fork on the edge of my plate, I took the papers, unfolded them, and felt my breath catch in my chest as I read the caption: CONTRACT FOR PURCHASE. Scanning the first paragraph, I blinked twice, then read the words again. "You're selling me a house?"

"Yes. It's a property Jonathan and I owned. It was his wish that you have it."

"He died fifteen years ago," I said. If it was Jonathan's wish for me to have it, I asked myself, still a little stunned, why was my mother making me *buy* it?

"Yes, and I have been waiting for you to show some responsibility before giving the property to you."

"This isn't a gift," I said as I read the terms. "You're *selling* it to me."

"People rarely appreciate what they get for free. I'm transferring the house to you at well below the appraised value," she pointed out. "The lot alone is worth a fortune. I'm selling it to you for twenty-five thousand."

My mother wasn't given to random acts of kindness. There had to be a catch. "I don't have twenty-five thousand dollars."

"How much do you have?"

In the bank or in outstanding loans? Admitting to the former would be less painful. "I've got twe—ten thousand dollars saved." Close enough to true. I'd gotten my bonus check on Monday, and other than the car lease, I hadn't spent a penny of it in four days. That was saving. Kinda.

"You can give me that as a down payment, and I'll hold a mortgage for the other fifteen."

"Why?"

"Why what?" she asked as she elegantly lifted a fork full of lettuce to her lips.

"If you've had this property for years, why sell it to me now, and why offer to let me make payments for the outstanding fifteen thousand?"

My mother's face pinched with impatience. Well, the parts that hadn't been Botoxed pinched. "Most homeowners carry a mortgage, Finley. It's far better than paying rent. In the end, you will have something to show for all those monthly payments."

The tiny hairs on the back of my neck prickled as I read the address. "The house is on Palm Beach. Nothing there costs twenty-five thousand dollars."

"The house might need a little work. There is some hurricane damage."

I looked up and met her gaze. "How much hurricane damage?"

"I'm hardly a contractor, Finley."

13

"If I give you all my cash, how am I supposed to fix hurricane damage? Or pay the taxes? Or the insurance?"

"If you don't want it . . ." Her voice trailed off.

"Of course I want it. I'm just a little confused. What's the catch?"

She shrugged slightly. "No catch. Well, except for paragraph eleven."

Moistening my fingertip, I quickly turned to that section. "If I ever want to sell the property I can only sell it back to *you* for the original purchase price?"

"It has sentimental value. It was the first piece of property Jonathan bought when he came to Florida. Oh," she added, smoothing a lock of chestnut-colored hair off her chemically wrinkle-free forehead. "And paragraph twelve."

Reading further, I discovered that in the event I sold the house back to my mother, I'd forfeit any money paid to her, as well as a one-time assessment of 5 percent of the appraised value of the home. "So, worst-case scenario, if I decided I didn't want the house, I'd lose my ten-thousand-dollar deposit plus whatever mortgage payments I made plus another however much for the assessment?"

She shook her head. "Conservatively, we'd be talking about an additional fifty to one hundred thousand. But that would only be an issue if you reneged on the deal prior to paying off the purchase price or—"

"Or what?"

"Or if I die first. Obviously, the house would be

yours free and clear in the event of my death. That's in paragraph seventeen."

This is the point in the conversation when I'm supposed to cry, *"No, Mom, don't die!"* but the best I could muster was a slight tilt of my head. Thank God this conversation wasn't being taped. No court in the land would acquit me if she suddenly croaked. I didn't want her to die, but I did want to know what was behind this unexpected show of generosity. "I'll have one of the attorneys look at this when—"

"I'm afraid I need your decision now."

I blinked. "Right now? Why?"

"The house has been vacant for about six months."

"Vacant? Who was living there?"

"Do you remember Melinda Redmond?"

"Jonathan's assistant?"

My mother nodded. "She rented the house after she had her epiphany."

"What epiphany?"

"Fifteen years ago Melinda decided to get out of advertising and devote herself to children. Can you imagine?"

Yes, Mom. Some people actually like their children and don't see them as disappointing burdens. "That's quite a change."

Sighing heavily, she said, "Melinda paid more attention to those children than she did to caring for the home. I had no choice but to ask her to leave."

"You evicted a foster mother?"

She nodded. "Yes. Which has created this opportunity for you, Finley. And a responsibility. Given the fact that you just tossed aside your future with Patrick, I need you to demonstrate that you're capable of taking on responsibility. Of making important decisions."

"This is an important decision," I agreed, wishing I'd ordered something a lot stronger than iced tea. "One I shouldn't jump into without thinking about it."

"What is there to think about?" she countered. "I'm offering to sell you a home in a prime location on the beach at a fraction of its fair market value. I've already spoken to your bank, and they'll give you a home equity loan for any repairs with the house as collateral. In the event you fail to meet your obligations, I've agreed to guarantee the loan. All you have to do is sign some papers at the bank. I've arranged for a line of credit up to two hundred thousand dollars. I will cover the taxes and insurance until you pay off the fifteen thousand dollars you owe me. That payment is set at two hundred fifty dollars per month. Since I have a long-standing relationship with the bank, if you borrow the maximum amount I've guaranteed, you're looking at a combined monthly payment of about seventeen hundred. How much is your rent?"

"Fifteen hundred."

"So," she said smugly. "For two hundred dollars a month, you're actually working toward owning a sizeable asset."

I felt a vine-covered pit opening beneath my feet. I smelled my own fear. My mother never gave anything without weighing her options. If it was good for my mother, it was bad for me. I knew that. It was a given.

But, damn. The offer sounded so tempting. I could find two hundred extra dollars a month. Right?

A homeowner. A house right on the beach. The payments sounded doable. The sell-back terms sucked, but if I took her up on her offer, I wouldn't *want* to sell the house back to her.

Run away, I told myself. "I-I know."

"I'm your mother, Finley. Are you insinuating you can't or won't trust me?"

Yes. "No, of course not. But I'd like to have Becky take a look at the contract." Becky was a contracts attorney at Dane, Lieberman, and Zarnowski and one of my best friends.

"I want this resolved now, Finley. Accept my generous offer, or don't. Make up your *own* mind."

Oh, boy. "Okay. Where do I sign?" Becky didn't trust my mother any more than I did. And she wasn't going to be happy that I'd contractually bound myself to buying a house without her going over the contract with a lice comb first.

"Then let's get Julianna over here." My mother raised her hand in the direction of the maitre d'.

"Who's Julianna?"

"She works here at the club. She's a notary. Philippe can be a witness."

I heard the sound of a train barreling over me, and my mind flashed an image of my body flattened on imaginary tracks. I'd come to Iron Horse Country Club for a simple lunch, and in under an hour, I was signing a contract and writing a check.

An hour later, still dazed, I walked into the lobby

of Dane, Lieberman, and Zarnowski. Margaret Ford was planted behind the horseshoe-shaped mahogany reception desk, Bluetooth tucked behind her right ear. She glanced over at me, then made a production out of checking her watch. Yeah, yeah, like I needed her snarky expression to tell me I was twenty-seven minutes late getting back from lunch.

"Messages?" I asked.

"No."

I turned and headed for the elevator. Other than arranging for a site appraisal on the Melanie Dryer estate, my afternoon was pretty light. By the time I reached my office on the second floor, I was dying to get a look at the house I'd just bought.

The faint scent of lavender from a plug-in air freshener mingled with the strong aroma of coffee. After dropping my purse in a desk drawer, I filled my mug with the dregs from the carafe and navigated my way to a satellite photograph of Chilian Avenue. I was still having a hard time wrapping my brain around the idea that I was the owner of a home on Palm Beach.

My fingernail tapped impatiently on the arrow key, annoyed that the satellite photo was so fuzzy. All I could really make out was a basic outline. The roof of my house was approximately one-tenth the size of the garage on the neighboring property to the left. And smaller than the pool of the house to the right.

So what. It was right on the beach, and it was mine. Well, mostly mine.

As much as I wanted to race out and see the house, I decided it should be a celebration. And who better to share my newfound land-baron status with than my nearest and dearest? I emailed Becky, Liv, and Jane, sure that if I called them I'd spill my guts and spoil the surprise. In less than five minutes, I had confirmations from all three.

I called the appraiser, then devoted my attention to surfing for decorating ideas. My friend and neighbor, Sam Carter, is an interior designer, and he would probably cut off my fingers if he knew I was picking colors and furnishings unsupervised. His disdain wouldn't be wholly unwarranted. The décor in my apartment lingers somewhere between yard sale and college dorm. Sam was at some home show in Vegas, but I was sure that once he saw the house, he'd have strong opinions.

Hell, I wanted to see the house. Glancing at my Kuber watch, I pressed my lips together. It was only a few minutes after three. Drumming my fingers on my desk, I glanced at my open case files, deciding which one I could use to my best advantage. There was no way I could get past surly Margaret and her file room flunkies without a viable excuse.

Margaret's been stationed at that desk for twenty-five years—probably one of the things that's made her so bitter. That and she resents the fact that I make more money than she does. In Margaretville, lawyers should earn the big bucks and the rest of us should be paid according to seniority. Coincidentally, that would make her the highest paid non-attorney member of the staff. But I was the one with the degree. And I was the one who'd just brought five new clients to the firm. As far as I was concerned, she could go suck her Bluetooth.

With a draft of the Jessup estate accounting tucked into the pink alligator leather tote I bought as a consolation gift after my last confrontation with Patrick, I scooted my chair back, clicking the button on the wireless mouse to hibernate my computer, and made a stealthy exit.

"THIS IS *YOURS*, FINLEY?"

It was hard to hear Becky Jameson's voice over the excited thudding of my heart in my ears as I closed the car door. The magnitude of this moment made it hard for me to remember how to breathe normally.

The idea that I was a homeowner before I hit the big three-o qualified as a major milestone. And not just any home. My new abode was a darling cottage on the north end of Palm Beach. *The* Palm Beach.

"Yep," I said as I hoisted my tote and purse higher on my shoulder.

Becky lingered by the car, whistling softly as she gave the exterior a once-over. "What's the catch?"

I believe those were my exact words.

Becky's tone echoed the uneasiness knotted in my stomach. We'd been friends since college, so like me, she was stunned when I told her that my mother had sold me the house for a fraction of its value. "The contract she had me sign was really straightforward," I insisted. I had the five-page document tucked inside my tote.

I focused, transfixed, on the tidy turquoise cottage with a small front porch and coral accents that, as of a few hours ago, was my new address. Like Weezie Jefferson, I'd moved on up. The Palm Beach address was a huge step up from my apartment in West Palm. Under normal circumstances, it was also far beyond my meager means.

Becky slipped her sunglasses down on the bridge of her perfect nose and gave me one of those "I'll bet" looks. She was a little miffed that I'd made my first real estate transaction without so much as calling her for advice.

Which I would have done if my mother hadn't put a ticking clock on the transaction.

"Are we going in?" Becky asked as she moved around the front of her car toward the house.

"We have to wait for Liv and Jane."

Becky lifted her auburn hair off her neck and twisted it into a messy knot. "Great. You get a house and I get heatstroke."

"Let's walk around back," I suggested.

The small yard circling the building was landscaped, and the grass was freshly mowed. A small, uneven stone pathway led around the side of the single-story home. Someone had recently planted white flowers in the flowerbeds that rimmed the house. Hopefully that someone would keep it up, since I have the blackest thumb in all of south Florida. I didn't make eye contact with the plants, afraid they'd pick up on my botanical death ray and die on the spot.

Other than a cement slab, the backyard was nothing more than a glorious slope of sand leading straight into the Atlantic Ocean. The surf lapped softly on the deserted shoreline, sending a cooling, salty breeze to greet us. I slipped off my shoes and felt the cool, fine-grained sand beneath my feet. Besides a few clumps of sea grass, nothing impeded my glorious view. On either side of my beach—I paused to repeat that in my head: *my beach*—the neighbors had privacy fences with some sort of vines growing over them for aesthetic purposes. I didn't care; the small red flowers perfumed the air, enhancing the whole experience.

"This is my sand," I said as I wiggled my toes.

"I'm pretty sure the sand belongs to the state," Becky remarked, hooking the straps of her wedges over one finger.

Unlike me, Becky didn't have to resort to online auctions and outlet shopping. Thanks to her JD, she earned a decent salary. "Want a roommate? This view is incredible," Becky sighed. "This place has to be worth a few million, easy."

True. It was one of the few prime beach-front cottages still standing. Most of the small lots in Palm Beach had been gobbled up by developers. Cottages like mine—I got a rush just hearing that thought in my brain—were practically extinct.

"You could flip this place and—"

"No, I can't," I explained. "That was one of the provisions my mother put into the contract."

"You can't sell it?"

I shrugged. "I can, but only back to her. Apparently she has a deep emotional attachment to this place even though she never lived here. She had the same tenant for most of the past fifteen years, but six months ago, Melinda left. It's been vacant ever since."

"Melinda? You knew the tenant?"

"Kinda," I said, shading my eyes as the sun behind me painted the surf gold. "She was Jonathan's assistant in New York and then somehow went from that to fostering kids. My mother didn't give me the details, just that she evicted her."

"That's cold," Becky remarked without surprise. "Where is your mother now?"

I turned and looked at my friend. "How should I know? And what difference does it make?"

"None, I guess. But I'm having a hard time with the notion that your mother just had you write a check and handed you the keys. No warning, no nothing?"

I shrugged. "A random act of kindness. Who cares what her motives are? Bottom line? I have a beautiful, three-bedroom oceanfront house."

"What other restrictions did she put on the sale?"

I waved my hand dismissively. "Just general stuff about maintaining it properly, blah, blah, blah. Oh, and"—I lowered my voice, hoping it would drown in the sound of the waves—"I can't borrow against it for anything other than maintenance and repairs."

Becky shook her head. "She dangled the bait and you impaled yourself on the hook."

"Look around you," I said. "I could work for the

23

next gazillion years and I'd never be able to afford this place."

"Can you afford the taxes and the insurance?" Becky countered.

"I don't have to until I've paid off fifteen thousand I owe my mother. Can you go pull the wings off a different butterfly?"

Becky raised her hands in surrender. "You're right, I'm sorry. This is a huge thing, and I'm sorry for pissing on it."

We started back toward the house. "How much do you think a total face-lift will cost?" I asked.

"How much have you earned in the past nine years?"

"You're still pissing."

"Sorry."

Olivia Garrett and Jane Spencer were walking up the pressed concrete driveway as we came around the house. Liv was balancing a champagne bottle and a picnic basket. Jane raced toward me, grabbing me in a tight hug that lifted me off the ground. Jane's very athletic. In fact, we met at the gym. We pretended to be friends so we could take advantage of the two-for-one special. The friendship had lasted. The gym membership, at least for me, had been a one-visit thing.

Jane is an accountant who looks more like one of the Pussycat Dolls. Her hair is long and dark. Her smile is brilliant, and she has a body that looks better than the airbrushed models in fashion magazines.

Liv owns an event planning business with her

partner, Jean-Claude. She's as smart as she is beautiful. There's something exotic about her features that makes men literally stop dead in their tracks. If I were a lesbian, I'd definitely go for Liv.

Spreading my arms, I said, "Welcome to Chez Tanner."

"Oh my God!" Liv gushed.

"It's perfect!" Jane practically squealed before covering her mouth with her hands. "I hear the ocean. I'm so jealous, I hate you," she added, and then she looped her hand through my arm. "Finley, this is so great."

As we walked to the front door, I felt my pulse quicken again. I fumbled inside my purse, feeling for the loose key I'd carefully tucked into the side pocket. My hand was actually shaking as I inserted the key, then I heard the unmistakable click of the dead bolt sliding open.

As soon as I pushed open the heavy teak door, I was slapped in the face with the foulest odor in the history of stench.

"What is that smell?" Becky gagged.

The alarm chirped seven times before I pressed the code to disarm it. Not an easy task, given the fact that my eyes were burning from the rancid fumes and I suddenly realized that my bare feet were wet. Looking down, I realized that I was standing on moldy, squishy carpet that was foaming as if having some sort of convulsion.

From the outside, the cottage looked fairly pristine. The inside looked like a scene straight out of *Extreme*

Makeover Home Edition. Exposed wiring hung from the ceiling. Not a light fixture to be seen. Probably a good thing, since the standing water would have conducted current and we all would have been electrocuted.

I wondered if my mother had actually evicted Melinda or if she'd left of her own volition. Probably the latter. The house looked as if nothing but cursory repairs had been done in the three years since back-to-back-to-back hurricanes had slammed into Palm Beach.

"What is that?" Liv asked through her fingers, pointing at the wall.

Some sort of brown gunk dripped from the bowed ceiling until it met a furry patch of black mold leeching up from the mildewed carpet.

"It's alive," Becky mocked in a horror flick impression. "I can't believe a tenant put up with this."

Neither could I. Bravely, I walked through the living room toward double glass doors. My fingernail polish chipped as I battled the latch to unlock, then push open, the door. Blissfully, fresh air whooshed though the house, allowing us to stop using our hands as protective masks.

Sucking in a deep breath, I turned to see that I was standing in the center of a breakfast nook. I was no expert, but I was fairly sure the grout between the ceramic tiles covering the floor wasn't supposed to be black. Nor was the kitchen counter supposed to have a crack in the granite that looked a lot like the San Andreas Fault. A grimy square outline marked where a stove had once been connected. Three of the cabinet doors were missing, as was the refrigerator.

Liv said, "Who would let a piece of primo real estate like this go to hell in a handcart? Sorry, Finley, but this is a dump."

"A dump smells better." Becky's voice was muffled by the hand she still had clamped over her nose and mouth.

"The mold might be toxic," Jane suggested somberly.

Crying seemed like a good idea. "I hope it kills me quickly," I said, hating that my voice cracked.

"Hang on," Becky said, coming over to put an arm around my shoulder. "It's still a beautiful location. It just needs some TLC."

"Are you on LSD?" I asked. "The whole place has to be gutted."

"And?" Becky prompted.

I blinked a few times, my mind in hyperdrive. She was absolutely right. I started looking around. Really looking. If I started from scratch, I could turn the place into my dream house.

"I could make this whole back wall doors and glass," I said, excitement budding in my stomach. "A sleek kitchen with a wine chiller."

"You'll need a lot of wine to forget about the mold," Jane said. "How could anyone live here?"

I shot her a stern look. "I don't know, but I guess that's why my mother arranged for my bank to give me a home equity loan for repairs. I knew there was a catch. I feel like a fool."

"Don't," Becky said. "Look on the bright side. The place has potential. Forget the mold for now."

"You're right. I can get rid of the skanky carpet. Hardwood floors, maybe?" Leaving my shoes, tote, and purse on the counter, I went off to explore.

My friends followed along, crouched behind me so that we looked like the Tin Man, the Lion, and the Scarecrow on their way to see the great and powerful Oz. There was a small powder room off the hallway. The toilet bowl and sink were missing. "At least I won't have to pay to have them removed," I said, thinking aloud. Farther down the hall I found two small bedrooms opposite each other. There was another bathroom, sans shower stall. The master bedroom was at the end of the hall.

"It's small," Liv said. "How many foster children lived here at one time?"

"No clue," I answered absently. "I can take down this wall," I suggested. "Combine the master bedroom and one of the other ones. I can build a killer closet and maybe do a spa bath."

Jane wandered over to the accordion doors lining one wall. As soon as she touched the scratched knob, the door fell off its tracks. The closet was narrow, and the rod was missing. She laid the cheap door on the floor, stepped over it, and walked into the adjoining bathroom.

Coming up behind her, I placed my hand on her hip and moved her to one side. It looked like something you'd find in a youth hostel. Tiny tub, sink affixed to the wall. Mirror hanging above the chipped sink and a toilet sandwiched in between. There was a narrow rectangular window mounted in the shower stall near the ceiling line. Judging by the blistering of the plaster, I was already resigned to the fact that it leaked.

"So," I said as I rejoined Liv and Jane in the bedroom. "I guess I'll need a Home Depot credit card."

"No," Jane scoffed. "You need an Extreme Home Makeover." Her green eyes glinted mischievously. "The team can do the house and I'll do Ty Pennington. Deal?"

"I get Ty!" Jane called as she headed back toward the smaller bedrooms.

"Was that champagne you brought?" I asked Liv.

She nodded. "And some fruit and cheese. I didn't bring an ice bucket because I thought—"

"C'mon," I interrupted, leading Jane and Liv back down toxic alley to the kitchen. "You coming?" I called to Becky as we passed the smallest bedroom.

"Be right there."

So what if my new house was uninhabitable? It didn't have to stay that way. I had my apartment, so it wasn't as if I'd have to sleep in moldville. "Sam will help."

"We'll all help." Liv started gathering up the picnic basket, and I grabbed the champagne. "Jane, run out to my trunk and grab the blanket. We can have drinks on the beach."

Jane half ran, half hopped across the living room mush, muttering curses as she went.

I heard a loud bang and yelled, "Becky, what are you doing?"

"Trying to open the frigging closet in here," she called back.

"Leave it. We're going out to the beach."

"I can make this work," I told Liv a few minutes later as I twisted the metal net off the top of the champagne bottle. Using the hem of my skirt, I eased the cork loose without losing a single bubble.

"Nice," Liv complimented as Jane arrived and spread the blanket on a level patch of sand.

Looking back at the house, I had a zillion ideas running through my head. Okay, so I was discouraged, but I was also excited by the challenge. "I wonder how much it will cost."

"Won't be cheap," Jane said as she held up a flute for me to fill. "But you can't go wrong."

"I can't?"

She shook her head. "It's location, Finley. Since you barely paid anything for the property, whatever you put into this place, you'll get back at least fifty times over. Palm Beach real estate is a great investment. If this place was built prior to 1929, I can even help you apply for some tax deferment programs and rehab grants."

"Really?"

"You'll need a contractor," Liv said. "Though I'm all for calling in Ty Pennington."

"I'll keep that in mind."

"Get a hot contractor," Jane insisted. "You don't want some old, fat guy with a bad comb-over and his butt crack showing."

"To Finley's new status as a land baron. And to hot contractors," Liv said, raising her glass.

"Shouldn't we wait for Becky?"

"Naw, we'll just refill our glasses."

I grinned at Liv, enjoying the soft tickle of the dry champagne as it washed over my tongue. "The lease on my apartment isn't up for another three months. Think that's enough time?"

"Probably not. You need to talk to someone who knows construction," Jane said. "What about Liam?"

"He's still on my To Be Avoided list."

"I thought what he did was gallant," Liv sighed, then popped a grape into her mouth. "Any other guy would have screwed your lights out."

I wish. My cheeks felt warm. I'm not sure whether it was because I was imagining Liam and myself together or remembering that he'd declined my offer to do just that. "Sam probably knows someone."

"True, but I doubt he knows anyone as hot as Liam McGarrity."

"Sure he does."

Jane shot me a glare as she reached for a wedge of cheese. "*Heterosexual* hot guys."

Liv reclined on her elbows, her gaze fixed on the house. "Are you going to name it?"

"Name what?"

"The house. People on Palm Bach name their houses. You know, Hidden Palms. Restless Waters. Something beachy and pretentious."

"You really think I need to call my house something?"

Becky rushed out and said, "This place is a crime scene."

"It is not. It just needs a redo."

"No," Becky said in a single, clipped syllable. "I mean it's an actual crime scene."

"So someone stole the appliances and some of the fixtures. It's not like—"

"No, Finley! Call the police. I just found a dead guy in the closet."

*Whoever said dead men tell no tales didn't
have a dead person stuffed in their closet.*

two

꘠

"THAT IS DISGUSTING," I said, speaking over the
lump of revulsion lodged in my throat.

That was a partially visible body protruding
from a half-rotted box shoved into the back corner of
the master bedroom closet. Even more disgusting was
the state of the corpse. The arm hanging out of the
trunk was almost all bone, but from what I could see
from my vantage point, the skull still had long brown
hair attached in places. "I don't think it's a dead *guy.*"

Becky gagged, backing into me as she retreated,
hand over her mouth. "Of course it's a guy. It has an
opposable thumb. See?"

Looking at the curled, fleshless fingers, I agreed
that the remains were human. "Look at the hair,
though," I said. "I think it's a dead girl."

"Girl, guy, who cares? Dead is dead. We have to
call the police," Liv insisted. "Let them figure out the
gender *after* they get it out of here."

"I think we should wait outside," Jane quavered,

her voice shaking slightly. Understandable, since she was already falsely arrested for murder earlier this year. "Does anyone remember what I touched?" She pulled a tissue and a trial-size container of Purell from her purse and wiped down the doorknob. "Where I might have left prints?"

"Don't worry about that," Liv said. "There's no way we can get into trouble for this. That poor soul has been dead for too long."

"But we should definitely wait outside," Jane insisted.

"We should," Liv agreed. "If only to get away from the creepy factor."

"Let's go." Becky backed out of the room.

I wanted to be right on their heels, but I waved them on, an odd tightness in my throat as I fixed my gaze on the small round object clutched in the deceased's curled fingers. My heart seized in my chest as I focused on the familiar green enameled palm fronds just visible through the cracks in the finger joints.

Glancing over my shoulder to make certain I was alone in the room, still battling my revulsion, I made a first, tentative grab for the medallion. I got within a hair of the skeleton, then snapped my hand back while swallowing the squeal of serious *eewww* in my throat. It took three tries until I was finally able to grip the medallion with my fingernails and give a tug. The medallion came loose, as did the forefinger of Dead Girl.

I grimaced as the bone dropped to the floor, then rocked back and forth before settling against my instep. I leaped away from the bone as if it might bite me, all the while wondering if I could be charged with some crime for de-fingering a corpse.

Putting aside any thoughts of the legalities of my actions, I inspected the medallion cupped in my hand. Though it was badly tarnished I could tell it was silver and approximately two inches in diameter. The side facing up was familiar. It bore the green enameled palm fronds and polo stick logo of The Palm Beach Polo Club. Adrenaline raced through my veins like a triple shot of Brazilian Roast. I knew I had to turn it over to the police, but I hesitated as a million fears, questions, and possibilities raced through my mind.

"Stop making yourself strange," I chided in a whisper. "What are the chances?" I slowly flipped the medallion. My heart fell to my feet as I read the inscription . . .

Love you, Daddy. F.A.T.

I'd had those words engraved on the medallion myself. A gift I'd given nearly twenty years earlier. A memento to Jonathan for being named Club Player of the Year at The Palm Beach Polo Club. I hadn't seen it in forever. I'd assumed my mother had either thrown it away or tucked it into one of the zillion boxes she had in storage units all over the county.

So how did a gift I gave Jonathan when I was ten end up in Dead Girl's fist? Did my mother know? No. My mother wouldn't cross the threshold of a place in this condition, let alone go ferreting through closets.

Melinda would have to know. Hard to believe she'd moved out without checking the closet. I glanced at the skeleton again. Maybe not. I was no expert, but based on the way the skeleton was shoved in between the exposed framing, it almost looked like the skeleton was a recent addition. Except that she was holding Jonathan's medallion.

Distant sirens split through the silence of the early evening. Panic welled up inside me. I didn't know how my long-deceased stepfather's medallion had ended up in the hand of a corpse, but I figured it was something I wanted to keep to myself until I had answers.

Knowing the police would be there in a matter of seconds, I freaked out wondering where to hide the thing. They were sure to go over the house with a fine-tooth comb—which surely would include my purse and tote—so I had no choice but to sneak it past them. Unfortunately, neither my adorable skirt nor my cute cami had pockets, and I'd left my suit jacket in Becky's car. The only viable hiding place was my bra. Quickly, I stuffed the cool medal, covered no doubt with dead person cooties, into place and rushed out to join my friends.

My first mistake was making eye contact with Becky. One look and she knew something was wrong.

"What did you do?" she asked.

Her question-slash-accusation drew the attention of my other two friends. Suddenly I had three pairs of eyes trained on me just as four police cars came screeching to a halt. One, I noted, parked on the lawn, leaving deep tracks in the grass.

As fully armed officers descended upon us, I could only remain mute and hope it wasn't called a wonder bra for nothing. And as if robbing a corpse wasn't bad enough, an unmarked West Palm Beach car arrived a fraction of a second later. Palm Beach does have a police force, but it's small, and I could only conclude that for serious matters such as dead people, they called for reinforcements. Unfortunately for me, out stepped Detectives Steadman and Graves.

They hated me.

Graves, who looked a lot like the star of the Ving Rhames cable remake of *Kojak,* had a body of solid muscle and the personality of a toad. His partner, Detective Steadman, was one of those women who confused being assertive with being a bitch. She was square and compact, a lot like SpongeBob. Having a history with the two detectives didn't bode well for any of us. Particularly Jane, who, I could see, had started to shake. Not that I could blame her. These were the same detectives who had dragged her off to jail and charged her with Paolo Martinez's murder.

The fact that she was exonerated probably screwed with their case closure rate, not to mention the fact that it must have caused them some personal embarrassment. At any rate, neither detective looked too happy to see us huddled together in the front yard.

The feeling was mutual, but I slapped a smile on my face and tried my very best to appear grateful for their presence. "It's in there," I said, pointing toward the house. "I mean, *she's* in there."

Steadman went inside with the other officers.

Graves was expressionless as he took out his notepad and pen. He wore an ill-fitting white shirt. It wouldn't have been ill-fitting if he'd (a) worked out less, or (b) gotten a decent tailor. He was so muscle-bound that the girth of his own lats hindered his movements.

"Ladies," he said, though there wasn't much sincerity in the greeting. "Name of the deceased?"

"Dead Girl," I answered, proving my mother's assertion that I couldn't pass up an opportunity to be a smart-ass. In my defense, it's a nervous condition. The more scared I am, the more sarcastic I get. Becky elbowed me in the rib cage.

"The remains are skeletal," Becky explained in a very lawyerly, reasonable tone. "There could be identification with the remains, but as soon as we discovered the body, we exited the house and called you."

Graves made a note, then looked at me again. "But you think the victim is female?"

"Based on the hair," I replied. "Then again, nobody's seen Fabio for a while, so I guess—*umph*." Again Becky slammed me with an elbow to the ribs.

With a cock of her head, Becky took Graves and steered him a few feet away. Liv had one arm around Jane and was patting her hand with the other. "We can't possibly be suspects," I said, mostly for terrified Jane's benefit. "It takes more than three hours for a human body to turn to bones."

"She's right," Liv told Jane, then gave her a gentle squeeze. "They'll go after the previous owner—"

"Who would be my mother," I said. I was suddenly filled with conflicting emotions. My wounded inner child didn't object to the idea of my mother being grilled like freshly caught tilapia, but my DNA demanded that I warn her. Or at the very least, let her know what was happening. Only problem? My cell was in my tote and my tote was on the kitchen counter. In addition to letting her know that she should expect a visit from the police, I also had a few questions of my own about the medallion. The last time I saw it was just after Jonathan died fifteen years ago. It was lying on top of his dresser in the bedroom of their Palm Beach home.

Not this place, but a massive, twenty-five-thousand-square-foot house about a mile down the beach. After Jonathan's death, my mother lived there for another five years, with husband number two. She sold it after marrying husband number three. He came with a thirty-thousand-square-foot house. It was a trade up.

The sound of a car engine backfiring caused me to jump. Even knowing I was nothing more than the innocent bystander who happened upon a body, I was more spooked than I thought. I glanced over my right shoulder in the direction of the noise.

Just behind the police cars, a familiar '64 Mustang coughed another cloud of blue smoke before the engine was turned off. For an instant, as my last encounter with the owner of the Mustang replayed in my mind, I seriously considered running into the house and joining the skeleton in the closet. I look way better in Lilly Pulitzer than I do draped in the memory of one of my worst personal humiliation moments.

Rhonda Pollero

As Liam McGarrity stepped from what I could only generously describe as his car, I donned the expression I normally save for the occasional drunk frat boy spewing a really bad pickup line. He'd told me he was in the process of restoring the thing. He'd also told me he wasn't interested in having sex with me. Forget the car. The way he'd rejected me still stung.

Don't get me wrong, I've been rejected. Mostly by credit card companies and my mother. You'd think I'd be able to let it go, but for some reason hearing Liam tell me to take a hike stuck in my craw. And I don't think I even know what or where my craw is.

"Now that is a thing of beauty," Liv sighed softly as Liam walked toward us.

"Beauty fades. Asshole is forever," I muttered through my tight smile.

As usual, Liam was dressed in jeans, a faded Tommy Bahama shirt that was at least three seasons old, Reef sandals, black hair mussed. I suspected the not-so-ex Mrs. McGarrity was the musser as I pretended not to be affected when his deep blue eyes locked on me.

The fact that he looked like he had . . . might have . . . could have . . . probably . . . maybe just rolled out of his ex's bed was as irritating to my ego as my own foolish desire to run my fingers through his hair. Hair, schmare. There wasn't an inch of his six-foot-plus frame I didn't want to run my fingers through, and I hated myself for being such a jerk. Worse yet, I didn't know if my strong desire was real or if I just wanted to prove to him that he'd missed a great thing when he'd sent me on my way. How masochistic is that?

"What are you doing here?" I asked, wishing it didn't sound so pissy.

"Heard your name on the scanner. Wondered what you'd gotten yourself into this time. Liv, Jane," he added with a slight nod of his head, though his gaze never left my face. "Anything I can do to help?"

Hold me? Kiss me? Get eaten by sharks? Biting my tongue first, I held out my hand. "Can I use your cell?"

Unclipping it from his waistband, Liam handed me a cell phone that was big and bulky and I half expected to be rotary dial. It was a far cry from the sleek iPhone I'd just bought for myself—another breakup consolation gift. "Thanks," I said, then turned my back and dialed my mother's number.

"You've reached 561-blah-blah-blah." I sighed heavily as I waited for the answering machine to beep. "Mom, if you're screening, pick up. There's a major problem with the house and—"

I heard a quick click of the receiver being picked up. "You own the house, Finley," my mother said without preamble. "I am not your landlord, so any problems are yours to handle. It's called being responsible and—"

"I don't think my responsibilities include the skeleton in the closet."

"All older homes have histories, Finley."

"I didn't mean a metaphorical skeleton, Mom. A real one. Why did you really evict Melinda? Did you have any suspicions? Did she happen to mention—"

"Suspicions about what? I only knew the woman through Jonathan. If she left the place in disarray, that's your problem."

Through gritted teeth, I said, "A skeleton is not disarray. Like it or not, you need to tell me what you know so I can tell the police why there's a Dead Girl in the closet of the house you sold me."

"I can assure you, I have no knowledge of any . . . dead person. The fact that you think I could be involved—"

"I don't. I just need you to tell me how to get in touch with Melinda. She's the one the cops need to talk to."

"Since I haven't spoken to her except through my lawyer, I have no idea how to reach her. Why are you assuming Melinda would know anything about a skeleton? It's probably the work of one of those miscreant children she housed."

"She has to know something, since the Dead Girl is holding Dad's—" I shut up the instant I saw the detectives at the front door. Cupping my hand over the mouthpiece, I said, "Call your lawyer. *Now.*"

"Holding Jonathan's what?" my mother asked. It was the first time I could remember hearing genuine fear in her tone.

"The police are going to want to talk to you."

"Why?"

I rolled my eyes. "You just sold me a house with a dead person in it. I may be wrong, but I'm thinking they'll have a few questions for you."

"There's no need to be sarcastic, Finley."

"I'm trying to be helpful by giving you a heads-up."

"And you think I had something to do with a crime? That's absurd. I'm not the one with the criminal history in this family, so why would I need a lawyer?"

Detective Graves was walking toward me. "Fine. Don't call your lawyer. Call your travel agent."

"Why?"

"Have her recommend a trip to a place where you can't be extradited back to the U.S. to face murder charges."

"Murder char—" I snapped the antiquated cell phone closed. I'd done my daughterly duty.

"Who were you calling?" Graves asked as the mobile crime scene unit drove onto the other side of the lawn, leaving more deep grooves in the freshly laid sod.

"My mother," I told him, meeting his narrowed gaze with one of my own.

"You and your friends are going to have to go to the Palm Beach police station and give statements."

It was a relief hearing I wasn't going to be dragged back to West Palm for interrogation. "My purse is in the house."

"It will be returned to you at the station. After the crime scene techs get finished. The cars, too."

"Can I at least have my shoes?"

Graves frowned and jogged back inside, returning in a flash with my damp, *expensive* shoes dangling from his beefy forefinger.

I looked at my brand-new BMW. Liam was leaning against it, his arms folded in front of his chest. I was curious when I saw him glare down one of the officers stationed in the driveway. Officer—I strained to read the nameplate pinned on his uniform shirt—Diaz was glaring right back. My heart fluttered a few times, touched that Liam was, albeit passively, showing support.

In a matter of minutes, Jane, Liv, Becky, and I were driven to the station. It was a far cry from the dank, gray station in West Palm. It looked more like an office building, complete with art on the walls and the distinctive feel of a professional decorator's hand.

Not unexpectedly, we were separated, and I was instructed to follow a tall, lanky male officer through the door clearly marked NO UNAUTHORIZED PERSONNEL BEYOND THIS POINT.

With an authentic smile on his face, he politely held a padded chair out for me. If he hadn't been dressed in a blue polyester uniform, I could easily have mistaken him for a well-trained server.

"Can I get you anything, Miss Tanner? Coffee, a soft drink?"

"Coffee would be great, thank you."

"How do you like it?"

"Intravenously."

He laughed. "I'll be right back."

He also lied. My toes tapped nervously against the marble tiled floor as five, then ten, then thirty minutes ticked off the clock mounted between two avantgarde paintings with small cards taped just below the lower right-hand corner. Jumbled nerves and building irritation inspired me to walk over and inspect the artwork. The small cards indicated that the paintings were on loan from a tony gallery and available for sale. Only in Palm Beach.

As casually as possible, I tugged at my bra strap, feeling the warmth of the secreted medallion against my skin. I kept trying to think of a reason for why and how the medal had found its way into the hand of a skeleton. For that matter, how had the skeleton gone undetected all these years?

Hearing the click of the doorknob, I turned to see the officer carrying not the cup of Styrofoam tar I'd been dreading but a molded cardboard holder with an iced latte tucked into one of four compartments.

"Sorry it took so long."

"Well worth the wait," I said, greedily taking the latte from him. If you had to be trapped in a police station, Palm Beach was definitely the way to go.

He had a clipboard tucked under his arm, and as soon as we settled into our assigned seats, he pulled out a pen and began asking me benign questions. Name, address—I gave him the one to my condo, unsure when I'd get the nerve to return to my dream/nightmare house on the beach.

"Marital status?"

"Single."

"Dating anyone?"

I blinked. "How is that relevant to the investigation?"

He grinned up at me. "It isn't. I was trying to sneak it past you."

"You're hitting on me?" I didn't know whether to be flattered or furious.

He shrugged. His shoulders were narrow and boney. His hair was blond and neatly cropped. His charm was marginal. Other than being thirtyish and bringing me a decent iced coffee, there wasn't a single thing about this guy that landed him on my radar.

"That would be a violation of departmental protocol," he explained. Wink, wink, nod, nod. "No offense intended. But if you're not doing anything on Friday night—"

"I'm in the middle of a celibacy thing," I cut in.

Reaching into his pocket, he pulled out a business card and passed it across the carved cherrywood table. "Feel free to give me a call if you change your mind."

"Can we move this along?" I asked, pulling the card close and using it as a coaster.

If he was disappointed, it didn't show on his tanned face. For some idiotic reason, that stung. First Patrick, then Liam, and now Officer Kiss-ass. I was starting to wonder if I was destined to spend the rest of my life internet dating.

His cell phone chirped, and he had a brief conversation that consisted of "Okay," and "I'll let her know." Holding the phone away from his ear, he said, "Your friends have finished giving their statements. They want to know if you want them to wait for you."

Knowing that Jane was probably totally freaked, I shook my head. "I'm good." I was irritated that my interview was taking so long, but I had learned the hard way not to annoy the police. Even when the police annoyed me. And this guy was in danger of leapfrogging over Graves and Steadman as my least-favorite law enforcement officer. The only thing preventing me from putting him at the top of the list was the latte, and I was almost finished with that.

It took him another thirty-nine minutes to complete the questionnaire, then he went and got a tape recorder and listened as I recounted how we'd found the skeleton. I was left to trace the logo of the coffee shop with my fingernail while my statement was typed, then presented for my signature.

I read it, signed it, and stood up. "Thanks for the coffee."

"Wish I could take credit for it," he said unapologetically. "Some guy dropped them off for you and your friends."

As fast as possible, I left the police station. It was fully dark, but the parking lot had lights attached to tall poles. I looked around for my car, or at least for a familiar face to take me back to my car. Tucked into the half dozen cars in the parking lot, I spotted Liam leaning against my new car, one foot resting on the front bumper. His half-primer, half-putty car was in the spot next to mine. He brought a long-necked bottle of beer to his lips and, judging by the sharp angle of the bottle, took the last sip.

"There are laws against having open containers of alcohol," I said. "Why are you here?"

He smiled and my stomach knotted. I was torn between wanting to slap the smile off his face and kissing him senseless. I hated him for making me feel like this.

He flung the empty bottle into a Dumpster a good ten yards from where we stood. The sound of the glass breaking echoed in the still night.

"Thanks for the coffee, Liam," he teased. "That was a really decent thing for you to do, and I really appreciate it."

"I'm eternally grateful," I said flatly. "You want to get off my car? I'd like to go home."

"Wanna tell me what you lifted off the deceased?"

I felt my cheeks grow warm and was thrilled that it was too dark for him to see the guilty blush. "What makes you think I—"

"I heard what you said to your mother."

"Eavesdropping is rude."

He shrugged and rose to his full height. I hated that I had to tilt my head back to compensate for his height. "Have it your way," he said as he turned his back and moved toward his car.

"Thanks for bringing me my car," I said, finding it easier to talk to his back.

"I didn't. The cops towed it here. The bill's on the passenger seat next to your purse."

three

I WAS TIRED, ANNOYED, AND jonesing for coffee—three really good reasons why I should have
done the smart thing and called it a night. It's rarely
a good idea to have a face-to-face with my mother
when I'm not at my peak, but I knew I wouldn't be
able to sleep until she explained why my stepfather's
medallion was clutched in the skeleton's hand.

As I merged onto I-95, I ran possibilities through
my mind. After a twenty-minute drive to the swanky
Singer Island high-rise, I still couldn't come up with
a single scenario that explained where I'd found the
medallion.

As usual, I parked right in front of the polished,
deco-styled, twelve-story building. In the spot clearly
marked DELIVERIES ONLY, ALL OTHERS TOWED. I felt
a resurgence of irritation as I glanced down at the
tow receipt on the passenger seat. Cutting the engine, I decided it was a statistical impossibility that
I would get towed twice in the same night. Besides,

49

I almost always used this spot. It was a convenience and an excuse not to have to walk all the way from the visitors' lot. It was just to the right of the polished stone steps that encircled the beautiful, lighted fountain and led up to glass doors with heavy brass handles. A gentle breeze lifted a light spray of water into the air.

When I reached the top step, a security guard glanced up, gave a little nod of recognition, then buzzed me in.

"Hi, Ted," I said, hoping he wouldn't notice that I had to glance down at his nametag.

"I'll call your mother and let her know you're on your way up," he replied, reaching across the ornate desk.

"Thanks." I walked through the four-story atrium toward the dual elevators. Tucked between the elevators was a gigantic bouquet of freshly cut and professionally arranged flowers.

As usual, my issues of being a failure as a daughter joined me in the elevator. In the amount of time it took to travel from the lobby to the penthouse, I made a lengthy mental list of some of the ways in which my mother considered me a failure. First and foremost, she couldn't forgive me for not going to law school. Forget that I didn't want to go to law school. That was immaterial. What made that decision such an unforgivable sin was her perception of how it reflected on her. Then there was the twenty-nine and not married thing. Given that she was prowling for hubby number six, she couldn't understand why

I didn't marry someone—*anyone*—even if it didn't work out. I felt myself smile at the skewed logic. My mother would rather see me divorced than perpetually single. If I was divorced, at least then—according to her—it meant I had tried.

The elevator dinged and the doors slid open just as a Muzak version of a Tom Jones tune began. My palms were sweaty. That always happened when I was about to enter my mother's penthouse. I always morphed into a stupid sixteen-year-old right at the threshold. Must be a mother-daughter thing. Or maybe a spider-fly thing.

Before I had a chance to ring the bell, the door opened and I was greeted with an icy glare. It's weird, because my mother and I have exactly the same aqua-blue eyes, so it's kinda like being glared at by yourself in some twisted alternate reality.

"Do you know what time it is?" she asked, tightening the belt on the blue silk La Perla robe Lisa had given her for Mother's Day. Needless to say, the robe had made my gift of an orchid look like an afterthought.

"Ten-o-five?"

I took a deep breath, knowing it would be the last filtered air I'd put in my lungs for a while. My mother was quite fond of Imperial Majesty No.1. At $2,100.50 an ounce, you'd think she'd use it sparingly. Wrong. I practically choked on the heavy scent as I walked through the foyer and into the living room.

The penthouse is very formal. Lots of earthy colors, floral watercolors, and the creepy Grecian statuary—

most of them headless—that had scared me senseless as a child.

Glancing into the kitchen, I saw three teacups and demi torte plates next to the sink. Crooking my thumb in that direction, I asked, "Graves and Steadman?"

"Lovely people," my mother commented as she sat on the sofa across from me, hands decorously in her lap, back straight. "Couldn't have been more polite."

"You had a tea party with the police?" I slumped down in the closest chair. "The same officers who arrested me not that long ago?"

Mom shrugged. "They were doing their job, Finley. Knowing you, I'm sure you went out of your way to antagonize them." She paused and tucked a strand of auburn hair back into place. "It's like you have some sort of mental illness when it comes to dealing with authority figures."

This wasn't going well. "You served tea and canapés to the people who handcuffed me and stuck me in a cell not once but twice, and you think I'm the one with a screw loose?"

My mother's face scrunched, but only those facial muscles that were low on Botox cooperated. "What do you want, Finley? I've got an early appointment tomorrow, and I'd like to get some sleep."

I ignored my mother's look of disapproval as I fished inside my bra and pulled out the medallion. Placing it on the coffee table between us, I steered it around a vase of lilies. "The victim was holding this."

My mother gave the item a cursory glance. "What victim?"

I quelled my strong urge to reach across the table and shake her. "The murdered girl in the closet of the house you just sold me."

My mother sighed like a pro. Technically, thanks to her years on stage, she is a pro, so the overly dramatic response fell within the bounds of normal. "Where did you get the idea she was murdered?"

"Gee, call me crazy, but burial in a closet was my first clue."

"The police told me they didn't find any evidence of foul play. It's their position that the poor woman was a vagrant and simply took refuge in a vacant home. Melinda moved out six months ago. As I explained to the police, other than the security patrols, there wasn't anyone checking the house on a regular basis. Whoever the dead person was, she probably had pneumonia or some other homeless person illness and crawled in the closet to die. While that is sad, it is hardly cause for alarm." Her eyes narrowed. "Nor is it cause to back out of our agreement."

I rubbed my hands over my face and counted silently backward from one hundred. I made it all the way to seventeen before I was sure my tone and expression would meet with her approval. "None of that explains the medallion."

"I haven't seen that silly thing for more than a decade," she said with a dismissive wave of her hand. "If I'm not mistaken, it was one of the items stolen when the Palm Beach house was robbed eleven or twelve years ago—though God only knows why a thief would bother with that piece of costume jewelry."

"Burgled," I corrected absently.

"Excuse me?"

"Robbery is stealing by threat or intimidation or violence. Burglary is breaking and entering for the purpose of theft."

"Did you come here to argue semantics?"

"No. I'm trying to figure out how a medal I gave my father ended up in the hand of a skeleton shoved in a box in a house I just bought from you."

"How should I know?"

"You *owned* the house."

"As I explained to the police, I never had anything to do with the place. Jonathan originally bought it as an investment but then decided it was better to turn it into a charitable endeavor. We had a property management company handle day-to-day things. After Jonathan died, I kept the same management company."

"Back up," I interrupted. "What was charitable about a rental property on Palm Beach?"

Another deep sigh. "Because of the tenant. Jonathan rented the place to Melinda for a pittance and wrote the difference off as a loss. His choice didn't sit too well with the upper crust on Palm Beach, but Melinda and Jonathan had worked together for years, so he supported her devotion to those ill-bred children. They did agree that Melinda would limit herself to four children at any given time. It was Jonathan's way of trying to avoid trouble with the neighbors.

"Unfortunately for them, the society types couldn't very well take action against Jonathan. Can you imagine the bad press if they attempted to ban a foster mother from the island? Look at the fallout when Donald Trump raised a large American flag. They sued him, but the public sided with patriotism. The old money residents are not fond of publicity, especially when it shows them in a bad light."

"Why am I only hearing about this rental thing now?"

"It was none of your business. Other than the occasional Christmas card, I had no interaction with Melinda. Beyond that, you'd have to ask my accountant or the property management company if you want more details. I've never paid much attention to business affairs."

Unless it was how many shares of stock were put into her portfolio by a soon-to-be-ex husband. "So what changed?"

"What do you mean?"

"If you were getting a huge tax break, why did you stop renting the place?"

"It was turning into a headache. The neighbors were complaining more and more frequently, that sort of thing. Seven months ago I had the property manager give Melinda notice."

"Out of the blue?" I asked. "No wonder she stripped the place."

"You got a house out of the deal," my mother reminded me.

I had a sinking feeling she'd be reminding me of

that a lot. "And a skeleton," I said. "Let's not forget that hidden perk."

"If you want to renege, Finley, I suggest you—"

"I don't want to renege; I just want to know how a gift I gave my stepfather ended up in the hand of a skeleton."

"Maybe he left it in the house."

"But you said it was stolen."

"I assumed it was. My insurance company asked me for a list of missing items after the break-in. It wasn't with Jonathan's things, so I assumed the burglars took it. Obviously, he lost it in that house and the vagrant found it. I think your recent crime-fighting spree has warped your mind. There's nothing untoward about that medallion turning up in a house Jonathan visited occasionally."

I wanted to press her for more details, but when she stood up, I knew I was being dismissed. The cops got tea and canapés. I got the old heave-ho. Before she showed me to the door, I was able to wrangle out of her the name of the property management company. Marc Feldman would be one of my first calls in the morning.

It TOOK A WHOLE lot of MAC concealer to cover the dark circles I was sporting after a fitful night of being chased by skeletons that morphed into my mother and back again. Pretty scary dreams. On the plus side, since I'd gotten up just after 4:00 a.m., I'd already downed a pot of coffee, so my energy level was pretty high as I pulled into the parking lot of Dane, Lieberman, and Zarnowski.

I noticed two things right off: (a) I was still five minutes late, and (b) one of the hottest guys I'd seen in all twenty-nine years of my life was parked one car away. Maybe there was life after Patrick and Liam after all. If not life, I mused as I watched him lift a box out of the trunk of a sleek black Porsche, definitely sex.

Of course, he turned and caught me staring at him. With that face and that body, I didn't much care that I'd been caught with my eyeballs in the cookie jar. He was the anti-Patrick—tall, slightly muscular, jet-black hair and eyes to match. He smiled back, making him the anti-Liam.

I reapplied lip gloss just to kill time. I wanted to make sure I headed for the door at the same time as Gorgeous Guy. A completely intentional, accidental meeting might just cure my dating dry spell. He smoothed his tie out of the way, then pulled a third box from his trunk. They were those cardboard put-it-together-yourself things that I have yet to master. His looked pristine.

Was it possible that the work gods had smiled on me and I was a Honda Accord away from a new estate client? I put him somewhere in his thirties, definitely within the parents' estate zone. He was definitely from out of state. Floridians didn't wear black Hugo Boss slacks and Ike Behar black shirts. At least not in the daytime when the temperature was already nearing eighty and it was barely past nine.

As soon as I saw him reach to close the trunk, I stepped out of my car and slipped my most recent purchase from the Coach outlet in Destin on my shoulder. It was from the SoHo collection, and the pink was a perfect splash of color to complement the gently pre-owned Ralph Lauren ruffled black and white shirtdress I'd picked up on eBay. The dress retailed for over one-fifty, but I'd gotten it at less than a quarter of that, even after adding in dry cleaning to get rid of any remnants of pre-ownership. My round toe pumps came in handy, adding a couple of inches to my five-foot-three frame.

"Need some help?" I asked, casually strolling in his direction.

"That would be great." He handed me a box by the press-thru handles. It barely weighed a pound.

After folding his suit jacket over the top box, he hoisted everything and started toward the door. He had an exceptional butt. And I was happy to trail behind, drinking in the scent of Acqua Di Giò eau de toilette, one of my all-time favorite men's fragrances. I hurried around him, quickly admiring his broad shoulders as I reached for the door handle.

"Thanks," he said.

Recognizing the remnants of a New York accent, I instantly started planning our dating future. Of course dating a New Yorker would mean Christmases in the city, Broadway plays—hell, I'd almost reached that romantic moment in a hansom cab, where he was offering me a signature blue box from Tiffany's, when Maudlin Margaret's voice turned into a total buzz kill.

"You're late."

You're bitter. "Traffic," I lied.

Margaret pushed back her chair and came out from behind the horseshoe-shaped reception desk. I half expected her to have a whip or something. I wouldn't put corporal punishment past Vain Dane.

"You must be Mr. Caprelli."

"Guilty," he said, placing the boxes on Margaret's sacred ground and offering her his hand. "Mrs. Ford, right?"

She batted her lashes. "Call me Margaret, please."

My stomach turned at the sight of her flirting with my possible future husband. Peeking around the torso of Mr. Caprelli, I asked, "Messages?"

Margaret reluctantly turned her gaze on me. "Mr. Dane wants to see you in his office at nine thirty."

"I'll take that," Caprelli said as he turned and took the box from me. "Thanks for your help."

"I can carry this for you, just tell me who you're here to see."

"Not necessary. But thank you . . . ?" totally hot Caprelli asked.

For a split second, the question hung in the air as I tried valiantly to remember how to speak English. "Uh, Finley."

"Thanks, Finley." He punctuated the greeting with a smile that made my knees more than just a little weak as I turned and walked across the lobby to the elevators.

Crap. I went up to my office on the second floor. I had ten minutes before I had to answer the call of the senior partner. My guess was he'd seen the snippet in the morning paper about the skeleton in my house. Dane, Lieberman isn't a large firm, but it's a prestigious and discreet one. My hopes that he'd missed the small article were dashed, so I spent what little time I had preparing my own defense.

This wasn't the first time I'd gotten into trouble with Vain Dane, but he could hardly hold me responsible for a vagrant climbing into my house to die.

After pouring a generous mug of coffee from the pot under the credenza behind my desk, I opened the bottom drawer and pulled the medallion out of my purse. Flipping it over and over in my palm, I was still perplexed. I placed it next to my mouse pad, then powered on my computer. I scanned my emails, and my heart sank when I saw the high bid on a Rolex box go beyond my means. Since I'd given my mother almost all of my money for the house, I was back to hunting for parts for my build-it-from-scratch Rolex project.

I noticed two emails from Liam and took great delight in deleting them unread. There wasn't anything he had to say that I wanted to hear. Or read. Or whatever.

Gulping down a huge hit of coffee, I grabbed a legal pad and pen, then dutifully marched toward the elevator. The executive offices were on the top floor.

When the elevator opened, I was greeted by the sight of a beautiful spray of flowers in the center of the waiting area, which was designed like a wagon wheel. Each spoke went to a different attorney's office or conference room. Thomas Zarnowski, the founding partner, was mostly retired now. I missed him. He'd hired me seven years ago and actually liked me.

Ellen Lieberman, the first and only female partner, had her office and conference area to the left. Calling her a female partner was a bit of a stretch. Her long, curly hair turned gray years ago; she favored shapeless, flowing dresses with four slits—one for her head, one for each arm, and one for her unshaven legs to share. She lived in Birkenstocks, often wearing them with thin socks. I never went to her house, but I had this picture in my mind of a cluttered condo with lots of books, a single chair, a TV tray, and sixty cats.

Vain Dane's office was directly in front of the elevators. His secretary had a huge desk, and she sat behind it like a sentry. I smelled the flowers as I passed by, then just as I reached the secretary's desk, I smelled Acqua again. My heart fluttered just remembering my future fiancé.

"You may go in, Miss Tanner."

"Finley is fine," I told her for the umpteenth time. I could tell she was mentally tossing the suggestion in the trash as I started down the long hallway leading to Dane's opulent office.

The strong scent of leather greeted me as I gently knocked on his partially open door.

"Come."

Sit. Speak. Plastering a smile on my face, I walked in clutching my legal pad to my chest.

Dane looked annoyed. He didn't get up from his custom-upholstered leather chair. He just sat there, fingers steepled, glaring as I slowly walked forward. Behind his massive desk was a wall of windows, and I wondered how much of a running start I'd need to break through the glass and plunge to a painful but relatively quick death. My suicidal thoughts were cut short when Caprelli stood and turned in my direction.

Somehow—and no, I don't know how—my heel caught one of the loops in the carpet, and for a flash of a second, I lurched forward before tossing my legal pad and grabbing for the first solid thing my hands encountered. That thing was Caprelli. I regained my balance and maybe 20 percent of my dignity as he guided me to one of the chairs across from Dane's desk. "Thank you," I mumbled as my cheeks grew hot.

Caprelli handed me my legal pad, and I adjusted myself on the edge of the seat. Grabbing the pen I'd tucked behind my ear, I sat poised and ready. For what I had no clue. It wasn't as if I could take shorthand, and Dane didn't usually farm out work to me. At least not since the Evans estate debacle.

"Finley Tanner, this is Anthony Caprelli."

"We met earlier," I said, offering my hand, "though not formally."

"Tony," he said as his large, masculine hand swallowed mine.

My heart rate increased when I lifted my eyes to his. They were dark and rimmed with perfect lashes. His complexion was dark as well, very Mediterranean and marred by just a few lines around his eyes that managed to make him even more attractive.

"Finley." My own name came out in the froggish croak that even I didn't recognize. I cleared my throat and said it again. "Finley." Better. Well, not really. I remembered then that I had told him my name earlier in the lobby. Between my inability to remember my own name and a near-miss pratfall, he was probably already thinking I was a ditz. *Great.*

Breathe in, breathe out. Breathe in, breathe out.

Tony took his seat, crossing one leg over the other and casually grabbing the ankle.

"Given the last few months," Dane began, leaving out the words *"of you screwing up,"* "Ellen and I decided to bring in a new partner to expand the firm's areas of concentration. Tony will be heading up a criminal division, and he'll need support staff."

Like an overeager kindergartner, I wanted to yell, *"Pick me! Pick me!"* but I refrained. "I'm happy to help wherever you think I can do the most good."

I could sense that Dane wanted to roll his eyes. "Any duties you take on will be in addition to your responsibilities in estates and trusts."

"Not a problem." True, I could practically do estates in my sleep after seven years.

"When did you last do litigation support?" Tony asked.

"I did an internship at the public defender's office."

Caprelli's smile waned. "An internship? When?"

"In college."

He shook his head slightly and let out a long, slow

breath. Then he turned his attention to Dane. "I was hoping for someone with more recent litigation experience."

"I know. Ellen and I agreed that with a few continuing education courses at the community college, Finley will be up to speed in no time."

"What?" I asked.

Vain Dane slipped two sheets of paper across his desk to me. "The firm has already paid your tuition. You have classes on Tuesday and Thursday evenings from six to nine forty-five."

Legal continuing ed classes? God, please let this be a hallucination. A bad dream. Something, *anything* but those wickedly boring courses put together by the bar association meant to keep practicing attorneys up on the latest rulings and treaties in a given area. In reality, they were mostly populated by paralegals and legal secretaries. Continuing education certification in a specific area allowed the firm to charge a higher rate for work done by support staff. The last time I did CE courses, the instructor was about five years beyond his expiration date. Dane, Lieberman might have been paying the tuition, but I wasn't going without a minimal fight. "I've got . . . *things*."

"We will, of course, pay you overtime while you're in school so long as you maintain a B average," Dane decreed.

"I just bought a house, and it needs a lot of work and—"

"Upon completion of your course work, you'll receive a twenty percent raise."

My get-out-of-debt antennae went up. "How long will the certification classes last?" Maybe Tony would help me study. *Naked.*

"Six weeks."

I can do anything for six weeks. Except have a life. Not that I have much of one now. "Twenty percent? Consider me a cooperative coed."

Twenty percent and Tony at the end of the tunnel. Working with him was almost worth the loss of personal time. As I sat there, I couldn't stop thinking about my hunky new boss. I winced. The boss part could present a problem. I wouldn't have a problem having a relationship with my boss, but that didn't mean Tony would feel the same way. Still, he was checking out my legs during the meeting, so there was hope on the horizon.

Feeling as if I'd just sold my soul to Vain Dane for a dating prospect, I made my way back to my office. On the plus side, I didn't trip on my way out even though I had a hard time taking my eyes off Tony. On the minus side, I arrived at my office to find Liam sitting in my chair, drinking out of my coffee mug, with his feet propped up on my desk.

"Go. Away," I said, slapping his feet to the floor.

He chuckled softly, which only irritated me more.

He put the coffee mug down. "You're a very hard woman to help."

"I don't want your help. I don't want anything from you," I insisted as I rounded my desk fully prepared to roll his ass right out of my office and dump him into the hallway.

He stood, and we ended up toe to toe with little more than a hairsbreadth between us. My body started to tingle when I locked eyes with him. Very slowly, he lifted his hand and traced a whisper of a trail along my jawline. It felt as if my heart would explode in my chest, and it was hard to keep up the pretext of being completely immune to him. Correction. *Impossible.*

"Don't do this."

"Do what?" he asked as his fingertip found the rapid pulse point at my throat.

I swatted at his hand. "Don't touch me. Don't help me. Just go play with your ex-wife."

He pulled a rumpled, tri-folded sheet of paper out of his back pocket. "I could do that, but then you'd never know what the ME found out about your skeleton."

I started to grab for the paper, then remembered I wasn't five. "It isn't my skeleton. So what did the ME find?"

"I'll show you mine if you show me yours."

"What?"

Liam reached over and picked up the medallion I'd left on my desk. "Is this what you took off the dead chick?"

I pressed my lips together and glared at him.

He flipped the medallion in his palm and started nodding. "I can see why. Can't be too many F.A.T.s out there. Any idea why the deceased had it in her hand?"

"You've seen mine, so now I get to see yours, right?"

He handed me the paper. There was a lot of medical jargon that I could look up later, but what I wasn't finding was a cause of death. "How did she die?"

"Undetermined, but that's not the interesting part. Read the third paragraph."

I did, but unfortunately that was part of the medical jargon, and I barely understood more than something had something to do with something that had to do with signs of crystallization and something else to do with dehydration. "I give. What is supposed to be jumping out at me?"

"That's just a preliminary report, but it appears that your skeleton is pretty well traveled."

"Excuse me?"

"Before she took up residence at your place, your dead roommate was in a humidity-free environment, then frozen and finally boxed up and placed in your closet."

Men are like PMS—they irritate you
for no reason.

four

S O THIS IS A homicide?" My adrenaline
surged, though it was tempered by the
knowledge that Vain Dane wouldn't like my
being mixed up in a murder. Again. With *wouldn't
like* being the understatement of the year, even
though this was different. This time the murder
had come to me and not vice versa, but I suspected Dane wouldn't appreciate the semantics.

Liam shook his head, and the signature lock of
black hair fell forward. My fingers twitched, wanting
nothing more than to brush the hair back into place,
followed immediately by ripping off his clothing
and . . . *focus!*

Easier said than done when his body brushed
against me as he stepped around the desk and sat in
one of the two chairs opposite mine. In an attempt
to redirect my thinking, I tossed the legal pad on the
credenza, then poured myself another cup of coffee
before settling into my chair. "What happens next?"

Liam was grinning at me. Not in a good way. He was mocking me. "What?" I snapped.

"Ever hear the expression NHI?"

I shook my head.

He leaned forward, poured half of my coffee into his mug, then took a swallow. I'm not sure what about him annoyed me the most: I just knew that the list was growing. Showing up unannounced, commandeering my desk and my favorite coffee cup, touching me just to get a rise out of me—which totally worked—or knowing that when it came to crimes, he knew more than I did. No wonder Vain Dane was sending me to the legal version of GED classes.

"Cop speak for no humans involved."

"That's harsh."

"That's reality," he countered. "Your skeleton has been dead for ten to fifteen years, give or take. Guesstimate on her age at the time she died is between thirteen and sixteen. No skin on her hands means no fingerprints. The clothing they found with the body had labels. The items were sold exclusively at Wal-Mart. Impossible to trace. She had perfect teeth, so that's probably a dead end."

"Was she a runaway? Maybe someone reported her missing."

"They've inputted the relevant information into the system, but nothing popped so far. You have to remember," he said, then paused for a sip of pilfered coffee. "Somewhere around seven hundred fifty thousand kids go missing every year. Multiply that times the ten to fifteen years since your skeleton died, and you're talking a whole lot of files to cross-check."

"So you're telling me the police aren't going to do *anything*?"

"Officially? They'll release a press statement and promise to make this case a priority."

"Unofficially?"

"They know the chances of closing a case this cold are practically nil. It'll get filed alphabetically someplace between who cares and why bother." He stood, swallowed the last of his coffee, and said, "By the way, you might want to stop deleting my emails unread."

"Who gave you permission to go snooping in my computer?"

"Didn't so much as take a peek. Didn't have to."

How could a man I'd never even kissed know so much about me? It was annoying as sin. "Then take the hint."

"Fine. I'll stop sending you names of reputable contractors. I'm sure you'll be great at tearing up mildewed carpet and ripping out Sheetrock."

"I'm not helpless," I insisted, knowing full well hell would freeze over before I ruined a fifty-dollar manicure doing DIY. "I'll take a second look at those emails. Thank you."

"Not a problem. See ya."

"Wait!"

He paused in the doorway, turning to glance back at me. "For what?"

"What about the dead girl? What will the police do?"

"Nothing."

"How can the police do nothing? We're talking about a teenager. She was someone's daughter or sister."

He shrugged. "Unless *someone* reported her missing, or you turn over that medallion to the cops to use as a clue, there's not a lot the police have to go on." He glanced down at his watch. "Gotta go. I've got to see a guy about a thing."

Always with the *thing*. Quelling the childish urge to throw something at the back of his retreating head, I fell back into my seat. There was no way I was going to hand the police something that might place guilt on my late, incapable-of-defending-himself stepfather. At least not yet. Grabbing up the phone, I dialed Becky's extension and asked her to come to my office.

"Ellen just dumped a mountain of work on my desk. How about lunch?"

"I'll take what I can get."

"Cheesecake Factory?"

"Sure. I'll meet you there around one thirty. The lunch rush will have died down by then."

I made similar calls to Liv and Jane, then Googled Marc Feldman to get his telephone number. My call was answered on the second ring by a pleasant female voice. I explained who I was and asked for an appointment, only to be told that Mr. Feldman had a heavy schedule for the day and would only be in the office after three. Thanks to the Google info, I knew his office was an easy five-minute walk from mine, so I arranged to meet him at three thirty.

I needed to file my deed at the courthouse. According to an email from Jane, I also had to pick up forms for a homestead exemption, some sort of tax thing she promised to explain at lunch. There were some other things I had to do for Dane, Lieberman at the courthouse such as open an estate and get letters of appointment for the executor, and I'd finally finished the initial asset inventory on another case. Plenty of time to get all that done and then meet my friends for lunch.

I was just about to head out when Tony Caprelli knocked on my open door. He'd loosened his tie and rolled up his shirtsleeves. His hair was mussed, as if he'd been raking his fingers through it.

"Got a minute?"

My mouth was dustbowl dry, so I just nodded and pointed him to the chair recently vacated by Liam. Then my brain started doing the inevitable comparisons. Tony was a little shorter than Liam, but he was definitely the better dressed of the two. Both had black hair, but I could tell Tony had his cut regularly—and not by some hack in a strip mall, either.

"You didn't seem too thrilled about taking a couple of refresher courses," he said.

Working with you and a raise sealed the deal. "Was I supposed to?"

He smiled, and I noticed a really sexy dimple on the right side of his face about an inch to the right of his very sexy mouth. Liam didn't have any dimples. But he did have those incredible blue eyes. Tony's eyes were nice. Brown, but nice.

I started imagining him on the precipice of passion. I'd bet my impending raise that those eyes turned the color of rich, imported chocolates, sensual and sinful. I wondered what it would feel like to have his large, square-tipped fingers touching me. The temperature in the room rose along with my interest. Who wouldn't be interested? The guy was gorgeous, smart, financially stable, and three feet away from me.

"I guess not. Victor gave me your personnel file."

I tried not to groan or grimace. "Dull reading, I imagine."

"Anything but," he said, lacing his fingers behind his head. "Why'd you stop at a bachelor's degree? You had the grades, and your LSAT scores would have gotten you into the law school of your choice."

"Have you met my mother?" Jesus, just what I needed—a third musketeer jumping on the Finley-could-have-made-something-of-herself bandwagon.

"Let me guess, she's less than thrilled by your career choices."

My shoulders relaxed, and I leaned back in my chair. "That's putting it mildly. Luckily for her, I have a sister whom she can brag about for days on end."

"An attorney?"

"Pediatric oncologist."

He whistled. "That would be a tough act to follow."

"I wasn't the follower, I was the leader. Lisa's three years younger than I am and about to marry a doctor. If you're keeping score, that's Lisa two, Finley zero."

He laughed. "You did good work on the Evans investigation."

My heart skipped a self-congratulatory beat. "Thank you."

"And on the Spencer case."

"Thank you again, but you must not have read carefully. Mr. Dane fired me in both instances."

"And rehired you," he said.

"Only because I brought new clients to the firm."

Tony shook his head. "Victor Dane isn't an idiot, Finley. He knows you're bright and very capable. So does Ellen Lieberman. She told me you mastered complex contracts in under a week."

It felt really good to have someone compliment my work. It also felt really weird. Especially since I'd just planned my day to include a long lunch and personal errands all on Dane, Lieberman's dime. I felt a little guilty, but not guilty enough to change my plans. I was grateful, not stupid. I did do good work. I just had a limited work ethic.

"Have any questions for me?" he asked.

Do you put out on the first date? "No, sir."

"Don't call me 'sir.' 'Tony' will do just fine. I'm taking the morning to get settled in, but I'd like to meet with you at three thirty."

While I was minorly excited that Dane, Lieberman was branching out into criminal law, did they have to flipping do it at three thirty? "That would be fine," I lied.

"Great. See you in my office then." He rose and started for the door.

"Where exactly is your office?"

"Fourth floor. I think it used to belong to Mr. Zarnowski."

My heart skipped a beat. "He's not coming back?"

"Apparently not, if they've given me his office."

"The fourth floor is for partners."

He paused in the doorframe and glanced back at me. "Yeah, I know. Guess we'll be ordering new letterhead."

Becky was going to be frosted. She'd been working like a slave for five years with a single goal in mind—making partner. As I called Feldman to reschedule, I silently prayed Ellen would tell Becky before lunch. I didn't want to be the bearer of bad news, especially not to my dearest friend in the world. I also knew there was no way I could stay mute through lunch if she didn't know. Crap.

Not when the new partner was Tony. After he left, I imagined what kind of wedding we'd have and what our children might look like. Foolish, yes. But out of the question? No. Okay, so I'm iffy on the children part, but if Tony came back and asked me to marry him in the next five minutes, I think I'd say yes. He was positively made to order. Putting the whole employer-employee thing aside, he definitely piqued my interest. He was gorgeous, polished, and *so* not Liam McGarrity. The employer thing wasn't really an issue. I knew three or four paralegals, administrative assistants, and secretaries who'd ended up marrying their bosses. I could be happy going from support staff to pampered spouse.

As I went back to packing for my jaunt to the courthouse, I wondered how my life could have changed so dramatically in less than twenty-four hours. The last thing I did before leaving my office was to slip the medallion into my purse.

The police might not care who the teenage girl was or how she died, but I did. And I wanted to know how she died holding Jonathan's medallion.

"I'M STARVING," JANE SAID when she joined me near the podium. "How long is the wait?"

"Ten minutes," I said, holding the plastic square thing that would buzz, flash, and vibrate as soon as our table was ready. My stomach gurgled as the scents of dozens of different foods floated all around me. I was eyeing the cheesecake case, trying to decide which decadent dessert I'd order to go. In my life, cheesecake for dinner was a totally acceptable entrée.

Liv and Becky arrived a few minutes later, just as the plastic thing started to buzz and flash. "Great timing," I said, following the waiter as he led us through the large, busy restaurant.

Jane and I shared one side of the booth, while Becky and Liv settled in opposite us. The food was great, but the restaurant tended to be noisy, so we all leaned forward on the polished wood table. One look at Becky's gloomy green eyes confirmed she'd heard about the new partner.

Liv, as always, was cheery and telling us about her latest coup—her company, Concierge Plus, had landed the Semple-Gilmore wedding reception contract. "Ask me what the budget is?" she asked, her eyes wide with excitement.

Jane, always the accountant, sighed, "I don't want to know. It always amazes me when rich people spend a small fortune to celebrate marriages that have the shelf life of arugula."

Liv's perfect lips pressed together in a perfect pout. Not uncommon, since Olivia Garrett had perfect everything. Thank God she's my friend—if not, I'd have to hate her for being so incredibly beautiful. Even the waiter, who I was sure was gay, couldn't keep his eyes off her as he asked for our drink orders.

Ignoring the waiter, I said cheerfully, "Liv's going to do such a spectacular job on the wedding that both parties are going to have her cater not only their divorce but also all future weddings. It's job security."

Liv said "Damn right" and opted for champagne while the rest of us ordered the tropical iced tea. Champagne sounded good, but I was pretty sure Tony wouldn't appreciate my showing up for our first staff meeting with a blood alcohol level of point-five.

Toying with the paper band holding her utensils together, Becky guessed, "Five million."

Liv shook her head, then focused on me.

"The supermarket chain Gilmores?" I asked.

She nodded.

"Seven million."

"Ten," Liv practically squealed with delight. "Can you imagine?"

"No," we all said in unison. Actually, Becky added the f bomb, but I figured that was more a result of her mood than anything else.

"I thought you got passed over on that event last year," Jane said.

Liv nodded. "I did, but it turns out the bride felt that the previous planner wasn't treating her with the appropriate amount of deference due a Palm Beach debutante."

"Maybe because she isn't a Palm Beach deb?" I suggested. "Wasn't Terri Semple Gilmore's secretary or something?" The image of Tony flashed through my head.

Liv grinned. "She was his secretary's secretary. Rumor has it she sabotaged the secretary, took her job, and six months later, she had a whopper of an engagement ring on her finger."

"Guess there's hope for all of us," I said on a long breath. "I think it's easier to break out of jail than to break into Palm Beach society."

Liv leaned in closer and whispered, "Rumor also has it that if Papa Gilmore was still alive, he'd nix the nuptials in a heartbeat."

"Lucky for her he died last year," Jane said.

Becky added, "You mean lucky for Liv's business."

I could sense Liv's feelings getting hurt by Becky's lack of enthusiasm, so I figured it would be best for everyone if I interceded. "Dane, Lieberman hired a new partner, and they tagged me to work for him."

All eyes turned on Becky. Quickly I said, "His

name is Tony Caprelli, and he'll be heading the new criminal division."

"That sucks," Liv said, patting Becky's hand. "You've worked your fanny off for that firm."

Becky shrugged. "I'm not a criminal specialist."

"Tell me they at least gave you a raise," Jane said.

Becky's eyes met mine. "Nope, that would be Finley who got the raise. Congrats, by the way." Her sentiment was sincere, but it lacked enthusiasm. Totally understandable.

Holding up one hand, I waved it furiously. "Don't congratulate me. The raise came at a very high price. I have to take classes at the community college two nights a week."

"You?" Liv asked, barely able to keep her laughter in check. "You hate school, you always have. Besides, don't you have to rehab your house? Or at least get rid of the skeleton?"

"No one seems too interested in the girl in the closet."

"So they know it was a girl?" Becky asked.

I nodded. "A teenager, according to Liam."

The minute I said his name, three sets of eyes widened, and they stilled in silent anticipation. "He came by my office."

"And?" Liv prompted.

I shrugged. "And nothing. Can we get back to the house?"

Reluctantly they nodded.

"Good. So this new job opportunity will earn me some much-needed overtime, and the raise will come in handy, since my new house is a money pit."

"Speaking of handy," Jane said as she reached into her large Coach tote. "I made a list of contractors."

I took the piece of paper, then turned. I stared at my friend for less than thirty seconds before she broke and spilled her guts. "Okay, so I didn't *personally* put the list together. Liam has some contacts, and it's always wise to get references before you start any home improvement project."

"That man has it bad for you," Liv opined.

"No, he doesn't," I replied. "He just derives some sort of sick pleasure from toying with me. I'm completely immune to him."

"Liar," Becky muttered. "If he walked in here this minute and crooked his finger, you'd go running."

"Trust me, his finger won't be crooking anytime soon."

"What would you do if he did?" Jane asked.

Run through fire. "Turn him down. The guy has too much baggage. There's the whole thing with the ex-wife. I'd understand why they spend so much time together if they had kids, but they don't. Which can only mean one thing—he isn't over her, and after wasting the last two years of my life in a dead-end relationship, I'm not going to make that mistake again."

"Who said anything about a relationship?" Becky asked. "Just hook up with the guy. Do the friends-with-benefits thing. Great sex does not require happily ever after."

"Says the woman who hasn't had a date since the Clinton administration," Liv inserted.

Becky scoffed. "Please, Liv, give me dating advice. I haven't had the nerve to tell you until now, but my whole life I've dreamed of being with a man who is over thirty and still lives with his parents. How is Garage Boy?" she asked, humor dancing in her eyes.

"Ladies," Jane warned. "Can we all just agree that right now none of us is doing very well in the relationship department?"

We spent the rest of our lunch chatting, mostly about the best way for me to go about attacking the remodeling of my new house. Jane came totally prepared with applications to get me all sorts of grants and tax breaks. Before leaving, I ordered a slice of cookies and cream cheesecake to go.

Becky lingered with Jane and Liv. I hurried back to the office, knowing full well that Margaret would be lying in wait. If she could, I think she'd attach one of those GPS ankle things they put on prisoners to me. Instead, she had to settle for snarling at me when I came through the front door.

"Any messages?" I asked, though I kept walking. Margaret made a point of letting my calls go to voice mail.

So her "Yes" caught me off guard.

Turning on the balls of my feet, I walked to her desk and held out my hand, expecting one of those pink message slips. Instead, she just smiled . . . well, her version of a smile, which is much more like a sneer. "Mr. Caprelli had to reschedule your three thirty."

"Until?"

"Seven," Margaret practically sang with unabashed joy. She reached down and handed me a small slip of paper. "If that's a problem, he said for you to call him on his cell phone. I told him to expect a call."

I'll bet that wasn't the only thing she said.

Reluctantly, I had to give my nemesis props as I went to the elevator and took some of my frustration out by slapping the button for the second floor. If I blew him off, I'd be playing right into Margaret's trap. But seven o'clock? What part of 9:00 to 4:59 didn't Caprelli understand? Thank God he was smoking hot, or I would have blown him off.

I added his cell number to my iPhone, then tossed the slip of paper in the trash. For the third time, I called Feldman's office, and this time I got lucky. Apparently, one of his meetings had been rescheduled as well, and, according to his secretary, he could see me in thirty minutes. Normally I would have agonized over what case could get me past Margaret without her dialing Vain Dane to report me AWOL, but this time I didn't bother. I breezed past her with nothing but a wave of my hand. I'd more than make up for any time I missed by staying late.

Feldman's office was a small, brick building squashed in the middle of Clematis Street. A fresh coat of white paint brightened the brick, as did the tropical coral shutters flanking the windows and doors. His name was stenciled on the door in simple block print.

As I opened the door, a tiny bell chimed. My nose was assaulted by the strong smell of sauerkraut and corned beef with a hint of kosher pickle. For a minute, I wondered if I'd walked into a deli or a property management office.

Standing next to a vacant desk with my documents tucked into my tote, I heard a noise down the hallway and looked in that direction. A short, dumpy man hustled toward me, wiping mustard from his tie in the process.

"You must be Finley," he said as he switched the soiled napkin to his left hand and extended his right.

I didn't want to be rude, but I wasn't thrilled with the idea of shaking hands, although I did it anyway. Thankfully, I had some Purell in my purse. "Mr. Feldman."

"Call me Marc," he said, squeezing my hand.

He had a bad comb-over, and his mustard-stained tie fell about three inches shy of his waistband. Okay, it wasn't the tie's fault: he had one of those protruding bellies that had me dying to ask when the baby was due. Instead, I followed him back to his office.

Sty was more like it. Papers were stacked high, some in folders, some loose, and all of it teetering precariously to the left. Half of his desk and all of his waste paper can were filled with fast food and/or candy wrappers.

In an attempt at gallantry, he removed an untidy pile of file folders sandwiched between newspapers and God only knew what else, and dumped them on the floor. Then he brushed a Tootsie Roll wrapper off the chair before offering it to me. I had a hard time imagining my mother in this hovel, but it did explain why she had little to no interaction with Feldman.

"What can I do for you?" he asked, then shook his head. "I'm assuming this has something to do with the body they found in the house?"

I nodded.

"I'll tell you the same thing I told the cops. Last time I was inside the house was a good seven months ago, when I served eviction papers on Ms. Redmond. Did a walk-through when she left six months ago, and there definitely wasn't no skeleton in the closet."

That meant someone had put a ten- to fifteen-year-old skeleton in the house after Melinda Redmond moved out. Taking a pad out of my tote, I asked, "What do you know about the former tenant?

"Melinda Redmond? She worked for the ad agency in New York that handled Mr. Tanner's business account. Found Jesus or something and started some one-woman crusade. She impressed your father so much he agreed to rent the house to her and her kids for a fraction of the going rate. I thought she was a nut job." Blinking once, he met my eyes. "No disrespect to your father's memory, of course."

"None taken." My mother had a penchant for being overly dramatic. I had to verify what she'd told me. "So why was Melinda evicted?"

Feldman reached behind him and jerked open a dented metal file drawer, pulling out a folder that was about three inches thick. "Why wasn't she evicted sooner is a better question." He opened the file. "Citations from the city for failure to maintain the property. Citations for noise complaints. Citations for open burning. Failure to pay rent on time. Late fees accruing interest. Your mother had to pay to lay down sod and paint the exterior to avoid the city's fines. Spit and chewing gum repairs, but we had to do something to stop the fines. It really got bad about twelve months ago."

My heart sank as I imagined my daily lattes being drained by the money-sucking house. "How so?"

"The house was severely damaged by the hurricanes last year. We'd schedule a repairman, and Redmond would cancel the repair. Stopped returning calls. I don't know what happened, just that she let the house go to hell in a handcart. Excuse my French. It wasn't until I worked the deal with the developer that your mother finally signed off on the eviction."

"Deal?"

He nodded. "Until last week, when your mother had a sentimental change of heart, I was all set to sell the property to one of the neighbors. The house was scheduled to be bulldozed next week. The guy already had plans drawn for a pool and guesthouse to be built on the site."

"Did the tenant know that?"

"Sure. I told her we were tearing the house down. I might even have told her we'd do it with her still inside."

"Bulldozing the house might have obliterated all traces of the skeleton," I said, thinking aloud. "So the tenant, Melinda Redmond, could have put the skeleton in the closet."

"Not necessarily. The permit was applied for several months ago. Public record. Anyone could have read about the demolition, gotten the address, and stuffed the bones in the closet."

"How easily?"

"It's all online and published in the *Palm Beach Post*."

"Do you happen to know where I can find Ms. Redmond?"

He shrugged. "Call the county."

"Why?"

"She was a foster mother. They should have an address on her, but hey, this is Florida. She wouldn't be the first foster parent to go MIA."

Owning a home is like getting a puppy; you
love it, but you keep finding crap everywhere.

five

As I walked back to my office, I tried to
drum up a memory of Melinda Redmond. I
had some vague recollection of meeting the
tall, pretty brunette at Jonathan's office when I was
about twelve and our family going out to dinner with
her once or twice. I hated to think she'd been having
an affair with him.

Who was I kidding? My mother would have
smelled an affair from across the Atlantic Ocean, and
Jonathan would have paid dearly for a transgression
like that. Hell, as memory served, husband number
four had strayed, and my mother had gone the extra
mile and filed a civil suit against his mistress for
alienation of affection. Of course the suit had been
dropped within a day of being filed; it had merely
been the club she'd used to beat every penny out of
the poor guy.

No, there was no way Jonathan had cheated with
Melinda Redmond. But not having all the pieces

yet inspired all sorts of suspicions in me. I couldn't wait to get to my computer to do a little cyber-digging.

Unfortunately, I had to wait. My first priority was hiring a contractor for the remodel. Even with my raise and the overtime, it was going to be hard to pay a mortgage and my rent simultaneously unless I blew off a few VISA payments in exchange for collection agency phone calls. I'd been down that road and was in no hurry to incur the wrath of the debt gods again. No. I was going to have to cut *something* out of my monthly expenses. What could I live without? New shoes? Needed those. My Rolex parts? Nope. Had to have those. That cute Betsey Johnson dress? Had to have that. The only thing I absolutely, positively could do without was—*food.*

I'd have to think about this a bit longer. On to more important and immediate issues.

Using the list Jane/Liam had provided, I called the first name. Happy Handyman Harold answered on the first ring. "Hi, um, Harold." I assumed neither Happy nor Handyman was his given name. "This is Finley Tanner."

"Already spoke to Liam. I'm just finishing a job now and ready to head over to your place. I can pull up and remove your carpet before it gets dark. Anything else will have to wait till tomorrow."

"That would be great," I said, not wanting to question my good luck. Inexpensive contractors in Florida don't have a stellar reputation, but I didn't think Liam would send me to a serial killer. "Is there any chance you could swing by my office for the key? I've got a late meeting."

"Anything for a friend of Liam's."

"Anything?"

"Hell, yeah. Er, sorry, ma'am. Liam, he's a good guy. Talked the state's attorney into knocking my last felony down to a misdemeanor. I'd be doing a full dime at Martin Correctional if he hadn't helped me out."

"Great," I said with far less enthusiasm.

"Don't you worry, though. I haven't touched a crack pipe in going on seven years."

"Good for you," I said, at a complete loss for anything more profound. *My contractor is a felon.* So . . . what? The truth of the matter was that there was nothing in the run-down house that could be ruined, and the floor had to be taken care of before I could move in. The rarely used practical side of my nature reared its head.

"What time will you be coming by? I'll meet you in the parking lot so you don't have to trek all the way up to my office." *Where people will see you and wonder why my new best friend is a recovering crack addict.*

"Twenty, thirty minutes."

"See you then."

I called one of the interns on the first floor and had him race to the hardware store down the block to have an extra key made. Call me cautious, but I didn't relish the idea of giving my only key to Happy Harold the Dope Fiend.

I was half tempted to call Liam and ream him a new

one, but then I remembered I was completely tempted in other areas. So the safest course of action was to have as little interaction with the guy as possible.

I ended up tipping the intern twenty bucks, not because I was feeling generous, but because I was buying his silence. I don't actually have any authority over the interns without prior approval from one of the attorneys, and none of them would have approved of my sending the eager twenty-three-year-old on a personal errand.

Happy Harold wasn't what I expected. He was worse. He pulled into the parking lot in a possibly green pickup that spewed and coughed blue smoke. He stepped out wearing filthy denim overalls and a sweat-stained wifebeater T-shirt. He smelled like a sneaker. To heighten the stench, he had an unlit cigar stub wedged in the corner of his mouth. Judging by the presence of acne on his forehead, he was probably close to my age, but tanned, leathery skin and a jagged scar down the right side of his face made him look more like fifty.

He offered his dirty hand, complete with grime-encrusted nails. At the same time he smiled, revealing a single yellowed tooth. But that wasn't the kicker. The guy had on a wedding ring. He had one tooth, a rap sheet, and a wife. Life really wasn't fair.

In my second Purell moment of the day, I handed him the spare key and gave him directions to the house. "I don't have a Dumpster yet," I told him.

"No problem. If you're just going to toss the stuff, I can probably find a use for it."

"Consider it yours," I said. "What do I owe you for removing the carpet?"

He grinned and rolled the cigar to the opposite corner of his mouth. "Fifty bucks ought to cover it. Once I've given the place a look-see, I'll do up a real estimate."

I opened my wallet and discreetly pulled out fifty dollars. Pretty silly, since I'd just given the guy a key to my house. Being overly cautious that he might see how much cash I had on hand was probably the least of my worries.

I returned to my office and sent Liam a very insincere thank-you email. He replied, but I deleted it and turned my attention to the internet.

In less than five minutes, I had three newspaper articles and a White Pages listing for Melinda Redmond with a zip code in North Palm Beach. The first thing I read was a ten-year-old human-interest piece on her that practically nominated her for sainthood.

After leaving New York and a lucrative job in advertising, she'd devoted her life to providing care and nurture to troubled teens trapped in the Florida foster-care system. There was a small, grainy black-and-white photograph of the woman I kinda remembered surrounded by a half dozen teenagers. I filled in my credit card information and requested a copy of the picture.

News photos often have the names of the people listed on the back. That a woman who cared for teenagers had lived in *my house* and the skeleton of a teenager had been left in *my house* was just too coincidental. I tried to think of scenarios that would explain why a killer would have kept the body. *And* kept moving it. *And* not notice Jonathan's medallion. I did a quick online surf and found an answer to my last question. Apparently, *death grip* wasn't an expression; it was a fact. If a person dies with a closed fist, it stays closed. Kinda creepy in a factoid way. The keeping and the moving were things I couldn't explain.

A shudder danced along my spine at the mere thought. The Everglades were within easy driving distance, so why not dump the body there? I hunted for an answer to that question on the Net and found it rather easily. Apparently, alligators prefer live meat or, at a bare minimum, a fresh kill. Who knew those disgusting things were picky eaters? Over the years, many bodies dumped in the Everglades have been retrieved and identified, thanks to the discerning palates of the native reptiles.

So the killer had to have been smart enough to know the feeding habits of alligators, or was a student, I quickly surmised after navigating to the Florida school curriculum page. The local ecosystem is a big part of high-school science. So another possibility was that one teenager had killed another teenager in Melinda's care. That possibility raised more questions than it answered. Melinda would have noticed if one of her kids had gone missing. Right? If so, why hadn't she reported the missing teenager to the police? Or the state would have noticed, albeit eventually, that Melinda had been one teen short. And if the state had noticed or Melinda had made a report, why hadn't anything shown up when the police had searched for possible matches to the skeleton?

None of that explained the frozen part or the climate-controlled part of the ME's findings. I sat back in my chair and chewed on the tip of my pen as I tried to come up with a logical series of events that would explain everything, including my finding Jonathan's medallion in the corpse's hand. Nothing leaped to the forefront.

Well, unless you counted Tony Caprelli, who was standing in my doorway tapping his watch.

"Oh, gosh," I said apologetically as I quickly clicked my computer into hibernate and grabbed my purse, a pad, and a pen. "I was in the middle of something and lost track of the time." And my cheesecake dinner was still untouched in the employee refrigerator, so he could expect some serous stomach rumblings.

"Obviously," he said.

I followed Tony to the elevator, and then into Mr. Zar—*his* office. Someone had already scraped the gold lettering off the door. To my utter delight, I smelled freshly brewed coffee and immediately decided to forgive Tony for violating my sacred out-by-five policy.

The furniture was the same, but in a single day, he'd turned the ambiance of the office from elegant masculinity to relaxed family playroom. Everywhere I looked, I found framed photographs of a little girl ranging in age from toddler to maybe nine or ten. There were macaroni works of art, crude drawings—mostly rainbows—and clay art projects that held paper clips and pushpins. She was obviously his daughter; the resemblance was unmistakable.

The other obvious thing was there didn't seem to be a Mrs. Caprelli.

"Her name is Isabella. She's ten going on thirty," he said as he motioned me into a chair.

"She's beautiful."

"Thanks. Sorry about the last-minute change in plans, but I had to interview a housekeeper."

"Single father?" I asked, unashamedly fishing.

"Yeah," he answered as he sat down and pressed the heels of his hands against his eyes for a minute. "I've had her in a camp for a week. Not her favorite thing. But enough about my domestic disturbances. I wanted to talk about the kinds of cases we'll be handling."

"Criminal cases."

"Yep. The state's attorneys win about ninety percent of their cases. So get used to losing."

"If you'll excuse me for saying, you're pretty cavalier about innocent people going to jail."

He shook his head and smiled. That whole dimple thing was really distracting.

"What makes you think our clients will be innocent?"

"I just assumed—"

"Mistake number one. This leads me to rule number one. Never ask a client if he or she is innocent."

"Why not?"

"Because then I'm stuck with a single fact pattern to argue in court. It's always better to leave your options open, since you never know what a prosecutor will throw at your client. Criminal law is all about leveling the playing field. The state has a police force and labs and all sorts of things at their disposal to assist in prosecuting an individual. The defendant only has us. My job is simple. Rule number two—make the state prove its case, not the defendant prove his innocence."

"You make it sound like a game," I said, remembering quite distinctly how it felt to be wrongly accused of a crime.

"In a lot of ways, it is. It's like chess. It's a combination of skill and strategy."

"Not guilt or innocence?"

"That's God's job, not mine. Rule number three—no child-killer cases."

"Isn't that contrary to rule number two?"

"Yeah, but they're my rules, so I get to make adjustments. Margaret showed me the morning paper. So what's the deal with the skeleton in your house?"

Leave it to Margaret to throw me under the bus. "It violates rule number three. The ME's report says the deceased was a teenager."

"Know anything about it?"

"No, how could I? I'd owned the house for a matter of hours before we found the thing in the closet."

"But it was your mother's house, right?"

I leaned forward and placed my palms flat on his desk. "A house she never set foot in. If you're concerned, call Detective Steadman or Graves. They interviewed her last night. Why do you care?"

"Because Victor indicated that you'd probably do or say something that might require the firm to become involved. I just want to be prepared."

I was starting to get annoyed. "How can the firm get dragged into anything? It's my understanding that the police don't work up a sweat on a case this cold."

"But you will," he said. "Victor wanted to make sure I reminded you that what you do reflects on the firm."

Screw his cute dimple. I went past annoyed to completely pissed. "Consider me reminded."

He shrugged. "Of course I told Victor I thought that was a ridiculous position to take."

"W-what?"

"Jesus Christ, Finley. If I'd bought a house with a skeleton hidden in the closet, you can bet your a— fanny I'd want to know the who, the how, and the why."

I was stunned. Until this second, Becky had been my only true ally at the firm. Now it appeared as if handsome Tony Caprelli was on my side too. Color me impressed. And surprised.

"Really?" I relaxed and sat back in my chair.

He nodded. "I can't imagine how disgusting that was for you and your friends to stumble upon. That said, I need you to focus on taking classes—not on solving puzzles, or, worse, interfering with a police investigation."

My cheeks grew warm.

"But not scary enough," Tony continued, "to keep you from disturbing the corpse, though, right?"

I opened my mouth, then snapped it closed. Was he reading my mind?

Again, I got a dimple smile. "Liam McGarrity mentioned it during his interview."

"Interview?" I repeated, as if English had been a new language.

"Part-time at first. A good defense attorney has to have a good investigator. Is there a problem?"

Hell, yes! "Of course not," I lied.

"Don't get sidetracked over this skeleton thing. *Dead* and *murder* aren't always synonymous. There could be a perfectly logical explanation for how the skeleton ended up in the closet."

"I'm sure that's true."

"Liam mentioned that he thought you took something off the body?"

"If I tell you, wouldn't that sidetrack me?"

"Yep. Just call me curious. It'll take some time for me to bring in clients, and who knows? Maybe I can help."

I hesitated, then eventually reached into the side compartment of my purse. I pulled the medallion out of its silk hiding place. "She was holding this."

After inspecting it, Tony asked, "When did you give this to your father?"

"Stepfather," I corrected, as if that was somehow relevant. "About twenty years ago. His team won the CV Whitney Cup Championship. It's a big deal among polo enthusiasts. I bought the medal for him and had it inscribed."

"And you last saw it . . . ?"

"I'm not sure. I think it was when my mother was married to Enrique Rossi. He was a retired polo player and raised Thoroughbreds in Argentina. They split their time between Palm Beach and his family's other estate outside Sao Paulo. I know that before Jonathan died, he kept it in a small cedar box on his dresser."

Oddly enough, Tony was taking notes. "Where was this?"

"Their home on Palm Beach." I gave him the address. "My sister, Lisa, and I were shipped off to boarding school about a month after Jonathan died. We only came back for holidays and a few weeks in the summer, so I'm not positive if I saw it last before or after Jonathan's death. It was a long time ago."

"Your mother told the police it was stolen."

"It could have been. I know the Palm Beach house was robbed. It freaked my mother out enough so that she closed up that house and moved to New York for a while. Then Jonathan died and my mother married Enrique and she was back in the polo circle again."

"So Enrique was your mother's next husband. Could he have taken the medallion?"

I shook my head. "No. Enrique was husband number three. Jonathan was her first husband. He died and she married Jake Halpern. That didn't work because she was trying to recapture her youth by sleeping with one. Jake was handsome, but he only married my mother for her money. Jake was in his early twenties, and as soon as my mother figured out his motives, he was history. It lasted *maybe* four months.

"Next came Enrique. He was my mother's age, only Enrique couldn't keep it in his pants, so she divorced him. Got half his family's lands in the divorce.

"My mother wised up and set her sights on . . . shall we call them more mature men. Enter Kirk Browning. He was a nice guy. Some sort of retired insurance broker. He died seven months after they got married. Never had kids, so his whole fortune went to my mother.

"Her last husband was Carl Johnstone. I'm not sure what he did, he was long retired by the time he married my mother. They were sailing around the world on his private motor yacht when Carl suffered a massive heart attack."

Tony was grimacing.

"When I say it out loud, it sounds pretty bad, huh?"

"Marrying your mother can be hazardous to your health."

"Yeah, but you've got to give her points for trying," I joked. "Even with Jake and Enrique, all she was trying to do was reclaim what she'd had with Jonathan."

"So you don't think there's any connection between this Melinda Redmond woman and any of your mother's subsequent husbands?"

Vehemently I shook my head. "If my mother so much as thought any of them were involved with another woman, she would have jettisoned them from her life in a heartbeat. That's her style."

"Is that what she did to you?"

"No, not exactly. I'm her daughter, so she can't shun me without explaining it to the DAR and the Junior League, so instead, she opted to cut me off when I decided not to go to law school. If I change my mind and/or if I marry someone 'suitable,' then she'll reconsider her position."

"And here I thought only Italian mothers interfered. Part of the reason I moved to Florida was so my mother would stop setting me up every Friday night."

"I hate blind dates."

"Ditto," he said, pouring us both mugs of coffee. "Only in my case, she falls on the 'Isabella needs a mother' sword."

Hell, we were spilling our guts, so I might as well go for it. "There's no Mrs. Caprelli?"

"Not since September 11, 2001."

My heart squeezed in my chest. "I'm sorry."

"The worst part is Isabella doesn't remember Maria."

There was a sad, distant look in his brown eyes that touched me. While I hadn't lost Jonathan to a national tragedy brought about by fanatics, I knew what it was like to lose a parent. "But you do, and you'll remind her," I offered.

He let out a long breath. "Not sure how we got so far afield."

"I'm using the skeleton as a starting point."

Tony frowned. "I thought we just agreed that you weren't going to let this whole skeleton thing distract you from your new responsibilities."

"It won't. But what I do on my own time . . . ?" I let that hang in the air.

He shrugged. "Any idea where to go next?"

I shook my head. "I'll figure something out."

"If it was me," Tony said as he stroked the faint shadow of stubble on his chin, "I'd arrange for a private autopsy. The ME's office is good, but they've got a lot on their plate, so they sometimes miss minute traces of foul play. A cause of death would be helpful in establishing your time line. A second autopsy might even give you an ID." Tony glanced down at his watch. "I've got to run. I promised Izzy I'd tuck her in." He stood and came around the desk.

He was very close. The coffee scent of his breath washed over my face as I felt the heat coming off him. I'm not psychic, but I can certainly tell when a man is looking at me with interest. Yep. Tony's dark eyes locked with mine, igniting a spark in the pit of my stomach. My whole body tensed. I was waiting for something, but I didn't know what that something was. Much to my disappointment, Tony reached for my hand. Much to my pleasure, he held it a few seconds longer than necessary. Maybe planning our wedding wasn't as far-fetched as I'd thought.

"Thanks for coming by," he said, his eyes fixated on my mouth.

I knew what he was thinking. Hell, I was thinking the same thing. The offices were deserted, we were consenting adults, and there was definitely a connection. The only reason a man looked at your mouth was a prelude to a kiss. I was at an unexpected crossroad—reach for him or play it safe and walk away.

Depleting most of my self-control, I pivoted and took a slow, deliberate walk down the hall. I didn't need eyes in the back of my head to know Tony was checking out my butt. That knowledge alone was enough to put a smile on my face. I'd won the first round.

Twenty minutes later, I was pulling into the driveway of my uninhabitable home. I'd expected to find Happy Harold the Crack Head. Instead, Liam was seated on the front porch, uncorking a bottle of my favorite red wine.

"You're trespassing." I watched as he pulled a hunk of cheese and a baguette from a bag he'd partially hidden behind his back. My empty stomach rumbled. *Traitor.*

"Nice to see you too," he replied. "Wine?"

"Yes, thank you." I sat next to him on the top step. "The stench is gone," I remarked as I glanced over my shoulder through the open door. "How come there are lights on? Wait, how come there are lights?"

Liam shrugged. "I made a trip to Home Depot and called Florida Power and Light and had service turned on. Oh, there'll be a onetime fifty-dollar security fee on your first month's bill."

"Don't your need my Social Security number to do that?"

"Yep."

I bit off a hunk of bread, chewed it, then swallowed it along with some wine. "Is there anything about me you don't know?"

"Nope."

"In case you were wondering, that's very irritating."

"Want me to take my wine and food and leave?"

"No." I turned and offered him my sweetest smile. "I want the wine and food to stay. You're welcome to leave anytime."

"I had to check on Harold's work."

I drained my plastic cup. "Thanks for sending me a drug addict."

"Recovering."

"Whatever. He has b-u-l-l and s-h-i-t tattooed on his respective knuckles."

"Popular prison tat."

"That's reassuring and screams professionalism." I stood and stepped over the wine bottle and went inside the house.

The mushy carpeting was gone, revealing partially rotted wooden subflooring. In the center of the dining room was a small, neatly swept pyramid of debris.

It wasn't until I sensed Liam behind me that I ventured down the hall to the master bedroom. Harold had pulled up the carpet and carted off the closet doors. As he had done throughout the house, Liam had placed an inexpensive, shadeless table lamp in the center of the room.

"Still spooked?" he asked.

Hell yes! "No," I replied as I rubbed the goose bumps on my arms. "Okay, maybe a little." I knew all I had to do was lean back and I'd be in his arms. I also knew that was a dangerous idea. Once burned, twice stupid. "So how did you finagle a job out of my new boss?"

"Tony? He called me. Offered a decent retainer."

"He's paying you to do nothing before he even gets his first client?" I asked as I turned quickly and went back into the less creepy part of the house.

"Isn't he sending you to school before he has his first client?"

How did he know all the comings and goings in my life? I rolled my eyes, and in the process, they fixed on a small, yellowed scrap of paper in the debris pile. Ignoring Liam completely, I went over, crouched down, and examined it from a few different angles. "Looks like it might have writing on it."

Unlike me, Liam wasn't the least bit squeamish about flicking aside the bug carcasses and other disgusting things to retrieve the paper. As he unfolded it, dust rained down to the floor.

Ragged edges indicated it had been torn from a pad or notebook. "What does it say?"

"Nothing. It can't talk."

I groaned at his bad joke and took the paper by the edge. In faint, barely legible printing, I could read only a few words:

Dear Sir: I'm sorry. I should have done this sooner but . . .

"What do you think this means?"

"Could be part of a suicide note," Liam suggested. "Assuming part of her suicide plan was to move around a lot after she offed herself."

I jabbed him in the ribs with my elbow. Not hard,

but enough to make my point. "Or . . . maybe whatever she should have done sooner got her killed."

"Or the note was written by any one of dozens of people who've lived in this house over the last fifteen years. Or one of their friends. Or one by—"

"Did I mention you were trespassing?"

"I'm just suggesting you keep this in perspective. Until we know who she was and/or how she died, it's impossible to tell what is or isn't important."

"I'm starting with Melinda. I called earlier and I'm having lunch with her tomorrow."

*If lying doesn't work, you probably
aren't doing it right.*

six

I AWAKENED THE NEXT MORNING to the irritatingly happy chirping of birds and a retina-burning shaft of sunlight slicing through my bedroom drapes.

My modest, rented apartment was on the ground floor of a complex in Palm Beach Gardens. It had a decent-sized bedroom and bathroom, but I chose it mainly for the walkout patio. The walkout wasn't as impressive, comparatively, now that I owned a house smack on the sugary sands of the Atlantic Ocean.

On autopilot, I got up, shuffled to the kitchen, and flipped on my coffeemaker. Leaning my elbows on the counter, I listened to the lyrical sounds of water seeping, then spitting, and then finally hissing to let me know the brew cycle was complete.

I poured a cup, then wandered over to the sliding glass door. Using my bare toe, I kicked free the dowel I used as added security, pushed the silver lock to the open position, and slid the door a few inches.

Warm, balmy air caressed my skin and lifted my hair off my shoulders. This was one of those days that convinced people to move to Florida. It was just past nine, little puffy white clouds drifted in off the ocean, and the thermometer hovered somewhere around eighty.

My place was fairly neat. The throw was balled in the corner of the sofa, right where I'd left it after watching the late news, and the television screen could have used some dusting, as could the coffee table, but my caffeine levels weren't high enough yet for me to contemplate chores.

As for most working people, Saturdays were catch-up days for me—laundry, groceries, all the mundane but necessary things that had to be done if I wanted to avoid a public nudity charge and the prospect of garlic-stuffed olives being my main meal of the day.

I rested my head against the doorjamb and looked critically at my furnishings. Until now I'd been content with my eclectic—definition: affordable—furniture, but I wanted more for the beach house. Closing my eyes, I imagined a casual yet chic blend of white with hints of . . . *other* colors. Nothing I could pull off without serious professional help.

Grabbing my phone, I pressed the speed-dial code to my friend Sam's place. His apartment was above mine, and I'd noticed his car in the parking lot the night before. He was a professional. He'd help me turn my cottage into a showplace.

"What?"

"Good morning to you too," I said, sipping coffee.

"It isn't morning, Finley. It's the middle of the night."

"On the West Coast, but now you're home. Time to readjust your internal clock and welcome a new day."

"Screw you, Mary Poppins."

"Fine," I said as I twirled a lock of hair around my forefinger. "You go back to sleep and I'll go shopping for furnishings for my new house all by my lonesome."

"Did you say new house?" Sam's voice no longer sounded foggy and distant.

"Yes, I did, but you obviously need your rest. Sorry I bothered you."

"I'll be down in five minutes."

It was more like twenty, but that suited me fine. It gave me enough time to brush my teeth, apply makeup, and knowing that I had a lunch with Melinda Redmond, pick out a casual but fun white Betsey Johnson dress accented all over with tiny cherries. I had one white cork-soled wedge on when the doorbell chimed.

I hopped over to the door, checked the peephole, then let Sam in. I managed to get the second shoe on just before he grabbed me in a big hug and swung me around the room. Of course my shoe left a scuff on the wall that I knew would be deducted from my security deposit, but I didn't care.

Sam was about five-foot-six, with brown eyes—tweezed brows, of course—and brown hair always styled perfectly with product. This morning, he'd chosen pale blue and green madras plaid shorts and a pale blue collared shirt. It didn't take a rocket scientist to guess his sexual orientation. Not that I cared. Sam had been my neighbor for years; long enough to know that neither one of us was any good at picking men.

He sat at one of the three mismatched stools at my bar while I told him all about the house, pausing only to refill his coffee mug or to eat a handful of Lucky Charms cereal right out of the box. One of the advantages of living alone is the freedom to eat what you please when you please. Lucky Charms pleases me.

"But all the remnants of the dead girl are gone now, right?" he asked uneasily.

I nodded. "Liam and I were there until almost ten. Not a bone in sight."

His brows arched. "With Liam? Until ten?"

"In the kitchen? With the wrench?"

"C'mon, Finley. A guy that hot and all you do is drink wine and break bread? Way to wuss out."

I leveled him with a glare. "I won't hire you as my decorator if you don't stop mentioning Liam."

Sam clapped his hands with excitement. "What's the budget, and when do we start?"

"Jane's working on a budget for me. You know better than to expect much, but we can head over there now and have a look around. You'll have to follow me, because I have a lunch date with the woman who used to rent the place."

Sam's fingers gripped my upper arm. "But she could be a killer. You can't meet her alone."

"Who said I was going to be alone?"

Sam sighed. "With hot, chivalrous—"

"I thought we just agreed we would not mention Liam's name."

He tossed me one of those childish superiority looks that was often accompanied by sticking out his tongue, but apparently he contained the urge. "*I* wasn't the one who mentioned him. Is this new too?" he asked after I pressed my keychain and made the BMW chirp.

"Yes. See all the stuff you miss when you go out of town?" As we were about to get into our cars, the FedEx truck zoomed into the parking lot and stopped right behind my car. The logo alone was enough to reignite the anger inside me. I'd probably associate FedEx with my breakup with Patrick for all time. However, the smiling face of the deliveryman quickly doused my irritation. He handed me a flat nine-by-twelve envelope, and I signed his bulky computerized thingy with its tethered pen.

I zipped open the tab and carefully removed the photograph from the envelope. It was much clearer than the one I'd seen on the *Palm Beach Post*'s website. This larger, eight-by-ten version made it possible for me to read the names typed neatly at the bottom of the photo.

Sam looked over my shoulder as I read. Unfortunately for me, Melinda Redmond was the only name listed. The others were simply identified by initials. "Crap."

"Maybe she can tell you herself at lunch," Sam suggested.

"Maybe," I murmured.

Just in case we got separated, I gave him directions to my cottage on Chilian Avenue. I still liked saying "my cottage." So much so that as I drove the twenty minutes from West Palm, over the bridge to Palm Beach proper, I must have said it a hundred times. I had homeowner's Tourette's.

I don't know whether it was the midday light or the fact that I'd accepted the condition of the house, but for whatever reason, I felt excited as I pulled into my driveway. From the outside, and only because of city ordinances, the place looked darling and pristine. I made a mental note to ask Jane how much it would cost to add a pool. Something small that could be heated during the winter months, when it often dipped below seventy.

Sam arrived even before I closed my car door. He grinned, then his bottom lip quivered, then tears started streaming down his cheeks. "I can't believe you're going to move. What if they rent your apartment to some old hag, or worse, homophobic frat boys?"

I patted his shoulder. "Or they could rent it to some incredibly hunky gay guy. Or a nice girl with an incredibly hunky gay brother. You never know."

He sniffled once, then regained his composure. "This is happening way too fast for me, but okay. Let's see what we've got to work with."

As soon as I opened the front door, Sam gasped.

"It looks like pictures I've seen of cells for Tibetan dissidents."

He started to turn away, but I spun him around and gently shoved him inside. "Look. Look at that beautiful view."

"Look," he said, pointing up, "look at that rotted ceiling joist. Geez, Finley, this place should be condemned."

"I think it was, but that's irrelevant now. Just give me ideas. You know my taste."

"Such as it is," he said without bothering to cloak his censure. Taking a notebook and pen out of his man purse, he strolled though the kitchen, shaking his head and making some sort of *tsk-tsk* sound while I followed along like an obedient tracking hound. He wrote as he walked.

A few times he stopped to make a frame with his hands, then moved along. It wasn't until we were on our way back to the kitchen that he opened a door I assumed was another closet.

Stink billowed out of it. Moldy, musty, humid stench. Feeling along the wall, I found a switch and flipped it. It wasn't a closet but a small garage partially filled with trash bags, scraps of wood, and an old gas grill minus the propane tank. I put that tidbit in the plus column. A single cement step led down to the garage floor. Next to the step was the rusted outline of a rectangle. I had no idea what had caused the stain, and quite frankly, I didn't care.

I was about to turn off the light when a piece of green and black striped fabric sticking out of one of the bags caught my eye. As I walked toward it, I heard Sam say, "Don't open anything. There could be raccoons or snakes or God only knows what in those bags."

Okay, so fear threatened to overtake my curiosity. But I figured there couldn't be a second body in here. Could there? Carefully, using my forefinger and thumb, I was able to tug the fabric free from the rusted twist tie holding the bag secure. Out popped a worn and torn T-shirt in a junior size 2. While it wasn't from one of the pricey shops that defined Worth Avenue as the Rodeo Drive of south Florida, it wasn't from a superstore either. It was vintage Abercrombie and Fitch.

"Stop playing in the trash, Finley."

Using the tip of my toe, I stabbed at a few of the two dozen bags, and it felt to me as if they were all full of clothing—or, at the very least, soft stuff. No bones, thank God. "I'll have Harold open these and sort them."

"What on earth for? It isn't like you'd wear vagrant people's castoffs."

If he only knew. But he didn't. I kept my eBay and outlet shopping habits to myself.

"There might be a clue in here."

"What kind of clue?"

"I don't know." I shivered. "Let's go back inside the house."

Sam went out to get a large sketch pad from his car while I wandered out onto the beach. I'd gotten within a few feet of the surf line when I saw a flash of light out of the right corner of my eye. Turning in that direction, I shielded my face and thought I caught a glimpse of something or someone crouched down in the three-foot-high sea grass that separated my house from my neighbor's. But after I blinked and my eyes refocused, I didn't see anything. Probably a bird or one of the sacred, federally protected turtles that lay eggs on the coast. I shook my head. It was probably nothing but the play of light against the foliage and my own fears screwing with me.

When I rejoined Sam, he was busy pacing off the size of each room. I helped by writing the length and width as he called out the dimensions. It was nearing eleven, and I had to meet Melinda Redmond at Bimini Twist just west of the Turnpike at noon. "We need to move this along."

"Decorating is an art. You can't hurry art," he said as he continued to sketch.

"Okay, then lock up when you're done."

"You're leaving me here alone?"

"Sam, we've opened every door. No bonus skeletons. Besides, Happy Harold is coming by, and you two should probably get together regarding any interior walls you want taken down."

"How about all of them?"

"How about you remember that I'm already hemorrhaging money?"

"I will use all of my decorating genius to turn this place into a seaside palace. But Finley, there are some serious structural issues that have to be addressed."

I kissed his cheek. "I trust you."

"Do you trust Happy Harold?"

Liam does. "Jury's still out on that one. I'll call your cell when I'm done with lunch. Thanks," I said, waving over my shoulder, walking down the steps and disarming my car alarm at the same time.

I was already contemplating macadamia nut–crusted sea bass as I turned left on Okeechobee Boulevard and eventually crossed the bridge connecting Palm Beach to the mainland. Like it is in most subtropical locales, as soon as you cross the railroad tracks, estate homes give way to more humble abodes. The crisp smell of the ocean is replaced by the choke of car exhaust, and bus and truck diesel, and it's occasionally relieved by the smell of freshly mowed grass.

Pockets of abject poverty coexist side by side with manicured gated communities. The telephone listing for Melinda had a North Palm Beach address. Probably one of the tidy small homes off A-1-A. I felt for her. A home in North Palm was not exactly a step up for her.

Eventually Okeechobee turns into a ribbon of strip malls, payday loan offices, liquor stores, and auto dealerships. The area west of Florida's Turnpike is more sparsely populated, thanks in large part to the number of private ranches and corporate orange groves. The ranches are slowly evolving, moving away from beef cattle production to more lucrative, swanky equestrian centers.

Bimini Twist is a large restaurant that serves good food. Me? I'd have picked one of the zillion or so restaurants with a water view, but that's just me.

My heart skipped a beat when I spotted Liam's car as I pulled into the lot. Hard to miss the 1964 Mustang, with its putty quarter panels and mismatched tires. I didn't recall inviting him to join me for lunch. However, it was five after twelve, so I grabbed my purse and the news photo and went into the dimly lit restaurant.

My mouth watered at the smells as a polite twenty-something hostess led the way to where Liam sat with a woman. Her back was to me, so all I could really see was shoulder-length dark brown hair and a few inches of a strapless Shoshanna ivory and white sundress. That sucker retailed for somewhere in the vicinity of three hundred fifty dollars, so either Melinda was a closet outlet shopper like me or the foster mother thing paid more than I thought.

As I approached the table, Liam stood, looking calm and casual in his chino cargo shorts and faded tropical shirt. I plastered a smile on my face but glared at him. My irritation didn't seem to faze him.

Melinda just turned her head, and the minute I saw her dark blue eyes I felt an instantaneous sense of recognition.

She smiled up at me. "I'm not sure I would have recognized you after all this time, Finley. You've turned into a stunning woman."

Talk about a passive-aggressive greeting. I was tempted to respond, *"Really? You look the same except for all those wrinkles."* Instead, I answered with a polite "Thank you," as the hostess helped push my rattan chair close to the square, glass-topped table.

"How is your mother?" Melinda asked.

I was cataloging every inch of her face. I remembered her as a young woman, but clearly she was over fifty, and, as far as I could tell, she hadn't had anything done except an eyelid lift. An unusual thing in Palm Beach. Most women start plastic surgery in their midthirties. "Fine." I switched, trying to get a personality read on the woman, but I couldn't. Other than the questionable greeting, which in all fairness, I could have taken the wrong way, she was open and polite and, well, likeable.

"I was horrified when I heard what they found at the house," Melinda said as she shoved a paper umbrella away from the rim of her glass to take a sip of what I guessed was some sort of tropical rum concoction.

The server appeared, handed all of us menus, and took my drink order: "Iced tea, thank you." After the server left, I ran my fingernail around the rim of my water goblet and agreed. "It was pretty disgusting."

"Mr. McGarrity showed me photographs of the house, and I can assure you, it looked nothing like that when I left." She reached down, grabbed her purse, opened it, and handed me a folded receipt. "See? I even had it cleaned and the carpets shampooed. They charged me extra for cleaning the appliances, which proves they were in the house when I left. The only items I left behind were some clothing, but I made arrangements with a local charity to pick up the donation."

"The donations are still there, but the appliances are definitely gone."

Melinda looked at me. Her eyes shone with apology and a hint of anger. "I wouldn't be surprised if Marc Feldman trashed the place intentionally."

"Why would he do that?"

"First," she said, raising a finger, "he made the last few months of my tenancy unbearable. He wouldn't fix anything, or if he did, his repairmen did a half-hearted job that lasted a week or two."

"So you think he was forcing you out?"

She nodded. "Well, none of us knew that your mother would transfer the property to you, so I think Marc's master plan was to force me out by neglecting the place, then earn himself a tidy commission selling it to a developer. It's a darling cottage, Finley, but let's face facts. It sits on prime Palm Beach ocean frontage. A smart investor would level the cottage and either sell the lot to one of the adjoining neighbors or build something more lavish on the site. And with all due respect, your mother never impressed me as a woman who would give away such a valuable asset."

"It was required generosity," I explained, feeling the tension in my muscles abate. "Until yesterday, I didn't even know about the cottage. It was Jonathan's, and according to my mother, it was his wish that I have it."

Melinda smiled apologetically. "That sounds more like the Cassidy I knew when she was married to Jonathan."

"What made you leave New York and completely change your life?" I asked.

"Have you ever felt as if you were destined to do something?"

Only if you count my Rolex project. "Not really, no."

She looked almost wistful. "I still remember the minute it struck me. I was running in Central Park." She smiled. "I still run, just not as far and not as fast." She paused and sighed. "I saw this woman yelling and screaming at a child, completely out of control. Slapping him, knocking him to the ground. Something just came over me. I marched up to her and threatened to call the police. Well, she explained to me that the little boy was her foster child, so the police wouldn't care.

"I'd passed a police officer, so I ran back, found him, and insisted he do something to help the little boy. So he goes to the playground and has a two-minute conversation with the woman. Then he just walked away."

"He didn't do anything?" I asked.

Melinda shook her head. "Basically told me the kid said she wasn't hitting him, and without a victim, he couldn't do anything."

"Then why not stay in New York and help kids there?" Liam asked.

"That was my plan, but when they did the home study they said my one-bedroom apartment was too small to allow me to take in children. I went to Jonathan for advice." She stopped and gave my hand a squeeze. "He was a brilliant businessman, and I thought he might help me."

"A house on Palm Beach is more than help," Liam remarked.

"Yes, it was," Melinda agreed. "But Jonathan knew about my surgery. He paid me for the six weeks of work I missed without batting an eye. He knew I could never have children of my own." She looked directly at me. "He adored you so much that I always believed he did it because he knew how easy it was to love a child who had no biological connection to you. I loved my foster children very much."

"What happened to you and the kids in your care after you left?" Liam asked.

Melinda fiddled with the pendant hanging around her neck. I was pretty sure the pinkish-orange stone was a padparadscha sapphire. Not cheap. "Losing my home of sixteen years pretty much forced me to give up my kids." Bowing her head, she sniffed, then fished a handkerchief from her purse.

She wore the same stones in her ears. Very matchy-matchy. Very expensive. "How many children have you fostered?" I asked.

Melinda's expression changed almost instantly. "Over the past sixteen years?" She tapped a perfectly manicured peach fingernail against her chin as she thought back.

It gave me an opportunity to get a better look at the ring and earrings that matched her pendant. "You have beautiful jewelry," I commented as my tea was delivered.

Melinda held her hand at arm's length, then touched her earrings and finally clutched the pendant in her hand. "Thank you. It's paste, of course, but I like it."

"Love the color, paste or not. Where did you find the pieces?"

"At a swap meet in Pompano Beach."

Liam leaned close to me and asked, "Are we going to count foster children anytime soon?"

Melinda blushed. I just grinned at him and enjoyed the fact that he was having to suffer through girly chitchat.

"Between thirty and forty," Melinda said. "Some stayed for years, others just for a night or two."

I pulled the decade-old photograph out of the envelope and passed it to her. "I found this photo in the *Palm Beach Post* archives. You were getting an award for your hard work. Do you remember these kids?"

Her head tilted slightly as she smiled, nostalgically tracing the six faces with the pad of her forefinger. "I'd forgotten about this," she said without taking her eyes off the photograph. "I forgot about that story," she mused as she scooted her chair closer to mine. "This young lady here on the end is Bridget Tomey. She was only with me for about a month. An emergency placement until the Department of Children and Families caseworker could convince her mother to file the necessary papers to keep her boyfriend out of the house. He liked to use Bridget and her mother as punching bags."

Her finger moved over the next face. Male, Hispanic, and obviously very close to aging out of the system. "This is embarrassing. I can't recall his name. I just remember he was short-term, because as soon as he moved out, another boy moved in. I was only authorized for four children at any given time."

"There are initials on the bottom," I prompted. "C.L.?"

She shook her head. "I can't place him, but maybe his name will come to me," she said as she kept looking at the photo. "The girl next to him," she said, tapping a slightly overweight blonde with vacant blue eyes, "is Megan Landry. She was a hard case."

"How so?" Liam asked.

"Drug-addicted mother, absent father. The mother would get clean for a few months, regain custody, and then start using again. Sad, really." She continued naming the kids in the picture. "Then I'm sure you recognize her," Melinda said, smiling proudly as she pointed to the tall, slender brunette on the end.

Taking the picture, I stared at the image for several seconds, then shook my head. "Sorry, I don't."

Melinda leaned close to me and whispered, "Well, she has had some work done in the ten years since that picture was taken. The bump on her nose and a little enhancement to her lips. But I'm sure she'd prefer that that didn't become public knowledge. She's got enough trouble, with the tabloids calling her a gold digger and all."

I blinked and scrutinized the photo again. "I still don't know who she is."

"Terri Semple," Melinda said, barely above a whisper.

"The one about to marry the Gilmore grocery heir?" I practically choked out.

Melinda beamed. "Yes. And it couldn't happen to a more deserving girl. Well, woman, though to me she'll always be the gangly, shy twelve-year-old who came to live with me."

"Terri Semple was in the system?" Liam asked.

"Difficult home life," Melinda said. "Her mother left her with her grandmother and took off. The grandmother had a stroke. Terri cared for the woman until she died. Twelve years old and a mother nowhere to be found. She hadn't been to school for more than two years. But she was smart. Worked hard and caught up to grade level in less than six months. Terri always was a quick study."

After she answered Liam, I asked, "How long did she live with you?"

"Seven years. Until she aged out."

The waiter returned, took our orders, hurried away. As soon as he left, Melinda continued reminiscing. Through it all, I got two dozen names out of her, with another half dozen partials. I was discreetly texting the names to myself.

It turned out to be a lovely lunch. When the check arrived, much to my surprise, Liam picked up the tab. He surprised me again when he looked directly at Melinda and asked, "So any idea who the girl found stuffed in the closet might be?"

If at first you don't succeed, destroy
all the evidence that you failed.

seven

🦜

MELINDA APPEARED NOT ONLY shocked but also appalled by the bluntness of Liam's question. Too shocked and too appalled. Nothing about her seemed to fit. Great clothes, perfect accessories, classy, polished; none of it said foster mother. I was having a hard time reconciling what I knew with what I saw. I couldn't help it. I had a sneaky suspicion based on absolutely nothing but gut instinct that Melinda knew something. Maybe not the name of the skeleton, but *something*.

Her perfectly made-up face flamed, and her eyes glinted with anger. "I haven't the first clue," she snapped, spine and syllables stiff.

"Please think back," I said, trying to smooth over Liam's thinly veiled accusation.

"I kept close tabs on my kids," Melinda said evenly before sipping her drink. "DCF made unannounced visits to check on their health and welfare. Believe me, if someone went missing, I'd have known."

"Unless you didn't want one of your charges to get into trouble," Liam suggested. "If they screwed up while in your care, wouldn't a group home be the next stop?"

Melinda nodded. "My kids knew that too. Yes, some of them were challenges, but they eventually came around. Most of them knew the system inside out, so they knew better than to walk away from a good thing."

"So you're saying all your foster kids were success stories?" Liam asked.

"Success is relative," Melinda said, her tone flat. Clearly she wasn't thrilled with the line of questioning. Too bad. Right now she was the only one with answers, and I had no choice but to milk her for answers. She turned her gaze on me. "I learned that working for your father."

"Jonathan was very successful," I countered defensively.

"Yes, he was, but not every single one of his advertising campaigns worked. And I'm not saying the failures were his fault. Sometimes it's the product that's the problem. The campaign for New Coke didn't work because no one liked New Coke, not because the advertising was bad. Every now and then I'd get a kid too damaged to help."

"What'd you do with those kids?"

"I didn't *do* anything, and I resent the accusation. I've spent most of my adult life helping young people, not harming them." In a theatrical move that would have given my mother a run for her money, Melinda tossed her napkin on the table. "Nice to see you again, Finley." She turned on her Jimmy Choos and regally marched out of the restaurant.

For a second I watched her weave her way between the tables, righteous indignation in every line of her body. I turned back to Liam. "Well done. Haven't you ever heard of asking nicely? Now she'll probably never speak to me again."

He shrugged. "She wasn't going to tell us anything more anyway."

"And you know that how?"

"I'm pretty good at reading people."

"Yeah, well, you just alienated the only person who *might* know the identity of the skeleton."

"She knows," he said.

"Again I ask, you know that how?"

"She didn't ID the boy in the photo."

"That's it?"

"That and fifteen years as a cop, seven of those as a homicide detective." He flashed me a crooked smile that made my heart skip a beat. "Sorry, Finley, but c'mon, we both know you aren't exactly the best judge of people."

Heat flashed on my cheeks. "How long do you plan on throwing Patrick in my face?" I picked up the photograph from the table and stuffed it back into its envelope.

He leaned forward, close enough so I could feel the heat of his breath on my neck. He smelled like soap and the ocean breeze, which made me think of things other than the present conversation. Dammit. The man was insidious. "I wasn't *talking* about Patrick. I was thinking about the way you came to my house that night. You assumed I'd—"

I looked pointedly at my watch. "Gotta go." I stood so fast I nearly knocked my chair backward. "I have to get back to the house. Thanks for lunch." The memory of the way I'd tried—and failed—to seduce Liam chased me from the restaurant as if my butt was on fire.

Gravel spewed from underneath my tires as I tore out of the restaurant's parking lot. On my way back to the cottage, I ran through a drive-thru and grabbed a double-shot latte. To assuage my annoyance, I added whip. Caffeine with a fluffy mountain of whipped cream was my anti-anxiety drug of choice.

The sun was a raging circle of fire almost directly overhead. I closed the sunroof, then dialed Sam. "Hi. Are you still at the house?"

"Yes," Sam said, his mood irritatingly chipper. "Harold and I are working out some of the renovations."

"That's great, but don't do anything until I hear from Jane and—"

"She came by and dropped off a budget and some bank stuff you need to sign."

"How tight is it?"

"We can't do everything I'd like, but when can you be here? I went and got my laptop so I could use ArchiCAD to do a 3-D plan. I think you're going to be very pleased."

"On my way now."

I tempered my excitement by reminding myself that whatever money I pulled out of the cottage for the home equity loan would translate into higher monthly payments. Still, it was hard to contain my growing exhilaration as I crossed the bridge and made the left toward Chilian.

Harold's truck was parked in the driveway behind Sam's LeBaron convertible. The front lawn was littered with clumsy stacks of clothing, and I noticed a dark green Dumpster on the right side of the house.

Putting the car in park, I cut the engine as Sam came bounding out of the house like an excited puppy.

After surveying the mess, I pushed my D&G sunglasses—75 percent off because of a missing rhinestone I'd carefully replaced—up on my head. "I thought the point was to improve the property."

Sam waved a dismissive hand at the clothing. "Harold's airing that stuff out."

"Why?" I used a handy paint stick to lift a plaid something off the top of the pile. Ew! If everything else was as bad as the shirt, the clothing was all well worn and/or stained and/or so out of fashion even a homeless person would balk. I tossed the shirt back on top of the heap.

"Doesn't matter." Sam grabbed my forearm and pulled me past the outdoor closet. The sound of a power saw buzzed, forcing him to yell to be heard. "Your bedroom is going to be a showplace."

In just under three hours, Harold had knocked out four walls and was busy sawing the larger pieces of debris into smaller ones. Sam's laptop was out on the back patio, beyond the reach of the toxic dust field kicked up by the power tool. Harold waved to us as we walked through the house.

Sam had his extra-wide-screen Mac open on a cooler that was serving as a table in the middle of four plastic lawn chairs arranged on the patio.

"We're going with a plastic theme?" I asked.

"I made a Walgreens run," Sam said. "I needed a surface to work on, and in case you didn't notice, it's hot as hell. Without a fridge, there's no place to keep water."

"Sorry, I didn't think about that."

"I did. And you owe me fifty-six dollars and change."

"For a cooler and four chairs? Four ugly plastic chairs?"

Sam sighed heavily. "Plastic usually is ugly, but that's a different conversation. These are from Jane," he said, pulling a stack of papers out from under a pair of women's shoes he'd used to keep them from blowing out to sea.

As I took the papers, my eyes fixed on the heel of the shoes Sam had used as a paperweight. "Whose shoes?"

Sam clutched his chest. "Oh, dear God, tell me you aren't thinking of recycling shoes from the skanky collection."

So I could examine it more closely, I lifted one shoe with the paint stirrer I still held. "These were in the bag?" I asked.

"Yes," Sam said, plucking it from my hand. "As your friend, I can't allow you to consider adopting a ten-year-old pair of used Enzos."

"Were there other shoes in the bag?"

"No. And you're not focusing." He pointed to his eyes with two fingers, then waved them in front of my eyes to get my attention.

"The heels are scraped," I said, running my finger over the deep, vertical, even gouges in the beige leather.

"Color me shocked. Used shoes in crappy shape."

I continued to examine the shoe, then did the same with its mate. "They're in near perfect shape except for the heels."

"So have them fumigated, take them to a cobbler, wear them, and I'll mock you about them forever. Could we *please* get to the rehab?"

Something about the scuffed shoes bothered me, but Sam was right, so I reluctantly placed them on the ground and gave the financial documents my full attention.

Apparently, I was going to open a line of credit and draw against the house's value. Not exactly comforting. Dollar signs swirled around in my head as I read Jane's neatly typed columns. My friend knew me well enough to know math wasn't my strength, so she'd gone the extra mile to make a payment chart that about gave me a coronary. Running my fingertip less than halfway down the chart, I said, "Right about here I'll have to get a second job just to cover the interest on the debt."

Sam patted my shoulder. "Even with the structural repairs, we aren't going to need that much. But God," he said, "what I could do with this place if we used the whole four hundred grand."

I shrugged away from him. "Don't even dream. Christ, Sam, this place is a frigging money pit. Think that's why my mother gave it to me?"

"I wouldn't put it past her. But we can do this, Finley. It'll be a little tight while you're paying for the condo and the mortgage, but as soon as we can get you moved in here, you'll actually be paying less per month than you've been paying in rent."

Somehow, that knowledge wasn't much of a comfort. Not when I glanced back at the unlivable shell of a cottage. My shoulders slumped. "It will take months and a few small miracles to make this place livable."

Sam kissed my forehead. "Look on the bright side. We've already gotten rid of the skeleton, and Harold is a fast worker. I'm betting we can get you in before the end of the month."

It was my turn to do the kissing. Pinching Sam's cheeks, I planted one right on his mouth. "I love you."

"You'll love me even more when you see the plans." Scooting two plastic chairs together, he excitedly sat me down and started tapping buttons until suddenly a three-dimensional replica of my house filled the screen. Using the touchpad, he spun the image, then zoomed out and focused on the deep coral-colored front door.

Much too slowly for my liking, he moved toward the entrance.

"Ready?" he asked, his brows teasingly raising and lowering.

"Open the virtual door already!"

The door opened, and I swear I heard the sound of a choir singing the "Hallelujah Chorus." My breath caught and tears welled in my eyes as I sat forward to get a better look at the wide entry hall, with its pale, coral-colored tiled floor and walls. A narrow, whitewashed table against the right-hand wall held a spray of sea grasses in a clear glass vase, which were reflected in the enormous mirror. Beyond the hallway was a large room, a great room I presumed, that had a wall of windows overlooking the beach and the ocean beyond. One could stand at the front door and see the beach. So frigging cool.

"Loving it," I murmured. "Gimme more."

Sam did whatever was necessary to move me forward. Before I could take in the great room, I looked at that entire wall of windows and the view. "Oh, Sam." *My* view. *My* living room. I wanted to move in right that second. Sam had given me pale teal walls, the floors the same peachy-coral tile as the entry hall. The big, squishy, invite-all-my-friends-over furniture was covered in white slipcovers, and a teal and deep coral area rug looked soft under bare feet. Bless his heart, Sam had even tossed deep teal throw pillows covered with branch coral all over the sofas. Sam was all in the details.

"Kitchen?"

"Sure." I didn't cook, but who knew? I might

develop new habits when I—"Wow!" The cabinets could house the entire Calphalon collection.

"Lots of storage," Sam murmured as he moved the view so I could see what he'd done. Stainless steel, whitewashed wood, and a hunk of black granite one could see light reflected in, on the center island. Sleek, modern, and warm. I could easily see myself hanging out with the girls, sitting on the chrome bar stools sipping a glass of wine.

"You're amazing," I told him, not taking my eyes off his monitor.

"Ready for bedroom one?"

I loved the two guest bedrooms done in various shades of his chosen palette of white, coral, and teal. One bedroom had a bit of lime green in the bedspread; the other he'd made into an office done in a pinker shade of coral and a deeper green with just a few touches of teal. Very Lilly Pulitzer. Without tearing my attention away from my fabulously decorated house, I asked, "I need an office why?"

"So you have somewhere divine to sit while you write all the checks you'll need to write. Master bedroom?" he asked after he'd shown me the guest bathroom, which was gorgeous, with ocean-colored glass tiles and a square, contemporary-style opaque glass sink perched on top of a minimalist floating counter.

The master bedroom was every master bedroom fantasy I'd never had, come to 3-D life. "Holy shit . . ." The room was plush, luxurious, and looked like an expensive, high-end hotel room. The only color in the room was the deep teal walls. Everything else was white. The white-draped bed looked big enough to entertain on.

Sam showed me the remodeled master bathroom, with its expanse of glass looking out over the water and a steam shower. It was all drop-dead gorgeous.

"Let's go check out outside."

"Let's . . . Jesus, Sam," I said on a half laugh, my eyes practically eating what I was seeing. "Do you think I won the lottery?" The patio was tiled and looked wet. I swear I could hear water lapping. An infinity lap pool overlooked the beach, and, set a bit closer to the house, a hot tub steamed. Sam had even tossed a couple of white toweling robes over the wrought-iron chairs, and he'd added two wineglasses on the deck of the tub.

"Who am I having over?"

"I can lead you to water, but I can't make you drink," he said dryly. "You like?"

I made him show me the house three more times before I managed to tear myself away. I averted my gaze from the messy reality of it all. I had to keep Sam's vision in my head at all times. Especially as I wrote checks and basically signed my life away.

I rose off the plastic seat with a small sucking sound and kissed Sam my savior on top of his head. "You're a genius."

He grinned. "So true."

"I'll treat you to Chinese."

Sam shook his head. "Thanks, but I've still got some things to talk over with Harold."

"How about I have something delivered? Or I could stay here and keep you company?"

"Eating is a distraction. Having you looking over my shoulder is a bigger distraction. Thanks, but I'll get something. You just move along and let me create some magic."

Sam stayed behind, because who could argue against magic? I didn't understand most of what Sam and Harold discussed—well, except for the part where I was paying for everything. After a quick stop at China Moon for some take-out moo shu, I fantasized about the day I could take my food back to my polished black granite counter. Somehow I just knew it would taste better if I was sitting on a sleek bar stool with the sound of the ocean keeping me company. Pushing my premature fantasy aside, I went back to my condo.

A huge spray of pale pink roses studded with baby's breath stood guard at my front door. Normally flowers thrilled me to no end, but I knew before I got out of the car that these particular flowers would do nothing more than piss me off.

Again.

With my moo shu in one hand, I snatched up the envelope from the forked plastic holder and ripped the card out.

I miss you. Love, Patrick.

"Well," I said, gathering up the vase and carting it across the parking lot before lobbing it into the trash bin. "I don't miss you."

I didn't miss him. Well, maybe I did miss him a

little. Well, maybe not *him* so much as being in a relationship. Intellectually, I knew I'd done the right thing dumping him, but truth be told, I was lonely. Okay, so maybe desperate was more accurate. I probably only had a few weeks left before I'd have to make a discreet trip to one of those places that sold battery-operated boyfriends in a box. Not a pleasant thought. Neither was a life of celibacy.

Walking into my apartment with lukewarm Chinese as my date made me feel pretty damned pathetic. It was Saturday night, and the high point of my evening was destined to be breaking open my fortune cookie. Which, I discovered as I placed the bag on the counter, was going to be a problem, since I heard the cookie crush under the weight of the container.

I thought about changing my clothes, but my rumbling stomach convinced me food was a higher priority. I pulled the carton out of the bag. Using my teeth, I tore the paper off the single-use chopsticks and went over to the couch. Kicking off my shoes, I tucked my legs up and jabbed the chopsticks in the box while I reached for the television remote control.

Feeling comfy, I debated a few seconds before going back to the kitchen for a drink. I poured a generous amount of wine into a glass and told myself it wasn't completely lame that I was alone on a Saturday night.

My mind conjured a picture of Tony Caprelli. Weird that I'd think about my boss on a weekend.

Well, not so weird given those dimples. They were some fine dimples. I wasn't sure if lusting after Tony was better than lusting after Liam. I decided not to lust at all.

Thinking about my conversation with my mother, I decided I could check into the robbery of her home. Palm Beach wasn't exactly a hotbed of criminal activity—unless you counted tax fraud disguised as creative accounting. There was just something off about a robbery more than a decade ago with the medallion ending up in the hand of Dead Girl. Couldn't hurt to watch reruns of *Law & Order* and do a little investigating.

Wine in hand, I retrieved my laptop from the bedroom. I could see a slice of light beneath the closed closet door and silently berated myself for leaving the light on. I flicked the switch off; I couldn't afford to waste money by leaving lights on all day. I went back to the living room. The network news was ending, and my computer—which I'd scored at less than half its retail price on an eBay auction—powered up. Well, it started to power up, but then the screen went blank. Obviously I'd left a light burning but had forgotten to charge my computer—a minor annoyance that felt magnified given the sad-ass way my evening was unfolding.

I called Jane but got her machine. Then I remembered she had a date. I thanked her for all the budget stuff, trying to sound breezy when I was well on my way to a serious pity fest. I tried Becky next, but her line went directly to voice mail. I was fairly sure she didn't have a date; she was probably at the office, trying to keep up with estrogen-less Ellen.

Calling Liv would have been a waste. Her company was handling the big hospice fund-raiser. Nope, it was just me, moo shu, Chris Noth, and some mildly erotic thoughts. *That* man could zip me into a body bag any day.

I went into my bedroom to retrieve the power cord for my computer, when a sudden, strong breeze whipped up the curtain. Glancing to the right, my whole body froze when I noticed the open window. I knew I hadn't left it open.

Standing very still, only my eyes darted around the room. Nothing was out of place. The bed was made . . . well, the comforter was pulled up and the throw pillows were just where I'd tossed them.

The more normal it seemed, the more my heart raced. Taking a calming breath, I searched again. Nothing was out of place. Maybe I had opened the window and just forgot.

Grabbing the phone off the nightstand, I crept slowly into the bathroom. I flooded the small room with light. With the shower curtain pulled back, I knew there wasn't anyone hiding in my shower. I began to relax, letting out the breath I hadn't realized I'd been holding.

"I'm not only lame, I'm scaring myself shitless," I muttered as I went back into the bedroom.

Then I focused on the closed closet door. I don't normally close that door. I swallowed a lump of fear and reached for the knob. The shape of the outline was unmistakable.

A noose hung from the light fixture. It swayed slightly under the weight of a skeleton dangling from the loop.

I needed to be calm, muster some bravado.

Screw bravado. I screamed and ran for the front door.

*I think crime pays—the hours are good,
and there are often opportunities for travel.*

eight

I WAS OUTSIDE, SUCKING IN deep, calming breaths of heavy, humid air. My heart was pounding so hard that I thought it might crack a few ribs. I was bent over, hyperventilating and shaking as if I'd been in the final stages of some neuromuscular disease. I needed to get a grip.

I heard the shuffle of footsteps and smelled Bengay, witch hazel, and vanilla extract. I didn't have to be psychic to know it was my upstairs neighbor, Mrs. Hemshaw. The Bengay and witch hazel were for her arthritis. The vanilla extract was her version of perfume. I turned to find the eighty-three-year-old coming toward me with a very big gun clutched in one crepey, arthritic hand. The other hand held the edges of her housecoat closed.

Bracing my hands on my knees, I said, "Don't think we need the gun."

"I heard you scream," she said, waving the barrel around as she spoke.

"There was a break-in at my apartment," I explained, standing, taking my hand, and guiding the gun so it pointed down and away from me.

Given the fact that Mrs. Hemshaw was eighty-three and her glasses were as thick as muffin tops, I didn't think a weapon was a good idea. Besides, there was nothing to shoot. Besides me.

My neighbor made a *tsk-tsk* sound. "Pretty young thing like you shouldn't live in a garden unit. Crime just waiting to happen."

We'd been over this before. "I need to call the police."

"Already done," she assured me. "And I'll give them a good long piece of my mind, too. Called earlier when I heard noises and knew you weren't home."

"Earlier when?" I asked.

"Lunchtime. Saw a patrol car cruise through the parking lot, but no one bothered to get out and take a look around."

There were two possible explanations for the police blowing her off. Possibility one was Mrs. Hemshaw had the local sheriff's office on speed dial. She reported everything from cars running the corner Stop sign to stray dogs walking across the common areas. She often did this after downing a fifth of Jim Beam. Once a month, on the day she received her Social Security checks, she liked to sing show tunes on the balcony in her undies.

Possibility two was that they'd recognized the address. I wasn't much more popular with the West

Palm police than Mrs. Hemshaw was. Maybe I would be more popular if *I* stood outside in *my* undies.

Faint sirens grew closer, and in a matter of minutes, two patrol cars, lights strobing, careened into the parking lot. I was relieved to see they were uniformed officers. The last thing I wanted or needed was another confrontation with Graves or Steadman.

The officers opened their doors, then crouched behind them, weapons drawn. "Put the gun down slowly," one of the officers said over the speaker.

Mrs. Hemshaw planted a hand on her hip. "Do you believe this? They think I'm a criminal."

I smiled at her and held one hand up to the officers while I gently tugged the gun free from Mrs. Hemshaw. Well, maybe not all that gently. The old girl didn't want to give it up. "We'll just put it here on the ground," I told her.

As soon as I'd disarmed Mrs. Magoo, four officers ranging in age from early twenties to late fifties crowded around. I noticed they'd all holstered their weapons, but none of them had snapped the leather strap. There was still a slim chance I could get shot.

The youngest officer used his toe to kick Mrs. Hemshaw's gun well out of her reach. In a this-will-be-funny-later moment, I had a vision of Mrs. Hemshaw making a dive for her gun.

"I'm Sergeant Jennings," the oldest officer said. "What seems to be the problem?"

"I had a break-in," I explained.

He grabbed the radio clipped to his shoulder and

called for crime scene techs and someone from rob-bery-homicide. "You ladies wait with Officer Stevens while we check the apartment."

"He's long gone," I said, though the three officers ignored me. "And nothing was stolen."

Officer Stevens grabbed up Mrs. Hemshaw's gun, clicked a few things, and the cylinder opened. "It isn't loaded."

"It isn't?" Mrs. Hemshaw asked, confused. "I won-der where I put those bullets." She started shuffling back toward the staircase.

Officer Stevens started to grab for her, but I caught his shirtsleeve and did my best pleading-pouty face. "You've got her gun. If you need to talk to her, she's right upstairs."

He shrugged. "I guess she can't get far."

Since my neighbor was racing away at the speed of snail, I guessed not.

The three other officers came out of my apartment. "All clear," the eldest said. His eyes met mine. "I'm as-suming the skeleton in the closet started all this?"

I nodded.

"Hey," he began, rubbing his chin, "are you the same Finley Tanner who reported a different skeleton in a different closet a few days ago?"

His question made me sound like a serial victim. Again I nodded. "Different closet. Is there any way to identify the body inside?"

The sergeant's lips twitched, then surrendered to a smile. "Yes. It's from Florida Party. The price tag is still connected to the wrist bone."

I blinked a couple of times and then asked Jennings, "It isn't real?"

"Resin," he explained. "Popular at Halloween."

I went from scared to pissed in record time. "Why would someone *do* that?"

The officer shrugged. "Just a prank."

Crossing my arms, I felt my blood simmering. "Not funny. Can we go back inside?"

"I'll have the forensics people dust the bedroom window, and we should do a walk-thru to see if anything is missing. But don't get your hopes up, Ms. Tanner. Even if we find prints, I'm betting they belong to some fraternity punk and we won't have them on file."

Ignoring the moo shu, I went into the small kitchen and made a pot of coffee. The scent of a Southern pecan roast filled the air and blanketed me with some measure of comfort. Before my DeLonghi pot finished brewing, a team of CSIs wearing little booties and carrying matching metal tackle boxes and computer gear arrived and went to work in my bedroom. A creepy sense of déjà vu danced along my spine as I pulled coffee mugs down from a cabinet.

Stevens declined, but the other three officers gladly accepted my offer of coffee. From the fridge, I grabbed a small container of cream and set it on the counter, then found the sugar and set it next to the cream. Pulling the last clean teaspoon from my flatware drawer, I figured they could share.

"Maybe now would be a good time to have a look around the apartment?" Jennings suggested. "See if anything is missing."

One sip of coffee relaxed the tension between my shoulder blades. "Sure." Since my kitchen is roughly the same size as a boat galley, it was easy enough to confirm that whoever had left the fake skeleton hadn't carted off the collection of vintage Troll dolls I kept on the kitchen windowsill. It's an accidental collection started back in my college days. I'd buy one every time I had a lousy date or a relationship implosion. In four years I'd managed to amass an army of more than fifty of the naked dolls with their straight, neon shock of hair. I'd just added a new one—The Patrick Troll.

I didn't bother to explain the odd grouping; instead, I walked into the adjoining living room and checked the most likely targets. TV, DVD, iHome—all present and accounted for. Based on the accumulated layer of dust, no one had so much as breathed on them.

Cupping my coffee mug in prayer hands, I walked into my bedroom, trailing my contingent of officers. I swallowed a groan as I saw the black fingerprint powder smeared all over the wall with the open window. I knew from experience it was a bugger to get that stuff off. Another potential deduction from my security deposit.

I went to my nightstand and found my blank checks neatly stacked in one corner. As discreetly as possible, I ran my fingertip beneath the stack. The medallion I'd taken from the real skeleton was still tucked beneath the papers.

Moving to my dresser, I opened the top drawer and found my Rolex parts in their respective baggies. Next, I checked my jewelry box and found everything undisturbed. Sadly, that did it for my valuables.

"What about the other drawers?" Jennings asked.

"Just clothes," I answered, not thrilled with the idea of three police officers having a private viewing of my panty drawer. "Nothing of value."

"Got a hit," one of the CSIs called excitedly.

He was on his haunches, looking at a really cool split computer screen comparing fingerprints.

"How can you know already?" I asked.

The young man looked up at me, then pointed to a small rectangular piece of equipment connected to his laptop. "Lift them, then scan the lifts into the computer mainframe. Then the computer takes over, comparing the prints against those in our database."

His gloved fingers hit a few keys. "And the winner is . . ."

We were all scrunched together to get a view of the name.

"Tanner, Finley Anderson." He glanced back up at me. "Your prints are in the system?"

"Unfortunately." I shivered at the memory of being incarcerated, albeit briefly. Knowing my fingerprints were in the system didn't exactly make me feel all warm and fuzzy. I took a long swallow of coffee to calm my nerves.

"Well," the CSI said, "saves me the trouble of taking exclusionary prints from you."

"Always glad to help," I muttered.

His laptop beeped. "Got another one."

Again, I watched and waited for the computer to spit out a name. "Lachey, Patrick Michael. Printed for a pilot's license."

My eyes grew wide. "He's my ex-boyfriend."

"Amicable breakup?" Jennings asked.

"If you don't count the cactus incident, I guess."

"Cactus incident?" Jennings repeated as he scribbled furiously in his small notepad.

Sighing, I waved my hand. "A parting gift." Well, it was *kinda* true.

"If he's your ex, why would his fingerprints be inside your apartment?"

"Because I don't do windows. Patrick was definitely a weenie of a boyfriend and a schmuck of a human being, but he wouldn't hang a fake skeleton by a noose in my closet."

"How can you be sure?" Jennings challenged. "The story in the *Post* provided enough detail that anyone could have hung that skeleton in your closet."

The CSI came out of my closet with the resin skeleton and its noose in separate paper bags.

"Got another hit. Doe96-5, John."

"What does that mean?" I asked.

"I pulled a print from the sill, and it matches a partial print found at a crime scene in . . . 1996. Print was never matched to a perpetrator."

"But what does that *mean*?"

"We can only match prints already in the system. Unless the person has been arrested, served in the military, or had to have prints taken for work or something like that, they get filed as John Does."

"When was the last time you washed the windows?" Jennings asked.

"More coffee?" I replied.

"Naw, we're close to done here. Just a few more questions."

"Let's go back to the living room," I suggested, then led the way.

I refilled my mug, then sat on the sofa. Jennings scooted the ottoman over, licked the pad of his thumb, and flipped to a new page in his notepad.

"Any enemies I should know about?"

"My mother."

"Excuse me?"

"Bad joke," I corrected. "The office manager where I work hates me, but I can't see Maudlin Margaret or her file room flunkies pulling something like this. She's more the passive-aggressive kind of enemy."

"No other, er, men who might have issues with you?"

"Sam thinks my taste in decorating is criminal."

His smile reached all the way to his rather bland brown eyes. "You're not taking this very seriously. It'll help the investigation if you give us something to go on."

"I would if I had anything, but I honestly don't. I've been involved in a couple of murder investigations, but they both led to arrests. And you have to admit, it is a little coincidental that fingerprints from a robbery thirteen years ago match prints on my window."

"Sometimes a coincidence is just a coincidence. What do you do for a living?"

As little as possible to earn my paycheck. "I'm an estates and trusts paralegal at Dane, Lieberman. All of my clients are dead."

He laughed. "Very amusing. But I'm assuming the dead clients have families, other people not always happy with the division of property?"

"Sure," I said on an exhale of breath. "But that's really rare. Most of the beneficiaries are getting something for nothing. They normally leave my office with a check and a big hairy grin."

"Any unhappy widows or children lately?"

"The real widows are always unhappy," I explained. "They're grieving. The Botoxed trophy wives, well, let's just say their grief is proportional to the dollar amount of their inheritance. The last time I had a contested will was over a year ago. The baby widow—as memory serves, the deceased was four years younger than her grandfather—contested a bequest to the first wife. They fought for a while, and then agreed on a settlement. Baby Widow was forced to accept a piddly twenty-six million."

Jennings whistled. "Do all your cases deal with that kind of money?"

I shook my head. "Maybe sixty percent. The other forty percent is normal people's estates, setting up college funds, doing family trusts."

Jennings flipped his notepad closed and stood.

I stood as well. "So what happens now?"

"I'll run upstairs and have a chat with Mrs. Hemshaw. But I'll be honest, Ms. Tanner."

"Finley."

"Finley," he said as he shoved the pad into the breast pocket of his shirt. "This has all the earmarks of a cruel but harmless prank. Still, I'll have the watch commander order a cruiser to keep a closer eye on this place. You should consider getting better locks on your windows."

"Thanks," I said, extending my hand.

He gave me his business card. "Give me a call if you have any more trouble. If anything breaks, I'll let you know."

"Thank you," I repeated as I stood by the door and the group filed outside.

Once I was alone, I checked every lock on every door and window. Still a little spooked, I hunted for things to jam in the window tracks. I spent the better part of an hour duct-taping pens together to make sticks to prevent the windows from being opened. Well, they probably wouldn't hold, but at least I'd hear them snap if my skeleton freak decided to come back.

I reheated my dinner, then multitasked by channel surfing and powering up my laptop. Just for good measure, my cell phone was on the sofa next to me. Every so often, I was distracted by movement outside my sliding glass doors. Palm fronds swaying on the breeze, gecko skittering across the patio—everything inspired a stab of fear.

"Get a grip," I muttered. I had every light burning,

including the floodlight mounted over the back door. So much for cutting corners on my Florida Power and Light bill. Every shadow had me itching to call Liam and ask him to . . . *what*? Nope, there was no way I'd call him to play protector.

When I went into the kitchen, I peered through the dusty blinds, hoping to see Sam's car in the parking lot. No such luck. Not that it mattered. Sam, bless him, is a bigger girl than I am. At best, he'd probably try to subdue an intruder by wrapping him in tulle.

Going back to the sofa, I logged into eBay. If anything could get my mind off the skeletons—a word that should never be plural, by the way—it was a cruise through the online auctions for new Rolex parts. I found a couple of links, but the end dates for the auctions were days away. Only eBay novices place bets days out from the end of an auction. No, the smart way to do it is to wait until the last minute of bidding, then swoop in and grab the item away from the high bidder. I clicked them into my *watched items* files and switched to searching for new clothes.

The rational side of me knew I should be conserving every penny, but the put-upon side of me knew I was going back to school on Tuesday night. Like a six-year-old, I decided a new dress might be just the thing to make the first day of school tolerable. Tolerable was going to cost me, though, because I'd have to use expedited shipping to get anything before Tuesday.

The eBay gods were smiling upon me. In under a minute I found an adorable, worn once, Juicy Couture silk dress in my size. I winced at the two-hundred-dollar minimum bid, but the painterly circles and scalloped hemline called to me. With just a hair of hesitation, I typed in my bid but didn't hit the Submit button. There were still four minutes until the end of the auction and no bids listed. I couldn't risk alerting other professional eBayers to my interest.

Opening a new internet window, I logged into the *Palm Beach Post* archives. I searched for robberies on Palm Beach covering the Melinda foster care years up to six months ago, when she lost the house. There were literally hundreds. Narrowing the search, I entered the zip code for the 33480 area. Unfortunately, I quickly learned that as the population of Palm Beach County swelled, so did zip code boundaries. This wasn't going to be as easy as I thought.

I spent three and a half minutes constructing a time line of zip codes for the area, then flipped back to eBay and submitted my bid. As I'd feared, my two-hundred-dollar bid was rejected as too low. Quickly, I raised it to two fifty, but that was rejected as well. Disappointed, I muttered, "You win," to ClothesHorse2 and decided a Sunday trip to the Gardens Mall was my best alternative.

Opening a Word document in the background, I began cutting and pasting three dozen robbery articles into a single location.

The sound of my cell ringing made me jump. Glancing at the iPhone screen, I read Liam's number and chewed my lip as I debated answering. Screw it—I let it go to voice mail, which I ignored as well.

A minute later I received a text message from him: I'm standing outside your front door.

I texted back: Go away.

Instead, he started pounding, and, fearful that Mrs. Hemshaw might take up arms again, I reluctantly went and opened the door. A crack. With the safety chain attached.

He smelled male and comforting, but I knew from experience that didn't mean safe. "What?"

"Heard you had another skeleton in your closet."

"It wasn't real."

"Heard that too," he said as he raked his fingers through his hair. "Still, I figured you might be freaked out."

"You figured wrong," I said with more conviction than I felt.

"Let me in," he said, clearly irritated.

Okay, so I was totally trapped between a rock and a Liam place. If I didn't let him in, I'd practically be admitting that I didn't trust myself around him. If I did let him in, there was a possibility I'd prove that to be true.

Closing the door, I slapped the chain off and yanked the handle. Pivoting on the balls of my feet, I walked back to the living room pretending that I didn't care if he thought I looked good in my Betsey Johnson dress. Or that he noticed my freshly pedicured bare toes before I tucked my legs beneath me on the sofa.

If he did, it didn't show as he casually sank down next to me. "What are you doing?"

Trying not to think about the fact that your thigh is

brushing against my knees. "Since you alienated Melinda, I'm looking into robberies. My mother said the medallion was stolen, and it happened while Melinda was living in the cottage. I really want to know who that girl is . . . *was.*"

He lifted his arm and rested it on the back of the sofa. My heart skipped a beat when he absently wrapped a lock of my hair around his forefinger. The temperature in the room felt as if it had vaulted twenty degrees. Perspiration trickled between my breasts as my stomach knotted in a tight ball of desire.

Correction. A tight ball of *stupid.* I swatted his hand away, which, judging by the curve of his smile, amused the hell out of him.

"You're over the rebound period," he said, his voice an octave deeper as he began leaning toward me. "New rules."

Placing my palms flat against his chest, I stopped his forward motion. "Don't."

Those blue eyes locked on me and drew me in like a tractor beam. "Don't do this?" he asked, pressing his lips to my collarbone.

"Yeah."

"Or this?" he asked as his hot mouth trailed upward until I felt his tongue against my lobe and his warm breath tickled my ear.

"Yeah."

"Okay," he said easily. "Wanna let go of my shirt?"

Only then did I realize that I'd grabbed the front of his shirt and was practically clinging as every nerve ending in my body quivered with desire. "Yeah."

"Got any beer?"

"In the fridge," I said, biting the inside of my cheek so my body would focus on pain rather than pleasure. I watched him stroll into the kitchen. More accurately, I zoomed in on how his faded jeans molded his particularly fabulous butt and muscular thighs. "Bring me one too, please," I said, hoping more alcohol would addle my brain.

"I wouldn't have pegged you as a beer drinker."

"I'm not, but I didn't think you'd mix me a Cosmo."

"Happy to."

"Okay, then I'll take the Cosmo." Screw beer—a 100 percent alcohol drink was far more expedient than a beer. Besides, as far as I was concerned, the only difference between beer and urine was temperature. Oh, and I knew beer was the not-so-ex-Mrs. McGarrity's beverage of choice.

Thinking about Ashley doused me like a cold shower. I might be past the rebound stage, but Liam's life was still tangled with his ex-wife's. The last thing I needed was a man with baggage.

He delivered the Cosmo and I took a sip. It burned sweetly down my throat, bringing with it some liquid sanity. I motioned to his beer with my glass. "Feel free to take that with you when you leave."

He smiled. "Tossing me out?"

"Yes. I'm working."

He tipped the bottle and took a drink. "You'd rather work than fool around?"

Um, no! "With you? Yes." The lie rolled off my citrus-liquored tongue with ease.

He drained the bottle. "Your call. Lock up after me."

I should have been thrilled that he made a speedy departure. Instead, I leaned against the cold faux-wood door and guzzled my Cosmo to drown my loneliness and the residual desire that still had my insides all twisted.

The man made me crazy, and the last thing I needed was more crazy in my life. What I needed was mindless entertainment.

After placing my glass in the sink, I went into my bedroom and stripped off my clothes, pulled my hair into a ponytail, and washed my face. Going to my dresser, I opened my lingerie drawer and rummaged around, looking for the new stuff I'd bought last week. "Son of a bitch!" I muttered.

My intruder had left the skeleton but taken my brand-new-tags-still-on La Perla thongs. "Great, just what I need!" The image of some frat boy wearing my expensive panties on his head really frosted my cookies.

*Nowadays anyone who isn't in debt
isn't trying hard enough.*

nine

AT LEAST YOUR INTRUDER had good taste in lingerie," Becky said as we strolled past the fountain in front of the Gardens Mall.

I'd valet parked by the entrance next to the Brios, knowing without even discussing it that the two of us would have dinner after I replaced my pilfered panties.

"Where to first?" she asked.

I was itching to take the immediate right into Crate & Barrel, but I didn't dare. Whatever money I'd decided to blow would be on new school clothes and replacement undies. "Victoria's Secret."

As it turns out, it would have been cheaper to buy the Juicy Couture dress at full price at Nordy's than it was to do my back-to-school shopping. I came within seventeen dollars of the five-hundred-dollar limit on my Victoria's Secret credit card.

"Sephora?" Becky asked, her green eyes glinting.

"Absolutely. A new shade of lip gloss will cheer me up."

"Doing Liam would have cheered you up more," Becky said quietly as we waited by the glass elevator.

"I knew I shouldn't have told you about that."

"Sure you should have." Becky and I stepped into the elevator. "It's the closest I've come to foreplay since the Clinton administration."

I laughed, glad we were alone in the elevator. I was pretty sure a stroller-pushing mommy would have been horrified by our conversation.

"Don't repeat that," she said. "I already get enough grief from the other girls on my pitiful social life. Speaking of Liv and Jane, how come they didn't join us?"

"I haven't called them yet," I admitted as we exited the elevator and turned toward Sephora. "I know they'll both freak out, and it isn't exactly something I want to shout from the rooftops."

"Did you give your thirty-day notice at your condo?"

My shoulders slumped. "Not until Harold gives me a completion date. After yesterday, I'm half tempted to call and tell him to work around the clock."

Becky was eyeing the fragrance row. "You can stay with me."

I gave her arm a squeeze. "I know, thanks. But I'm not going to let a silly prank rule my life. I went out this morning and bought metal protective bars and industrial locks for the windows and the sliding door. Installed them myself without breaking a nail."

Becky laughed. "Practicing to be a homeowner already, eh?"

"I think I was more motivated by the memory of my dresser drawer and that stupid skeleton."

I detoured over to the display of new lip glosses from Stila. Unable to decide between a sweet watermelon shade and a deeper, bright fuchsia, I bought them both.

We spent the next two hours meandering through the designer shops and upscale department stores—Coach, Tiffany's, Nordstrom. Of course, I punished myself by going to visit the couture section. A mannequin was wearing the adorable, painterly circled, silk sundress with the scalloped hemline. I stood there admiring it as one might admire a Matisse or a Rembrandt. Debt sucks.

Unlike me, Becky was free to purchase three new dresses and four pairs of shoes. I felt a pinch of envy, but that was nothing new. Unless I took a stealthy detour to the clearance section, I was done shopping. Odd that I felt just fine telling Becky all about some guy raiding my panty drawer, but I couldn't bring myself to let her know that I couldn't afford full retail. We'd been friends for more than a decade, but admitting my shopping secret to my best friend would make it too real.

Eventually, after we loaded the packages in my car, we were seated alfresco at the Brios. Becky ordered a gin and tonic, while I opted for a San Benedetto iced tea. This was one of the few restaurants that carried the Italian import, and since I was driving, I went nonalcoholic. Reading the stack of fifteen-year-old police blotters I'd printed out promised to be mind numbing enough.

"What do you think about Tony?" Becky asked as she ran her fingertip around the rim of her glass.

"Tony the man or Tony the guy they just brought in as a new partner?"

Becky frowned. "Can you believe they just decided to open a new division and brought in an outsider?"

"I'm sorry." This was the first chance I'd had to tell her that since learning about Caprelli joining the firm. "I know it sucks for you."

Becky blew out a breath and twisted her more-red-than-brown auburn hair into a knot at the base of her neck. "Caprelli is a rainmaker. He'll bring in business and make the partnership shares bigger."

"You bring in business," I countered.

"Criminal cases can generate hefty retainers. Contracts, while lucrative, don't usually command hundred-thousand-dollar retainers."

I felt my eyes grow huge. "That's what he charges?"

Becky nodded, then lifted her menu as the waiter arrived. She ordered the pasta special, while I, still hearing my mother's unflattering comment about my four-pound weight gain, went for a large salad. Twenty-nine, and my mother was able to remote control my diet. *Pathetic.*

"He was a big deal in the New York DA's office," Becky said. "Then after his wife died, he went to work for the largest criminal defense firm."

I ripped a hunk of warm bread from the basket but passed on the herbed oil dip. "Think he's still in mourning?"

"I can't tell. I'd respect it if he is, but if he isn't, did you catch those dimples?"

"I dreamed about them," I joked. "But he's got a kid."

Becky waved her fork for a few seconds. "That could be a plus. Skip the whole pregnancy thing but still have a family with the added bonus of no ex-wife to fight over alimony, custody, and visitation every six months."

"That's a little cold."

"It's practical," Becky insisted. "Marrying a widower is way less complicated than playing stepmother to a child whose parents are divorced. How many stepmothers do you know who are loved and cherished by their stepkids?"

"Jonathan," I answered quietly.

Becky groaned. "Yes, my point exactly. Your stepfather never had to compete with your biological father."

"Whoever he might be."

"My point exactly. It would be the same kind of deal with a guy like Tony."

"Have you met the daughter?"

"She was in yesterday."

"And?" I prompted, my interest genuinely piqued.

"She's polite. A little on the shy side. About as beautiful as a kid can be. She'll break a lot of hearts growing up. Then marry an equally pretty man and have a bunch of pretty children."

"Aren't you rushing ahead a bit? Isn't she, like, ten?"

"Yep, but I have a good eye for this sort of thing."

"Being such an expert on children, of course."

"At least I didn't waste two years on lying Patrick."

"Touché."

"Is he still trying to weasel his way back into your life?"

I nodded.

"Wearing you down?"

I waited to swallow my mouthful of salad and then said, "Nope."

"Really?" Becky pressed.

"He sends me flowers every week and he's called a couple of times."

Smacking her hands on the armrests of her chair, Becky frowned at me. "He's getting to you. I can see it in your eyes."

"He wasn't *all* bad."

"No, he was all liar. C'mon, Finley, you have to be strong on this one. Past behavior is always the best indicator of future behavior. And his sucked."

"I know," I admitted, folding my napkin and placing it to the right of my half-eaten meal. "I just hate being single."

"Welcome to my world."

"Sorry."

"You don't have to be single, either. One crook of your little finger and Liam would come running."

"With Beer Barbie right behind him."

"You don't know that," Becky said for the millionth time. "Maybe they're just happily divorced people."

"Divorced with benefits."

A mischievous grin curved Becky's lips. "So offer him a better benefit package."

I WAS HAPPILY STUFFING the third handful of Lucky Charms into my mouth as I picked up a document on the Palm Beach robberies. So much for any plans for getting rid of my four bonus pounds. On the plus side, with my fancy new locks and metal bars jammed in the tracks of all the windows, I felt completely safe and secure.

I'd changed into a pair of cotton ladies' boxers with cute pink hearts on them and a matching spaghetti strap top. To complete my ensemble, I pulled on a pair of aloe socks I'd bought online. Cracked heels were the kryptonite of cute sandals, and besides, I just liked the soft feel.

To go with my Lucky Charms, I made a fresh pot of strong coffee and settled into my bed, with all the throw pillows behind me for support.

Reading the crime beat is about as interesting as reading the ingredient list on a bottle of cough syrup, but I couldn't think of any other way to find out if the skeleton and the robbery at my parents' house were somehow connected. Popping a marshmallow clover into my mouth, I focused on the oldest cases first. Most of the things listed were a line or two, giving me little more than stuff like "A break-in occurred in the such-and-such block of S. Ocean." Quickly, I printed out a map of Palm Beach, went into my kitchen junk drawer, and retrieved a set of Sharpies. Using a different color for each year, I started marking the locations of the robberies.

Information on the first few years didn't yield much, but slowly a pattern started to emerge. After 1994, all the robberies took place within a five-mile radius of my cottage. Maybe the cluster meant something, but without specifics about mode of entry, items taken, dates, times, et cetera, it was tough to find anything tying the robberies together.

About three hours into my task, I came across an article written in May 1996. The credited reporter's name was Justin Kearney. Aided by an unnamed law-enforcement informant, he claimed the robberies were linked by the way the robbers had entered the homes and that there was strong evidence to indicate inside help.

Glancing at my bedside clock, I decided ten thirty wasn't too late to phone the only person I knew who knew everything. The question was, could I call Liam without caving and asking him to come over?

"McGarrity."

"How do I get my hands on the actual police reports for robberies on Palm Beach from January 1993 through May of 1996?"

"Hi, Liam, is this a bad time?" he mocked.

"Is it?"

"No. Why do you need the reports?"

I heard an annoying female giggle in the background. It shouldn't have bothered me, but it did. Was it Beer Barbie Ashley, or did he have some other woman? "So how do I get the reports?"

More silly girlie giggles. "Give me an hour or two and I'll get back to you."

"Thanks," I said, and pretty much slammed the receiver back on its cradle.

Knowing that he was spending an hour or two having sex with God-knew-who really screwed with my confidence. On the bright side, at least we were both getting screwed. Only I wasn't enjoying mine at all.

I did discover that in a two-hour-and-seventeen-minute span you could consume an entire box of Lucky Charms and a half carton of cookie dough Häagen-Dazs. Oh, and three pots of coffee. It was almost 1:00 a.m., and I was on such a sugar and caffeine high that it would be hours before I could even consider falling asleep. Like some sort of sick stopwatch, every fifteen minutes my mind conjured a vivid image of Liam sweating up the sheets.

I hated him and I hated myself. I hated him more. A soft knock at my door startled me. Seeing Liam through the peephole flat out shocked me.

Removing the chain, I yanked the door open and tilted my head back so I wouldn't break eye contact. "What are you doing here?"

From behind his back, he pulled an eight-inch stack of file folders. "Police reports?"

"How did you . . . forget it," I said, taking the files and standing there in awkward silence. "Was there something else?"

"I used to be a cop, remember? I thought you might want my help deciphering some of that stuff."

"You thought wrong, but thanks," I said breezily as I derived great pleasure in closing the door on his handsome face. I slipped the chain in place, then listened for the unmistakable belch from the motor of his Mustang.

Silence.

Looking out the peephole, I saw him leaning against the doorjamb. I winced, knowing it would only be a matter of seconds before I crumbled and let him inside. I winced because obviously he knew I'd let him in too.

Resigned, I opened the door and led him into the living room. As I placed the folders in the center of my coffee table, Liam cozied up right next to me. I turned and gave him my best back-off glare.

He was impervious. Sitting, he grabbed me around the waist and planted me next to him. My top had ridden up slightly, so his large, callused hands made contact with my flushed, traitorous skin. He was still wearing jeans and one of his signature Tommy Bahama shirts, making me feel ridiculously underdressed.

"Let me go put on some clothes and makeup."

His grip tightened. "You're fine as you are."

Not a compliment, not criticism. Pent-up desire was eating my brain like some sort of parasite. "I don't feel very professional like this," I insisted, twisting away from him and practically hurdling the coffee table and ottoman to get to my bedroom.

In record time—twenty-two minutes—I switched to shorts and a baby doll top over one of my new bras and thong. With so little time, I had to do the blush on cheeks and lids with a little mascara and some lip-gloss thing. Almost by habit, I squirted some Lulu Guinness on, then picked up my laptop and marked-up map on the way back to the living room.

"Very colorful," he commented as he looked at my map.

I explained the color scheme, then asked, "Are these in chronological order?" as I pointed to the folders.

"Yep. When do you want to start?"

"January of '93."

Liam grabbed a folder. "January second at nine in the morning a call came in from the housekeeper at 101 El Marisol."

"Wait!" I grabbed the folder from him and scanned the two-page report. "That was my mother's and Jonathan's house. He died in April of that year."

"Sorry about your stepfather, but I thought that might get your heart started. The housekeeper showed up at her regularly scheduled time and found one of the east-facing doors—that would be the beachside—open. Since none of the Tanners were in residence, she checked the house and found jewelry, a coin collection, and several small statues missing."

"Part of the headless collection," I said. "My mother has always had a thing for headless bronzes and ceramics," I explained.

"There's a detailed list on the second page."

I had vague memories of some of the jewelry and several very specific childhood memories of watching Jonathan add pricey and rare coins to his beloved collection. Turning the second page over, I didn't find what I was looking for. Either the housekeeper hadn't thought to include it or it wasn't one of the items taken by the robbers.

"The medallion you took off the skeleton isn't on the list," Liam said. "I already looked. The info on how they got in is pretty interesting, though."

"They broke in the back cabana door," I said after I read the report.

"Yeah, the only door *not* connected to the state-of-the-art alarm system," Liam said dryly. "They were either lucky as hell—which I don't believe—or had some insider information. That makes more sense. Who knew that door wasn't armed?"

"My mother, me, Lisa, Jonathan, Trinnie—she was the housekeeper. The pool guy, I can't remember his name, but sometimes he came in to leave a note or something. I was a kid, so I don't really know. I do know Trinnie was like family. I can't imagine her fronting for a ring of thieves."

"Know where she is now?"

"Sure, she's in an assisted-living facility in Tequesta."

"Think she'll talk to us?" Liam asked.

"Absolutely, but I don't think you'll like her answers."

"Why?"

"Alzheimer's. She worked for us from the time I was three. I visit her once a month, but she doesn't have a clue who I am."

"Guess we move on to the particulars of the next robbery."

Liam and I pored over the files. As time went on, the thieves grew bolder and better. Sometime in 1995 they graduated to safecracking, landing themselves cash as well as the high-end merchandise, jewelry, and art they'd been carting off.

"That really screams inside job," Liam commented, his tone more serious. "They didn't ransack the houses, they knew right where to go to find the safes. And the choice of what to steal is the connection."

"How?"

He moved close enough that his warm breath tickled my bare arm. "You've got this stack," he said, patting the smaller pile. "Standard stuff, TVs, small electronics, the kind of stuff that can be fenced in a nanosecond."

"Okay."

"Then there's these." He hit the larger pile. "They took stuff that would require a specialized fence but would bring top dollar."

"And fit in a backpack," I offered.

"Statues fit in a backpack?" he asked.

"The ones taken from my parents' house would. They were originals, but I don't think any of them were more than five or six inches high."

"Okay," Liam said, stroking the dark stubble on his chin.

I tried not to think about the stubble that was sexy as hell. This was no time for my brain to take a detour. "So we should eliminate the robberies where run-of-the-mill stuff was taken and concentrate on the specialized stuff."

"Right."

It wasn't until I got to one in May 1996 that a tingle danced along my spine. "Seems the thief made a mistake on this one. Left a partial print on the handle of a safe they drilled."

"Gotta love felons, eventually they screw themselves."

My excitement tempered. "They never matched the print to anyone."

"Until yesterday."

My head whipped around and I said, "What?"

"You're going to get a call from Sergeant Jennings in the morning. This print matched the one on your windowsill."

"And you were keeping this a secret why?"

"I wasn't keeping it a secret. When I was getting copies of the files I overheard one of the Palm Beach cops on the phone with Jennings. He was confirming a print match to a May 1996 robbery. I think it's time for you to back off. Let the cops find the guy who broke in with a skeleton and left with your panties."

"How did you know that? I didn't even tell the cops."

"Becky was worried you weren't taking the situation seriously."

"So she called you?"

"She thought it might be a good idea for me to keep an eye on you."

"She thought wrong." Of course my conviction faltered as I imagined Liam on my bed. "So the person who broke into a Palm Beach house also did the skeleton thing in my closet and took my panties?"

"Yep. Only the cops don't know his name. He's still a John Doe, and he's still close. Close enough to have read the *Post* article about the skeleton in your new house." Liam hooked his finger under my chin and forced me to look at him. Deep lines of concern were etched into the corners of his eyes. "When I find John Doe, I'm willing to bet he'll be able to identify the skeleton."

Keep your friends close but
run from your enemies.

ten

M Y ALARM SOUNDED IN a distant fog, and
it wasn't until I lifted my head that I realized I was lifting it off Liam's lap. His
eyelids were half-open as he looked down at me
with those sparkling blue eyes. Not a bad way to
start a day.

"Sorry," I said, sitting up and stretching. "When
did I fall asleep?"

"Sometime around Christmas of '96."

"Wiseass." I slapped his thigh as I got off the sofa
and went to make coffee. My brain was no match for
Liam without a serious hit of caffeine.

When I heard my alarm go silent, I turned and
found him coming out of my bedroom.

Who knew it could be more awkward waking up
with a guy you *hadn't* slept with?

"Coffee will be ready in three minutes and seventeen seconds."

He chuckled. "No time. I've got a thing."

Again with the *thing*. Direct hit to my warming libido. "Have fun."

"Lock up after me," he said, pausing at the entry to my kitchen.

His broad shoulders nearly filled the space as he lingered, waiting for something. A hug? A kiss? A go cup of java? So what did I do? Something cool and sophisticated? Of course not. I waved. I freaking waved like an inept teenager. Lord, but that man brought out the very worst in me.

I did wait until he was out the door; I locked it and replaced the chain before letting out an embarrassed groan.

Four hours of sleep hadn't left me feeling perky, and a shower did little to wash the lethargy from my body. Wrapped in a towel, I bent down and picked my clothes off the floor. Before depositing them in my near-capacity laundry hamper, I lifted them to my face and drank in the scent of him. It was male and appealing and . . . "Get over it!" I hissed at myself.

I downed a second cup of coffee, then went to my closet and, realizing time was getting away from me, grabbed a belted Kenneth Cole print skirt I'd found online for under fifty bucks and a plain white cotton top from Target. Okay, I'm not normally a Target shopper, but it was cute and I'd cut the tags out in hopes of forgetting my foray into discount shopping for the masses. I know, I'm a snob, but I have an aversion to buying clothing in the same place I can grab a gallon of milk. Not that I ever grab a gallon of milk, but if I did . . . well, I didn't want it in the same bag as my clothing.

I chose a pair of Stuart Weitzman satin platform sandals. They were not really my color—deep emerald green—but they worked with the splashes of green in the skirt and they were first quality. They were a gift from my mother. She loves emerald green. I have a whole shelf in the top of my closet with emerald green sweaters, belts, nightgowns—you name it, she's given it to me. I suppose pink isn't in her vocabulary. Then again, we have completely different coloring. She's a brunette with a medium complexion. I, on the other hand, am a fair-skinned blonde. Other than our eye color—somewhere between blue and aqua—no one would ever peg me as her daughter. Which, come to think of, I'm okay with.

If I ever happen across Mr. Finley or Mr. Anderson, I suppose one of them will be a fair-skinned blond. Had to come from somewhere.

I abused concealer trying to hide my dark circles, then carefully applied my makeup. A pair of gold hoops and I was good to go. Almost. I had to transfer my essentials, lipstick, wallet, and cell phone to a small Coach bag that went with my outfit—I was tired, not incapable of accessorizing properly. Grabbing up its matching tote, I jammed the police reports and my colorfully annotated map inside. I was about to leave when I spun around, wiggled the mouse on my computer, and hastily emailed my working document from the newspaper archives to my work account.

In just over an hour since the alarm sounded, I was filling my travel mug and then out the door. I dumped the tote in the backseat, put the travel mug in its holder, and muttered a curse as I went back into my apartment for my sunglasses.

Even making record time, I still managed to pull into the parking lot at Dane, Lieberman at 9:05. I considered anything before 9:30 on time. Margaret, the self-appointed gatekeeper of punctuality Hell, considered on time to be 8:59. I braced myself for the Margaret glare as I struggled to balance everything and open the door.

I smelled him a split second before Tony reached over me and grabbed the door. I loved the smell of Gucci Pour Homme II. The olivewood base made it one of the sexiest men's scents to come down the pike in a long while. It smelled expensive and masculine.

"Thanks," I gushed without turning around. "I'd make a pretty lousy Sherpa, huh?"

"What do you have there?" With his longer legs, he was even with me on the third step.

"Stuff on the robberies. I promise I'm not sidetracked, just going to work on my lunch hour." I was having a morning glare-off with Margaret.

"Your classes start tomorrow. I hope you'll show the same commitment to the learning experience that you've shown to the skeletal remains."

I could practically see Margaret's gotta-know-everything antennae poke up from the back of her head. "Here are your messages, Mr. Caprelli," she said as if Sandra Dee was stuck inside her saggy, fifty-five-year-old body. She slid a small, neat pile of pink squares across her desktop.

"Tony," he corrected as he lifted the strap of my tote off my shoulder. "This weighs a ton."

"Good, I can claim I worked out this morning."

Margaret snorted, but she tried to cover it with a little cough.

"Do I have any messages?" I asked, quelling the childish urge to flick her in the Bluetooth.

"Yes. A Sergeant Jennings called. He asked that you return his call as soon as possible."

I didn't rate a pink square, neat or otherwise. "Thank you."

Tony escorted me to the elevator and went so far as to carry my tote to my office. "That wasn't necessary," I insisted, taking the tote and placing it next to my desk with a thud.

"Want to tell me why a cop is looking for you?"

I told him about the break-in, conveniently leaving out the panty part and Liam's involvement.

Tony's expression was impossible to read. Other than a slight pinch between his brows, I couldn't tell if he was sympathetic or irritated. "Is Jennings the officer handling the break-in?"

I nodded. "I'm sure it's just routine follow-up."

"Keep me in the loop," he said, then left.

I wasn't completely sure what he meant by "loop"—only that it somehow sounded ominous. And distracting enough to keep me from checking him out in his tailored black suit. I consoled myself with the knowledge that the day was young.

Following my routine, I made coffee, checked my interoffice mail and my voice mail, and reached for my phone to return Jennings's call.

I was put through immediately. "Thanks for getting back to me," he said, his tone a bit perturbed.

"I had a couple of things here that took priority," I explained. Besides, I already knew what he was going to tell me.

"We matched the prints to a cold case in Palm Beach."

"One of a series of robberies?"

"Yes, how'd you know that?"

Not sure if Liam had gotten the files legally, I hedged, "It was a break-in, so logically, the prints would match a robber. And the crime-scene tech told me the John Doe in your computer system was from 1996."

"Oh, right. I'll keep you posted if anything breaks."

"Thanks," I said, and hung up. Jennings didn't sound too optimistic.

Before I tackled unpacking the police reports, I retrieved my cell phone and pulled up the text I'd discreetly sent myself during lunch with Melinda.

I opened a new document on my computer and began typing the names of the foster children Melinda had given me. I was on the first name when the intercom buzzed.

"Yes?"

"There's a Sam Carter here to see you," Margaret complained. "He isn't on your appointment sheet, but—"

"Send him up, please," I interrupted.

Scooting my chair back from the desk, I walked slowly to the double elevators. Sam hadn't been to my new office, and, positive Margaret had probably greeted him like an invading cockroach, I wanted to be there when he stepped onto the second floor.

After a brief wait, the elevator dinged and the circular light next to elevator one illuminated. The doors slid open slowly, then Sam stepped out and smiled when he saw me waiting.

In one hand, he was carrying a legal-sized leather-zipped portfolio. His man purse was clipped to his trim waist. In the other hand, he balanced a molded cardboard tray with two venti drinks from Starbucks. The gift of coffee was always welcomed and appreciated.

"Hi," I greeted, placing a quickie kiss on his mouth. "Want me to carry anything?"

"Nope, I'm balanced," he answered. "So." He lowered his voice. "I heard from Mrs. Hemshaw that you had a busy weekend. The police were there. *And* Liam spent the night? You have to tell me everything."

"Hush!" I placed a finger to my lips, then turned and led him to my office.

Sam stood in the doorway; his expression amounted to one big disapproving frown. "How can you work in such bland surroundings?"

Looking around, I realized that there wasn't any art on the walls, and I wasn't one for cluttering my desk with photos. I used to have one of Patrick and me on vacation in the Caymans, but that went the way of the cactus. There was a paralegal on the opposite side of the building who had turned her office into a paisley palace; Mary Beth was one of those crafty people who, when not wielding a hot glue gun, was hosting home parties. She'd done me a favor on the Evans murder, but so far, I'd been able to dodge her invitations. Sitting in her house with a bunch of other women playing word games wasn't my idea of a good time.

Home parties aside, she was the queen of organization, making sure coworkers' birthdays were remembered and baking stuff for the staff lounge. She'd even decorated her office at her own expense.

"Forget it," I told Sam firmly. "I don't decorate what I don't own. If Dane, Lieberman wants to spring for a new coat of paint, they can have at it. Your job is the new house."

Somewhat reluctantly, Sam took the empty chair across from me and unzipped his portfolio. "Harold and I worked out a three-stage plan," he began, placing papers in neat piles.

"How much?"

He put his hands on his hips and tossed me a warning glare. "We're well below budget. Will it kill you to let me do my presentation?"

I leaned back in my vented leather chair and happily sipped my steaming vanilla latte. "Present away."

"Phase one is demolition," he said, passing me a neatly typed list on his business stationery.

Renting Harold and a Dumpster was going to run me about thirty grand. Dollar signs swirled in my head, and my grip on the coffee cup tightened. "Okay."

"Phase two is construction. That includes electrical, plumbing, and adding the pool and spa."

The number of one hundred six thousand dollars burned my tired eyes. "Could we consider using candles?"

"Trust me, Finley, that's cheap. Then there's the actual finishing and decorating. This includes cabinetry, painting, furnishing and window treatments."

"One hundred seventy-five thousand?" I choked out. "Is the paint liquid gold?"

Sam let out an irritated little grunt. "You liked the design when I showed it to you on my computer."

"I wasn't laying out three hundred grand when I looked at the 3-D version."

"There are some areas where we could cut corners, but in my professional opinion, that would be a mistake."

"And carrying that size loan isn't?"

"Interest rates are low. Besides, Jane says a home equity loan this size will actually be forty dollars less than your rent payment is at the condo."

Hearing that calmed me a little. "Okay. So what's the time line?"

Sam smiled and wiggled his brows. His brown eyes sparkled with an excitement that was infectious. "The demo will be finished by this afternoon. Thirty days to move in, give or take."

"Really?"

"Sure. There might be a few things that take

longer—like the pool—but so long as you don't mind living there while some of the finishing work is being done, you can plan on moving in by the end of next month." Sam clapped his hands. "Can you believe it?"

Sucking in a deep breath, I swallowed a squeal of sheer delight. "No. I'm so thrilled."

Sam's smile dwindled. "It isn't going to be the same when you leave."

"I'll miss you too," I said, reaching over to squeeze his hand. "But we can have sleepovers. I didn't miss the fact that the guest bedroom has some remarkable similarities to your bedroom."

He sighed heavily. "I knew you'd want to make me feel welcome, right?"

"Absolutely."

He pulled out three contracts, which I read and happily signed. That done, he put everything back in the portfolio, rested his elbows on the edge of my desk, and rested his chin on his folded hands. "Now dish."

"You'll be disappointed," I warned. "It was a platonic, *accidental* sleepover."

He rolled his eyes. "Talk about a wasted opportunity. Geez, Finley, you had that magnificent male specimen all to yourself and you went platonic? I think you need to see a doctor."

Sitting up straighter, I said, "My apartment was broken into. The creep hung a fake skeleton in my closet and stole my panties. Forgive me if I wasn't in the mood for a come-back-and-bite-me roll in the hay."

"I think two years with Patrick screwed with your perspective on screwing. Sex doesn't have to lead to happily ever after. It can just be good old recreational fun."

"Liam does work for this firm. Probably a lot more now that we're adding a criminal division. The last thing I want to do is run into a guy I *used* to sleep with on a regular basis on my way to grab my lunch from the employee fridge."

"You don't pack a lunch," Sam volleyed back. "I'm not saying fall in love with the guy." He lifted his hands in mock surrender. "All I'm saying is worse things could happen to you than hooking up with Liam McGarrity."

"Hooking up with Tony Caprelli," I muttered, wondering where that thought came from.

"You met someone? Tell, tell!"

I explained all about Tony's joining the firm. By the time I finished, Sam was shaking his head. "Sleeping with the boss is a guaranteed recipe for disaster."

I nodded agreement. "But you haven't seen his dimples," I added wistfully.

"You've got a loan. You can't afford to get fired. Oh, Jane told me to tell you to meet her at Bank of America on Okeechobee at one to sign the papers and get the checks you'll use to pay the draws on the remodel."

"Then it will feel real." *Real scary.*

"Be brave," he offered as he came around my desk and gave me a soft kiss on the cheek. "Gotta run. I'm meeting Harold at the house in a little while."

I stood and came around the desk. "You and Harold are getting pretty chummy."

"He's a decent guy. Married to a real piece of work."

"You met Mrs. Harold?"

"She helped with the demo. I can tell you," he continued as we walked to the elevators, "you wouldn't want to meet her in a dark alley. She's one scary chick. And I'm using that term in the broadest possible sense. Her biceps are bigger than her breasts and she's got linebacker shoulders. Solid as a rock and about as friendly. Maybe she wouldn't be so mannish if she didn't shave her head. Naw, she'd still look butch."

"Thanks," I said as he stepped into the elevator.

"How about drinks tomorrow night?"

I scowled. "Can't, first day of school, remember?"

He was chuckling as the doors slid shut.

Back in my office, I returned to the chore of compiling the partial list of Melinda's foster kids. Bridget Tomey, Terri Semple, Megan Landry, Carly Branson, Abby Matthews. I typed in the initials C.L. and wondered if Melinda might have remembered the name of the young man in the photo by now. As I dialed, I prayed she was over the snit brought on by Liam.

"Hello?"

"Hi Melinda, this is Finley."

"Yes?" I felt the chill freeze the phone line.

It felt weird to talk to her twice in three days given the fact that I really didn't know her that well. It was more like I knew of her. "I was wondering if you remembered the name of the young Hispanic kid in the photo. C.L.?"

I heard her let out an annoyed breath. "No."

"Could you contact DCF? I assume they keep a list of your foster children."

"Is that really necessary?" she asked. "Besides, DCF isn't the most organized governmental agency. It could be a taxing process to get them to go through their records."

"It would really be a big help."

"That isn't my understanding," she replied quickly. "A team of detectives came to see me right after our lunch and I told them there was no skeleton in the house when I lived there. They didn't seem all that worked up about your discovery."

"I think there's going to be an independent autopsy." *That I'll probably end up paying for.*

"What for?" she snapped.

"Just checking to make sure the ME didn't miss anything. As you've pointed out, the authorities aren't taking this very seriously."

"So why are you?"

"She was buried in my house," I said, growing a little miffed myself. "I'd at least like to know her identity. Will you help me? Please?"

"I'll think about it. I'm helping Terri with her wedding, so my life is a little busy right now."

"It would really, *really* mean a lot to me." I figured it might be a good idea to bring out the only card I had in my deck. "I know if Jonathan were alive, he'd appreciate you helping me, since he was instrumental in helping you by providing a home where you could foster your kids."

"I'll get to it as soon as possible," she said, though I sensed less hostility. "I've got another call waiting," she said. "Bye, Finley."

Another call my ass. There'd been no telltale click from call waiting. I rubbed my forehead, wondering why she'd lied to me. "Maybe she was tired of being bullied," I said as I stared at the list on my computer screen.

Reluctantly, I added her name to the list. Minimal past relationship aside, I had to admit Liam was right. I didn't know how I knew it, but I knew Melinda was hiding something.

But why?

And for how long?

The first day of school is exciting if you're five.
If you're twenty-nine, it's just humiliating.

eleven

GLANCING DOWN AT MY Not-a-Rolex watch, I had just enough time to make a quick phone call before an unexpected lunch with Tony. I'd discovered the sticky summons on my monitor when I'd arrived.

My office. 12:15. Bring your research. Tony

Quick went out the window when I reached the first level of automated phone system Hell. DCF had nothing on Dante when they designed the decidedly user-friendly information line listed in the front of the state services directory. After selecting my language of choice—English, though I had to admit Creole sounded more interesting—I navigated through eight more levels of options until I could finally ask to speak to a human being.

"Department of Children and Families, Mrs. Podbeilski speaking. How may I help you?"

I introduced myself, making sure to drop in the fact that I was calling from the small but prestigious law firm of Dane, Lieberman. Then I asked, "What's the best way to get a list of children fostered by the same mother starting roughly seventeen years ago to about six months ago?"

"You file a request."

That seemed far too easy. "I need the children's names."

"Assuming you have a valid cause—suspicion of abuse, negligence, that sort of thing—we can release limited information."

"How limited?" I asked.

"We can't give you medical records or Social Security numbers, just confirmation of dates and placements when the children are under our care and custody."

"No subpoena?"

"Not for the confirmations. If you wanted unrestricted access to the files, well then, yes, you'd serve the main office with a subpoena. A hearing would be set and a judge would determine if the request for access would violate the privacy rights of any minors involved."

Unrestricted access would have been my choice, but just getting the list would have to do for now. "How long does it take to process a request for the limited information?"

"Seven to fourteen days."

My shoulders slumped under the cloak of disappointment. "Is there any way to expedite the process?"

"For an additional hundred-dollar fee, yes."

"How soon could I get the information?"

"If you pay for overnight delivery, we could have it to you tomorrow. I can send you a PDF of the form by email. Fill it out and provide a major credit card number."

"That would be great, thanks."

"Will there be anything else?"

"No, thank you." I placed the receiver back on its cradle.

After five minutes, I started impatiently hitting the Send/Receive icon on my email. Nothing. Damn.

My cell rang. More accurately, it played the Wicked Witch's theme from *The Wizard of Oz*—*da-da-da-da-da-da-da-da*, a special ringtone I'd created for my mother.

"Hi, Mom."

"Am I so insignificant in your life that I had to read about your latest escapade in the morning paper?"

Since I hadn't seen the paper, I quickly opened a new internet page and Googled my name. A two-line report of the break-in at my complex was listed, including my last name. "Sorry."

"Really, Finley. In the last few months you've made quite a habit of drawing attention to yourself."

"Do you think I called Rent-A-Robber? Someone broke in. And I'm fine, by the way."

"Do not take that tone with me," my mother warned. "I've decided to go up to Atlanta to visit your sister. We still have a lot to do for the wedding, and of course now I'll have to find a way to explain to the

Huntington St. Johns why the maid of honor is constantly cavorting with unsavory criminals."

"Just tell them I couldn't find any savory ones."

"Your sarcasm is unwarranted. Oh." She paused, and I heard the jingle of bracelets; she must have been switching hands or something. "I also received a troubling call from Melinda Redmond this morning. Why are you hounding her?"

"I took her to lunch and asked her for some information. Hardly on the same scale as Abu Ghraib."

"Well, I want you to stop it immediately."

"It's nice to want," I sighed.

"Your sister doesn't talk to me like this, Finley."

Ironically, my sister didn't talk to my mother all that much. She was far too busy working and planning her upcoming nuptials to David Huntington St. John IV. David the Fourth—also a doctor—was a male version of my perfect sister. In eight short weeks, they'd have their perfect wedding. Then maybe some perfect children followed by finding a cure for cancer or eradicating world hunger or something.

"I'm sorry," I said on autopilot. "When are you leaving?"

"This afternoon. I should be gone a week or two, so please water my plants."

I swallowed a groan. Plant duty was expensive. My mother's collection of prized orchids hated me. I assumed they'd started formulating plans for a mass suicide the instant my mother had dragged out her luggage. My brown thumb and I were no match for her plants, so I'd have to swing by my mom's place, photograph them, and order replacements to swap out before she returned. I have no idea if my mother was any the wiser, but I suspected she knew, and relished the fact that as a plant-sitter, I sucked.

After ending the call, I clicked the Send/Receive icon once more, to no avail. Since Tony was in the mood to offer some free advice on what to do next, I gathered all my robbery records and headed up to the top floor.

The weight of my tote bag bit into my shoulder and had me listing to one side in order to compensate during the short elevator ride. As I stepped onto the floor, the executive secretary looked up without so much as a smile, then tapped one of the intercom buttons on her phone. Tony's voice came over the speaker.

"Miss Tanner is here."

I wanted to roll my eyes. I'd worked in the same building with the woman for seven years, and she had yet to call me by my first name.

"Send her in."

"You may go in," she said, then returned to her keyboard.

The cut flowers on the center table of the executive office smelled fresh and wonderful. Not as fresh and wonderful as Tony, but definitely a close second.

His relaxed smile was a nice change after my mother's phone call.

"I'm assuming those are the police reports on the Palm Beach robberies?" he asked rhetorically as one of the interns slipped in and silently delivered two chef salads and Diet Cokes. He left as quietly as he'd arrived.

I didn't know whether to be impressed or irritated. Had Tony ordered Diet Coke because, like my mother, he'd noticed the few extra pounds I'd put on? Did my clothes look too tight? How humiliating was that?

"Yes. I've followed your directive. I did all of this on personal time. You're welcome to check my time sheets. My billable hours are current and up from this time last year." It's never too early to start posturing for my next raise.

He leaned back in his chair, grabbing one of the cans in the process. A lock of brown hair slipped forward and caught in his lashes. Almost absently, he smoothed it back, then flipped the tab on his soda. "I trust you."

It was a simple statement, but my gut reaction was fairly complicated. As nice as it was to chat about work, I couldn't help wondering how he felt about me. He was definitely sending out vibes, but nothing about his posture changed. No body language to help me read the man. Nothing. Nada.

Frustrating. I'm not stupid enough to make a move on a guy I barely know. That didn't mean I couldn't fantasize about it. Especially since he seemed quite content to let those liquid chocolate eyes of his roam over my face and upper body. Subtle but not invisible.

The air between us seemed taut, and I felt anticipation begin to pool in my stomach. As the minutes clicked off in silence, I found it harder and harder to think of him as my boss. I was definitely sizing him up as potential date material.

He broke the tension when he sat up straight and looked at my tote bag. "I should have sent one of the file people to get those police reports," he said apologetically. Moving out from behind his desk, he relieved me of my tote and set it in one of two burgundy chairs opposite his desk.

"It wasn't a problem."

Tony retook his seat, leaned back, and laced his fingers behind his head. The action caused his polished cotton, monogrammed shirt to pull tight against his chest and arms. A little thrill slithered along my spine. Dimples and a great body. And great cologne and—Oh my God! A Rolex Cellini Prince watch was strapped to his left wrist. He had the 18k Everose gold model with the rayon flammé de la gloire Arabic numerals on a black leather band with a gold clasp. It was a new model based on rectangular designs first produced in the 1920s. Top of the line, sleek, expensive, and impressive as hell to a Rolex wanna-own like me.

He cleared his throat, bringing me out of my fog of envy. "Sorry," I said. "Nice watch."

"Thanks, it was a gift."

That was all he was going to give me? Not the who, the why, or the what for? Crap, no wonder he'd hired Liam on sight. They shared the same not-giving-out-any-personal-info attitude.

I pulled out all the work I'd done over the weekend, completely comfortable not telling him that

Liam had helped, and put it on his desk. After bringing him up to speed on the pattern of the robberies, I said, "So my next step is to see if I can find some link between the locations of the robberies. Lawn services, pool maintenance workers, meter readers, whatever. Something besides geography ties these robberies together."

"I agree," he said. "Excellent work."

I smiled. "Thank you."

"Liam called this morning. Told me all about the fake skeleton and the, um, theft. What kind of precautions are you taking?"

My smile faded. "New security bars. I'm moving in about a month, and my new house will have an alarm system."

"Add video cameras and manned monitoring."

"That's not in my budget," I admitted with a laugh I hoped would cover my embarrassment. "Speaking of which, I have to sign loan papers at the bank. I was planning on doing it during my lunch."

Tony shook his head and chuckled. "You did a lot of work over the weekend, Finley. You can take the salad and the soda to go. I didn't mean to cheat you out of your lunch hour."

Apparently, no one had told him my definition of lunch was closer to two hours. And that didn't include banking. "Thank you." I was still tempted to jump over the desk and kiss him. With tongue. I was totally loving my new boss. Fearful that I was reading him wrong, I contained myself as I gathered my salad and drink. "Thank you for lunch."

Swiveling his executive leather chair around, he grabbed the pile of papers from the credenza, stuffed them in my tote, and turned back to me. "I got this about an hour ago," he said, handing me two crisp pages.

Before I read the first word, I knew I was looking at an autopsy report. I'd seen hundreds of them during my tenure in estates and trusts, but this was only my second private autopsy. There was a big X over the C2-3 spine.

"My skeleton died from a compression fracture of the neck?" I asked. "Isn't that a relatively common injury people suffer diving into shallow water?"

Tony nodded. "Very good. It's also an effective way to asphyxiate someone without leaving the telltale broken hyoid bone." He rose and came around the desk and went behind me. I felt his palm flatten against the back of my head, fingers splayed. His other hand rested on my shoulder. "The killer would have to fold the person, probably to a seated position, and then apply pressure to the back of the skull," he said as he gently pressed my head forward until my chin touched my chest. "Enough pressure would literally cut off the windpipe, and the victim's death could look like, well, an accident."

For a few nanoseconds after he released me, I still felt the heat of his touch. Not with the same intensity I felt Liam's, but my body definitely reacted to him. Great, nothing like getting all hormonal over two of the least appropriate men possible.

"So, she was definitely murdered?"

Tony shook his head. "The pathologist will only go so far as to commit to probable. There are more findings," he said. "The victim was Caucasian, between the ages of sixteen and eighteen. The partial mummification allowed him to take tissue samples that prove the body was kept in a low-humidity environment, as well as frozen for a period. The county ME missed the partial remains of her stomach contents."

I gulped back the urge to gag.

"At or near the time of her death, she'd eaten licorice. The red rope kind. Hair follicle tests confirm she was a recreational drug user. Cocaine."

"How can this not be classified a murder?"

"With this fact pattern? If it were my case, I'd argue that the person died accidentally and any other injuries or irregularities occurred postmortem. At most, any defendant might be charged with misdemeanor illegal handling and disposal of a dead body. That's a fine and brief probation."

"Why a climate-controlled environment and a freezer?" I asked, thinking aloud.

"Assuming it was murder, it might indicate nothing more sinister than the killer moving the body around to avoid detection. Most killers don't like to be caught."

"So why stuff her in my closet?"

Tony took a sip from the open can of soda on his desk. "I called the permits department, and two weeks ago a demo permit was issued for your beach house."

"That can't be right. My contractor—" Okay, that

was a stretch, but it sounded better than having a convicted felon working for me. "He applied for the demo permit this morning."

"The name on the first application was Marc Feldman."

"My mother's property manager," I explained. "Depending on who you ask, he either intentionally ran the place into the ground or saved it from destructive tenants."

"I've lived here long enough to know that beachfront property is pricey and hard to come by."

"It was a delayed inheritance," I explained. I had no idea why my mother had suddenly decided to fulfill Jonathan's wishes, and I didn't dare question her motives. I only knew that in her mind, she was doing me the grandmother of all favors. I was sure she had convinced herself that making the practically condemned home my problem was but another responsibility-building exercise that coincidentally solved a problem for her.

"Finley?"

"Sorry," I said, coming back into the present. "Did the second autopsy provide anything that helps to identify the girl?"

"Three healed forearm fractures. All spiral."

I squeezed my eyes shut for a second to focus my limited recall of a How to Recognize Abuse seminar I'd attended four or five years ago. "That's the twisting kind, right?"

"Most common type of fracture seen in the arms of physically abused children."

"The kind that might end up in foster care," I murmured.

"This, if true, ties your skeleton directly to your house."

I let out a frustrated breath. "DCF won't release medical histories on the kids fostered in my house."

"So bypass DCF and try Medicaid."

"Because?"

"There has to be a record of a medical examination when the girl went into the system. Being a minor without financial means, that examination would be processed through Medicaid. But that's not the next step. It would take decades to go through Medicaid records for the last fifteen-plus years. First you need to narrow the search to females Melinda fostered who fall in the age range of the second autopsy and add a couple of years on either end. An autopsy on such old remains isn't as accurate as one done near the time of death."

"I'll get on it," I said.

"Keep me posted. Leave the tote bag. I'll have these files and a copy of the autopsy reports brought down to your office." Then he smiled. "You should probably head to the bank."

Checking my watch, I realized he was right. "Okay."

"Have your alarm company contact my secretary. Since you'll be doing a lot of work for me, Dane, Lieberman will cover any additional security costs."

"That's very nice of you."

"Not nice, practical," he said with a shrug. "Since the firm is covering the cost of continuing ed courses for criminal litigation, it's just prudent to protect the investment we're making in you."

Put like that, it didn't sound nice, just pragmatic. So what? Bottom line: Tony was worried about me—kinda—*and* I was getting beefed-up security. Given my experience over the weekend, that was fine by me.

"To SIGNING AWAY YOUR soul," Jane said as she lifted her glass of champagne.

My hand was still cramped from signing dozens of documents, but I was really touched that my friends had arranged for a surprise you're-carrying-major-debt lunch at Saito's Japanese Restaurant in City Place. They made exceptional sushi, as well as various yummy things from the hibachi grill. Even if they served dirt, I still would be grinning from ear to ear at the thoughtfulness of my three best friends.

Good thing I hadn't eaten the salad; I just needed to remember to take it out of the lounge refrigerator so Tony wouldn't know I'd doubled up on lunches.

"My impending poverty and I thank you," I replied as we clinked glasses.

"I'm so excited for you, Fin," Liv said as she tucked a strand of dark hair behind her ear. "It's going to be great."

"And I'm sure your undies will be safer in your new home," Becky mumbled into her glass.

"I couldn't believe it when Becky told me what that creep did," Jane said, visually shivering as punctuation.

As usual, Jane was clad in a tight, lacy bustier,

form-fitting skirt, and FM heels. The cherry-red demi sweater covering her shoulders was what took the outfit from pole dancer to proper. Liv was across the table from me. She must have had morning meetings, because she was in a tailored Chanel summer suit in a stunning shade of turquoise that matched her exotic eye color and flawlessly perfect features.

"I was afraid I might miss this," Liv said. "Apparently some committee at Bethesda-by-the-Sea thought it would be a good idea to paint the interior of the church the week before the Semple-Gilmore wedding. That's the reason she fired her last wedding planner. He okayed the painting. Terri is frantic. She definitely doesn't want paint fumes mingling with the twenty thousand roses we'll be using to decorate the church and the grounds."

Bethesda-by-the-Sea is *the* church to be married in. When Donald Trump married his third wife there in 2005, he dropped a few million and wagged a few gossip tongues. The old-money rich don't like it when the new money shines a spotlight on their private enclaves. The Episcopal church definitely fell under that purview. Built in 1889, which for Florida is seriously historic, the neogothic structure that dominates the intersection of County Road and Barton Avenue was added in 1925 and has served the religious needs of the filthy rich ever since.

Every so often, the church holds events that are open to the public, but they result in impossible parking and long lines.

"Candlelight service?" I asked wistfully.

"Of course," Liv said. "Terri wants very traditional romance, soft lighting, soft colors and has an almost pathological attention to detail." Liv frowned. "What she doesn't want is publicity. I'm still struggling to get her to understand that I can control a lot of things, but paparazzi, celebutante junkies, and telephoto lenses make it virtually impossible for me to keep things low profile."

Twisting the gold and coral bracelets on her wrist, Becky scoffed. "She's marrying the hottest gazillionaire in the country. Does she really think the rest of us don't want a peek at that?"

Glancing around, and then leaning forward and lowering her voice, Liv said, "She's a little weird. I mean, she's a big wad of contradictions. She's demanding and aggressive and, well, loaded with street smarts, but anything in the tabloids or even the legit press makes her nutty. What does she expect? She went from secretary to fiancée of the World's Most Eligible Billionaire Bachelor. Of course people want to know how a nobody pulled off that Cinderella scenario."

I waited until the server delivered our lunches and refilled our glasses before asking Liv, "Do you think you could convince her to talk to me? Completely confidential, of course."

"Sorry, Finley," Liv said without hesitation. "I don't want to do anything to jeopardize this job. This is going to catapult Concierge Plus to the next level."

"Sorry I asked."

Liv smiled, reached under her chair, and produced an expertly done gift bag, which she passed to me.

"What's this?" I asked, gently pulling pink tissue from the bag.

"You're not just a new homeowner," Becky said. "You're a coed again."

They'd bought me pink and lime green pens, pencils, and notebooks. On the bottom of the bag, I found a vintage Nancy Drew thermos. "How sweet." I looked from face to face. "You all do realize I'm going to the local college and not kindergarten, right?"

"Who cares?" Jane said. "The pink pen with fuzzy ball top lights up."

"That won't draw attention to me," I replied dryly. I had visions of looking like Cher from *Clueless,* only fifteen years later. "Thank you."

Liv reached across and patted my hand. "Don't forget to write your name in marker in all of your sweaters."

Yanking my hand away, I said, "Thanks for the tip."

"You know," Becky began as she settled back in her seat, sipping her second glass of champagne, "the benefit of going back to college at your age is the expansion of the dating pool. At your age, you can choose from both the students and the teachers."

"I'll keep that in mind," I lied as I checked the time. "Sorry, but I've got to get back to the office."

All three of them looked at me, stunned. Tilting my head to one side, I pressed my lips together for a second. "C'mon, I have to be careful. I can't afford to give Margaret a reason to let Vain Dane dock my pay."

Becky grinned. "From what I hear, Tony has your back."

"When did you start listening to office gossip?"

"When I paid ten bucks to enter the office pool on when you and Tony will hook up. By the way, if you could sleep with him on the twenty-eighth, I'd be beholden."

BY FIVE O'CLOCK, I was packed up and ready to leave the office. I'd caught up on a complicated trust document, and around 2:30 p.m., the PDF from DCF had finally landed in my inbox. I completed the request, filled in the payment information, and sent it back to Mrs. Podbeilski by 2:37 p.m.

The combination of a champagne lunch and four hours of sleep caught up to me as I dragged myself out to my car. Seeing the gift bag in the backseat mitigated the irritation of knowing I had to swing by my mother's penthouse on the way home. I had to take pictures and measurements of her plants so I could pass the information on to my replacement supplier, Ricardo. A couple of the plants showed early signs of impending death. Before leaving, I raided my mom's fridge and went home with a great bottle of chilled Chablis to go with my Tony-supplied chef salad.

Once I was home and had a glass and a half of wine in me, I ate about half the food before calling it a night.

I felt renewed the next morning. Good thing,

since, shock of shocks, Mrs. Podbeilski had over-nighted me two small boxes of files.

In a matter of minutes, I was greedily pulling neatly labeled file folders from the boxes in my office. Though each file was thick, much of the information had been redacted by thick, black lines. My spirits plummeted before I realized that there were initials and dates on the tabs.

In addition to five names Melinda had given me at lunch, I had another twenty-two sets of initials. Again I felt the weight of defeat, until I started reading the pages and realized DCF didn't redact pronouns. In a matter of minutes I knew Melinda had fostered seven males and fifteen females long-term and another three dozen overnight emergency placements.

It suddenly dawned on me that it was strange that the state of Florida allowed coed foster care in a relatively small home. I did a quick Net search and discovered that single-sex foster homes were preferred but not always available. The state didn't implement mandatory single-sex foster homes until after 2003. With one mystery solved, I went back to work on the contents of the box.

The third folder I took from the box made my heartbeat skip. C.L. I did a quick search and discovered that there was only one C.L. in the bunch. This had to be the C.L. from the photograph. Before I read C.L.'s file, I hunted down the other names Melinda had identified at lunch just by using their initials. Then I leaned back to flip through the pages on C.L.

There was a photograph clipped to the first page.

The boy looked to be twelve or thirteen, Hispanic, but it was the sad, vacant, expressionless black eyes that pulled at my heartstrings. The picture was taken when he entered the foster-care system, but according to the caseworker's notes, he was fifteen when he went to live at the house on Chilian Avenue. Melinda was his seventh foster mother in just over two years. He was living with her when he aged out in 1997. And apparently the state of Florida didn't keep tabs on former foster children, so I had no idea where C.L. ended up.

I closed the file. Sad as his case was, I wasn't looking for a male foster child. My skeleton was female.

I stopped to refill my coffee cup and to silently berate myself for thinking in terms of *my skeleton*. She wasn't mine, but I was becoming obsessed with uncovering her identity.

It took me all morning and a good hunk of the afternoon to whittle the possibilities down to white females who fit the approximate age range. Not knowing when she'd died was the worst handicap, but there wasn't a thing I could do about that.

Opening the document I'd started yesterday, I ended up with a list of sixteen potential victims based on the information I culled from the extremely limited records. Other than a child's initials, birth date, eye color, hair color, weight, and height at the time of intake, I didn't have much else to use as a filter.

Law firms pay a lot of money for databases, Lexis-Nexis being the major one for research. Plaintiff-Defendant database probably came in second, but my personal fave was the vital statistics database. I was authorized to use it in my estate work so I could order death certificates or birth records or certain Medicaid records, DMV records, and credit checks to hunt for AWOL heirs. I wasn't technically supposed to use it for my own purposes, however.

Starting with the first set of initials, I discovered an Abby Andrews with the exact birth date as the A.M. I found in the DCF files. A couple more clicks and I knew Abby was married, living in Daytona Beach, Florida, and had given birth to twin sons two months ago. No way was she my skeleton, but that didn't mean she didn't know who the skeleton was. I put her file in my "to be interviewed" pile.

E.B. turned out to be Eve Bradley. Her Florida driver's license had expired in 2000. I moved her file to the opposite side of my desk; she was one I'd have to trace through all fifty states. If that yielded nothing, I'd have to go international.

Carly Branson's file landed on the floor. She died in a car accident at twenty-two.

J.B. was Jill Burkett. She had dropped off the radar just before aging out of the system. I put her file in the "more follow-up" pile.

Repeating the process, I ended up with three other well-documented deaths, all drug-related; current addresses for five more former foster children and two others whose trails ended when they aged out of state supervision.

It wasn't until I rolled my head around on my stiff neck that I realized it was five thirty-five. My class started at six. The college was a good half-hour drive away. *Son of a bitch.*

Grabbing my purse, I scrambled out of the building and pointed my car toward I-95. As I reached the entrance ramp and began to circle up onto the highway, I eased my lead foot off the gas and applied the brakes to compensate for the sharp curve. The pedal went all the way to the floor.

I reached for the emergency brake just as my car jumped the small curb. Suddenly the air bag slammed into my face and my car was spinning like a top before going airborne. I heard the sound of metal scraping pavement, felt a hard thud, then nothing.

*They say people who play with fire get
burned. Me? I get incinerated.*

twelve

I DON'T THINK I LOST consciousness, but if I did,
it couldn't have been for more than a second. In
addition to the suffocating nylon of the deflating
front and side air bags, there was a lot of pressure on
my hips and chest and left shoulder. It made perfect
sense, since I was hanging upside down.

I heard tires screeching to a halt and figured it was
probably less dangerous outside the car. Like a cat
trying to free itself from a sack, I began to claw at the
air bags. Shoving, stuffing, mushing—anything to
give myself room to breathe, find the door handle,
and bolt.

Now that the immediate danger was over—I
hoped—I automatically started to cry. Tears of panic
rolled into my hairline, a very strange sensation. The
scent of gasoline filling the car's interior scared the
crap out of me.

"Hello?" a man's voice called.

"I'm here! I'm stuck."

"Hang in there. I've called for help."

The next person I saw, albeit upside down, was a paramedic, who crawled through the tight metal sandwich on the passenger's side of the car. Using his elbows, he worked his way in, carrying a brace, a blanket, and a banana bag.

"I'm going to snap the collar around your neck," he explained after introducing himself as Nick Something-or-Other and explaining that the driver's side of my car was buckled and I might get jostled around a bit while they worked on freeing me from the wreckage. "Take deep breaths," he instructed, reaching behind himself. This time, one of those plastic lengths of tubing with the little nostril things was in his hand. "One early indicator for the possibility of going into shock is the body slowing to shallow breathing. I'm going to give you some oxygen—again, just as a precaution, because I don't want you going into shock. How are you feeling, Lindsey?"

The tube had an awful medicinal/antiseptic/plastic smell. "Finley, not Lindsey."

"Sorry."

The blood pressure cuff inflated, tightening again. "I *really, really* want to get out of here," I said, unashamedly begging him with my eyes and the pathetic whine in my voice.

Nick smiled. "I want that too, but we have to do it the safe way. You could have a spinal cord injury, and a sudden movement, like me cutting your seat belt and you falling uncushioned to the roof of the car, could result in exacerbating the injury. So what do you—"

The deafening noise of something that sounded like a chain saw roared into my left ear. Nick grabbed my hand and held it as the car rocked and shook to the harmony of metal being peeled off the frame. Unable to help it, my tears began again. I'm sure it wasn't more than a few minutes, but it felt like days until four firefighters in full gear opened the side of my car like a can of tuna.

Nick was joined by another paramedic in a navy, short-sleeved uniform. Neither one of them looked much older than teenagers, but both men had well-muscled arms and strong, callused hands. And I loved them both for rescuing me.

Somehow, they managed to get me out of the car in an upside-down sitting position. Based on the cool draft I felt high up on my thighs, my skirt wasn't covering much. Great. Traffic was at a dead standstill, and any number of gawkers were probably filming my girl parts for webcast on YouTube.

I was placed on a stretcher, and the minute I was righted and lying flat, I saw stars and the clouds in the sky swirling and twirling. My instinct was to rub my eyes, but they'd already strapped my hands beneath the blanket covering me as I was wheeled inside a waiting ambulance. In a matter of minutes, I was inside the busy ER at St. Mary's Hospital on 45th Street. A chipper nurse came in, her shoes squishing on the linoleum floor. Her photo ID was clipped to her scrubs, and a stethoscope decorated with teddy-bear pins hung loosely around her neck. "Hi, I'm Rita," she greeted me, rolling the tray table to the foot of my gurney and opening a large three-ring binder. She asked me for some information, helped me change into a gown, put my clothing in a bag with my purse, and checked my vitals before finally peeling back the sheet on my left arm.

Then and only then did I notice a blood-soaked piece of gauze taped just above my elbow. "I didn't even know I was hurt," I said, limited by the neck brace still clipped in place.

"It's not bad," Rita assured me, adding a reassuring smile that went all the way to her blue eyes. "A few stitches, maybe. And a few more on your leg."

Tossing the blanket aside, I sat up enough to look down at my legs. There was another piece of bloody gauze covering the side of my left knee. "Why doesn't it hurt?"

"It will eventually," Rita promised. "They gave you some meds in your IV on the way in. Once they wear off, I'm sure you'll feel some discomfort."

The longest part of the process was waiting for the full-body X-rays, then having the radiologist on call give the okay for the neck brace to be removed. Instead of being taken back to the ER, I was wheeled into the suture room. It was a long, narrow room with a dozen or so areas, with tracts of curtains diving the space. A different nurse who looked more stern than Rita came in a minute or two later. "Can you rate your pain on a scale of one to ten?"

"A one," I answered. My cuts burned, but as long

as no one was poking and prodding my injuries, it wasn't a big deal.

"Good, because your private physician can't get here for about another half hour," she replied.

"You must have me confused with another patient. I don't have a private physician," I informed her. On the very rare occasions when I needed an antibiotic or something, I normally went to one of those walk-in places. The only doctor I saw on a regular basis was my gynecologist, and his specialty didn't extend to arms and legs.

She looked at my chart again. "According to the people in the waiting room, they've arranged for a Doctor Adair to come in to do the sutures."

"What people, and who is Doctor Adair?"

She looked at me as if I'd just asked her to donate a kidney. "He's one of the best plastic surgeons in South Florida. The arrangements were made by a woman and a man who came in while you were in X-ray. Press the call button if you need anything."

"Can the people in the waiting room come back and sit with me until the doctor gets here?"

She nodded, and as soon as she left, I scooted down in order to reach the plastic drawstring bag that held my purse. The closest thing I had to a mirror was the small rectangle in my silk lipstick holder. "Ugh," I groaned, then feverishly began to finger-comb my hair.

"Why am I not surprised that you're primping," Becky teased, reaching out and giving my right hand a squeeze. "Thank God you're all right."

Liam loomed behind her. I felt his eyes scan my entire body, and then some of the deep lines between his brows relaxed. "There are easier ways to get out of going to class."

I grimaced. "Yeah. Not exactly going to win me any points with Tony."

There was a flash of something in Liam's eyes, but it was gone when he asked, "So, what happened?"

Leaving my left arm immobile—I was fine with the minimal amount of pain and was in no hurry to irritate the gash—I pressed the fingers of my right hand against my forehead. "I was late for class, probably going a little faster than the posted twenty-five-miles-per-hour limit, when I went into the on-ramp too fast and couldn't stop."

"Finley," Becky chided. "I'm sure you'll be getting a visit from the state police accident investigators. Do not incriminate yourself by admitting you committed a moving violation. Not unless you want to pay damages to the other six cars involved in the accident."

"What?" I asked. "Please tell me no one was hurt. God, if I—"

"No one was hurt," Becky assured me.

"But smart money says they'll all develop whiplash as soon as they visit personal injury lawyers."

"Why would they do that?"

Liam scoffed audibly. "Hit by a BMW driven by a chick with a Palm Beach address? Once they get copies of the police report, their friends and families will convince them to see ambulance chasers and chiropractors."

"I can't afford to get sued," I said, feeling fresh tears well in my eyes.

"You're insured, right?" Becky asked as she sat on the side of my bed.

"Yeah."

"Then you'll be fine," Becky reassured me. "Your insurance company will defend the suits. Worst-case scenario, they'll raise your premiums."

Again, I thought. "Great."

A tall, lanky man dressed in designer casual wear arrived. He was thin, with expensively cut and styled brown hair and a spray-on tan. "Don Adair," he said, grabbing up my case binder, then weaving past Liam and reaching across Becky to shake my hand.

Becky stood and said, "Thank you for coming, Doctor. Finley, we'll be in the waiting room and come back when you're all stitched up."

Adair examined both injury sites and offered me a smile. "Nice clean edges. In three months or less, you won't even have scars to remind you of tonight."

"Sounds good. How did . . . who contacted you?"

"Liv Garrett called. Concierge Plus did my daughter's sweet sixteen party." He went to the sink, washed his hands, then collected a chrome tray with a blue cloth draped over it before rolling a stool to the left side of my bed. "Liv was amazing. Have any children?" he asked as he snapped on latex gloves and inspected the syringe, two suture kits, and scissors in vacuum-sealed casings. A nurse came in and stood by the opening of the curtains.

"No," I said.

He chuckled softly. "Well, let's just say that there wasn't a lot of sweet in my sixteen-year-old. Don't get me wrong," he continued as he started work. "I love her. You might feel a little pinch from the lidocaine. But she changed party themes a dozen times and was, um, difficult, to say the least."

Little pinch? It burned like hell, and I had to summon up all my willpower not to yank my leg away. "Liv thrives on difficult," I agreed through partially gritted teeth.

"Sienna is the poster child for difficult. She's a typical, overindulged only child. But she's our baby, and neither my wife nor I seem to be able to say no to her." Dr. Adair chuckled and proceeded to sew up the cuts on my knee and my arm. After instructing me to call his secretary next week to schedule an appointment to have the stitches removed, Dr. Adair shook my hand and left.

Now that I was all put back together, I wanted to leave. I was contemplating using the call button when two big, bulky state troopers appeared at the foot of my bed.

Their uniforms included big gun belts with nightsticks and handcuffs that jingled with the smallest of movements. One officer, Gutierrez, had one of those faces that gave away nothing. The other one, Kasey, had a shaved head. Both men had bulging muscles that inspired instant fear.

Kasey turned a knob on the radio clipped at his shoulder, silencing the squawk. Gutierrez followed suit. "Do you feel up to giving a statement, Miss"— he flipped open a notebook—"Tanner?"

"Sure. But I may be a little fuzzy on the details," I hedged.

"Understandable," Kasey said with a nod. "Any idea who did this?"

Now I actually was fuzzy. "Did what?"

Kasey frowned. "You don't know what caused the crash?"

My lead foot? "Not exactly, no."

The officers exchanged looks that gave me goose bumps.

"What?"

"Your car was tampered with. More specifically, the brake line was punctured. You might have tried to apply the brakes, but nothing happened?"

"Yeah, that happened."

"Any thoughts on who might have wanted to do this?"

"Couldn't a nail or some sort of road debris have punctured the line?"

Kasey shook his head. "A clean puncture. If your car was in motion at the time the line was cut, we would have seen ragged edges at the puncture site."

I shivered. "I have no idea who would do something like this." The Panty Thief? Stealing my undies was one thing, trying to kill me another. Same guy? Different guy? Bad enough knowing one person wanted to scare me, terrifying to think there might be *two* of them.

"We understand from the sheriff's office that you

had an incident at your home over the weekend, and that you recently ended a long-term relationship?" Kasey probed.

I spent the better part of thirty minutes trying to convince the state police that there wasn't anyone in my life, past or present, who could or would do such a thing.

Kasey flipped his notepad closed and put his card on the tray table. "If you think of anything that might help the investigation, call me. Is there someone you can stay with when you get outta here?"

First choice Liam, second choice, Tony. Third choice, nothing came screaming to the forefront. "Is that really necessary?"

"Yes. Miss Tanner, someone out there wants you dead."

I'm not afraid of anything until
something scares me.

thirteen

A FTER RE-DRESSING IN MY bloody clothes and signing a bunch of forms, I was taken by wheelchair to the exit, where Becky's blue hybrid— her nod to decreasing her carbon footprint—idled.

Refusing assistance, I got into the passenger's seat and tucked my purse on the floor behind my legs. "Thanks for hanging around," I said. "I didn't relish the idea of taking a taxi home."

"I think you should stay at my place for a while."

I gave her a genuinely grateful smile. "Thanks, but I've slept on your futon before. I'm saying this with nothing but love, but it's like sleeping on a medieval rack."

"I'll give you the bed."

"Not necessary. If you don't mind taking me by my apartment, I'll pack a bag and go stay at my mother's."

"Did you suffer a major head injury? You'll go crazy before you finish sharing your first cup of morning coffee with her."

"She's out of town. Plus it's a secure building, and I know where she keeps the spare set of keys to her Mercedes. Solves my transportation problem and provides security."

Becky pulled out of the hospital and steered toward my apartment. "I had one of the interns pull the surveillance tapes from the parking lot. He's dubbing a copy for the cops and another one for me. Hopefully The Panty Thief is on the tapes."

I'd completely forgotten about Dane, Lieberman's parking lot cameras. "Hopefully is right. I'm scared."

Becky patted my shoulder. "I know you are, honey. We're all scared *for* you. We all feel useless, too."

"The state police think it's Patrick."

Becky groaned. "They won't after they meet him. He doesn't have the balls for this, and like I told them, he wants you back, not dead."

My mind was swimming, and my thoughts fractured as each new wave of fear crashed to the forefront. "But he does know about brake lines and engines."

"C'mon, Finley. I loathe the guy, but even I know he'd never do anything like break into your apartment and steal your panties and leave a fake skeleton. Nor would he tamper with your car."

"What if he didn't mean for the brakes to fail. Just, *I don't know,* cause a fender bender? Maybe he thinks if I get scared enough, I'll turn to him."

"Well, I'd be happy to call him and let him know that I am ready, willing, and able to superglue your butt to a chair to keep that from happening."

"You're right, I'm being crazy. Where did Liam go?"

"Who knows," Becky said on a rush of breath. "Got a call on his cell, and then said he had to see a guy about a thing."

"God, that's an infuriating habit."

"I don't know. There's something sexy about a man cloaked in mystery. Add that to his God-given sexiness, and he's one fine specimen of a man. If he wasn't interested in you, I'd be on him like a cheap suit."

"He is *not* interested in me," I assured her.

"He is. And you know he is. This is me, Finley. I see the way the two of you try not to look at each other. The room steams up when the two of you are together."

"Let's change the subject," I insisted as I fidgeted in my seat. I filled her in on all the stuff I'd been doing to try to identify the skeleton from the Palm Beach house.

"I hope you told all this to the police," Becky said. "You start investigating Melinda the Foster Mother and coincidentally really bad shit starts happening?"

"They already knew most of it from talking to the deputies that responded to the fake skeleton, and they said they'd be talking to Graves and Steadman about the real skeleton tomorrow." Fatigue settled in, and I pressed back against the headrest. "FYI, you're wrong about Melinda. My family has known her since I was a kid."

"But until last week, you hadn't seen her in years. People change."

"True, but I'm just having a hard time thinking she

changed so much. Granted, I was young, but I remember her giving Lisa and me gifts at holidays and birthdays. Jonathan invited her for dinner several times. So I think it's safe to scratch her off the suspect list."

"But you said she was acting weird. Maybe she has an accomplice who doesn't want or like you stirring up the past."

My gut told me it wasn't Melinda who had tried to kill me, but I was pretty sure Becky wouldn't be interested in my intuition.

We spent about an hour at my place while I changed, packed, grabbed my laptop and all the chargers I needed for my various electronics. Then we headed to the office to pick up the dubbed security tape from the intern.

It was pitch-black, and the air was completely still. While Becky unlocked the door, I was keeping diligent watch for some unknown bogeyman. My heart was pounding by the time we entered the building, locking the door behind us.

"You're shaking," Becky said, her green eyes filled with empathy.

Taking a deep breath, I let it out slowly. "Guess I'm a little more spooked than I thought."

"Makes sense," Becky said, draping an arm around my shoulder as our respective heels clicked and echoed in the empty foyer on our way to the elevator. "Are you sure you don't want to stay with me? Just for tonight?"

"I'm sure. Besides, my mom's place is closer to work."

"Closer to work? Who are you, and what did you do with my friend Finley?"

Forgetting the stitches, I gently jabbed my wounded elbow into Becky's ribs. "Ow!"

"God smote you for being mean to me," Becky joked. "Besides, I think—and I know I can sell it to the partners—you should take tomorrow off. Christ, Finley, you rolled your car six times across three lanes of I-95. They had to use the Jaws of Life to get you out of the car."

"I can't afford it."

"Have you used up all your sick days?"

"No."

"Well," she said, clearly frustrated. "You need a day of rest and relaxation. Isn't there a spa in your mother's building?"

"Yes."

"Be nice to you."

I was convinced. "Okay. I need a couple of things from my office," I said as I stabbed the button for the second floor. "I'll meet you in your office in ten or fifteen minutes."

"'Kay."

Wincing every so often, I put several of the foster care files into my tote. Sitting at my computer, I emailed the relevant documents to my personal account, then powered off the computer. I wasn't sure if I would actually work on my sick day, but I wanted the files on the foster children just in case. That thought stopped me in my tracks. When had I become the kind of person who works outside the office?

Maybe the stuff they'd put in my IV had turned me into some sort of Stepford Employee. Now *that* was a scary thought.

Becky frowned at me when I arrived carrying my tote. "You only have one good arm," she reminded me.

Ignoring the criticism, I pointed to the shiny gold CD sliding into her CPU tower. "Is that the video?"

"Yep. You sit here and I'll stand."

"I got three stitches, not a partial amputation. Besides, the lidocaine is still working its magic."

"Fine, be a pain in my ass."

Her coral polished fingernails worked the keyboard, opening the media file and selecting Play. The first scene on her flat-panel screen was time-stamped before 8:00 a.m. More than an hour before I'd even arrived at the office. "Can we speed it up?"

"We might miss something."

Leaning against the edge of her desk, my eyes fixed on the screen. At four times normal speed, we watched employees and clients come and go. I had to squint to even venture a guess at the identities, and I worked with these people. "How come we can film the surface of Mars with total clarity, and video surveillance footage is so dark, grainy, and crappy?"

"Because the nation spends billions on those cameras and Victor Dane paid less than two hundred dollars for this system. And that included installation," Becky answered.

"Nice to know he's so concerned about our safety."

"He only did it to get a break on the property insurance."

That was the Vain Dane I knew and loathed. "Slow it down!" The time indicated the image was captured a few minutes after two o'clock in the afternoon.

Becky slowed the playback, rewound it a few frames, then played it in slow motion. The quality of the image was terrible, and about all I could make out was a guy moving between my car and Vain Dane's Hummer3. More accurately, I saw a bulky human who was *probably* male, based on his gait, but his face was completely obliterated by the bill of a baseball cap.

His image dropped between the two cars for less than a second. "He could be puncturing the brake line," Becky said.

"Or picking up a penny," I countered. "You can't even be sure it's a man. Is there any way to enhance this?"

Becky shrugged. "I can ask the IT people tomorrow. Or maybe the cops will do it as part of their investigation." Becky replayed the five seconds of footage, starting with the guy coming into the frame, bending down, then stepping through the landscaping to the sidewalk east, toward Clematis.

We continued the tape and discovered that a big brown delivery truck blocked the view of my car for more than seven minutes around four thirty. "There could be a dozen mechanics working on my car and we couldn't see them through that truck."

"Well, at least we got one guy on tape." She swiveled in her chair. "You look exhausted. How about I take you to the Witch's Castle."

I snickered. "And you have to stay long enough to help me cover all the headless statues with towels and napkins."

"What are best friends for?"

I WAS UP EARLY the next morning. Leisurely, I drank a pot of coffee and watched the sunrise from the terrace overlooking the Intracoastal. I bathed, keeping the dressings dry, and marveled that the minimal amount of soreness was easily eradicated by a couple of Tylenol I swiped from my mother's medicine cabinet. It was a beautiful day; bright sun, a few wispy clouds, and temperatures projected to climb to a comfortable eighty-two.

It was just before nine when my cell rang. "Hello?"

"How are you?"

The sexy, deep sound of Liam's voice traveled though me, settling in the pit of my stomach. "Great."

"Penthouse living agrees with you?"

"How did you know . . . scratch that."

"I hear you're taking the day off."

Actually, I was contemplating the almost four-hour round-trip drive to Daytona Beach to track down Abby Andrews, but I wasn't about to share that fact. "You heard right."

"Get a call from Jennings yet?"

"No, why?" A sliver of hope hung on that question. Nothing would make me happier than to hear that the sheriff's office had apprehended The Panty Thief.

"What do you know about fingerprints?"

"Everyone's are different."

"Right. There's an anomaly with one of the sets of prints they lifted from the windowsill at your condo."

"Anomaly?"

"Your boy Patrick have any birth defects?"

Mild irritation overtook hope. "He isn't mine, and no, not that I know of, why?"

"They lifted full finger and palm prints from the sill, but unless Patrick's thumbs are on the outside of his hand, the prints were a plant."

"I don't understand."

"Remember the vase of flowers you ditched that night?"

"Yes." I wasn't fond of Patrick, but tossing beautiful flowers had been difficult.

"Someone went to the trouble of lifting his prints off the vase, then transferring them to the windowsill. Obviously to throw suspicion on your ex."

"So when they did the transfer, they did it backwards?"

"Exactly. A stupid and careless mistake made by someone."

"Who would do that?"

"Someone who has done their homework on you."

Something in his tone changed. Alarm? Concern? Trepidation? I couldn't tell. "That's not a very comforting thought."

"Not meant to be. Listen, you should give serious consideration to laying low for a while. At least give the cops a chance to do their job."

Easier said than done. "Will they also pay my mortgage?"

"I can float you a loan."

"Pass, thanks." Debt and lust were not good bedfellows. "There are two armed guards downstairs."

"I've seen them. My grandmother could take them."

"Not until she got buzzed in and I gave the doorman a very small list of approved guests."

"I know that too. They wouldn't even let me in the building."

"Sorry, Liam. You didn't make the cut."

"Consider changing that," he said in a reasonable way that almost, *almost* sounded like a request. "When he heard about the brakes being tampered with, Tony put me on this full-time."

"What's *'this'*?"

"Finding out who wants you dead."

"I honestly don't know," I insisted. "But I'm leaning toward it has something to do with that skeleton at the beach house."

"Have you found any explanation of why the dead girl had your stepfather's medallion in her hand?"

"Nope. Have you had any luck with that partial note we found?"

"A little. The lab rats say the ink is consistent with the chemical makeup of mass-produced ballpoints manufactured from 1991 through 1999. Based on the moisture content of the paper, they would only say with certainty that the paper was more than five years old."

"That's some progress."

"Whatever. How scraped up are you?"

The minute I heard the word *scrape,* it was as if a lightbulb went off in my brain. "The shoes."

"What shoes?"

"The *scraped* shoes Sam found at my house. They were in with the clothing Melinda left behind when she moved out. I asked her about it at lunch, remember? She said she'd arranged for the stuff to be picked up by a charity but that didn't happen."

"And this is relevant why?"

"The backs of both heels were scuffed. Most women scuff the back of their right shoe more than the left. It happens when you drive."

"I'll warn women everywhere."

"The shoes I found were evenly scuffed. Is there any way the pathologist or someone can tell if those shoes would have fit the skeleton?"

"Yeah, there are some general tissue depths and muscle averages they use to calculate that sort of thing."

"If she perspired in them, there would be DNA too, right?"

"Yeah."

"The shoes are in the back of the closet in my apartment. Beige Enzos with one-inch heels. If they were the skeleton's, the scrapes could prove she was dragged around. If we prove that, maybe it will tell us who was doing the dragging."

"I'm on it. Stay safe."

NORMAL PROCEDURE AT MY mother's upscale building was to call down to the valet and have the car brought up from the garage. Being cautious, I decided to take the service elevator down and claim the emerald green Mercedes with its tinted windows myself. Of course, my mother's Bentley would make the long drive to Daytona more comfy, but my mother didn't leave her keys for that luxury with the valet.

I took my tote and purse along with me as I made my descent. The elevator compartment filled with the scent of my freshly sprayed Lulu Guinness, and I fussed with my hair and adjusted the filmy sleeves of my top in the mirror. I'd paired the bright lemon and lime patterned top with simple white capris to cover the bandage on my leg. The top was Lilly Pulitzer, one of my all-time eBay highlights—twelve bucks— and the capris were BSBCG, 80 percent off due to a black smudge of grease my masterful dry cleaner had removed with just three treatments. My entire ensemble cost less than forty bucks, and that included the shoes. I'd gotten the white striped Coach flip-flops for ten dollars at the thrift store. I'd sprayed them with Clorox Hard Surface, so any cooties were history.

The teenage valet was sitting in the metal chair with a pathetically thin cushion when I stepped out of the elevator. His cheeks flamed red as he tried to hide the skin magazine he'd been, well, *viewing*.

"The phone didn't ring, Miss Finley," he apologized, making me feel about a hundred years old.

"I didn't call. I'm just going to take the Mercedes out for the day."

"Um," he said as he leaped up and blocked my way. "Your mother left strict instructions that you weren't to use her car."

Twenty bucks got me over that hurdle.

The boring two-hundred-mile trip gave me an opportunity to think. And discover I'd developed a driving phobia. Every time a car came near me, my grip on the wheel tightened and I braced myself for a crash that wouldn't happen. My driving anxiety subsided at about the same time the navigation system told me to head east on International Speedway Boulevard.

Daytona was a shrine to auto racing, a sport I didn't understand. Hours of cars making left turns. I passed the Daytona Speedway on my right, then just after the airport, I was directed down a side street.

The minute I made the turn, I was sorry I'd made the trip. I wasn't exactly in an upscale neighborhood. The Mercedes drew stares as I continued to follow the instructions called out by the onboard computer. Eventually, it led me to Happy Shores Trailer Park. I slowed and leaned forward, trying to read the addresses painted on the mailboxes.

I circled the park twice before finally finding Abby's pitifully run-down trailer. Some of it was painted a pale blue; the rest was down to the bare aluminum. A warped plastic picket fence, about two feet high, surrounded the small lot. The roof of the attached carport was nothing but a square of rusted metal nailed into precariously leaning poles. An ancient Toyota was parked alongside the trailer.

My mother's spit-polished, emerald green Mercedes stood out like the bastard at a family reunion.

Lifting my glasses, I could just make out dual car seats in the Toyota. This had to be the place.

A couple of other residents, seated on porches or under tattered, faded awnings, craned their necks as I got out of the car and headed for the front door.

Such as it was. Sometime in the not so distant past, someone had kicked in the door. A hole was covered with some sort of fabric, and someone had taken a crowbar or some other tool and mostly straightened the doorframe.

Pulling open the screenless screen door, I knocked softly. Almost immediately, an infant started to cry. Then another.

A woman I knew to be in her early thirties—I'd seen her birth certificate—yanked open the door. A swirl of smoke drifted from a filterless cigarette that dangled from the corner of her mouth, and a diapered infant was balanced precariously on her opposite shoulder.

"I don't want any," she said, then started to slam the door.

I raised my palm before it shut completely. "I'm not selling anything," I said quickly, business card at the ready. "I'd like to talk to you about your time with Melinda Redmond."

She eyed me like a dog that had been kicked one too many times and took a long drag on the cigarette. "There's a name I haven't heard in a while," she said. "I've got two babies to feed and—"

"I'd be happy to help," I lied. Babies aren't really

my thing. They're fragile, helpless, and often puke without warning or provocation.

"Suit yourself," she said, turning and walking into the darkened, smoky trailer.

Suddenly, feeding a baby seemed like a walk in the park. The must-smelling trailer had a lumpy, torn sofa, a scratched coffee table, and a beat-up recliner. The window treatments were interesting. Faded sheets held in place with pushpins.

Abby handed me the baby, and I did my best to soothe him as I followed her the few steps into the kitchen. The stovetop was crusted with burned-on food, and one of the hinges on the oven door was broken loose. I was no appliance expert, but I was fairly sure it wasn't supposed to be like that.

A small sink was filled beyond capacity with dirty dishes. The draining rack next to the sink was also filled beyond capacity. I wasn't sure how she could tell the difference between clean and dirty.

"What's the baby's name?" I asked as Abby fished into the sink and pulled out a grape-stained, opaque yellow pitcher.

"That one's Michael. The other one is Matthew. I was stupid and named him after his loser father."

She scooped powdered something into the not-so-clean pitcher, moved some of the dirty dishes from the sink to the counter, and added some tap water.

As Abby poured the formula in bottles and heated them in a pan of water on the stove, I bounced slightly, patting the baby's back, and dissected his mother. Her brown hair was filthy and pulled back in a rubber band. The shorts she wore were about a size 6, but Abby was closer to a 14. What didn't fit in the shorts spilled out over the waistband, but then she'd just had twins.

"I bought the house on Chilian where you lived with Melinda," I said conversationally.

"That was a great house," she agreed. "Best digs I ever lived in."

Somehow, that info didn't come as a shock. "And Melinda?"

Abby shrugged. "She was okay. Weird, but okay."

"How was she weird?"

Abby traded out the stub of her cigarette for a fresh one. I bit back an incredible urge to tell her to stop smoking around the babies. In another time and place, I might have, but I needed her, and I didn't think she'd like me standing in judgment of her.

Abby handed me a bottle and a rag that I wasn't quite sure what I was supposed to do with, then motioned me to sit at her Formica dinette. Brittle plastic scratched through my slacks, but I did as she asked. It was actually easier to support the baby properly with the aid of the table.

Carrying him more like a football than a baby, Abby joined me at the table, laying the baby on her ample thighs so she could stuff the bottle in his mouth one-handed. Leaning and stretching, she was able to pull open the refrigerator and grab a can of beer from inside. "Want one?"

"I'm good, thanks. You were saying Melinda was weird because . . . ?"

She handled the flip-top with a broken thumbnail. "As foster parents go, she was one of the best. No boyfriends dropping by to cop a feel. She was pretty lax with the rules, like one of us breaking curfew. Or having sex with one of the rich kids. She'd let that stuff pass."

"You were having sex with the rich kids?"

Abby grunted. "Those rich guys used to love scoring poor, underage tail. They'd come sniffing around five minutes into their breaks from their fancy colleges."

"And Melinda permitted that?"

"I wouldn't go that far. But she had weird punishments."

"Like?"

"Vocabulary and memory exercises. Mandatory boring-as-shit field trips to museums or galleries. She used to say she was responsible for feeding our minds as well as our bodies and that thanks to some guy, we'd been given a unique opportunity to see how far we could go in life." Abby let out a humorless little laugh. "Yeah, right. Like any of us would ever wind up Palm Beach debutantes."

"Terri Semple is about to," I said at the same time I felt a damp spot on my shirt. Smelly formula was leaking out of the side of the baby's mouth. Too late I understood what the rag was for.

"No shit?" Abby said, then nodded. "I guess Melinda was right. Miracles can happen. Wow, she's the last one I would have guessed."

"Why?"

"She was kinda mousey and sullen. Kept clear of the trust-fund boys for the most part."

"What did she enjoy doing?"

"Coke. Not when I first met her," Abby clarified.

"When was that, exactly?"

"Sometime in the spring of '91, I think. She and Melinda were really tight. Tell the truth, I thought she was a bit of a suck-up. Then they had a falling out or something. Terri hit the coke pretty hard, and then one day, poof, she was gone."

"That isn't in her DCF file."

"I doubt Melinda ratted her out. Like I said, Melinda was pretty cool that way. She used to lie to DCF, tell them some of us were half brothers and sisters. Hell, most of us didn't know who our fathers were. So long as you participated in her self-improvement crap, she'd bend the rules."

"Such as?"

"There was this girl, what was her name? Jill, Jill . . ."

"Burkett?"

"Yeah. Jill Burkett was a total bitch. She'd go out and stay away for days at a time. Always had expensive stuff, so she was either turning tricks or stealing. She always claimed the stuff was a gift from one of her boyfriends, but c'mon, how many girls in foster care do you think had diamond stud earrings?"

"Do you know what happened to her?"

"She was still with Melinda when I aged out. I was only there a few months. Glad to leave, 'cause the last two months were pure hell."

"Why?"

"Carlos the loser Lopez moved in."

C.L.? I thought, almost giddy. "Carlos Lopez?"

"He was as nasty as they come and a total perv. He raped Kelsey Nolan in the bathroom a few times. I think she was only thirteen or fourteen. Kelsey told Melinda, but Jill, who must have been doing Carlos along with everyone else, swore on a stack that she'd witnessed the whole thing, and having sex was Kelsey's idea. Jill was always covering for Carlos, and Melinda always bought their lame-ass act."

"Why didn't one of you tell the caseworker?"

Abby laughed and lit another cigarette. "This girl Tasha tried to tell the DCF folks, but with Melinda *and* Jill vouching for Carlos, the caseworker decided the claim of rape was unfounded."

"Was Kelsey examined by a doctor?"

"Sure, but it wasn't like she was a virgin or anything. No one believed her then, and I doubt anyone would believe her now."

"She's dead," I said, placing the bottle on the table and the rag on my shoulder. I lifted the baby and patted him gently because, well, because I'd seen it done that way. "Drug overdose in 2000. Do you remember any other people you met while you lived with Melinda?"

"Some girl named Ava moved in the week before I left. Oh, and another boy. Don or Dan, something like that."

I'd have to go back and check the records to see if I could find those people. The baby burped, and I felt something hot and slimy drizzling down my back. I'm not sure how, but Michael had managed to bypass the rag and puke inside my collar. It was going to be a long ride home.

I would have put the baby down, but I didn't see anyplace clean enough for an infant. "How did Melinda feed your minds?"

"By making us read glossy magazines and auction catalogs. If you really screwed up, she'd make you memorize a numerology magazine."

"A what?"

"You know, coins."

"Numismatic?" I asked gently.

"Whatever. She caught me selling some weed, and I spent the next week staring at a book about Lydian Lions. Said if I wanted to earn money I had to start by learning about the first coins ever introduced to the world. After that, I made sure she didn't catch me selling again." With minimal care, she flipped Matthew over on her thighs and slapped his back until he burped. "Look, these two will only sleep for about an hour after they've been fed. I need to catch up on some Zs too. Mind leaving?"

"Of course not. Thank you for talking to me."

She put Matthew on the linoleum floor and took his brother from me. Matthew started to wriggle and fuss, but Abby just stepped over him as she led me to the door. "You gonna see Terri?"

I nodded. It wasn't definite, but I was pretty sure I could come up with a plan.

"You tell that brown-eyed bitch I said, 'You go, girl!'"

"Thank you again," I said as I negotiated the uneven concrete steps of the trailer.

"Say?" she said, grabbing a handful of my shirt. "I was real helpful to you, and I got two babies and my husband violated his probation last week. You don't happen to have any extra cash, do you?"

I reached into my wallet and handed her a twenty. If I'd thought it would go to the babies, I'd have been more generous. Abby, I knew, would blow it on beer and cigarettes. Probably before night's end.

I left Daytona, stopping at the first rest stop to clean off the baby hurl and to buy a beach towel so there would be a layer between the stench and the car's leather interior. I bought a huge coffee and headed south. On my way, I called the DCF hotline and anonymously reported Abby. She might have helped me, but she had no business being the sole caretaker of two helpless babies.

She was smart enough to figure out it was me. A shiver of fear danced along my spine. "Well done, Finley. Just what you need—another enemy."

Everything wears out eventually,
including your nerves.

fourteen

THE SECOND MORNING I woke at my mother's penthouse, I was sore and tired from the long car trip, but at least I felt as though I'd accomplished something the day before.

This is the problem with taking a sick day when you don't feel sick. Yesterday, I felt fine. Today, I just wanted to stay snuggled in the thousand-count thread sheets on the guest bed. Not an option.

Dragging, I managed to pull my act together and call down to the valet by 8:50 a.m. I'd be a few minutes late, but that wasn't anything new.

Being cautious, I waited inside the locked atrium until I saw the Mercedes swing around the fountain and the valet attendant hop out. Only then did I have the guard buzz me out of the building.

Something bright flashed to my left as I walked down the marble stairs to the waiting car. As I put on my sunglasses, I discreetly looked to my left and scanned the tall hedge along the five-foot stucco wall that divided my mother's building from the one next door. A man in coveralls and a cap was belted to a palm tree on the adjacent property. I was about to dismiss him as a tree trimmer when I realized he didn't have any equipment. Well, unless a camera with a telephoto lens was somehow helpful in pruning palm fronds.

He was at least thirty yards away from me, and what was I going to do? Run to the wall, rappel over it, and run the other ten or so yards, then shimmy up the tree to confront him in an eyelet dress and Jimmy Choo sandals? Not an option.

What I did have was the privacy of the car's tinted windows and a camera on my iPhone. My heart was pounding as I pressed the button to lower the driver's side window, then stealthily stuck my hand out and snapped several pictures. I did this while whimpering, "Ow, ow, ow!" because I'd pulled the stitches in my left arm.

I put the window back up and pushed my sunglasses up to see if I'd gotten anything usable. All three shots were clear and great, except the telephoto lens completely obstructed the guy's face. I cursed softly. If I sat there too long, he was sure to grow suspicious.

I couldn't confront him; that would be stupid. I couldn't get a decent picture, so I decided to steer to the end of the round drive and wait the bastard out.

Adjusting the rearview mirror, I found him still in the tree, camera pointed at the car. Using the pad of my thumb, I switched to the keypad and dialed 911.

"What is your emergency?"

"There's a man in a palm tree taking pictures of me." For some unknown reason, I was whispering as I kept my eyes glued on the tree hugger.

"Is he trespassing?" the operator asked.

"Yes. He's in a tree on the southwest corner of the parking lot for La Mirada."

"Your name please?"

"Finley Tanner," I said, feeling my heart plummet as the guy began to slide down the tree. "He's getting away!"

"Your location, ma'am?"

"I'm one parking lot over. You have to hurry!"

"Can you describe the man?"

"Heavyset. Hispanic, maybe. Wearing dark blue coveralls and a white baseball cap."

"What kind of coveralls?"

I rolled my eyes. "What does it matter?"

"Is there a possibility that he's part of a maintenance crew?"

"Yeah, 'cause it's so much easier to prune with a camera than a machete."

He had completely disappeared. "You know what? Forget it," I said, tossing the phone in my lap. I decided to turn right to see if I could catch sight of him. A bold move, but then again, I was protected by a couple of tons of luxury automobile.

Just as I turned, I saw a streak of blue climb over the wall on the far end of La Mirada. I pressed the accelerator and the car lurched forward. Just as I was about to pass the second wall, an older silver sedan darted out of the side street, missing my front bumper by less than an inch. I didn't get a good look at the driver, but I saw enough to know he was wearing a baseball cap.

I drove dangerously close to him, trying to read the license plate. "K-F damn!" He ran the red light at the intersection of Military Trail and Palm Beach Lakes Boulevard, and I had to make a snap decision. I laid on my horn and blew through the intersection.

The crappy silver sedan sped up, weaving in and out of the congested traffic, widening the gap as I drove more conservatively. I was blowing through yellow lights and he still managed to get ten car lengths in front of me. Of course, he'd managed that by driving a few blocks with two wheels on the sidewalk. The farther west we traveled, the traffic thinned, and I tried desperately to make up some of the gap.

I reached down for my phone, then really tested my multitasking skills. I was dialing Liam's number, trying to keep sight of the sedan, and negotiating traffic and stoplights. Adrenaline surged through my system, and my pulse was pounding in my ears.

"McGarrity," he answered.

"I'm chasing him!"

"Finley? Who are you chasing?"

"A guy in a silver sedan who was taking pictures of me a few seconds ago. He might be the same guy from the surveillance tape. He's got on a baseball cap and—"

"Have you lost your freaking mind?" he practically barked through the phone. "Stop it. Now. Let it go."

"But I only got part of his license plate."

"And that's a start. Geez, Finley, what would you do if you caught up with the guy? Or did you go to SWAT school yesterday?"

"I'm not trying to catch up to him, just get close enough to read the rest of his license plate. Damn," I said more to myself than to Liam. "I don't see his car anymore."

"Thank God for small favors. Where are you?"

"Near Lion Country Safari, I think."

"Turn around and go to your office. Now. I'll meet you there."

"DID YOU TAKE A really big stupid pill?" Liam asked when he jerked open the car door a second after I parked at Dane, Lieberman.

I glared at him from behind my glasses. "Easy for you to say. Your life isn't going to hell in a handcart thanks to some nut-job stalker."

He grabbed my tote and wrapped his arm around me, holding me close to him as we walked the dozen steps to the front door. "Let go of me," I hissed. The minute we were inside, I twisted out of his grasp. In doing so, my sunglasses went flying, crash-landing hard enough to pop one of the lenses. "Well, that's just great. What's with the manhandling?"

"It's called preventing a clear shot."

The blood stilled in my veins. "He had a camera, not a gun."

"This time," Liam said as he herded me up to my

office and practically shoved me into my chair. Bracketing his hands on both armrests, he got right in my face. "Do. Not. Leave. This. Office. Until. I. Come. Back. Clear?"

His warm breath fell on my face, but I hardly noticed because of the intense way he was glaring at me. This was a side of him I hadn't seen before. Angry, assertive to the point of, well, scaring me a little. "Okay," I said, glad my voice didn't betray me.

"If you so much as put one of your little polished toes over that threshold, I will personally nail the door closed until five o'clock."

Flattening my palm against his chest, I felt his heart pounding against his sternum. "Message received," I said, giving him a little shove. "Don't bully me."

Liam raked his hands through his hair, sucked in a deep breath, and let it out slowly. "I wouldn't have to if you'd exercise some common sense now and then."

Anger surged through me. "Bite me, McGarrity. I *was* using common sense. Getting a license plate number would allow me to identify the guy in the baseball cap. If I can identify him, the police could arrest him or something. For your information, I called the police. They blew me off. What was I supposed to do?"

"Nothing," he snapped. "That's what professionals are for."

"He was leaving," I argued.

Liam stepped away from me and leaned against the wall. His head fell back with a thud, followed by another. "So the cops can go to where you saw him in the tree. It's called a canvass. They ring every doorbell until they find someone who saw the guy or his car or some other evidence that allows them to track this guy."

"Sorry," I said without an ounce of sincerity. "I don't recall reading that in my How To Be A Victim manual. Oh, wait! There isn't one, so I'm kinda winging it, because I don't *want* to be a victim."

"Then let me help."

Those four words magically melted my anger and nearly brought me to the verge of tears. I don't even know why. Normally I loathe feeling vulnerable and avoid it like a service station restroom. Oh, God! Please, *please* don't let me get emotionally invested in this man.

"So help already," I told him. I wanted Liam to help me track down Carlos Lopez, the violent kid Abby Andrews had mentioned yesterday, but I had a strong suspicion that now wasn't the best time to tell Liam I'd made a four-hundred-mile round trip to meet one of Melinda's former foster children. As casually as possible I said, "I found out the name of the male foster kid in the newspaper photo whose name Melinda couldn't recall—Carlos Lopez. Can you find out if he has a record?"

Liam looked at me with a question in his eyes but didn't say anything. He nodded and walked away.

In my day away from the office, emails had backed up into the hundreds. Most things I was able to dispatch with a minimum amount of effort, though distraction cut into my speed. It wasn't until I got to the last few that my interest refocused.

The first was from my friend from Washington—Gretchen, at Medicaid. We became long-distance friends because one of my responsibilities in estates and trusts was to pay any outstanding debts of the deceased. If there were sufficient assets, I always made sure any Medicaid subrogation was paid. A couple of times, I'd found hidden assets, allowing Gretchen to recoup large payments. This was the first time I'd asked for anything in return, and she'd come through in spades.

She provided me a hyperlink and a password that would allow me access and save me weeks of cutting through governmental red tape.

I wrote back to her, thanking her profusely. I could think of about four statutes we were breaking by using this little shortcut, but hey, I had a determined killer after me, so breaking a few arcane rules didn't seem so terrible on balance.

The second was from Melinda and included an attached list of her foster care children, along with a brief note mentioning the fact that she'd seen the news and hoped I hadn't been badly injured in the car accident. I reread it, evaluating it for subtext.

My absolute belief that Melinda couldn't have a role in the dangerous train wreck that was my life was starting to erode.

Someone has done their homework on you. Liam's words echoed in my head. While I wasn't too happy with the possibility that Melinda wanted me dead, there was no way I could ignore the reality that Panty Thief might be getting his information from her. That unpleasant thought was buttressed by the resistance I'd sensed when we'd talked and in the detached tone of her email.

I twisted my hair up, then rummaged through my drawer for a clip. Pouring a fresh cup of coffee, I decided to work on Melinda's list first. It was a selfish decision. Reviewing insurance billings was about as appealing as watching tile being regrouted.

I compared Melinda's list, which did contain Carlos Lopez's name, against the files I'd gotten from DCF and found a few differences. Jill Burkett wasn't on Melinda's list and there was no Dan or Don or anything even close on Melinda's list. All her faults aside, Abby had seemed to be completely forthcoming, so I believed that a Dan or Don had lived at the beach house.

"So why the discrepancies?"

Maybe a review of the Medicare billings would break the tie. Gretchen's hyperlink and password worked without a hitch. In no time, I was typing Melinda's name as the guardian of record into the search criteria. A new webpage loaded. Melinda Redmond's name was on the top of the page, as was the address on Chilian Avenue. The rest of the text was divided into seven unequal columns across—patient name, date of treatment, physician, diagnostic code, billed charges, payments received, adjustments in billed charges.

I groaned. There had to be a couple of hundred separate entries. This was going to take some time. Then again, I had nothing but. Well, until my class started at six. I shuddered, remembering the crash that had kept me from the first night of school.

I winced, also remembering that I hadn't called BMW to report that the less-than-a-week-old 330Ci was a total loss. I placed the call, listening to 95.5 while I held for the lease manager.

"Hal Griffin."

"Hi Grif," I greeted. We'd done enough business for me to know his preferred nickname. "It's Finley."

"Hi. How's the new car working out?"

"Well . . ." I told him about the crash, finishing with, "So, the wreckage will stay in police impound until they find the person responsible."

"At least you weren't badly injured," he said politely.

"May I make an appointment to come in for a replacement?"

"Um, er, I'll speak to the general manager and get back to you on that."

"Is there a problem?"

"Not for me, but this is the third leased vehicle you've totaled."

"My insurance will cover the damage."

"I'll get back to you," Grif said.

I thanked him, though I'm not sure why, and hung up the phone. At best, I'd have the use of my mother's car for two weeks. Assuming she didn't get wind of the fact that I was using it without her permission; she might do something vindictive, like reporting it stolen. In a preemptive strike, I took the cowardly path of least resistance—I sent an email to my sister about the crash and included the photograph that had run in the *Palm Beach Post* so she'd have a visual of the severity of the accident.

I was careful not to share the fact that it was a result of tampering. I knew she'd tell my mother the news—they were close like that. I also knew that she'd mention I'd commandeered the Mercedes until I could arrange for a new car. The minute I hit the Send button, I knew I'd started a ticking clock. Lisa probably wouldn't read the email until late tonight, so I had a small window before my mother found out I'd broken her hands-off-my-car rule.

She'd probably throw an aneurysm if she knew I was staying in her penthouse. I gulped down a hefty amount of lukewarm coffee and decided not to think about that right now.

Time to start weeding through a decade and a half of Medicaid billings.

When my phone rang, I was secretly glad to postpone the task. "Finley Tanner."

"I'm selling the business and going to work at McDonald's," Liv said, her voice tight.

"Before you start asking if I'd like fries with that, Liv, care to tell me what's wrong?"

"Do you live in a cave?"

"I don't follow."

"Some reporter for one of those tabloid rags found an old picture of Terri Semple and ran it alongside her engagement portrait."

"And?"

"It's a visual thing. Pull the *Intruder* up on your computer," Liv said.

A few clicks and I was looking at the front page of the national rag. Of course the dominant photo was of Paris Hilton being, well, Paris Hilton. Then, along the right side, were smaller insets with other titillating—if inane—teasers. The top one was a photograph of a singer caught not wearing her underwear, *again*. The other was a side-by-side of Terri Semple with the tagline "Two-faced?"

I zoomed in on the pictures and was intrigued, in a sick way, by the differences. "Wow, how much plastic surgery *has* she had done?"

"Cut her some slack," Liv snapped. "She was seventeen when one picture was taken. She's in her early thirties now. Of course she looks different."

"Don't bite my head off." I asked gently, "Why is this your problem?"

"She's my client, Finley. She's very private, and after that rag hit the stands, she's now threatening to call off the wedding and fly to some remote island for a quickie wedding by some tribal officiate."

"Is that legal?"

"Finley?" Liv warned.

"Sorry. But c'mon, she's marrying the last Gilmore standing. I'm kinda hard-pressed to feel for her." An image of Abby's trailer flashed in my mind.

"She's coming over in an hour to further trim the guest list."

"So slip her a Xanax or something. You can handle her, Liv. Oh, thanks for sending me Dr. Adair. That was nice of you."

"You're welcome. Jane and I stopped by your apartment, but it was dark."

"I'm staying at my mom's place."

"And you think Terri needs a Xanax? You and your mother under one roof?"

"Keep the meds, my mother is in Atlanta."

"How are you feeling?" Liv asked.

Scared witless. "Great. Adair said you handled his snotty daughter, so do the same thing with Terri."

"His daughter wanted bling and flash. Terri wants privacy. I don't think I'll be able to calm her down by commissioning a pink Swarovski crystal tiara."

"You'll think of something," I insisted. "What about a bait and switch? Leave the current plans in place but do a whole new plan at a different location to throw off the gossipmongers?"

"Terri has her heart set on Bethesda-by-the-Sea."

"Then tell her to chill."

"Maybe if I ply her with candy . . ."

"Excuse me?"

"Don't ask. All I know is she's never without her stash. That's another problem. I have to find some way to wean her off the candy before the wedding. A bride with sticky red fingers and lips could potentially ruin the pristine white wedding gown the designer has been working on for almost eight months."

"Be glad it's candy," I said.

"Why?"

"I spoke with a woman who was in foster care with her. Terri has had worse habits than jonesing for candy in her past."

"Please," Liv began pleadingly. "*Please* tell me the person you spoke with wasn't Abby Andrews Young."

"How did you know that?"

"She's the one who sold the story and the photo to the *Intruder*. Some reporter called Terri for comment last night, so she called me at midnight to see if the PR company I hired could kill the story. Which of course they couldn't. Salacious sells."

"Oh, God, Liv. I'm so, so sorry. How can I fix this?"

"You had no way of knowing. I'll figure something out."

"I feel terrible."

"Don't," Liv said. "You've got enough on your plate. Compared to having a killer stalking you, Terri's crisis pales badly. Do you have a phone number for that Abby woman?"

"Yeah," I said, clicking over to another document. "Why?"

"If she was willing to sell her story to the tabloid, I can probably convince Terri to buy her silence when we meet in the morning."

I was still riddled with guilt an hour after talking to Liv. I didn't like knowing I was responsible, even innocently, for causing my friend problems. I made a new pot of coffee, then tried and failed to concentrate on the Medicaid information. I read a line or two, then winced just thinking about what I'd done and trying to think of a way to mitigate the damage.

I did have a bargaining chip, so I reached for the phone and dialed Abby's number. Instead of ringing, I got that fast busy signal indicating a problem with the line. My educated guess was her service had been shut off for nonpayment. I needed to talk to her. I was willing to bargain with the devil if it meant helping Liv.

Speaking of devils, Liam appeared at my office door, carrying a bag from TooJay's Deli in Palm Beach Gardens. "Lunch is served."

"What'd you get me?"

"Dill chicken salad," he said as he brushed papers aside and started removing Styrofoam containers from the bag.

That happened to be my favorite menu item, and I was half-tempted to ask him how he knew that. Then I remembered it was Liam. Somehow he knew everything. It was really unsettling, not to mention annoying as sin.

He took a seat across from me and balanced a second Styrofoam container in his lap, placing only his bottled water on my desk. He bit into an overstuffed BLT on whole wheat, while I opted to peel off the bread and eat only the salad.

It was such a girl thing to do. I was no different from every other woman out there: For some reason, we want a lunch date, but we don't want said date to actually see us eat.

Date?

Warning sirens rang in my head. Thinking of Liam that way would lead to nothing but complications I didn't need or want. I might not need complications, but I wanted him. However, to keep from admitting that little tidbit aloud, I'd be willing to gnaw off my own tongue.

I filled him in on my morning, concluding with

Abby's unreachability, and my lament over causing Liv business problems.

Placing his half-eaten sandwich back in the container and placing it on my desk, Liam leaned to one side to unclip the cell phone from his waistband.

In order to do that, he had to lift his shirt just high enough for me to get a peek at his solid abs. My mouth nearly went dry, and I had difficulty swallowing the food.

Rationally I knew it was perfectly normal to have this awareness of him. Only a corpse wouldn't be interested in exploring the chiseled contours of his body. But only an idiot would act on that interest.

"Hey," he said into the phone. "Would you check on a Volusia County phone line for me?" He motioned to me for the number. I pivoted my computer screen, and he read the number to whoever was on the opposite end of the call. In under a minute, he said, "Thanks, beautiful."

Beautiful? Inappropriate jealousy stabbed me in the gut. I concentrated on keeping my expression bland—not an easy task, since I was really curious about Beautiful. A current girlfriend? A past one? Friend with benefits? Some homely woman he was showering with kindness?

Stop it! My obsession with Liam was starting to mirror my obsession with identifying my . . . *the* skeleton.

"Thanks," he said.

"Shut off for nonpayment?" I asked.

He shook his head, which caused a lock of hair to fall forward. In an instant, his normally relaxed face turned stonelike, and his eyes narrowed slightly. In a deeper, softer tone, he solemnly explained, "Fire shorted out the line."

I got a sick feeling in the pit of my stomach. "Do you know anyone in Daytona Beach who could go to the Happy Shores Trailer Park?" I asked. I flipped my computer screen back around and gave him the exact address.

"Is Deputy Milton available?" He cupped his hand over the mouthpiece. "Want to tell me why you've gone stark white?"

As briefly as possible, I recounted my trip to see Abby, culminating in the call to DCF. "If she got drunk because I gave her twenty dollars and anything happened to those babies, I'll just die."

"Milt," Liam said, resuming the call. There were a lot of "uh-huh's" and "okay's" and "really's" before he thanked the officer and flipped the phone closed.

"Well?" I practically shouted when he didn't instantly start feeding me information.

"DCF took custody of the twins at eight last night."

I let out the breath trapped in my body. "And Abby?"

"Died about an hour ago from burns and smoke inhalation."

"Was she drunk?"

"Blood alcohol was point-two-six when she arrived at the trauma center last night."

I squeezed my eyes shut. "Giving her that money was tantamount to handing her a loaded gun. I *knew* she'd spend it on beer."

Liam shook his head. "They checked with the guy at the local liquor store. She bought a twelve-pack of malt liquor at eleven. The fire department was called to the scene at eleven thirty. When they arrived, the fire was well established."

"I met the woman, Liam. She could toss them back pretty quickly."

"How much did she weigh?"

"One thirty, maybe one forty."

"At that weight she'd have to have downed eight beers in less than ten minutes. Based on your description, she was probably drinking all day. Don't lay this on yourself. In fact, thanks to you, the kids weren't in the trailer."

"I suppose that's something." My appetite disappeared, and I felt like I was choking on regret.

"You saved two lives, Finley. That's more than just something."

"It had to be my fault," I said, hearing my voice crack as I blinked to keep my tears at bay. "I led *someone* right to Abby. Probably the same someone who tampered with my car." I swallowed some of my emotions and rested my face in my hands for a moment. I managed not to cry.

Then Liam was stroking my back, and my own guilt smothered me.

You can't be late until you show up.

fifteen

WHILE I PICKED AT my lunch, I made a quick call to Liv to let her know Abby would no longer be selling tales to tabloids. Like Liam, she absolved me of any culpability in Abby's death, deeming it more important that I had saved the babies from their self-destructive mother.

I smelled Tony's cologne a second before he arrived at my office carrying a tight roll of letter-sized paper in one hand. I quickly blotted my mouth with my napkin and moved my food to the credenza behind my desk. When I started to stand, he waved me back to my seat.

Taking the chair next to Liam, he scooted the chair back so he could sit with his legs straight off to one side. They were long enough so I could see the tasseled Italian loafers where his feet extended past the corner of my desk. He took a french fry off Liam's tray and popped it in his mouth, chewing quickly.

All I could think was man-buffet. Not trusting

my voice to be anything more than a libidinous squeak, I kept my lips clamped shut. My pulse rate increased, along with my discomfort. I was terrified that one of them, probably Liam, would read my carnal thoughts and tag me on it. But come on! A mere desk-width away sat two of the most handsome men I'd ever encountered.

Forgetting for a minute that neither was boyfriend material, I indulged myself in some comparisons. Laid-back Liam had that whole bad-boy thing going on. You know, the kind of guy you meet and tell yourself you're all it will take to tame his bad-boy ways. Then you find out he's cheating.

Conversely, Tony had polish. Not the creepy metrosexual kind, but the manlier expensive confidence that practically assured a comfortable future. He was security and permanence. The Tonys of the world didn't cheat; they worked on relationships and really understood the concept of commitment.

With these kinds of thoughts, I was definitely headed for commitment. To an institution.

"Hot?" Liam asked casually, eyes sparkling with amusement only I could see.

I shook my head.

"Your cheeks are flushed," Tony observed. "Maybe you should have spent another day in bed."

"No bed for me," I said, averting my eyes so I didn't have to suffer the taunt written all over Liam's face. "Work is keeping my mind off my recent string of bad luck."

"Before I forget," Tony began, "I called the college

and made arrangements for you to take the continuing ed course online."

"I don't mind going to class." In fact, I would happily get an early start and leave, um, now. *Anything that might explain me running and screaming from the twin temptations in my office.*

"That's not going to work," Tony said. One dark brow arched when he added, "Especially now that you've added high-speed chase to your resumé."

I felt myself blush from my toes to my scalp as I glared at Liam. "Tattletale."

His response was an amused half smile. "Obviously this guy knows your friends and family, so starting tonight, you'll be staying at Tony's."

My eyes practically popped out of my head. "I'm more the live alone type."

"You wouldn't be living with me," Tony clarified. "I did a short lease on a town house when Izzy and I came down from New York. I found a house pretty quickly, so the place is sitting empty."

The nervous tightness in my chest subsided. "Oh, okay."

"But you won't be alone," Liam said. "I'll be in the second bedroom."

I swallowed a groan. It wasn't that I didn't appreciate the heightened security, but did it have to be Liam? Couldn't I hire some private, short, fat, bald, married security guard? "Is a babysitter really necessary?"

"It is until the cops find Carlos Lopez," Tony replied. "Liam gave me his name. I made a deal with Victor when I took the partnership."

"Carlos Lopez? And what deal?" I asked.

"He added a criminal division but made you my problem." Tony unfolded the rolled papers.

My lust issues evaporated as I took the papers and read that the John Doe fingerprints left on my bedroom windowsill matched the ones on file with the North Carolina Department of Corrections for Carlos Lopez. "What did I ever do to him?"

"Tony and I agree that he most likely killed the girl stuffed in your wall," Liam explained.

"Okay. But that still doesn't explain why he'd come after me."

"You pressed for an investigation," Tony reminded me. "And you've been chasing down leads on your own. He probably sees you as a threat."

"So why don't the police go to his last known address and arrest him?"

Liam handed Tony the container with the rest of the fries. "His last known is more than three years old. I contacted North Carolina. They're sending a copy of his rap sheet. He completed his parole for an attempted rape charge and told his probation officer he was returning to Florida to be with his girlfriend. We confirmed he moved back to Florida four years ago, but then it gets sketchy. He lived with his girlfriend for a while but then dropped off the radar. Wherever he's been, it hasn't been with his baby's mama in Riviera Beach. She claims she hasn't seen him in over a year."

"That still doesn't explain why he sees me as a threat."

"Maybe it has something to do with the medallion," Liam suggested.

I glared at him. "There are like eight people in the world who know I found the medallion. And I promise you, a North Carolina felon is not one of them."

Tony's dark eyes narrowed, and his mouth pulled into a taut line. "Do you trust all eight?" he asked.

"Yes," I said crisply and concisely. "I don't know how the medal ended up with the skeleton. The two of you are included in that number, by the way. Assuming Carlos is the same guy who's been following me, he might have been at the beach house the day after I bought it."

"What?" Liam and Tony barked in unison.

"Again, at the time, I didn't think it was anything sinister. I thought I saw a guy or something crouched behind the sea grasses that separate my house from my neighbor. But when I looked more closely nothing was there."

"That doesn't fit," Liam said. "That's a day after the police blotter said the skeleton had been found."

"Yeah, and that first newspaper article said it was most likely the remains of a vagrant and the police didn't feel further investigation was warranted. That should have put Carlos completely at ease, not the opposite."

"Is there anything left in the house that Carlos wouldn't want you to find?" Tony asked.

"Other than a slip of paper that said someone was sorry about not doing something sooner and some bags of old clothes, no. Liam has the note, and I let the contractor gutting the house have the clothing. Oh, except for a pair of shoes. Liam has those too."

Tony turned to Liam, and I suddenly felt invisible as they talked.

"And?" Tony asked.

"The pathologist said the shoes, size seven and a half, would have fit the skeleton. He sent them to the lab to see if they can pull DNA from the lining."

Tony turned back to me. "What made you focus on the shoes?"

"They looked the way shoes would look if the person who'd been wearing them had been dragged."

"Which a guy at the lab confirmed," Liam added. "He found pieces of concrete and grains of sand in the scuff marks on the backs of the heels."

"Can he match any of it to a particular geographical area?" Tony asked.

"The cement is commonly used throughout the southeast, and the animal and shell particles in the sand are found from the Caribbean up through the barrier islands of South Carolina," Liam replied with a shake of his head.

"Tell me about the medal," Tony said.

"It might have been stolen from my parents' home in 1991. My mother doesn't remember when she saw it last, but it isn't listed on the inventory sheet from the police report as one of the items stolen."

"Have you looked through the other robbery reports?" Tony asked.

"Most of them." I didn't dare look at Liam. I was afraid he'd offer up the fact that I fell asleep in his lap, which was why I didn't finish. Thankfully, on that issue he kept his mouth shut. "I stopped to track down former foster children, and today I've been going through Medicaid billings."

Tony and Liam donned matching looks of surprise. It was quite the ego boost to have bested them both in at least this area.

"How did you get access?" Liam asked.

"Don't answer that in front of me," Tony warned. "It's best I don't know you used Dane, Lieberman resources for a personal matter."

"Okay."

Tony ran his hand over his lips. Nice lips, by the way. Totally kissable.

Then he asked, "Who have you been talking to?"

"The police," I began, ticking the names off on my fingers. "My mother, four of my closest friends, Liam, Melinda Redmond, and the late Abby Andrews."

"Late?" Tony asked.

"Died in a fire this morning," Liam said.

"Not before she sold a picture to one of those gossip rags." I explained what she'd done. "I'm sure she did it for the money, and I'm also sure they paid dearly. When it was placed next to the engagement photo of Terri Semple, it was Michael-Jackson-plastic-surgery creepy. New nose, new chin, brow lift, it was all there in vivid color. The bride is so not happy."

"Because?"

I smiled at Tony and his question. "Ever since Martin Gilmore, the Gilmore supermarket heir, proposed,

Terri Semple has gotten some rough press. She's been pegged as a gold digger, and now, at least from the snippet I read, the gossip magazines are claiming all the plastic surgery is to make her look more Palm Beach and less poor white trash."

"And that matters?"

I shrugged. "It matters to her. I think she's just embarrassed, because when she was interviewed following her engagement party, she claimed she hadn't had any work done. This was stupid, since you can't walk ten feet in Palm Beach without running into someone who's had work done."

Tony rolled his eyes. "Okay, let's get back to the plan. You'll go to the town house with Liam. You can work from there until they find Carlos."

"I'm supposed to stay there twenty-four/seven?"

"I will lock you in and make Starbucks runs if you promise to behave," Liam teased.

"I need clothes and—"

"Give Becky Jameson the keys to your apartment. She'll pack whatever you want and bring it here before you leave."

"I also have stuff at my mother's place, and I have to return her car."

"Becky can handle that as well."

I looked from Tony to Liam, then back to Tony. "Is any of this optional?"

Vehemently, Tony shook his head. "No wiggle room whatsoever. Until Carlos is in custody, this is how it has to be."

◆ ◆ ◆

"YOU DON'T HAVE TO look like I just killed your cat," Liam said, humor in his tone as he started the engine.

It took three turns to coax the engine to a coughing, sputtering, vibrating idle. The smell of hot motor oil spewed from the vents.

"I don't own a cat. Does this car have air-conditioning?" I asked, lifting my hair off my neck.

"Absolutely," he said, reaching in front of me to unlatch a clamp and then doing the same on his side of the windshield. Reluctantly, the top motored up and back.

Now the hot midafternoon sun was beating down on me. "That isn't air-conditioning."

"It is once we get moving," he said, gripping the gearshift and reversing the car through its self-made cloud of blue smoke.

I waved my hand in front of my nose as I gave the emerald green Mercedes one last, longing look.

Once we were on the highway, my hair turned into about a dozen stinging whips as it lashed my face. It took both hands for me to pull it into a tight ponytail, and even then, the occasional stray poked me in the eye or ended up stuck to my lip gloss.

Luckily, the town house was close by—just across from the Gardens Mall. Being within walking distance and not being able to indulge was like going to Egypt and skipping the Pyramids. Liam punched a code on the keypad and a metal entry gate swung open. He made two turns, then dug a garage opener out of his shirt pocket and pulled the Mustang inside.

He shut off the engine, but the car didn't die quietly. It belched twice more before clicking and hissing.

I followed him inside the town house, struggling to comb my fingers through my twisted, tangled hair. I put my purse and tote on the sandstone countertop. Liam deposited my laptop on the small table in a nook just a few steps away, then went back to the pad by the door and entered whatever code reset the alarm.

"Want to make a grocery list for me?"

"You expect me to cook?" I asked from across the counter.

He stroked his chin. "Naw, it isn't happening."

"What?"

"I can't visualize you in an apron. Well, I can if that's the only piece—"

I threw a dry, hard sponge at him before he could finish the sentence. The air between us was already crackling; I didn't want or need any more sexual tension. Not when I had no idea how long our living arrangements would last. "Coffee—ground fresh, please. Cream—the real stuff. Industrial-sized box of Lucky Charms. Need me to write it down?"

"Nope." He held up his keychain and shook a small remote device that dangled off the ring. "I can set the alarm from the garage. Don't open a door or a window. Not for anyone."

"Yes, master."

He pivoted and headed back out the door. "Feel free to slip into something slavegirlish while I'm gone."

"In your dreams."

"Don't I know it," he muttered just before the door closed.

It took less than five minutes for me to explore the second floor. Two bedrooms and one bath. I hope Liam didn't mind using the powder room. Actually, I didn't give a flying fig if he liked it or not. I have very stringent bathroom rules—no sharing. I'd take the master bedroom, and Liam could have the smaller room.

Selfish, childish decisions made, I went back downstairs and set up my laptop. If I couldn't go anywhere, might as well surf for bargains.

My cell phone rang and I got up, retrieved it from my purse, and smiled when I read Becky's number. "Hi."

"How's prison?"

"Sucky."

"I'm sure, but it's also the best idea under the circumstances. Anything in particular you want me to get from your closet, or do you trust me?"

She had impeccable taste. "Go for it. Oh, and when you get to my mother's place, would you water the plants and take the washcloths off the statues?"

"Consider it done. So what's it like?"

"I can see Nordy's from my bedroom window."

"That's not what I meant. With Liam?"

"He's irritating."

"He's hot. Is he there now?"

"No. Went to make a grocery run."

"Ohhh, you're nesting."

"No, we're sniping."

"Really?" Becky asked, almost giddy. "Does that mean Tony is still in the running? No pressure, but remember the twenty-eighth. The pool is up to four hundred at last count."

"Not going to happen," I assured her, then whined, "I can't stand this."

"You've only been gone forty-five minutes," Becky said with a laugh.

"Yeah, well, I don't have to like it." ·

"Before I forget, that Redmond woman came by the office looking for you right before I left."

"Melinda? What did she want?"

"I don't know. Margaret was taking a message, and you know how dangerous it can be to get between Margaret and one of those pink pads."

"I'm going to call her. I'll call you back."

I punched in the number to the office.

"Dane, Lieberman, how may I direct your call?"

"This is Finley. I understand a woman came by to see me?"

I heard the shuffle of papers. "Yes. She asked you to call her at this number."

"Thank you," I said, while repeating the number in my head. As usual, Margaret didn't return the pleasantry. I dialed the number she'd given me, and it rang six times before Melinda answered.

"I'm so glad they got in touch with you," Melinda said. Her voice sounded strained and anxious. "I need to see you."

"I can't get away right now. What's wrong?"

"Carlos Lopez called me asking for help. I know

the police are looking for him. They came by earlier today."

A chill slithered along my spine. "Melinda, under no circumstances should you—"

The muffled sound of a door opening came over the line, then a loud clatter, as if the phone had been dropped or thrown on a hard surface.

"Melinda!" I called repeatedly.

Straining, I listened to Melinda pleading with someone. "No! Don't! Carlos, I'm warning you for the last time—"

Bang! Bang, bang!

Ohgodohgodohgod. I'd just ear-witnessed Carlos shooting Melinda.

I don't have a license to kill; I'm still
waiting on my learner's permit.

sixteen

"M ELINDA!" I CRIED INTO the phone,
knowing it was futile.

There was a scuffing noise, and then
heavy breathing, then Melinda tearfully said, "God,
Finley. I just shot him. He had a knife, there wasn't
anything else . . . what have I done?"

"The smart thing," I said, trying to keep my voice
calm as my pulse pounded in my ears. "Are you at
home?"

"Y-yes."

"I'm going to hang up now and call the police, and
then I'll call you right back, okay?"

"Can you come over?"

I winced. "Yes. Let me call the police, and I'll be
there as soon as humanly possible."

I dialed 911, then called Liam's cell.

"Want Twinkies or some other nutritionally questionable food?"

"Shut up and listen," I snapped. "Carlos is dead."

269

"What?"

I told him what I'd heard and that I'd already called the cops. "I'll give you twenty minutes to get back here," I told him. "After that, I'm calling a cab so I can meet Melinda at the police station."

"You don't need a cab. I'll be there in ten."

"YOU'RE HEADED THE WRONG way," I told Liam as he coaxed the Mustang north instead of south toward the main West Palm police station.

"I called a friend of mine on my way to pick you up. Melinda is still at her house. Call Tony and have him meet us there too."

"What? She won't need a criminal defense attorney. I heard the whole thing. It was self-defense."

He took his eyes off the road and offered a chastising look.

"Right. Good idea." I knew from experience that innocence didn't keep the police from holding and/ or arresting a person. If it could be avoided, I wanted to spare Melinda the ordeals I'd suffered at the hands of the well-intentioned but myopic local law enforcement officers.

Tony picked up on the third ring. I gave him a quick recap of the shooting. "Will you come just to make sure her rights are protected?"

Without hesitation, he said, "Sure. What's the address?" I had no idea, but obviously Liam did. Holding the phone away from my mouth, I asked for the information.

"A community off Federal Highway. Jonathan's Landing."

My jaw literally dropped. Melinda lived in one of the most posh private communities in Palm Beach County. The homes averaged in the seven-figure range.

Tony's voice was in my ear. "Hello? Finley?"

"Um, sorry," I mumbled as I came out of the fog of my surprise. I rattled off the address, and, remembering he was kind of new to the area, I gave him general directions from Dane, Lieberman.

The exclusive, gated community was on the east side of A-1-A. Breathtaking flowerbeds, as well as a professionally designed and maintained fountain, marked the entrance. Liam made a right and pulled up to the stylish stone—and air-conditioned—guardhouse. In addition to several monitors and a computer, I could see the early news playing on a TV screen mounted inside. A uniformed man with a round face and a hefty paunch slid open a large window. With a single glance at Liam's PI badge, he asked, "Ms. Redmond?"

Liam nodded and tucked the badge into his shirt pocket.

The guard went to the computer, did something, then handed us a visitor's pass to be displayed at all times with directions to Melinda's residence. Like an alligator yawning, the gate arm rose slowly to let us pass.

Technically, Jonathan's Landing was an island, created by the Intracoastal Waterway snaking through the community—a community that included a private, deep-water marina, championship golf course, a tennis center, and not one but two clubhouses.

I smelled freshly mowed grass competing with sweet, heavy gardenia as we drove through a couple of promenade-connected villages. Part of my attention was on calling out directions. Another part was more curious than concerned for Melinda. She hadn't exactly embraced our reunion and had pretty much blown me off at every possible moment. Had it not been for the Carlos connection, I probably wouldn't have made such an effort.

The selfish part of me was gawking at the estate homes. The closer we got to the marina, the bigger the houses. I bet none of these people had ever come home to find a skeleton in their walk-in, air-conditioned closets.

As soon as we made the last left, he eased the Mustang to the right, parking on the street about ten yards from a half dozen police cars parked at angles on the opposite side of crime scene tape strung between mailboxes.

"How do we get past the crime scene tape?" I asked.

"Gimme a minute," he said, getting out of the car quickly.

My attention stayed glued to Liam's back as he approached the young officer charged with maintaining the perimeter set up to preserve evidence.

In a matter of seconds, the temperature in the car started to rise. I manually cranked down the driver and passenger windows and was immediately rewarded with a nice, fresh, floral-scented cross breeze.

Liam turned and waved me over. By the time I reached his side, he was holding the tape up for me to duck under. As we followed the sidewalk to the beigy-pink pavers leading to a ten- or twelve-thousand-square-foot house, I smelled the familiar, briny waters of the Intracoastal. "How'd you manage this?"

Liam slowed his long strides, allowing me to keep pace. "Told them I'd brought a witness."

Much to my chagrin, Detective Graves opened the right side of the double entry doors. He scowled when he saw me approaching. "Been expecting you," he said.

It sounded more like an accusation than a greeting. Not a surprise. "May I see Melinda?" I tried to peer around him, but his shoulders were as broad as the doorway.

"After you give me your statement. Let's stay outside for now."

"Could you at least tell her I'm here?"

"No."

Prick.

Graves pointed to a spot near the closed garage, as if I'd been some sort of hunting hound being sent to retrieve a dead duck. Arguing with him would be pointless, so I decided the best plan of action was to cooperate fully and quickly.

I was answering the third stupid question—my address, which the detective probably had memorized, so he was definitely busting my butt—when Tony arrived.

I stood there while they did the mutual introduction thing. The minute Graves heard Tony identify himself as my attorney and potentially Melinda's, I thought steam would come out of the detective's ears. "Miss Tanner claims to be a witness. I need to get her statement," Graves gritted out before turning his eyes on me and adding, "then verify her story."

"It isn't a story," I said, feeling confident, because not only did I have right on my side but I also literally had an attorney on my side too. I walked him through every detail of what I'd heard over the phone, then dug my iPhone out of my purse and showed Graves the screen of outgoing calls. Melinda's number was the most recent, and the time was prominently displayed. "AT&T can—"

The squeak of an unbalanced wheel drew my attention, so I glanced over my shoulder to see a battered gurney coming my way. A dull black body bag clearly outlining Carlos's corpse was creepy and a huge relief. I couldn't say I was sorry he was dead. I remembered the fake skeleton, the violation of my panty drawer, the stories Abby had shared, and the fear I'd heard in Melinda's voice as he'd made a move on her. Carlos Lopez was a blight on society and my personal bogeyman. I doubted he'd be missed.

"Hang on," Graves said to the ME's assistants, who were pushing the gurney. He stepped over and partially unzipped the bag. "Have you ever seen this man before?"

I swallowed a surge of bile as my eyes fixed on the surprisingly small hole dead center between his large, bushy eyebrows. With my hand clamped over my mouth, I moved from the macabre focal point of the gunshot wound to his torso. There was a second wound in his barrel chest. A large, dark stain made the navy coveralls look black.

"I didn't see his face, but I recognize the clothing. He was taking pictures of me this morning." Glancing around, I spied a silver sedan parked a few houses down and identified the car as the one I'd chased.

Graves rezipped the body bag and sent the body on its way. "Any idea why he was taking pictures of you?"

I shook my head. "Not a clue."

"Is there anything else?" Tony asked.

"She'll have to come to the station and provide an official statement."

"She will," Tony promised. "I'd like to see Ms. Redmond now."

"You can go in," Graves said. "Miss Tanner can wait for you here."

"Will you be questioning Ms. Redmond?" Tony asked.

"Of course," Graves answered. "She just killed a man."

Tony sighed. "Miss Tanner is my paralegal. That makes her part of Ms. Redmond's legal team, and it would be a violation of the Sixth and Fourteenth Amendments to the U.S. Constitution, as well as raising a *Miranda* issue for you, to interfere with Ms. Redmond's right to counsel."

"Fine, she can go in," Graves said.

I could feel his eyes on my back as I followed

Tony inside the house. I noticed three things right off: (1) the two-story foyer had two mirror-image curved staircases with black wrought-iron railings and was impressively huge; (2) the big pool of partially dried blood on the black and white marble floor was hard to miss, since we practically had to step over or around it as we walked in; and (3) next to the blood, a yellow plastic evidence marker acted as a beacon, drawing my attention to a knife with a large blade, serrated on both sides.

Tony asked the officer standing guard at the door where Melinda was, and we were directed to the left. Going down a hallway lined with arched niches displaying various pieces of art glass with gallery-quality lighting, we eventually entered a massive great room and adjacent kitchen.

It was a posh room, with four cream-colored sofas and five triple sliders that opened out to a large, screened lanai and an unobstructed view of the water. A two-level, in-ground pool included a grotto and waterfall off to the far side.

"Thank God!" Melinda leaped off the sofa and wrapped me in a tight embrace.

I kinda stood there, then settled on the not-actually-a-hug country club pat on the back. Cold air poured out of the ceiling vents, chilling my bare arms. Rising goose bumps pulled at my stitches, and I was afraid my teeth would start to chatter. The AC was aided by the presence of three ceiling fans spinning at warp speed. I stepped out of her embrace. "How are you holding up?"

Her blue eyes seemed vacant and glossy, but she attempted a small, forced smile. "I raised him for four years. I treated him like a son. He came at me, and I had no choice."

"I know," I said. "This is Mr. Caprelli. He's an attorney, and he's here to help."

She patted my cheek. Another awkward moment.

"Thank you, Finley. I knew I could count on you," Melinda said.

Not sure why or how, I thought, but I remained silent. After all, the woman had been attacked by Carlos, so I cut her some slack.

Detective Steadman was standing close, tapping the toe of her sensible shoe. I suddenly realized the one person missing was Liam.

Tony informed the detective that we'd need a little time alone with Melinda before she resumed questioning her. She was not happy.

Not that I cared. I hadn't forgotten the way she'd tossed me onto her cruiser and twisted my arms behind my back, then slapped handcuffs on me before whisking me off for booking. Her happiness was immaterial to me.

Melinda led us through the luxury appointed kitchen, past the paneled Dacor Epicure refrigerator, and a Fisher & Paykel two-drawer dishwasher. I was looking at thirty to forty grand worth of appliances and couldn't help but wonder how Melinda managed to live so high on the hog. I also wondered why she kept her house so frigging cold.

We ended up in a home office that was equally

well-appointed. I sat in one of four butter-soft leather chairs that matched the executive chair in front of a massive mahogany desk. The leather was cream colored, as in the great room, and art and large fresh sprays of flowers provided splashes of color.

Tony looked at Melinda and asked, "Do you have a pad and pen so Finley can take notes?"

Melinda opened one of the desk drawers and handed me a 5x7 pad and a gel pen, then settled into a chair. Nervously, she twirled a lock of dark brown hair around her forefinger and kept drawing her lower lip between her teeth.

"Walk me through it," Tony said.

Melinda took a deep, calming breath, then let it out slowly. "Carlos called me and said he needed my help. First time I've heard from him since he left my care when he turned eighteen." She turned to me and said, "Finley, I swear, I had no idea he was the one responsible for your recent troubles. Not until the police were here just after lunch. I hope you know that."

"I do." Even as I heard myself say the words, I wasn't quite sure they were the complete truth.

She pressed her fingertips against her forehead and took another dramatic, audible breath. "Carlos was a troubled kid, but we hadn't been in touch for years. That's why I was so surprised when he called out of the blue and demanded to see me."

"What do you think he wanted from you?" Tony asked.

She shrugged. "Money, maybe?"

"Why would he think you'd help him out?"

"I was the closest thing he ever had to a mother. I told him not to come here. To turn himself in."

"How did he know where to find you?"

"I'm listed in the phone book."

Tony leaned forward, resting his hands on his knees. "What did you do after he called?"

"I was going to call the police, but I guess I still had hope that I could reach him even after all these years. I knew he was in serious trouble and would definitely need an attorney. I tried calling Finley, since I knew she worked for your law firm, but the woman at the desk kept saying she wasn't available. Even though Carlos chose the wrong path, I hoped I could help him and get him to turn himself in to the authorities. Carlos didn't show up, so I went to Finley's office. I thought she could refer me to someone like you, and, of course, I wanted to let her know that he'd made contact. But she wasn't there."

"It would have been smarter to just call the police," Tony said.

She looked on the verge of tears. "I couldn't bring myself to betray him without at least giving him an opportunity to tell me why he'd tried to kill Finley. I honestly thought I could talk him into doing the right thing."

"Where was the gun?" Tony asked.

"In this pocket," she said, patting the right side of her silk slacks.

"You had it on you?" Tony asked, his expression unreadable.

"I wasn't planning on firing it. I just thought it

prudent in case I couldn't reason with him. Carlos is . . . *was* . . . a large man. He burst in here, slapped the cell phone out of my hand, and then I saw the knife and, well, Finley, *tell him*. You *had* to have heard the whole thing."

"I did."

Tony rubbed his chin. "There were no signs of a break-in."

Melinda's lower lip quivered. "All I can say is that I was concerned for Finley and must have forgotten to check the lock after I came back from the law office. Stupid, huh? But I don't normally lock my front door. You can ask any of my neighbors or Terri Semple."

"Does she come here often?" I asked.

Melinda gave a weak smile. "Of course. She and Martin gave me this house."

"Generous," Tony remarked.

"That's Terri," Melinda insisted. "Generous to a fault. So what happens now?"

"We'll all go to the station. First, I'll do my best to convince the cops that the shooting was justified. You're lucky you were on the phone when Carlos came in. However, if they do charge you, I can probably get a judge to agree to bond because of the mitigating circumstances."

Melinda blanched. "You think I'll go to jail?"

Tony shook his head. "Not if I can help it. Let's go."

As we headed back to the great room, I touched Tony's sleeve. He dropped back and I whispered, "Thank you. There's nothing worse than being an innocent person locked in a cell."

"You're forgetting the rules. I don't know that she's innocent."

AS IT TURNED OUT, it was a good thing I had to go to the police station to give a formal statement, since Liam's Mustang was gone when we came out of Melinda's house.

I ended up having to call Becky to take me back to my apartment.

"All my stuff is at the town house," I said as I got into her car.

Becky sipped on a latte, then set it in the cup holder next to the one she'd kindly brought for me. "I don't mind taking you by there."

"I don't have the code to get in."

"Can you call Liam or Tony?" she asked.

"Liam must have had one of his annoying *things*, and Tony is finishing up the paperwork with the state's attorney."

"I'm surprised they didn't charge Melinda," Becky said.

"Hummmm."

"What?" Becky prodded. "Something not right? Word back at the office is the shooting was justified."

"I know. I *heard* the whole thing happen just as she described to the police."

"But?"

"The blood was like two feet inside the door."

"Why does it matter where he bled to death? Personally, I'm just happy he bled. Now we know he can't hurt you."

"You're right," I agreed, wondering why I had the feeling that something wasn't quite right.

"You're lucky," Becky said as she pulled into the parking lot of my complex.

Liam was leaning against the trunk of the Mustang, arms crossed in front of his chest.

"Why is he here?" I groaned. And why did he have the ability to annoy me and excite me at the same time? "Why is the Mercedes here?" My mother's car was parked in the spot next to his.

While we parked, he popped the trunk of the Mustang and lifted out the clothes and other things from the town house.

"How did you get the car from the valet?" I demanded.

He gave me a lopsided grin, then said, "Why Liam, you thought of everything. Thank you so much."

I dug out my keys. "Thanks. Now tell me how you managed to get my mother's car."

"Fifty bucks," he answered as he followed me inside and unceremoniously dumped my clothing on the sofa. "For a hundred the kid would have let me hot-wire the Bentley."

"I've got to run." Becky came over and hugged me.

"Liar," I whispered in her ear.

"Selfless friend who hopes you get lucky," she whispered back.

Liam followed Becky out, then returned with

my laptop and files. "You don't exactly pack light, do you?"

"No."

I expected him to leave, but instead he pulled out his cell phone and sat on the ottoman. "I've got something I want you to see."

Yes, you do. You show me yours and I'll show you mine. Which is why I need you to leave before I do something I'll really regret. "What?"

He looked up at me. "You're pretty snippy."

"I'm tired," I lied. "Plus, spending time at the police station isn't my idea of a good time." *You, naked, well that's a whole different story.*

"Come look," he said, handing me his phone.

My heart pumped harder and faster as I scrolled through about a dozen photos. Some were from a distance, others close up. They all featured walls in some dank, nasty room. Taped on the wall were at least a hundred pictures of me, taken, based on my attire, over the last five days. They began with my first visit to the Chilian Avenue cottage and ended this morning.

A second wall was a mirror image, though I wasn't the subject. All those photos were of Terri Semple. "Where did you get these?"

"Pay-by-the-day motel off A-1-A."

"But how—"

"I saw the silver sedan parked on the street. There were some receipts crumbled on the floor. Went to check it out. Carlos has been staying there for the last three months."

"Think Terri Semple knows he was stalking her too?"

He shrugged; the movement pulled his trademark faded Tommy Bahama shirt taut across his broad shoulders. "Don't know."

I was trying not to notice things like that.

And failing miserably.

"She might have," I said. "Liv has always assumed she was so freaked about privacy because of the plastic surgery. But what if she was actually freaked by Carlos?"

"Speaking of Terri," he said, leaning to pull a quartered single sheet of paper from his back pocket. "Preliminary DNA results from the shoes."

Excitement surged through my lust-muddled brain, clearing away the lust. I grabbed the paper; his body heat still clung to the page. Unfolding it, I held my breath, certain I was about to discover the identity of the skeleton. I read the name. Three times. "Terri Semple? How is that possible? She's alive and well and about to marry a bazillionaire."

"You made an assumption about the shoes," Liam said. "Turns out you were wrong."

"I can't be wrong. The pathologist said the skeleton was moved around from place to place."

"But he never said she was dragged in *those* shoes," he pointed out with just enough amusement to make me want to scream.

He stood up and turned quickly. Suddenly we were face-to-face, and I was looking up into those piercing blue eyes. My heart stopped beating when he lifted his hand and ran his fingertip along the slope of my neck. I held my breath, sensing he was about to say something. Part of me wanted it to be *"Let's have sex."*

Instead he grinned and said, "We both know you can be wrong. Night."

I opened my mouth, but nothing witty or pithy came out. In fact, nothing came out at all. I stood there, mute, angry, and frustrated, and watched him casually walk out the door. After he did, I threw a pillow in his wake. Since I throw like a girl because . . . well, I am one . . . I didn't even come close to hitting the door. Instead, the pillow slammed into my coffee, splattering it over the floor, the wall, and most of the counter. *Shit.*

Ambition is the only disease that laziness can cure.

seventeen

THE NEXT MORNING WAS a study in contradictions. On the plus side, my stitches no longer hurt. On the plus-plus side, I was about to slip on a fabulous new pale blue Betsey Johnson dress with wide belt that was flattering to my waistline, if I did say so myself. New clothes are the tonic that cures all ills. I also had a killer pair of sling-back Coach shoes, white with darling Carolina blue bows accenting the peek toe. On the plus-plus-plus side, I didn't have a lunatic stalking me.

But I had to take the bad with the great. I'd mustered the nerve to call my mother to tell her I was using her car.

On the downside, the stitches itched and made shaving my left leg a challenge. My mother gave me twenty-four hours to return her car. Harold called me at dawn to remind me he'd be by later for a payment to cover materials costs. And I arrived at the office to find my desk piled high with neglected estates and trusts work, topped with a curt memo from Vain Dane insisting there'd be consequences if I continued to shirk my responsibilities. *"Consequences"* was his code word for docking my pay.

Even though the danger was gone, I still didn't know the identity of the skeleton, so I dragged the files into my office, just to have them sit, untouched, on the floor. They'd have to stay like that until I arranged for letters of administration for the LaGrange estate. Done by 10:00 a.m. Typed and faxed the court clerk an initial inventory of assets on the Salanis estate, which was already a week overdue. Done by 10:17. And completed the final accounting on the Preston estate. Still off by three frigging dollars at noon. I had a vending machine lunch of M&M'S and a can of Red Bull, then raced to the bank to get the money for Harold. His ratty truck was in the parking lot when I returned.

"You should come by the house after work," he said. "I should have the framing up by then."

"Great."

It was great. I was dying to see the progress, but I had to arrange for a rental car and find the math error so I could get the Preston thing filed by 4:30. The heirs were flying in from New Jersey on Wednesday to collect their inheritance. Until I could reconcile the bank account and get it approved by the court, I couldn't write those final checks.

On the eighth attempt, I finally found the number I'd transposed, and Preston was finished. A few minutes before 3:00 p.m., I was making my way over to the courthouse, happy to be out in the bright sunshine, listening to the palm fronds rustling on a soft breeze.

I waited until my favorite clerk was free, then presented my accounting and cajoled her into taking it to the judge for approval then and there. Because I make a point of sending her flowers on her birthday and Godiva at Christmas, it didn't take a whole lot of convincing to get her to bend the rules.

On my way back to the office, I called Enterprise and made arrangements for them to deliver a rental to my mother's building at 5:30. I was so organized I was scaring myself.

My butt barely landed in my chair before I was typing an email to Vain Dane to let him know I had cleared my desk. I sent it, then foolishly waited a few minutes thinking he *might* email me back acknowledging my Herculean efforts.

"Thank you for the positive feedback," I said to the screen. Jerk.

It wasn't that I didn't trust Handyman Harold; I really wanted to share the unveiling of my beach house with my friends. I called Becky's office, only to be told by her intern that she'd be in contract negotiations until midnight. Jane was my next call.

"Are you dancing around like a Munchkin singing, 'Ding, dong, the stalker's dead'?" she asked.

"I must admit, it is nice to be out from under a threat of imminent death."

"You should send that Redmond woman flowers."

"She's got the flower thing covered," I said, then

described the half dozen arrangements placed around the first floor. "For all I know she's got another half dozen upstairs. I'll have to think of something else." Maybe that would relieve the unexplainable prickle that crawled up the back of my neck whenever I thought about Melinda. I told Jane about the progress on the Chilian Avenue house. "We can go see the framing, then grab dinner."

"Oh, sorry," Jane said. "I've got a date."

I was disappointed, but happy for my friend. "With?"

"A guy I met at the gym. We're going ocean kayaking."

"A kayaking date? The guy better be hot."

"He's okay," she sighed. "I'm actually more looking forward to being out on the water for a few hours. Rain check?"

"Sure."

My final call was to Liv. Like Jane, she congratulated me on the demise of the threat of Carlos. Like Becky, she had to work. Concierge Plus was handling a charity dinner at The Breakers.

"Stop by if you want," Liv offered. "I'll slip you a couple of crab puffs and some champagne."

"I might," I hedged, not sure how my evening would unfold. It might be nice to just sit on the beach with a glass of wine, some cheese, and a baguette.

After hanging up, I looked at the clock, certain that it was close to five. I let out a groan when I saw it was just a few minutes past four. The only way I'd be able to leave early would be if I opened the window, climbed out, and shimmied down the drainpipe. Even then, I couldn't be totally positive that Margaret wouldn't be waiting for me.

I drummed my fingers on my desk while a half pot of coffee brewed. Checked eBay; nothing caught my fancy, so I logged into the Medicaid database and decided I could look around until 4:59, when I'd make a dash for the elevator. Thirty seconds to get down to the lobby, and I'd be at the car when the clock struck five.

Using the same insurance code manual I used for my estate work, I was easily able to decipher the medical information. I found a few billing errors. The government had charged one of Melinda's foster children for a prostate exam. Only problem? The patient was a twelve-year-old girl named Hilary McMasters. The second error raised an alarm in my mind, so I reread the entry.

According to the U.S. government, they'd paid three ER bills and related orthopedic charges for Terri Semple. All were for spiral fractures to the right arm. All while Terri was in Melinda's care.

Reaching into my credenza, I flipped through the file until I found the skeleton's second autopsy report. There it was, right in the third paragraph. Evidence of three healed spiral fractures to the right arm. "Son of a bitch."

Technically, it was conceivable that my skeleton and Terri Semple had each suffered the same injuries. They were both abused children, and it was a common injury when an unfit parent or caregiver twisted a kid's arm. Running my fingers through my hair, I weighed my options. There was a possibility that it was nothing more than a billing error. Somehow the skeleton's medical records had comingled with Terri's. The prostate exam proved the system was fallible.

I reached for the phone twice before finally making the call.

"Hi," I greeted.

"Finley," Melinda replied, her tone chipper. "I've been meaning to call you all day. I can't thank you enough for yesterday. And Mr. Caprelli. If it wasn't for the two of you, I might very well be sitting in jail right now."

"I'm glad everything worked out. Listen, I have a question."

"I already know what you're going to ask."

"You do?"

"The police asked me about the pictures in Carlos's motel room. Did Mr. Caprelli tell you?"

Mr. Caprelli had been MIA all day. I knew because I'd made a few calls to his extension and had kept getting his voice mail. Under the guise of acknowledging his help, I had almost worked up the nerve to invite him for a drink. Especially after all my friends had bailed on me. "Um, no. What about the pictures?"

"The police think he was stalking you and Terri Semple. My guess is he was following her around hoping to get an unflattering photo to sell to a tabloid."

That seemed like a stretch. He had hundreds of pictures, and, as memory served, lots of them were unflattering—and a few were of her sunbathing top-less at the Gilmore estate.

"He couldn't have been after me for money."

"I think he was fixated on you for your looks. Carlos always liked pretty blondes."

That seemed like a very lame reason to spend five days perched in trees or crouched in alleyways just to take my picture. Then again, he'd broken into my apartment when I hadn't been there, so maybe she was right and he was just—gross—an admirer. It didn't matter now. He was dead.

Speaking of which. "Do you remember Terri Semple breaking her arm three times when she was living with you?"

Dead silence.

"Melinda?"

"You caught me."

I knew it! I knew she was hiding something. "Doing . . . ?"

"You have to understand, there's a lot of red tape in the foster care system. Someone else needed medical attention, but there was a problem getting her Medicaid benefits transferred from her previous foster home. So I used Terri's card. I didn't have a choice. She needed medical attention, and I was struggling to keep food on the table with the stipends I got from the state. Can I ask how you found out about that?"

"I'm still trying to identify the skeleton in my house."

"And you think it was Jill?"

"Jill Burkett?"

"Yes. Troubled girl. And unfortunately, trouble often attracts trouble. She had a boyfriend who liked to beat on her. He was the one who kept breaking her arm."

Same injuries. Right time frame. Jill Burkett had to be the skeleton in the closet. "What happened to her?"

"She wasn't one of my success stories, I'm afraid. Kept running off with that horrible boyfriend. She'd come back, usually after a bad beating. Until the last time."

"When was that?"

"Wow," Melinda said on a breath, "let me think. She came in 1990, so it had to be sometime in '96 or '97. I don't know anyone she kept in touch with after she left."

"I think that's because she's the skeleton I found at the Chilian Avenue house."

"That's not possible," Melinda said vehemently. "I lived in that house for years after she left. Space was an issue. Believe me, someone would have noticed a body in a closet. *I* would have noticed. Why, the smell alone would have . . . well, you know what I mean."

I did. "You don't happen to remember the boy-friend's name?"

"Heavens no," she said. "Jill wouldn't tell me. If she had, I would have called the cops and pressed charges for the assaults. So, what happens now?"

"With what?"

"If you make the identification public, I could be charged with Medicaid fraud."

I sensed genuine fear in her tone. "I don't want to get you into trouble," I said. "I'll find some other way. Did she have any siblings? Someone who might be able to provide a DNA comparison or something?"

"I don't suppose you'd be willing to just let this go. Assuming it is Jill, she's been dead for more than a decade. Nothing good normally comes from dredging up the past. I'd be more than happy to cover burial expenses or anything you think might be appropriate to put this unfortunate situation to rest."

"I'd like to know what happened to her," I said, more for my own edification. "Someone murdered her."

"Probably that boyfriend."

"Why would a boyfriend keep the body all these years?"

"I shudder to think."

Glancing at the clock, I realized it was two minutes after five. "Listen, I've got an appointment, so I need to go."

Rudely, I all but hung up on Melinda. It couldn't be helped. I had to go to my mother's house to drop off the Mercedes and meet the Enterprise guy. Grabbing up my skeleton research and my purse, I dashed for the elevator.

AT 5:35 P.M., I was transferring those same items from the Mercedes to a utilitarian, nondescript white four-door coupe.

Driving in hideously slow Friday-night traffic, I crawled along I-95 to Palm Beach Gardens. It took me close to thirty minutes to go eight miles, but I finally reached the little French bistro in the newest addition of trendy shops and eateries known as Downtown across from the Gardens Mall.

After selecting a nice Brie and some crusty artisanal bread, I walked two stores down and bought some wine, a corkscrew, and a pair of glasses. I only needed one, but that wasn't an option.

Armed with dinner, I made one final stop before heading to Palm Beach. Using Military Trail as an alternative to the overly congested interstate, I detoured into one of the Walgreens that seemed to inhabit every other corner and bought a cheap sand chair.

The change at the house was nothing short of miraculous. Still, I groaned when I saw the Mustang already parked in the driveway. I was mentally exhausted and not in the mood to play head games with Liam. I wanted to be left alone. I needed to sort through the bits and pieces of the skeleton mystery that didn't quite seem to fit.

The whir of a power saw buzz traveled on the breeze coming off the beach. I entered the house and stopped short. Liam, gloriously shirtless, was hunched over the sawhorses, operating the power tool. A fine dust swirled all around him, and some of the shavings stuck to the sheen of perspiration coating his naked torso.

"Hi," Harold greeted me as he came down the hall.

Only then did Liam look up and find me standing on the threshold.

"Hi." I walked across the plywood subflooring and placed my bags on the counter so I could remove the chair I'd hooked in the bend of my elbow. I fixed my attention on Harold. "I'm here for my tour."

He offered a single-toothed smile. "Right this way."

Like a kid showing off birthday presents, Harold took me through the house, explaining as he went.

"This will be the powder room," he said, pointing to some tubes and a round thing. White PVC pipe zigged and zagged through holes drilled in the two-by-fours.

"Very nice," I fibbed. With nothing but boards nailed up every twelve inches or so, I couldn't tell where one room ended and the next one started. Maybe I'd do better when the drywall went up.

"Mr. Sam had me add this," he said, patting a boxy-looking thing under what I thought was my bedroom window.

"It's great."

"She has no idea what it is," Liam said. I turned to find him standing in what I thought might be the doorway, his arms raised, wrists resting against the framing.

Waving his arms in an inverted arc above the box shape, Harold said, "It's a window seat. Mr. Sam said you'd be able to watch the sunset from here."

Leaning over, I peered out and checked the view. The sun wasn't due to set for another couple of hours, but I got the gist. I could almost see myself seated on a padded surface, fluffy pillows at my back and my computer cradled in my lap. It looked like a very cozy place to hunt for Rolex parts, Lilly fashions, and un-loved Betsey Johnson dresses.

"It's going to be fabulous," I said, making Harold beam. "It's almost seven. You should call it a day."

"I don't mind long hours," he said proudly.

"She's giving us the boot, Harold," Liam said.

God, it was like he could read my mind.

"Oh, right. Sorry, Miss Finley, I didn't mean to be a bother."

"You're not a bother." Liam, on the other hand, was a big bother.

Harold insisted on carrying my chair out to the beach, while I uncorked my wine and generously filled one of the two glasses. They should have been washed first, but there was no running water, so the alcohol would have to serve as a sanitizer. Taking my bag and my glass, I headed out the new sliding glass doors, which, unlike their predecessors, opened and closed with a whisper. A large floral arrangement of two dozen pale pink roses and a few fragrant Star-gazer lilies, with a few sprigs of greenery, sat off to one side.

Slipping the handle of the bag up on my wrist, I bent to pull the envelope from the plastic tine. I nearly spilled my wine trying to get the card out, and when I did, I was sorry I'd expended the effort.

Congratulations on the new house. Love, Patrick.

"He's persistent."

The unexpected sound of Liam's voice so close to my ear startled me. This time I did spill my wine. A big red stain made a burgundy stripe right down the center of my pale blue belted dress. In a final insult, two drops splashed off a paver and stained the bow on my left shoe.

"Thanks a lot," I grumbled. "Do you have any idea what these shoes cost?"

"Probably more than my first car. I am sorry," he said with absolutely no remorse. "I didn't mean to make you jump."

"You did, and you ruined my dress and my shoes."

"I'll pay for the cleaning."

"You bet you will," I said as I kicked off my shoes and headed toward the beach.

Liam caught up to me. "What's wrong?"

I quickened my pace. "You just ruined a dress I've worn exactly once and a killer pair of Coach shoes."

"Hey," he said, moving to my right and gently but firmly grabbing my uninjured arm. He stepped in front of me, effectively blocking my way.

I stared straight ahead, at the dark hair covering his chest then tapering into a V as it disappeared into the waistband of his button fly jeans.

Crooking a finger beneath my chin, he tilted my head up. "What's wrong?"

"I've had a long day. I just want to sit on my little strip of beach, have a glass of wine, and relax."

He shook his head. "Is it the flowers from the pilot?"

Glancing around him, I called, "Harold, take those flowers home to your wife."

"I can't take those," he said. "They're yours."

"I don't want them. If you don't take them, they'll end up in that Dumpster."

"Well . . . um."

"She means it," Liam said without taking his eyes off my face.

"Okay, then. Thank you, Miss Finley."

Harold shuffled off.

"If it isn't the pilot—"

"It isn't. I'm just tired and I want to be left alone." I shrugged out of his hold.

Liam lifted his hands in mock surrender. "Fine. Just tell me why you're treating me like the enemy."

"Because right now, at this moment, you are."

I SPENT AN HOUR on the beach enjoying my wine and solitude, then I dragged the chair back up to the patio. I left it there, not really caring if someone stole the nine-dollar item.

Neither the wine nor the solitude had resulted in answering the question that was at the forefront of my mind: How did Jill Burkett's skeleton end up in my house?

I recorked the wine, laid the glasses on the floor of the backseat, and got behind the wheel. I headed south, to the Italian Renaissance–style hotel that dominated one hundred and forty acres of primo beachfront. It wasn't just a hotel. It was The Breakers. Built by Standard Oil tycoon Henry Flagler, it has hand-painted ceilings and stunning medieval tapestries hanging on the walls. Originally the private retreat of the American elite, it hadn't lost any of its charm or flavor in its one hundred plus years. The newest additions were a third golf course and programs for the spoiled children of the rich and famous. My favorite thing about The Breakers? The food, especially Sunday brunch, which ran seventy-five dollars. Running a close second was the spa. Best in south Florida, and even better if you opted for the outdoor, oceanfront hot stone massage.

I turned into the hedged driveway of The Breakers, self-parked—a rarity for me—then grabbed a file folder to hide as much of the stain as possible. I went to find Liv. I didn't want a crab puff as much as I wanted some club soda to try to salvage my dress. I might be in a contemplative funk, but that didn't mean I was going to sacrifice a dress I'd watched like a hawk, then swooped in on at the last moment and outbid my arch eBay rival, ClothesHorse2.

The Breakers was opulent and buzzing with conversation that was carried on the soft music from a three-piece band. I peered out into the courtyard. Liv's party was in full swing. I smiled for the first time in a while, happy to see the event so successful.

A waiter carrying an empty tray as if it held the crown jewels opened one side of the beveled glass doors. I stopped him and asked if he would get me a bottle of club soda. I knew he would. The Breakers' staff is renowned for their attention to their guests.

Technically, I wasn't a guest, but he didn't need to know that. I waited by the door until I caught Liv's gaze. She had a wireless headset on and a clipboard in her hand and somehow made that work while dressed in a sleek silk gown and matching drop pearl earrings.

Discreetly, she made her way around the fountain to where I waited. "I'm glad you came. Want me to have Jean-Claude make you a plate? We have free-flowing Cristal as well."

I pulled the folder away from my chest as if it was hinged. "I'm not fit to mingle with hoity-toities."

"Miss your mouth?"

"Liam did it."

Her exotic eyes grew wide. "He threw wine on you?"

"He startled me. It was an accident."

"I'm sure he apologized."

"He did, and I bit his head off."

Liv shook her head like a disappointed teacher. "So now it's your turn to apologize."

"I know. I will, just not tonight."

"Something wrong?"

"Yeah, but I'm not sure what."

Liv reached out and touched the back of my hand. "Carlos was the guy, right?"

I nodded, and the waiter appeared with my club soda. I thanked him, then gave Liv a smile. "Go enjoy the fruits of your labor. I'm going to slip into the ladies' room and blot this stain."

She gave me an air kiss. "Call me in the morning.

Maybe we can all get together for dinner or drinks or something."

"I will. The courtyard looks beautiful. You did a great job. Love what you did with the candles."

"Thanks."

I walked across the lobby to the ladies' room. The attendant gave me a white washcloth and offered to help me, but I was just as content to work on the stain myself. The room smelled of lavender with an undertone of night jasmine. Not a heavy perfume, just enough to continue the feel of luxury contained in every square foot of the Palm Beach landmark.

I heard the flush of a toilet, then one of the stall doors opened. I glanced up from my blotting and found myself staring at the reflection of Terri Semple in the mirror.

The people who put on the most style are the same people who put off the most creditors.

eighteen

TERRI WAS VERY ATTRACTIVE, tall, and slender, with dark blond hair twisted into a messy updo. She was tanned and moved like a goddess in an off-the-shoulder white gown with gold trim and embellishments.

When she went to wash her hands, I saw it. Her engagement ring included a five-carat pink diamond, courtesy of Harry Winston, that was set in platinum. I was surprised her arm didn't drag the ground under the weight of that sucker.

We did that little wordless, awkward, eyes-met-so-you-have-to-acknowledge-each-other thing.

"Good evening," she said with just a hint of Midwest accent in her diction.

"Hi," I said, trying desperately to think of some way I could strike up a conversation, and then ease into grilling her like the catch of the day.

She had the home court advantage. If I said the wrong thing, Martin Gilmore's fiancée could have me banned from the property faster than I could say boo.

As she shut off the water, she smiled again, this time revealing seriously bleached teeth. They were so bright that they matched her dress. Teardrop diamonds dangled from her earlobes. Another giant diamond teardrop hung from a thick gold choker.

The jewelry she was wearing was worth more than the treasuries of several emerging nations. She could probably hock a couple of pieces and end world hunger.

"Have a nice evening," she said as she accepted the cloth offered by the trained-to-be-invisible attendant.

Opening a small evening bag constructed of gold links, she removed a tube of lipstick and did a touch-up to the color on her dark red, chemically plumped lips. Just out of curiosity, I glanced in her purse and almost laughed when I saw a Tiffany compact sharing space with three shoestring ropes of licorice the same shade as her lipstick.

"Hang on," I said.

Her response to my request was a tight, impatient smile. "Yes?"

This was wrong in so many ways. My confidence was as soggy as the front of my dress, but I couldn't let this opportunity pass. "You're Terri Semple, right? We have a mutual *aquain-friend*. Melinda Redmond." So *friend* was a stretch.

She eyed me up and down, and even though she didn't say a word or change a thing about her expression, I knew I'd come out on the short end of the inspection. "Melinda's a wonderful person," Terri said.

She began to pivot on the balls of her Gucci Sevigny sandals with the darling ankle cuff and four-inch heels that left her just shy of six feet tall. "I'm Finley Tanner."

Bye-bye pivot. "You're the one who bought Melinda's old house, right?"

"Actually, it belonged to my father," I said. Babbled, really. I waved my hands in a pointless attempt to erase the inane detail. "We have something in common," I began again. "I'm assuming the police spoke to you about Carlos Lopez and his, um, photos?"

"Yes."

"Had he been in contact with you?"

She stepped a little closer, and I found myself backing up. If I didn't stop soon, I'd topple into the big basket of soiled washrags.

"I haven't spoken to Carlos in years. He's part of my past. A past that was painful and difficult to overcome. Unlike you, I didn't have a doting mother or Jonathan Tanner in my life."

Doting mother? Obviously, she'd never met my mother. And how had she remembered Jonathan's name so quickly? Maybe she was one of those people who remembered names. Maybe I was getting paranoid. "I was blessed," I replied. "I don't mean to dredge up unpleasant memories; I'm just trying to get some information on Jill Burkett. The two of you were in . . . *lived* with Melinda at about the same time?"

"I don't remember her at all."

"Really?" I asked, tilting my head to the side to

try to get a better read on the woman. Not possible; she'd already shown her hand when she'd said my stepfather's name. She was as cool and controlled as a statue. "Abby Andrews had some very vivid and, well, unkind things to say about her. She specifically recalled Jill being very cruel to you."

Terri's smile slipped into a sneer just for a fraction of a second. "That's quite possible. I simply don't remember, nor do I want to. Now, if you'll excuse me, I don't want my fiancé to become concerned."

Neither would I if I had a fiancé who came with hundreds of millions in banks all over the world that could and would buy me anything and everything. "I didn't mean to keep you. Enjoy the event."

She was almost to the door when I said, "Perhaps I could discuss this with you at a more appropriate time?"

"I don't think so," she said, then regally removed herself from the room.

I felt a little feisty after being dissed by that woman. So she'd hit the marriage lottery, but geez, she acted as if it had been her birthright instead of some freak occurrence. Just to make myself feel superior, unlike Terri, I tipped the attendant.

I ARRIVED HOME TO find a sealed manila envelope tilted against my door. I recognized the bold, masculine handwriting as Liam's, so I picked it up and carried it inside.

Knowing him, it was probably full of dry-cleaning

coupons or some equally stupid thing that, in spite of my best efforts, would charm me right out of my thong. God, I was starting to wonder if I had some sort of superpower when it came to picking a man to obsess over. Of course, that's minus the ugly tights and a silly cape, since everyone knows a cape makes a woman my height look even shorter. Why was it I kept falling for the wrong men? Not that I was admitting I'd fallen for Liam. I was starting to believe that if I was dropped into a room full of eligible, handsome men, I would find the worst possible match before I downed my first Cosmo.

I looked around my apartment and reassessed my opinion of myself. Here it was a beautiful Friday night, and what were my plans? Microwave popcorn and channel surfing. Topped off by some possible internet time. I was getting closer and closer to the bleak future of an unmarried, unhappy woman with sixty-four cats as company.

I fell face-first onto my never-made bed, stifling my groan in the pillow. I had half hoped to see Sam's car in the lot, but apparently, he had plans as well. Rolling over, I winced as the skin pulled around the itchy stitches.

"Enough," I told myself, getting up on my elbows. "Do something."

I slipped off my still-damp dress to discover that the wine had seeped through and discolored the white lace that trimmed my new bra. Thank you, Liam. The irony that the man had ruined my bra without ever touching me wasn't lost on me. I changed into jeans and a cute baby T with rhinestone accents. Barefoot, I took my stained clothes into the kitchen, plugged the sink, tossed the dress and bra in, and dumped a couple of liters of club soda over everything.

I made a pot of coffee. Once I had a nice steaming mug, I settled into the couch and powered on my laptop and the television. After a few minutes, I muted the TV. Liam's package sat on top of my skeleton files, so I debated which to tackle first.

"Who are you kidding?" I asked myself as I slipped my nail under the flap and broke the seal. Patience is a virtue, just not one I possess. Clipped to the top page was a short note apologizing again for making me spill my wine. A nice person would call him and say all is forgiven. A naughty person would add, *"Come on over."* I couldn't trust myself, especially when the mere sound of his voice raised my blood pressure several degrees.

The first few pages were documents from the North Carolina Department of Corrections. The more I read about all the horrible things Carlos had done—and knowing that they were probably just the tip of the iceberg—the less I was able to muster any sadness at his passing.

Earlier, while browsing through the stuff for the class I'd yet to attend, I'd read a statistic that on average, criminals got away with four crimes for every one they got caught committing. If that was true, Carlos committed his first felony in vitro.

While I was perusing Carlos's criminal record, I was halfheartedly watching an eBay auction for a pair of killer Jimmy Choo ankle boots. They retailed for six twenty, and the bidding was already up to three hundred with more than six hours to go. Too rich for my blood.

Blood that stilled in my veins when I reached a report from the Florida authorities that conclusively matched Carlos's fingerprints to the 1996 robbery *and* my break-in. He'd been positively identified as Doe96-5. There was a memo attached to the report stating that a clerical error had resulted in a failure by North Carolina to enter Carlos's prints into the AFIS system. Had they done that, Carlos would have been identified the night I'd come home to find the resin skeleton hanging in my closet.

The next item was the ME's report on Carlos. I tossed it aside unread. He was dead. That was enough.

Still suffering under the annoying suspicion that I was missing something parked right under my nose, I decided to make a bulleted list. It needed to be done, and besides, the Jimmy Choo bids had climbed to five fifty.

"You people are fools," I admonished the unseen eBay bidders. "They're listed as slightly worn and you're bidding the price to near-full retail. Amateurs."

I took a big gulp of coffee and tried to decide how best to organize my thoughts. "Start with what you know."

(A) I knew the skeleton was Jill Burkett, even if I couldn't tell anyone until I found a way around exposing Melinda's insurance fraud.

(B) I knew Terri Semple wouldn't help me, and

now that I was over being snubbed, I didn't blame her. I couldn't. Not when I had that big, glaring, *totally not my fault* blight on the record of my own past.

Speaking of which, I opened my email and sent Patrick yet another request to stop with the flowers. I would never know, or care, if he replied: I'd put the lying bastard on my Blocked Senders list. Any emails from him would go rot in cyber hell.

(C) I knew Carlos had been involved in at least one of the robberies in Palm Beach during the nineties. Chances were good he'd been involved in all of them.

I tried to remember some of what Abby had told me. What I remembered most was that Jill and Carlos had been tight. It wasn't a huge leap in logic to assume that Jill might have been his accomplice. Tapping my fingernail on the edge of my in-need-of-a-refill coffee mug, a question repeated in my brain.

Maybe the recent reduction in my caffeine consumption was screwing with my problem-solving skills. Okay, so *skills* was a bit of a stretch. When it came to solving a murder, I did some of my best work accidentally.

As I went into the kitchen, I vocalized the question, hoping that hearing it aloud might shake an answer free. "How did Carlos and/or Jill know what to steal?" A third accomplice, maybe? Someone with a knowledge and appreciation of the finer things?

I was just about to go back to my bulleted list when someone knocked on my door. Probably Sam; he often dropped in after a date when he saw lights blazing.

Couldn't have been much of a date. Not if he was home a few minutes after nine. Getting up on my tip-toes, I was surprised to see Melinda on the other side of the door. And she didn't look happy.

I undid the locks and opened the door. "Hi," I greeted her as she breezed past me, leaving a trail of perfume in her wake. "Please, do come right in," I muttered.

She stood in the center of my living room, arms crossed, Dooney & Bourke dangling off her forearm. Her face was scrunched, and her eyes narrowed, making it perfectly clear that she was pissed. "I *thought* we had an agreement."

"On . . . ?"

Huffing out a sharp breath, she answered, "About the skeleton thing. Terri called me, terribly upset after you accosted her at the charity benefit."

It was my turn to get a little huffy. "First off, I didn't *'accost'* her. I accidentally ran into her in a public bathroom. Secondly, if anyone has a right to feel put down, it's me. During our brief—and I'm talking *maybe* sixty seconds interaction, she was quite the statuesque snot."

"Because she has a lot to lose if you keep poking around in the past. You've changed. The Finley I used to know as a child was much more considerate."

Anger gurgled in the pit of my stomach. I felt like Jan Brady, only instead of "Marsha, Marsha, Marsha," my concerns were overshadowed by Terri, Terri, Terri. Screw that. Planting my hands on my hips, I met and matched Melinda's steely blue eyes.

"Tell Terri I said to pull up her big girl panties and get over herself. As for you," I added, my voice quivering with fury, "you're hardly in a position to cast stones about being considerate. Thanks to me, Tony made sure you didn't end up in jail for shooting Carlos. And I haven't told anyone about your little insurance scam. *Yet.*"

My not-intended-to-be-subtle threat effectively wiped some of the antagonism off Melinda's face.

I stepped to the side. "I want you to leave. Now."

Silently, her spine straight, she headed to the door, slamming it hard enough to cause a mini earthquake inside my apartment.

Guess I was off her Christmas card list. Melinda's overreaction lent credence to my lingering feeling that something about her wasn't quite right. Nothing else explained her odd behavior. Throwing herself between Terri and me made no sense. Her actions were too over-the-top to qualify as a de facto mother protecting her child. Especially since Terri wasn't a child but rather a woman creeping up on her midthirties.

In a very lame imitation of Jack Nicholson, I went to my computer and said, "You just screwed with the wrong marine," as I logged into the Dane, Lieberman mainframe.

Melinda might have attitude, but I had unfettered access to vital records and could run credit and background checks. I had the skeleton file, police and medical reports, at least a dozen other information sources, and internet search skills that would make Bill Gates proud. I switched to a Scarlett O'Hara impression, taking a bit of license with the famous movie quote. "With God as my witness, I will find whatever it is you don't want me to find."

In less than an hour, I had addresses and phone numbers for two more of the former foster children—Ava Patterson and Hilary McMasters.

Ava answered the phone on the second ring. I heard children and music in the background and spoke loudly as I introduced myself. Stretching the truth just a bit, I told her that she could either speak to me, or my law firm would ask a judge to issue a material witness warrant for her as part of the investigation into the murder of Jill Burkett.

"What does that mean?" Ava asked.

"It means you'll sit in a jail cell until it's time for you to give testimony."

"How long would that be?"

"No way of knowing, well beyond the legal one-eighty, eighty rule."

"What's that?" Ava's hardened tone was gone. Now she sounded panicky.

Another tidbit I'd read in my continuing ed course materials. "A criminal defendant must be prosecuted within one hundred days of being charged. Ever heard of the right to a speedy trial?"

"Sure. I've got kids and no husband. No way I can go to jail. When do I have to come give my statement?"

For effect, I shuffled some of the papers Liam had delivered. Thanks to my internet snooping, I knew Ava had a job as a receptionist at an insurance agency in West Palm, a position she'd taken less than a month ago. Using that knowledge to my advantage, I said, "I'm available Monday at eleven."

"I'm at work then."

"You'll have to take some time off. My schedule is completely booked. Since you're refusing to cooperate, I guess we'll have no choice but to contact that judge."

"I'm not refusing," she said, her voice choked with emotion.

I winced. I was bullying the poor woman.

"Can't we work something else out? I can come on my lunch break or during the evening."

"Again, Ms. Patterson, my schedule is quite full. Unless . . ."

"Unless what?"

"I suppose I *could* make an exception and meet with you this evening." I held my breath waiting on her answer.

"I can't leave my kids here alone."

I made sure to sigh into the mouthpiece. "My firm doesn't make house calls." I paused for effect. "Okay, I'll break with policy and come to you."

"Thank you," she fairly gushed. "Do you need directions?"

MY THIRD OUTFIT OF the day was the über-conservative navy and white Chanel suit normally reserved for mandatory brunches with my mother. My hair was pulled back in a no-frills ponytail, and I'd completed the all-business look with a pair of simple navy pumps.

The rental was equipped with a navigation system, so I had no trouble finding the small, single-story house on the dirt road in Greenacres. The car rocked as it lumbered along the rutted driveway until I parked next to an assortment of toys littering the lawn. Okay, lawn was a stretch. It was mostly sand with a few lonely patches of grass.

A floodlight partially pulling away from the wall lighted the crumbled sidewalk leading to the cracked step in front of the house. Slimy green moss blanketed much of the stucco around the door. I heard the clunk and hiss of a window air conditioner as I knocked.

I fully expected Ava to be a clone of Abby. I was wrong. She was a tall, heavyset woman with clean, coiffed hair and a layer of careful, if imperfect, makeup.

She wore shorts, a faded black shirt from a Metallica concert, and no shoes. She greeted me with a smile that was equal parts warm and weary.

Shooing two boys who looked to be about ten to twelve years old to their bedroom, she moved a game controller to the top of the television and offered me a seat on the sofa. The house was clean and tidy. The faint scent of chili hung in the air.

The chair next to the sofa squeaked when Ava sat down. "Would you like something to drink?" she asked.

"Coffee?"

While Ava went into the other room, I took a legal pad out of my tote; I retrieved a pen, balanced the pad on my knees, and crossed my legs at the ankles. The sleeve of my suit was irritating the stitches on my arm. The stitches on my leg were discreetly covered by a Band-Aid.

"Milk or sugar?" she called.

"Black is fine."

She returned, holding two mugs in one hand. Mine was placed on a veneered coffee table, while she kept hers with her as she retook her seat.

"Who was murdered?" she asked.

"Carlos Lopez murdered Jill Burkett," I explained.

Her brows drew together. "I saw on the news that he was killed recently by our foster mom. A justified shooting. Melinda walked away, so who is going on trial?"

"Carlos had an accomplice after the fact."

"Who?"

"Who do you think?" I asked. "You lived with him."

"Not by choice," she said, pain falling like a curtain over her expression. "But then, we never had choices."

"What can you remember about your time at the Chilian Avenue house?"

She blinked several times, and I wondered if it was her tell—an unconscious habit that indicated she was about to feed me some sort of lie. Too soon to know, but I'd be watching for it.

"Melinda was an okay foster mother. I liked living at the beach."

I'll bet you did. "Who lived there with you?"

She sipped her coffee. "When I first got there, it was Carlos, Jill, Terri, Abby, and me."

"Tell me about them."

"Jill and Carlos ruled the place. Cross either one of them, and you paid."

"How?" I asked.

"If you were lucky, Carlos would just smack you around."

Again, she did the rapid blink. I was right, it was a tell, but not the kind I expected. It was what she did when recalling something unpleasant. "And if you weren't?"

"He'd . . . *mess* with you."

Translation—sexual assault. My heart squeezed as sympathy for the woman settled in the pit of my stomach. "Where was Melinda?"

"Around." Ava's shoulders slumped, and it was like watching a balloon deflate from a slow leak.

"And Jill?"

"She wasn't as violent as Carlos, but she was often the instigator. I think they were doing it. If she got pissed, which happened practically daily, Carlos would act as her muscle."

"And Melinda did nothing?"

Ava shrugged and blinked some more. "I guess you could say she tried. If you towed the line, she'd take you on one of her field trips. If you screwed up, like missing curfew, you had to study one of her stupid arty things."

"Coin books?" I asked.

"Coins, statues, glass vases, paintings. I didn't take it seriously the first week. Not until the Friday test."

"You were tested?"

Ava nodded. "We'd all sit at the table, and Melinda would put color copies in front of us. She thought it was a unique family-type game and a way of teaching us about the finer things in life, but it was hard. I never did very well. Especially with the paintings. To this day, I get freaked out if I see a Maltese."

"Ma*tisse*," I corrected automatically as I made notes.

"Whatever. Besides, I couldn't compete with Terri or Jill."

"Why?"

"Jill studied those art books and auction catalogs all the time."

"And Terri?"

Ava shook her head. "I never saw her do it. But she had one of those memories. You know. See it one time and remember it forever. She was the nicest of them all."

Not in my book. "What about Jill? Do you remember when she left?"

"May of '96. Thank God."

"Know where she went?"

"Never heard from her again. Never wanted to. Jill might have looked like an angel, but she was pure evil. No conscience, no regard for others. Manipulative to the core. She'd glare at you and her eyes would turn almost black. Like a shark about to move in for the kill."

"Did she manipulate anyone other than Carlos?"

"Hell yes," Ava said, sipping her coffee. "When I first got there, I thought Jill and Terri were friends. That changed though, and Jill went out of her way to bust Terri's ass. As time went on, Terri got really quiet and reserved. She spent hours lying on her bed playing with this token."

"What kind of token?" I asked.

Ava made a circle with one hand. "About this big around, and it had trees on one side and I think something engraved on the other side."

My hand shook as I pulled Jonathan's medallion out of my purse. "Was it this?"

Ava turned it over in her palm. "Maybe. It was a long time ago. All I know is Terri kept to herself until Hilary arrived."

"Hilary McMasters?"

"Yeah. We used to call her Jill Junior. She was a total suck-up and imitated everything Jill did." Ava let out a little sarcastic laugh. "Actually, it worked out pretty well for Terri and me. Jill, Carlos, and Hilary would sneak out at night, leaving Terri and me in peace. We'd go to our room and do our own thing."

"What was your thing?" I asked.

She almost smiled. "I was into writing angsty teen-aged poetry. Suicide was a popular theme with me back then."

"And Terri?" I asked, watching her over the rim of my coffee cup as I drained the last sip.

She shrugged. "Daydreaming, I guess. All I know is she'd lay in her bed for hours playing with that token thingy." She handed me back the coin. "That could be it, but I never saw it close up. Like me, she had some secret hiding place. I slit my mattress to hide my poetry notebooks."

"Mom! Trevor took one of my cars!" a child screamed.

"I can't leave them alone much longer," Ava told me. "If I do, I guarantee a fight will break out."

"One last question," I said, standing as she did. "Do you know how to get in touch with Hilary? Her phone's been disconnected."

"I ran into her about three months ago. She was working at the Cracker Barrel in Stuart."

"Thanks."

Wanting is good. Wanting it for free is better.

nineteen

WHERE ARE YOU?" LIAM asked.

"Out having dinner," I answered, conveniently leaving out the part about being at the Cracker Barrel. And that my dinner had been a big slab of chicken fried steak, mashed potatoes, and fried okra. And that said yummy, calorie-heavy meal had been served by none other than Hilary McMasters.

"It's nearly midnight."

"I know. I've been able to tell time since the first grade. Is there anything else? It's rude to the other diners for me to chat on my cell." The other diners were four young men and a young couple who had that travel-weary glaze in their eyes. I'm sure none of them cared that I was on the phone, but what Liam didn't know couldn't come back to bite me in the butt.

"Did you get the stuff I left for you?"

"Yes. Thanks."

"You're taking the news awfully well."

Okay, so he'd gotten my attention. "News?"

"The tox screen from Carlo's autopsy didn't raise a red flag for you?"

I hated to admit a lapse to him, but I had no choice. "I didn't get to that."

"His blood alcohol level was off the charts."

"Based on the stuff I did read, I'm not surprised he abused alcohol before he went after Melinda."

"He wasn't drunk," Liam said. "He was obliterated. With that much liquor in his system, I doubt he could have found Melinda's house, let alone her door. I know you were on the phone and think you heard everything that went on, but—"

"I'm open to suggestions," I interrupted, then told him of our little standoff in my apartment. "Wasn't Abby drunk when her trailer caught fire?"

"Um-hum. Interesting coincidence."

A chill ran through me. "You think Melinda drove all the way to Daytona and got Abby drunk, then set the fire?"

"A friend of mine at the phone company checked. There's no record of Melinda calling Abby or vice versa."

"So, it might have been an accident," I said, almost disappointed to have such a promising lead shot down in a single breath.

"I didn't say that. Abby did reach out to Terri Semple. Called her five hours before the fire started."

"Something about her doesn't make any sense. Everyone I've spoken to who spent any time with Terri claims she was a sweet person."

"Which is why I had my phone company contact

do a little more digging. Right after Terri heard from Abby, she called a prepaid cell number."

"I happen to know those are impossible to trace."

"True, unless you happen to find the prepaid."

"Judging by your tone, I'm assuming you did."

"Not me," he said. "The ME. It was in Carlos's pants pocket when they inventoried the items on the body."

"So what happens now?"

"I thought I might take a trip to Abby's trailer park tomorrow. Ask around to see if anyone saw Carlos or his silver sedan the night of the fire. Wanna come?"

"Maybe," I hedged. "Can I call you in the morning?"

There was a brief pause, and then he asked, "What are you up to?"

"Who says I'm up to anything?"

"You're being evasive. That means you're doing something dangerous, stupid, or both."

"For your information," I said, not masking my irritation, "I'm thinking of dropping in on Terri tomorrow."

"Not a good idea. My gut tells me she's involved in this up to her eyeballs."

"Your gut may be right. But we'll never know until I have a chat with Terri."

"Too dangerous."

"It would be if I planned on meeting her at her home, but I happen to know she has a meeting at Concierge Plus tomorrow. She can't do anything to me there."

"What time?" he asked.

Still stung by the implication that I would intentionally do something stupid that would put me in danger, I gave him the time and hung up. Technically, I gave him *a* time. An hour after Terri's appointment time. Guess we'd see just which one of us was stupid.

As soon as I saw Hilary come out from behind the massive fireplace that hid the kitchen, I pulled a hundred-dollar bill I'd gotten from the ATM in the gift shop and placed it on the table.

Her washed-out blue eyes bulged when she saw the bill. "I don't think I can break this," she said, reaching for the money.

I slapped my hand on the edge of the currency and looked up to lock gazes with her. "It's all yours."

She eyed me suspiciously, placing one hand on her nonexistent hip. The woman was rail thin, with a gaunt, drawn face. The only word that came to mind was pathetic. She just had the look of someone who'd had a very hard life. Her teeth were stained yellow from tobacco, and she had the remnants of an orangish lipstick in the corners of her mouth when she smiled.

She smoothed the tight, thin sides of her dyed-too-often brassy hair and asked, "What's the catch?" Instantaneous distrust laced her tone.

"Fifteen minutes of your time."

She rolled her eyes. "Sorry, honey, but I don't turn tricks, my double shift is over, and I don't do chicks."

"Conversation only," I clarified.

"You a cop?"

"Do I look like one?"

She eyed me up and down. "In those shoes? No. What's the topic of this conversation that's worth a hundred bucks?"

"Jill Burkett."

She backed up. "Right. Like I'm dumb enough to do that. Keep your Ben Franklin."

As she started to walk away, I called after her and hurriedly yanked another bill out of my purse. "Ben has a twin."

Her lips pursed as she hungrily stared at the two bills I fanned out like a hand of blackjack.

After a minute of staring at the money, Hilary said, "Meet me in the back parking lot in five minutes."

I paid my check and noticed my hands were trembling, partly because I was hoping Hilary would tell me something that would explain how Jonathan's medallion had found its way from Terri's hiding place to Jill's hand. The other reason I was shaking was less complicated. I was scared.

My anxiety level doubled when Hilary failed to show after five minutes. For all I knew, she'd left by the front and ditched me by the kitchen door, leaving me to choke on the stench from the nearby Dumpster. Five minutes turned into fifteen, and I was ready to admit I'd been had when Hilary came around the building.

"Thank you for talking with me."

She held out her hand palm up. "One hundred up front. The other hundred when we're done."

Not exactly how I wanted to do it, but since she had me by the thong, I relented. "Here."

"So," she said as she pulled a cigarette out of her apron pocket, cupped a lighter to block the breeze, took a drag, and blew a steady stream in my face. "What are we going to conversate about?"

We could start with the fact that conversate *isn't a word.* Yeah, that was sure to win her over. "I want to know about the time you lived with Melinda Redmond."

"What part?"

"Carlos Lopez and Jill Burkett?"

"The Bonnie and Clyde of the system," she remarked as she drew on the cigarette, making the end glow orange.

"I heard you were friends."

Her eyes narrowed. "What's your angle in all this?"

"I bought the house on Chilian Avenue. It came complete with a skeleton in the closet."

She raised her hands. "I had a couple brushes with the law, but there's no way in hell you can pin a body on me."

"I'm not trying to," I insisted. "I'm more interested in what Jill and Carlos were doing."

"What weren't they doing?"

"I know about Carlos's inappropriate sexual behavior."

"Cop a feel Carlos," she agreed with a little laugh. "He was an amateur compared to my stepfather."

"And Jill?"

"Total bitch. But she had this . . . this *way* about her."

"Can you explain that?"

Dropping the cigarette to the ground, Hilary snuffed it out with her rubber-soled shoes. "If you didn't know better, you'd think she was legit. She could walk the walk and talk the talk and blend right in with the local snobs. Then without warning, she'd turn on you and without so much as blinking, tell Carlos to beat the crap out of you."

"Why did Carlos do her bidding?"

She cocked her head to one side. "Gee, let's see if we can think of a reason why a guy would do anything for a girl. He was a pudgy toad, and she was a goddess."

"It was about sex?"

"And drugs and pretty much whatever he wanted. Gold chains, Air Jordans."

"How could she afford those things?"

Hilary glanced at her watch. "Time's up."

I shook my head, holding my ground and my money. "No. I want to know about the robberies."

She seemed surprised but not shocked. "So we lifted stuff from the rich folks."

"You, too?"

"Sure, a couple of times. We got to keep part of whatever she got from the fence. First and only time in my life I had cash to spend. 'Course, most of it went up my nose."

Color me shocked. "Do you remember the last time you saw Jill?"

She shrugged. "Four years ago. Tried to hit her up for cash. We set up a meet, only Carlos showed up and did this." She pulled up her shirt and showed me a ragged, red scar on her belly. "Said if I ever contacted Jill again he'd gut me like a fish."

"I'm not paying for lies," I told her.

"I'm not lying. Think I'd slash myself with a box cutter just for something to do?"

"Not that. You couldn't have seen Jill four years ago. I was the one who found her remains. Two autopsies concluded she'd been dead for at least a decade or more."

Leaning back, she regarded me for several seconds. Then her lips curled into a smug smile. "You really don't know, do you?"

"Know what?"

In a swift and unexpected move, she snatched the second hundred out of my hand. "You'll have to figure that one out all on your own. Me? I'd like to keep on breathing."

I WALKED TO MY car with Hilary's words bouncing around in my brain. How could Jill be alive four years ago when her remains were at least . . . *Holy shit!*

Checking the dashboard clock, I debated calling any or all of my friends. I gave a passing thought to calling Liam, but it was after one in the morning. With my luck, Ashley would answer the phone, and I didn't want a reminder that he was still sleeping with Beer Barbie to kill the elation pumping through my system.

The only option was to call the police. They'd swoop in and make the arrests, totally stealing my thunder, but now was so not the time to be selfish.

"Nine-one-one, what is your emergency?"

"How do I get in touch with Detective Graves or Steadman?"

Slightly miffed, the emergency operator had me hold the line while she looked up their direct lines.

I thanked her, disconnected the call, then dialed the number she'd supplied while it was still fresh in my mind.

"Hello."

"Hi, it's—"

". . . have reached the desk of Detective Ed Graves. Please leave a message at the sound of the beep."

Beeeeep.

"This is Finley Tanner. Please call me back the minute you get this message. It's about . . . It's . . . just call me, please."

Before starting the engine, I tried Sergeant Jennings, with the same result. He was working days and not expected until 7:00 a.m.

I drove home, stopping once for an iced hazelnut coffee from the McDonald's drive-thru. I was way too excited to sleep, plus I wanted to go back through my skeleton files, knowing I had to print out proof to turn over to the authorities. And given what I now suspected, I knew exactly what to look for.

I arrived at my apartment thirty minutes later, and still Sam's car wasn't in the lot. I quickly scribbled a note insisting that he come see me the second he got home, then I ran up the stairs and went to my own apartment to get to work.

The first thing I did was delete my incomplete,

now useless list without saving it. I sipped on my coffee while simultaneously logging into the Medicaid records one last time. Clicking the mouse button, I sent the file to the wireless printer in my bedroom.

While the cheap-but-utilitarian inkjet slowly did its thing, I shed the Chanel suit, hung it up, and changed back into my jeans and T-shirt. Pulling the band from my ponytail, I shook my head and ran my fingers through my hair.

While I collected the pages out of the tray, I chanted, "Finley is a genius. Finley is a genius." Then I headed back to the living room and my laptop.

With my legs crossed, I pulled the machine into my lap and surrounded myself with the files. My sense of accomplishment soared as I typed the first line:

Terri Semple is actually Jill Burkett.

It fit. It explained almost everything. My new bulleted list was going to support my conclusion.

I didn't have all the answers, but I had a lot of pieces. The Terri Semple I'd met in The Breakers ladies' room wasn't the sweet, kind girl I'd been hearing about. What had Abby called her? A brown-eyed bitch?

"How did I miss that?" I chided myself. The woman engaged to Martin Gilmore had hazel eyes. Sure, they could be contact lenses, but my guess was no. Riffling through the files, I found Jill Burkett's DCF records, and sure enough, right there on the intake form, she was listed as having blond hair and hazel eyes.

I checked Terri Semple's file and found that the real

Terri, in fact, had brown eyes. "Score another one for me," I said as I added that information to my new list.

I'd probably have to show it to her for verification, but Ava's brief description of the "token" had to have been Jonathan's medallion. Which, of course, explained . . .

"No, it doesn't," I mumbled, frowning. Neither Abby, nor Hilary, nor Ava had implicated the real Terri in the robberies. If she hadn't been part of the theft ring, why had she died clutching a medallion stolen from my parents' home?

Sighing, I took a long sip of coffee. Caffeine helps me think. Real Terri could have found it and threatened to . . .

"Wasn't on the police inventory of things stolen." I was sorry to dismiss that idea as an available possibility.

And sorry I hadn't figured out sooner what was so obvious. The thought jogged another tidbit from my memory. I'd read almost that exact sentiment not so long ago. Hunting in yet another folder, I retrieved a photocopy of the scrap of paper Liam and I had found in the Chilian Avenue house.

Dear Sir: I'm sorry. I should have done this sooner but . . .

Idea revived! Just because it wasn't in the inventory didn't mean the medallion *hadn't* been stolen. Just that it hadn't been reported or fenced. I grinned like a giddy schoolgirl. "So Real Terri finds the medallion.

She was the nice, kind one, so it would make perfect sense that she'd write an apology and turn the medallion over to the authorities.

"Something that would have made Crazy Carlos and Mean Jill very, *very* unhappy." Carlos had had strength and well-documented rage. It wasn't much of a stretch to assume he'd overpowered Real Terri, causing the asphyxiation injury that had killed her. Most likely at Jill's urging.

"Jill did send Carlos to do her dirty work when Hilary tried to shake her down."

I kept adding conclusions and assumptions to my list. Then I thought I heard a car, so I raced to the door and glanced out the peephole, hoping to see Sam's car. No Sam's car—or any other headlights, for that matter. "Wishful thinking, Finley."

What I didn't get was how a couple of foster kids had become so adept at stealing. Or knowing which had been the high-value items.

The Friday Night game. My excitement faded a little. As annoyed as I'd been with Melinda, I really didn't want to know that she'd played a part in the robberies. As she was one of the few links I still had to Jonathan, I preferred her not having been involved.

Liam's information practically proved that Melinda had shot Carlos not in self-defense but in cold blood. "Which explains why the blood was just inside the door." I thought about the temperature in her house. That much AC probably skewed the time of death, but that was something I'd have to leave to the professionals.

Three soft knocks echoed through my apartment. "Finally," I sighed, abandoning my laptop.

Hurrying to the door, I looked out and saw Sam, who did not look happy. His date must not have gone well, I thought as I opened the door.

Sam rushed in, bumping into me, knocking me back several feet, nearly knocking me on my butt. "Hey, what's with—" My throat closed, choking off the words when I saw a man—no, Terri . . . no, *Jill* dressed as a man—standing in the doorway, holding a gun.

She stepped inside and slowly closed the door. Her long hair was tucked into a cap. Given her height, build, jeans, and loose-fitting Hawaiian shirt, any witnesses would identify her as a tall, lanky male.

Sam regained his footing and turned, partially shielding me behind him. "You can have our money," he said, starting to reach into the front pocket of his pants.

"That's okay, I have my own," she said as she lifted the small gun and fired once.

Sam crumpled at my feet even though I grabbed him beneath the arms. I fell under the weight, taking him with me. I immediately scrambled to my elbows as blood began to spill from a small hole just above his right eyebrow.

"Sam," I cried, shaking him gently and patting his cheek. "Why did you shoot him?" I choked, looking up at the woman.

She shrugged. "Because he was in the way of my real target and because I could. Get up."

Tears burned my eyes as I carefully rolled Sam's

limp body onto the floor. In the process, I felt the outline of his cell phone in his pocket and made the split-second decision to make a move for it.

It meant turning my back on Jill for a half second, and I half expected her to shoot me in the back. Palming the cell phone, I turned over while slipping it in the back of my waistband as I got to my feet.

Her gaze flickered to my sofa and she said, "Get it all."

I put the files in a pile, then unplugged my laptop's power cord. As I closed it, I hit the Print Screen key and hoped beyond hope that she wouldn't hear the wireless printer in the bedroom. "Where are you taking me?" I asked.

"A three-hour cruise," she replied sarcastically. "I'd prefer to shoot you right here, right now, but then the cops would get suspicious. Melinda had an intruder last night, and tonight you have one? Nope, they'd never buy it."

Arms loaded, I looked back at Sam's bleeding, motionless body and felt the warmth of tears streaking down my face and throat.

She poked me hard in the back with the gun as we left my apartment. "Across the lot," she said, hitting me on the right side of the head toward the familiar car. It belonged to Melinda.

"I would have opened the door for Melinda. You didn't need to use Sam, and you didn't need to kill him," I said loudly.

"Keep your voice down," she snapped, giving me another, harder whack in the head.

I felt something warm trickle into my ear, then down my neck into my shirt. Jill popped the trunk and directed me to put the files and my laptop inside Melinda's Lincoln.

With the gun still trained on me, she pulled a roll of duct tape out and said, "Wrists."

As if praying, which I was, I stood still while she secured my hands. Next, she led me to the passenger's side and shoved me into the front seat. The cell phone jabbed me, then slipped lower so that I was nearly sitting on it.

"Legs."

I complied, and she wrapped the tape several times around my ankles.

I had a dull sting where she'd pistol-whipped me, but any pain was lost when I thought about poor Sam. I cried softly as she drove onto the highway and turned toward Palm Beach.

"Shut up. What did you think would happen with all your nosing around?"

"I didn't think you'd kill my friend."

"Thanks to you, I've had a busy night. Luckily," she began as she pulled the cap off and her hair tumbled over her shoulders, "Martin is on a business trip, so I didn't have to wait to take care of loose ends."

"I'm not a loose end," I said. "I'm a person. A person who'll be missed. There's nothing you can do to me that won't cause suspicion."

"Melinda's been saying the same thing to me for years. God, she was a pain in my ass."

"Was?"

"Poor thing took a header down her staircase earlier tonight. Hit the marble and, well, her skull cracked like a coconut. The maid'll find her day after tomorrow. I'll get a call, pretend to be crushed. Host a lovely funeral for her, and no one will be any the wiser. And for the first time since Martin asked me to marry him, I won't be paying that bitch blackmail."

She drove one-handed, the gun lying in her lap in a loose grip. My eyes flickered between Jill's profile and the weapon. Testing the tape, I found it snug. I could move my fingers some, but I doubted I could get a grip on the gun and reverse our roles.

"Because of the robberies or because you killed the real Terri?"

"Very good," Jill said. "Except Carlos killed Terri."

"At your request, I'm sure. Ow!" She hit me in the mouth. When I tasted blood, I knew she'd split my lip.

"I also requested he get rid of the body after Melinda went to bed, so the moron stuck it in the garage freezer."

I remembered the rusty outline I'd seen on the floor at the beach house and realized it was a perfect shape for a chest freezer.

"The idiot gets up the next morning and the freezer is empty. Only he didn't tell me immediately."

"Melinda found the body?"

"Yep. She surprised me by moving it to a storage unit. She kept it there all these years, taunting me from time to time. It was her way of leveling the playing field."

"What playing field?"

"You're awfully nosey for someone who won't be alive long enough to share any of this."

I braced for another lash from the gun. Thankfully it didn't come. "I just want to know why I'm dying."

"Fair enough," Jill said as she stopped at the light at the base of the bridge to Palm Beach.

I considered reaching for the door handle, but in the amount of time it would take me to roll out of the car, she could empty the gun on me.

"So I'm thirteen or fourteen, and I meet one of the rich guys on the beach. Home from Yale for spring break. He takes me to his house. We take care of business, and on my way out, I wrap a vase in my beach towel. Melinda found it. At first, I thought she was going to turn me in. Instead, she flips the vase upside down and shows me the marks. It wasn't very valuable, just a decorator item. Then she hits me and says if I'm going to steal, I should steal the good stuff."

"Melinda trained you?"

"Me, then Terri, and eventually Carlos. Terri and I were pretty tight for a while. We shared everything. Secrets, guys, drugs. We'd spend hours in our room, eating red-rope licorice and comparing notes. Terri had a real eye for antiques and art. She always brought back the big-ticket items."

"It's good to have a skill."

This time I did get hit on the arm, right on the stitches, which instantly split. I guess my adrenaline was pumping, because I didn't feel any pain.

As soon as she crossed the bridge, she turned left

on Australian and shrugged off the big shirt, revealing a perfectly appropriate-for-sailing top with gold and navy trim. Obviously, we weren't headed for the Gilmore estate.

"If she was so good, why'd you and Carlos kill her?"

"She met this guy, found Jesus and a conscience. Carlos stole a medallion we couldn't pawn. Terri found it and was going to go to the cops. We were clearing thirty to forty grand a month, sometimes more. Especially after we learned to break in. Before that, we had to wait until one of us got inside one of the homes. I can't tell you how much sex I had just to have an opportunity to do recon on a mansion. We'd wait a few days or weeks, until we knew the house would be empty, then stroll down the beach, right up to the home. A few seconds and snap, we were in, out, and back home before those rich bastards knew what hit them. Once we aged out, I didn't give the robberies a second thought. Carlos went up to North Carolina for a family reunion, and then the dumb bastard nearly raped his own cousin. I figured he'd rot in jail. When I went to work at Gilmore, I had to use Terri's Social Security number, since she didn't have a criminal record and I did. Next thing I know, Melinda crops up. The minute Martin and I started dating, she tells me she's still got Terri's corpse and the only way she'll stay quiet is if I share the wealth.

"I didn't hear from her for a while, and then I think it was like ten seconds after Martin proposed before greedy Melinda demanded a house."

"The estate in Jonathan's Landing."

"Yeah. Only I refused to do it unless she gave me Terri's bones. She did, then once again, I asked Carlos to take care of it, and what does he do? Puts her *back* in the Chilian Avenue house."

"Good help is hard to find," I murmured.

"You don't know when to shut up, do you?" she asked as she whacked me so hard on the head that I saw stars.

Jill pulled into the Town Docks. My heart leaped when I saw a man up ahead. Jill cursed when she saw him too, and she shoved my head down so she could wave to the guy, who was unloading a cooler. If I raised my head or screamed, I knew she'd shoot me immediately. Weighing that against the option of living for a while longer, I didn't scream.

We drove all the way down to the last slip, where a massive yacht was moored next to a smaller—in comparison—sailboat.

"Slide this way," she instructed, grabbing my hair and pulling me across the console. She held me there for a few seconds. Even though it was still before dawn, the marina was well lit, and I suspected she didn't want to run the risk of being seen with me.

Another yank and my eyes watered as I nearly fell out of the car onto the gravel parking lot. She'd parallel parked, so it was pretty easy for her to drag me onto the smaller of the two boats.

I felt the phone slipping down the inside of my pants leg as I hopped along. By some miracle, I bent my leg enough to trap the phone behind my knee as we went aboard the boat. Thanks to the streetlamp, I read the name painted on a life preserver mounted on the deck of the boat. *Checkout.*

In the dim light on the waterside of the boat, Jill opened a wide bench and tossed life jackets onto the deck. Then she tossed me inside. I smelled wood cleaner, the ocean, brass polish, and my own desperation. Even with the sound of water lapping, I heard the snap of the padlock close.

I listened for footsteps, and when I was as sure as I could be that Jill had gone to prepare to take the boat out to sea, I grabbed my pants leg with my bound hands and jerked until I heard and felt my jeans pull free of the tape around my ankles.

I started to sweat as I bent and contorted in the tight space, furiously trying to get to the phone. It took some doing, but I eased the lump down until my fingertips felt the antennae. My back and legs cramped as I slid the phone out, careful not to let it catch on the adhesive on my ankles or, worse, fall out of my limited reach.

Tears of relief, fear, and frustration poured unchecked from my eyes when I finally succeeded.

Disentangling my body, I used the pad of my thumb to dial 911 as I rolled onto my back. As quietly as possible, I started to tell the operator everything and that I needed immediate help. I was nearly finished when the engines roared to life and I heard the hum of the rotary blades below the waterline.

"I'm on the *Checkout*," I told the operator again. "She's about to pull away from the Palm Beach Town Docks. It's a sailboat, but it has a motor."

"I've alerted the Coast Guard and the local police," the operator calmly said. "Just keep talking to me, Finley."

"We're moving."

"Can you tell which direction you're headed?"

"No. You have to send an ambulance to my apartment. She killed my friend."

"Tell me the address."

I did, gulping back sobs between each word.

"Help is already there," she said. "One of your neighbors called in a gunshot report almost twenty minutes ago."

God bless Mrs. Hemshaw. "Did they find Sam?"

Before she could answer, I heard the approach of sirens. The engine revved, the boat lurched, and I heard footfalls running toward me.

I was so scared that I dropped the phone and squeezed my eyes shut, fully expecting bullets to come splintering through the wood.

Instead, the lock jiggled, the top flew open, and a crazed-looking Jill grabbed me by one leg and one elbow, lifted me as if I weighed nothing, and tossed me into the dark, diesel-scented water.

*The best gifts in life aren't free; you just
have to work harder to find the price tag.*

twenty

I SWALLOWED MY FIRST GULP of oily salt water
as I kicked my legs to keep from drowning. I
was choking, coughing, and scared. There was
enough light from approaching police cars for me
to make out the *Checkout* racing out of the marina.
I opened my mouth to yell for help, but the wake
of a wave slapped me in the face and forced a second painful rush of water into my lungs.

I heard a splash in the distance, but my vision was
blurred from tears, water, and my tenuous battle to
remain conscious. The water rushed into my mouth,
and my nose and my chest burned from holding what
little breath remained in my body. I was blinded when
I sank lower. Just as I tried to process the fact that I
was going to die, I felt someone grab my waist and
shove me back to the surface. I coughed and sput-
tered, then let my head fall back against the solid body
of my savior. I would have thanked him, but my head
swirled into complete blackness.

Fat Chance

◆ ◆ ◆

"You're not making it up?" I asked Becky as she held my hand while Doctor Adair, my new cosmetic surgeon best friend, continued to put stitches above my ear.

She smiled and made a cross over her heart. "I swear to God. I'll take you to see him as soon as all your cuts are cleaned and tended. The weird part is," she began with a little laugh, "Sam got shot in the head, but you look worse."

"But he's not dead or brain injured or—"

"A .22?" Dr Adair asked.

"Yes," Becky answered.

I tried to look at the doctor and was instantly admonished to keep still unless I wanted a big scar. "How did you guess that?"

"If you're going to get shot in the head, that's the best caliber possible. It's a small projectile."

"But it still went into his face," I argued.

"I haven't seen the patient, but my guess is it entered the skull at just the right angle to clip the occipital bone, and that's enough to change the direction. Then the bullet travels around the skull instead of through it. Still, your friend was mighty lucky."

If he wasn't trussing me closed like a turkey, I probably would have kissed the doctor for explaining how Sam had survived with a relatively minor injury.

I, on the other hand, had stitches in my swollen

lip; stitches on both sides of my head; and a do-over set on my arm. My hair was damp and matted, except for the two places where the doctor had shaved it off to sew me up. I wasn't in any huge hurry to look in the mirror.

"What about Jill?" I asked as the doctor finished up.

Becky gave my hand a squeeze. "Last report I saw, the boat was surrounded by Coast Guard cutters. Looked a lot like Kennedy's blockade during the Cuban missile crisis."

"I don't think Jill will back down," I said.

"I don't much care," Becky said. "Is Finley free to go?"

"I'm off to write the discharge orders now. You will finish all of the antibiotic and use the ointment, and you need someone to check on you every hour for the next twenty-four hours. I stitched you up, but that has no effect on the concussion."

"We've got her covered," Becky insisted.

"Thank you," I said to the doctor, hearing the speech impediment as my numb lip continued to swell.

Nearly an hour passed before I was wheeled up to post-op to see Sam. He had gauze wrapped around his head, an IV in his arm, and his eyes were bruised and closed. Mine teared just remembering the sound of the shot and the acrid smell of gunpowder and burned flesh.

Liv was in a chair next to his bed, thumbing through a magazine. Jane was on the opposite side, resting her head on her folded arms at the edge of the bed.

Machines blipped and bleeped all around me as Liv stood to allow Becky to maneuver me in my wheelchair to his bedside. I ran the back of my hand along his cheek. There was something very comforting about the feel of his warm skin.

His eyes fluttered open, and he swallowed loudly. "I've . . . never . . . seen . . . so . . . hideous," he struggled to say.

I lifted my hand to cover my mouth. "I'm so sorry," I choked, tears streaking down my face.

"What?" he said, struggling and obviously in some sort of narcotic haze.

"If it wasn't for me, you'd never have been hurt."

He reached up and grabbed at my hand. "Crazy woman shot me."

"I stole your phone."

"Now that," he said, his voice scratchy, "you'll have to make up to me."

"I will."

"Go home. Sleep. I'm fine."

"You are a medical miracle," I corrected. "I'm sure they want to check you over thoroughly."

Becky came around to give him a kiss. "I left everyone's phone numbers with the nurse. You need anything—*anything*—and we're here for you."

Liv and Jane kissed him too. I couldn't; my puffy lip wasn't exactly well-suited for kissing.

As I predicted, Jill Burkett did not cooperate. Instead, with news helicopters buzzing overhead, the boat surrounded by about twenty-plus boats and ships, she stood on the deck, stuck the gun in her mouth, and tumbled into the water.

Me? I'd have left her for chum, but the authorities retrieved her body, ending the one-woman murder spree.

That was almost six weeks ago, but I still had the occasional nightmare and fading scars to remind me of my ordeal. Grudgingly, Vain Dane—with a push from Tony, according to the prevailing gossip—allowed me to work from home until Dr. Adair removed my stitches. It worked out okay, since my friends worked out a shift system so neither I nor Sam, once he got home from the hospital, was left alone.

Sam went back to work after a few weeks. And he started dating the nurse from the ER once he got back on his feet.

My mother came by when she returned from visiting my sister. Her main concern seemed to be that my scars wouldn't be healed by Lisa's wedding. Oh, and she gave me a bill from Total Plant Replacements, since all the inconsiderate traitors in her apartment died due to my abject neglect . . . even though said neglect happened while I was recuperating from a near-fatal attack.

Other than going to the grocery store in the wee hours of the morning—in the new, champagne-pink-colored Mercedes CLK convertible I leased—I laid low until my lip was back to semi-normal and I'd found a way to hide the re-growth where my hair had been shaved.

Patrick made the mistake of dropping by when Jane, who worked out religiously, was on duty. She was quite specific about which orifice he should shove his flowers up and gave him ten seconds to go away or she'd be the one doing the shoving.

Jane visited and made sure I kept current on my scheduled payments to Harold so the remodel stayed on track.

Tony sent flowers and a card. Or more accurately, his secretary arranged for the flowers. I knew this because the card was typed and I recognized the arrangement. It was the classic Dane, Lieberman employee floral spray. Tulips and daisies in a brightly colored vase. I'd probably sent a hundred of them in my years at the firm. I should have been grateful that they acknowledged my ordeal, but a small part of me was a little disappointed that Tony didn't drop by. Not that I wanted him to see me at my worst; it just meant that I'd misread the signals and he wasn't interested in me after all.

The most notably absent person was Liam. Not a call, not a card, not a peep. Guess he wasn't that into me either.

Tonight everything would change. Becky and Liv were taking me out to dinner to celebrate my return to visually normal. Jane was going to try to make it as soon as she finished a couldn't-get-out-of meeting.

In addition to the car, I'd splurged on a pale pink, sleeveless BCBG dress, with a ruffled collar and the most adorable pair of Zanotti heeled sandals accented with light pink crystals—to-me-from-me gifts for passing my online continuing ed course with the highest final grade in the class.

Because the ruffle was such a focal point, I slipped on a pair of gold hoops and added some bangles to each wrist. Deep fuchsia lipstick obliterated the scar, and two discreet hairpins ensured that the scars on my head were concealed.

I couldn't do anything but apply bronzer to the scar on my arm, but I was thrilled to see that the one above my knee was so faint that it was impossible to see.

When Becky came to the door promptly at seven on Saturday night, I was ready, except for switching purses to the oversized leather clutch I'd scored on an eBay auction.

"Ready to rejoin society?" Becky asked.

"I am. You look great," I said as I locked my apartment door behind us. In theory, I had another week until I moved into the beach house, but on a stealthy nighttime visit two weeks ago, I didn't see how that could happen. I'd worry about that next week. "New skirt?" I asked.

It was silk and in her signature shade of rust, with a leg-baring slit on one side. She paired it with a simple cream shell and lots of big, clunky, amber jewelry. I offered to drive. Wanted to, actually; it was a lot of fun to sit behind the wheel of the two-seater Mercedes, but Becky insisted that we take her environmentally friendly hybrid. That made her the designated driver, which was actually a plus for me.

"Marks?" I asked. The City Place restaurant was a spot we reserved for very special occasions.

"Nope. We found a new place."

"Where?"

"Chill. It's a surprise."

When she headed east on Okeechobee, I figured we were going whole hog and dining at one of the restaurants at The Breakers. But then she passed The Breakers and sped to Chilian Avenue.

"Oh. My. God," was all I could manage when I saw my house. Even before I got to the front door, I saw window treatments.

Liv greeted me with a big smile and a glass of champagne. "Welcome to Chez Tanner."

My jaw dropped. Sam, Liv, and Jane—the cagey liar—were inside, along with every stick of furniture. Every piece of art was hung. Every window was dressed. Fresh flowers adorned the table, and candles floated in the pool. Something wonderful was in the oven, filling the kitchen with the scents of thyme and lemon. The dining room table was set for six, and I was honestly stunned speechless by the transformation.

I went from room to room, *oohhh*ing and *ahhh*ing. It was perfect. I ran to Sam and gave him a big hug. "When did you do all this?"

"I am a limitless well of talent."

"You are," I agreed. "You shouldn't have been working so hard," I said as I gently ran my fingertip over his fading scar.

"I had help," he said.

I turned to my friends and smiled. They all shook their heads. Becky said, "Not us."

As if choreographed, the doorbell chimed. I liked it. It sounded expensive. I assumed it was Sam's new boyfriend.

I assumed wrong. Liam walked in, carrying a cake box. After the long absence, I felt as though I was being introduced to his handsome face for the first time. It was a special moment.

"Sorry I'm late. I had a thing."

Thing? Moment over.

"BECKY COULD HAVE DRIVEN me home," I said as I sat in the passenger's seat of Liam's Mustang, raising my voice to be heard over the rattle coming from some loose part. "My apartment is completely out of your way."

Even though it was dark, the dashboard provided enough illumination for me to see the sexy half smile and amused lines on his profile. "It's not a thing."

"Everything with you is a thing," I said as I nervously twisted my bracelets.

"Try, 'Thank you, Liam, I appreciate the ride home.'"

I sighed. "Thank you for the ride home. And thank you for having my dress cleaned and sent to my apartment."

"You already thanked me. You sent me a card. The scented pink envelope was a first for me."

"Mocking my stationery? Fine. Next time I'll scribble something on a napkin."

He laughed, which only seemed to pour fuel on

the conflicting emotions smoldering in my stomach. I twisted my bracelets harder and faster, relaxing only when he reached the parking lot in front of my apartment.

I tugged on the antiquated handle and stepped clear of the sputtering, I-don't-want-to-die engine, but not before it belched a big cloud of pungent blue smoke.

"You don't need to walk me to the door," I said, feeling the heat of his presence behind me as I nervously fumbled with the key.

Liam reached over my shoulder, gently covered my hand, and easily guided the key into the slot.

The door swung open, but I didn't move. My pulse quickened, and I could only manage small, uneven breaths. His body was against mine. I could smell him, feel him, and knew that all I had to do was turn around and all these months of wanting and wondering would finally end.

The better angels in my brain tried to shout down the needy demons urging me to go for it. As the seconds passed and I heard and felt his ragged breathing, I knew the demons had won.

Turning my hand in Liam's palm, I laced my fingers with his and wordlessly pulled him inside. The door closed and he turned me in his arms. "This is a lot better than the last time I had you in my arms."

"That was months ago," I said, sure he could feel my heart pounding in my chest.

He pulled back slightly and eyed me suspiciously. "You don't know, do you?"

"Know what?"

"Forget it," he said as his head dipped toward mine.

I raised my hand and placed a finger against his warm, slightly parted lips. "Tell me."

He shrugged and smiled. Not his normal smile, but an almost bashful one that really pushed me off balance. "It's nothing."

"No, it isn't. As soon as you tell me, we can get back to the kissing part."

Bashful melted into sly and sexy in the blink of an eye. "The last time you were in my arms was after Jill tossed you into the ocean."

The blinking of my eyes became literal instead of figurative. "I thought Fire and Rescue . . ."

He was shaking his head. "I heard about the shooting at your apartment and raced over. Sam's pulse was strong, and he tried to tell me something about a woman before he passed out."

"You left him there?"

"I called an ambulance. I found your list in the bedroom printer and called the cops, thinking Melinda had you. But she'd already been found dead, so I had the Palm Beach police run up to the Gilmore mansion. No one home but the help."

"You went to a lot of trouble."

He ran his finger along my chin. "You were in a lot of trouble."

"How did you get from the mansion to the marina? What clued you in?"

"Some guy loading bait onto his boat called the

cops to report seeing a woman drag another woman onto the *Checkout*. I heard that on the scanner and figured Gilmore Supermarkets and a boat named *Checkout* had to be a connection."

"You came for me," I said, almost teary.

"Right, so can we get back to the kissing part now?"

I reached around his neck and practically dragged his mouth to mine. He kissed me hungrily.

I was kind of aware that my back was against the wall. I was totally aware that his tongue was toying with the seam of my lips and his hands bracketed my waist. Even with heels, I pressed up on my toes, wanting, *no*, needing to feel every inch of him.

His thumbs were making dizzying little circles against my rib cage. Moving higher and higher until his palm tested the weight of my breast.

I moaned against his mouth and slipped my fingers between us, searching for a belt, buttons, anything that would start the process of separating him from his clothes.

His mouth moved from my lips. My skin felt flushed as the sense of urgency kept building and building, turning my insides into something molten and dangerous. I found the bottom button of his shirt and twisted it free. My hand snaked higher, over silky hair and cement-hard muscle.

Our eyes met for a minute, then he reached up, flicked open my earring, and tossed it to the ground. Using his teeth, he drew my lobe into his mouth while his hot breath tickled my ear. His hand wandered off my breast to the front of my dress. He made quick work of the closure and stepped back as he pushed the edges apart.

His gaze scorched my skin before he dipped his head and planted a thousand little kisses just above the lacey edge of my bra.

"No fair," I said, my trembling fingers unable to manage the buttons.

"Very fair," he said, running the tip of his tongue through the valley between my breasts. "If I let you touch me, this won't last very long."

"It doesn't have to," I insisted, grabbing his waistband and letting my fingers slip inside.

"Yeah, it does," he countered.

My heart was pounding so hard I thought it might rupture. Pounding, pounding . . . no, *knocking*.

Somewhere, my sex-fogged brain connected enough neurons to realize someone was knocking at my door. Tugging my dress closed, I nuzzled his neck and whispered, "It's probably my neighbor, Mrs. Hemshaw. I can get rid of her in a half second."

Liam closed his eyes, and his head fell back as he raised his hands so I could duck under his arm. I quickly redid some of my buttons and called, "Just a minute." Liam grabbed me around the waist and nuzzled and nibbled my neck. "I can't button buttons when you do that."

"I know."

Pushing his head away from me, I went to the door and opened it. "Sorry, I—*Patrick!*"

His smile ebbed when he saw my disheveled appearance. It completely disappeared when he looked past me and saw Liam.

"What are you doing here?" I snapped.

"Don't be mad," he said, returning his gaze to me. "I left my wife."

"I'm sorry," I said, genuinely meaning it. "But that doesn't change anything."

"I know," he agreed as he pushed his blond hair off his forehead. "I was hoping this would."

His arm came out from behind his back. I recognized the gold crown on the red square box. Rolex. Quickly, because he surely knew he had my full attention, he flipped open the top. Nestled inside was the watch of my dreams: the Ladies' Datejust with the pink oyster face surrounded by diamonds.

I swallowed both my shock and the urge to reach out and touch it.

"Patrick," I stammered.

"Take it, Fin. We both know it's the one thing you want most in the world. I want you to have it. I want you to have everything. And I want to be the man who gives it to you. Tell him to leave."

I was distracted counting the diamonds that circled the watch face. Shaking my head to clear my thoughts, I said, "Who? Liam? No!"

"Liam, yes," Liam mocked as he brushed past me.

I practically shoved Patrick to the ground to follow Liam. God, if he fell I hoped he didn't scratch the crystal.

"Wait!" I called as Liam reached the Mustang.

He had the door open and was standing behind

it, using it like a shield. I expected him to be angry, scowling, irritated, frustrated, possibly even hurt. I did not expect the calm, reasonable smile. "What?" he asked.

"I don't want you to leave."

"Irrelevant."

"It is my call. Patrick is my past. *You* saved my life."

"And I helped Harold finish your house on time and under budget."

I had a death grip on the door. "Thank you for that. For everything. Please, *please* don't leave like this. I want you to stay."

He leaned back as he slipped behind the wheel. "I want that too."

I threw my hands up. "Then get out of the car."

He hooked his thumb in Patrick's direction. "Seems like you and that guy have some unfinished business. I would be one selfish bastard to come between you and the thing you want most in the world."

Mustering all my nerve and choking on all my pride, I said, "No. I want you."

"It's good to want things," he replied, his palm reaching up and cupping my cheek. "Don't get all flustered. After all, I saved your life. I think that means you have to grant me three wishes."

"Staying is not one of your wishes?"

"It's all of my wishes," he said matter-of-factly as he started the engine. "And I'll be collecting soon."

I watched him drive off, crushing my libido under his balding tires. "Not if I collect first!"

acknowledgments

THANKS SO MUCH TO Maggie Crawford—a great editor I've learned volumes from already. Donna Bagdasarian and Maria Carvainis, great agents who remind me to be positive and for working so tirelessly on my behalf. And for Mo Bishop, Shirley Leonard, and all the folks at Mo's Danceworks who keep my daughter occupied so I can write.

Pocket Books proudly presents

SLIGHTLY IRREGULAR

THE STYLISHLY ENTERTAINING NEW
FINLEY ANDERSON TANNER NOVEL BY
RHONDA POLLERO

TURN THE PAGE FOR A PREVIEW OF

SLIGHTLY IRREGULAR. . . .

Coming in trade paperback from Pocket Books

The worst lies are the ones we tell ourselves.

one

FREEDOM WAS THREE HOURS away. Technically, two hours and fifty-six minutes of work time; two minutes to go through the motions of straightening my office—we have a cleaning crew and it isn't me—then two minutes to gather my belongings, hit the elevator, stroll through the lobby, walk out the front door, and insert my key into the shiny handle of my practically brand-new champagne-pink Mercedes CLK convertible. Since it was Friday, I might even consider shaving a few minutes off my exit plan.

Friday was the one day of the week when Maudlin Margaret Ford, the passive-aggressive firm receptionist (extra order of aggressive on the side), did not get her feathers in a twist when I ducked out a few minutes early. Any other day of the week and she'd be sounding the alert to the senior partner of Dane, Lieberman, and Zarnowski. Technically speaking, it was now Dane, Lieberman, Zarnowski, and Caprelli.

It's a small but prestigious law firm just off Clematis Street in West Palm Beach. Until a few weeks ago, I was exclusively an estates and trusts paralegal.

The elevator door finally blinked open and I stepped inside the small compartment, then pressed the number four. I'd been summoned to the executive offices. A summons used to have me shaking in my Jimmy Choos but not so much now that Tony Caprelli occupied one of the partner's suites.

I sighed and fiddled with the cloisonné clip holding my blond hair off my face. Before leaving my office, I'd carefully checked my lipstick—reapplied and then added some Stila gloss—and smoothed the front of my vintage Lilly Pulitzer dress. The circa 1960, pale periwinkle and spring green dress with ribbon and lace accents was—if I did say so myself—one of my finest bargain moments. I'd come across it on antiquedressing.com. Talk about a find! Classic Lilly with the metal zippers and original labels is well beyond my meager means, which had been made more meager by the hefty mortgage I was now carrying and my mostly maxed-out credit cards. The catch? The hem was faded and stained. A disaster for most women but since I'm just shy of five-four, it was a snap for me to have the seamstress at my cleaner's turn up a new hem without destroying the line of the dress.

Draped over my shoulders was a white cashmere sweater. It accentuated the cute white birds in the dress's print, and since the dress was sleeveless, the sweater saved me from turning into a cube of ice. Florida isn't the sunshine state, it's the over-air-conditioned state.

I had just enough time to check my reflection in the elevator's polished mirrored walls. I was wearing one of my favorite pairs of wedge sandals, white patent with seriously cute bows right at the peep-toe. My pedicure had held up nicely, the dark pink polish as shiny as my glossed lips. I couldn't help but smile. I'd turned bargain hunting into an art. Short of an inspection by Tim Gunn and Heidi Klum, no one would ever know that I was a walking, talking tribute to gently worn, factory damaged, and slightly irregular. And I wanted to keep it that way.

The elevator opened into a circular lobby where The—that's with a capital *T*—secretary sat sentry at her desk. She glanced up at me over the tops of her reading glasses, then pressed the button on her Bluetooth.

"Miss Tanner is here to see you," she said. "Yes, thank you." She lifted her head and met my gaze. "You may go in."

I quelled the urge to salute her; c'mon, the woman was so stiff she'd be a natural at Buckingham Palace.

"Thank you," I said, and headed toward Tony's office.

My heart rate climbed with each step. Tony had joined the firm a little more than a month ago and in that short amount of time, he'd generated quite a bit of interoffice buzz. While everyone else was buzzing, I was actually training to work at his side.

No, I didn't like the continuing education classes on litigation, evidence, witness preparation, or police procedure. I didn't like balancing all of that while renovating my new cottage. But I did like Tony. And not in an employer-employee way. The guy was hot. And polished and, well, perfect. He was more than six feet tall with dark brown hair and eyes the color of rich imported chocolates. He wore tailored suits, monogrammed shirts, and a top-of-the-line Rolex. A perfect man with a perfect watch. What more could a woman want in a man?

A date.

I sucked in a breath and let it out slowly. Therein lies the rub. I'm almost thirty, not thirteen. I know when a man is interested in me. I've caught Tony watching me when he thought I wasn't looking. His fingers have brushed the back of my hand a few too many times for it to be accidental. He's interested. But he's also my boss. This is yet another example of why dating sucks.

Life really isn't fair when I can re-create an iconic fashion statement from the 1960s but I can't seem to find a way to let my boss know I'd like to go out with him. There are times when sexual harassment laws totally get in the way of good old-fashioned get-to-know-you dating.

I considered slipping into the ladies' room quickly, painting "ask me out" in liner on my lids and then spending the whole meeting with my eyes closed. Naw, too desperate.

Then again, I am on the precipice of desperation. Since I'd dumped Patrick after wasting two years of my life on him, the only men in my life were the ex-convict who was still doing some minor finishing work on my house and Sam, my dear, dear friend who had worse luck with men than I did. And Liam.

Kinda.

A shiver ran along my spine as I conjured his image. Liam McGarrity is everything I never wanted in a man. Very little polish and way too much testosterone. But one look into those piercing blue eyes and I start to think I can rework him into the man of my dreams. The practical part of me knows better. The libidinous part of me doesn't care. Liam should have to wear a warning label around his neck—Danger! Man Needing Work. Keep out!

The only way I've been able to avoid the lure of those incredible blue eyes has been to keep my distance and screen my calls. So far, I've been successful. Who knows what will happen the next time we have to work together. And that time will come. Liam does a lot of the PI work for my firm. I won't be able to avoid him forever. I'll worry about that when—

"Sorry," Tony said as his hands grabbed my shoulders, keeping me from falling back on my butt.

He smelled good, so good that for a second his cologne rendered me mute. Or maybe it was the feel of his large hands gripping my arms. My sweater had slipped so the heat from his hands was against the bare skin of my arms.

"Is everything okay?" he asked.

"Yeah," I said, stepping back so I could pick up my sweater and the pad I'd dropped when I'd accidentally run right into him. "Sorry, I must have zoned out for a minute."

"Not a problem," Tony said, stepping aside to allow me to enter his office first. He looked good enough to eat in a dark, well-cut suit and crisp creamy shirt and dark blue tie. Very *GQ*. Very much the opposite of shaggy, rumpled Liam. Both men are sexy, but they're polar opposites in appearance. Both men, however, sent my pulse racing and my libido into hyperdrive.

Tony had a great office. Used to belong to Mr. Zarnowski but he was mostly retired now. Too bad for me. Zarnowski had hired me. He liked me. Unlike Vain Victor Dane, the managing partner who always treated me like some annoying insect bite he couldn't scratch but couldn't ignore. Or Ellen Lieberman. The woman who thinks I'm a slacker since I didn't go to law school. She seems to forget that I didn't go because I didn't *want* to go. I never wanted to be like her—working seventy hours a week with no life. And in her case, no access to proper hair care.

I started to clear a spot for myself on Tony's couch when he reached out and placed his hand over mine. "No need. This is going to be quick."

Turning slightly so we were face-to-face, I smiled up at him. "What do you need?"

"You."

The room spun for a second as my brain tried to wrap itself around that word. "E-excuse me?"

He took my hands in his and gave a gentle squeeze. "I have tickets to *The Magic Flute* tomorrow night."

"Nothing like a Saturday night with Mozart."

Humor flashed in his eyes and when he smiled, I was treated to a look at the near-legendary dimple on his right cheek. "Right, your mother was a singer with the Met."

"Yes she was. Now she's a professional widow, divorcée, or bride-to-be, depending on when you catch her."

"Sorry?"

I waved my hand. "Bad joke. My mother is very fond of getting married. She just has a problem *staying* married. That said, she made sure my sister and I were exposed to opera from birth."

"How do you feel about *The Magic Flute*?"

"I liked the Kenneth Branagh movie version. Very stylized, like a Target commercial."

Tony glanced at his watch. "I've got to be at the courthouse in ten minutes. Is there any chance you're free tomorrow night? I know it's short notice but—"

"Short notice is fine."

"Great," he said on a relieved rush of breath. "Can you be at my place at about six?"

"Absolutely."

Tony walked around to his desk and crammed some files into his briefcase. As he came around again, he gave my hand a squeeze. "Thanks, Finley. See you tomorrow night."

"At six," I called as he left in such a hurry that the collection of drawings piled on his desk fluttered.

I picked up the one that fell on the floor and placed it in the center of his desk. It was a pencil sketch of some sort of bird, but I didn't pay much attention to it. My entire brain was fixated on the knowledge that tomorrow night would be my first date with Tony.

"JUST LIKE THAT?" BECKY asked the next morning when we met at the Gardens Mall. "No preamble, nothing?"

"Preamble?" I said, laughing. "He wasn't writing the Constitution, he was asking me out on a date."

We were standing outside Crate and Barrel, waiting for our friends Liv and Jane.

Becky and I have been friends since college. We graduated from Emory together, then Becky went on to law school while I came back to Palm Beach and went to work for Dane, Lieberman. Becky joined the firm after graduation and I was thrilled to have my best friend back in town.

Becky is a smart, savvy attorney and clients love her. Male clients especially love her. For good reason. She's tall, attractive, and always put together. She's on a rust-orange-amber binge right now. She wears high-end, if conservative, clothing in various shades of rust or brown to set-off her reddish auburn hair. She tones down the tailored look with fun, funky jewelry.

Jane, on the other hand, doesn't tone down anything. Even now when she was fifty yards away in the parking lot I knew it was her. I met Jane at a two-for-one gym promotion. We pretended to be friends to get the better price. The friendship lasted. My membership at the gym did not. Jane exudes sensuality. She can't help it. She has long, dark hair and a toned body that most women would kill for. Everything up top is cut low and everything down below is hiked high. She's an accountant, though to anyone getting his first glance at her, he'd probably think she was one of the Pussycat Dolls.

Liv was with her, handing something—most likely a generous tip—to the valet attendant. Liv makes the rest of us look like trolls. She's a very successful event planner. Almost no one hosts a party or a wedding on Palm Beach without hiring Concierge Plus to handle the planning. Liv is an exotic-looking woman. She has eyes that match the ocean, clear turquoise, and midnight black hair. Kinda like a present-day Cleopatra. The biggest perk in knowing her—aside from the fact that she's a great friend—is she can slip us into a lot of the über-rich parties on the island.

Once the four of us were together, we made a mandatory swing through Starbucks. I was so excited about my first date with Tony that I'd had a hard time sleeping. I needed caffeine and a good concealer.

"He just asked you out of the blue?" Liv asked as we waited for our coffees to be placed under the pick-up sign.

"Geez! Why does that seem to surprise all of you?" I asked, minorly irritated.

Jane passed me my skinny vanilla latte. "Men aren't usually that spontaneous. Think about it, Finley. He emailed asking you to come to his office so he could ask you out? Why not go to your office?"

"Or for that matter," Becky said, "why run the risk of asking you out at work?"

"What risk?" I asked.

Becky rolled her eyes. "We all know there was no risk but Tony didn't know that. A smart guy—and he is that—would call you after work so there could be no misunderstandings."

"Like?"

Becky took a long sip of her chai tea. "Like his asking you out while at work could be construed as sexual harassment. You could claim you felt pressured to go out with him because he's your boss."

"That's ridiculous."

Becky's green eyes bore into me. "You'd better hope Dane and Lieberman don't hear about this. Especially Ellen. She'll freak out if she thinks he's risking creating a hostile work environment."

"Anybody ever tell you you're a major buzz kill?" I asked.

Becky raised her hands. "Sorry I mentioned it."

"Okay," I said, happy to have that bit of unpleasantness quashed. "It's got to be black. I'm thinking something subtle but I don't want to look like a mortician. Shoes and a clutch."

"Um," Jane began cautiously, "where does this fit into the budget we did for you?"

"Whatever I get for tonight, I'll wear to the rehearsal dinner. That cuts the cost-per-wearing in half right there."

"How many little black dresses do you have in your closet?" Liv asked.

"Not as many as you, and besides, classic never goes out of style."

"And Finley never gets out of debt," Jane grumbled.

I looped my arm though hers. "Lighten up. I'm splurging this once, then I promise to return to living like mortgaged-to-the-gills-Mary. Okay?"

"You're pulling equity out of your house. You have every right to do that. I'm just telling you, in my capacity as your financial planner, what I think."

"Fine. Then be my friend, not my financial planner."

Jane smiled. "Well, in that case, I say we go to Nordy's and find you *the* perfect dress."

"And shoes," Becky said.

"And purse, and maybe some new jewelry," Liv weighed in.

Three hours and four lattes later, I had a stunning BCBG Max Azria, belted one-shoulder sheath dress. It was fitted jersey and fully lined, and according to the saleswoman, required nothing but a thong.

I'd found the perfect shoes in a matter of minutes. Stuart Weitzman peep-toe silk satin platform slingbacks with a wrapped heel. The saleswoman raced over and grabbed the matching clutch as I yanked my debit card from my wallet. I found a stunning Judith Jack double strand pendant necklace and chandelier earrings to go with my new ensemble, finishing it off with three skinny bangles.

As I drove home, I didn't have buyer's remorse so much as I had paid-full-price remorse. If Tony had given me forty-eight hours notice, I could have put something together online, and even with expedited shipping, I wouldn't have spent nearly two thousand dollars. Then again, it was worth it. If I parceled the cost between the Tony date: one thousand; and the rehearsal dinner: one thousand. I had already cut the cost in half. If I could think of another occasion to wear it, I could keep dropping the CPW—cost per wearing—down to a more reasonable number.

Who was I kidding? I looked, I liked, I bought. The *veni, vidi, vici* of shopping.

I stopped on the way home and had my polish changed and a brow wax. Add another fifty dollars to my ever-growing debt. I'd rather add to my debt than have a straggler eyebrow hair. A girl's got to have priorities.

By two thirty I was on my way over the bridge to Palm Beach. Thanks to selling my soul to the devil—that would be my mother, the only living heart donor—I owned a very modest cottage on the beach. Thanks to my friend Sam, it was a showplace. It was sleek and beachy, comfy and posh all at the same time. Handyman Harold still came by almost every day to tighten something or hammer something else, but for all intents and purposes, my home renovations were finished and stunning. And had me several hundred thousand in debt.

My mother sold me a shack. I can't wait to see her reaction when she finally decides to accept my standing invitation. She's currently back in Atlanta helping my sister get ready for her enormous wedding.

I adore my little sister and I'm happy she found the man of her dreams. Proving her dreams are amazingly dull, by the way. David Huntington St. John IV is nice enough but he's a big geek. A very rich big geek but definitely not overly interesting. Of course my mother loves him. He's rich, he's a doctor, and his family is old money. He and Lisa met on one of those Doctors Without Borders things.

I'm all for my sister's humanitarianism but do you have any idea what it's like to have to compete with a perfect sibling? Lisa went to med school. Lisa made something of her life. My mother considers me a failure. Maybe I am but on the whole, I'm a happy failure.

I lingered in my spa tub, allowing the warm water to relax my first-date tension muscles. First dates always make me tense. It's like opening a can and not knowing whether there's a diamond in the bottom or if a dozen springy fake snakes will explode out of the top.

Tony didn't impress me as the fake snake kinda guy.

I carefully applied my makeup, savoring every second of the anticipation that was building in the pit of my stomach. I wasn't looking forward to sitting through *The Magic Flute,* but imagining all the delicious ways the evening could end made the notion of sitting through opera as a vehicle for comedy more palatable.

I was really pleased when I finished dressing. The only thing that would have made it perfect would be a pink oyster-face Ladies' Datejust Rolex. Unfortunately, I didn't own one. Yet.

I was well on my way, though. Since I couldn't afford the actual watch, I'd begun collecting parts on eBay.

Grabbing a black pashmina from my closet, I took my keys and headed out to my car. It was a beautiful night but there was no way I would sacrifice my perfectly coiffed hair by putting the top down. Convertibles, lip gloss, and long hair don't mix well. I punched Tony's address into the onboard GPS and after a second, a map appeared and a cheerful male voice with a touch of a British accent began giving me instructions. Twenty minutes later I was following the signs to The Falls at Lost Lake. I wouldn't have pictured Tony as a golf course community kinda guy but as I scrolled through the keypad at the gate, I quickly came to "Caprelli" and pressed the button.

"Yes?"

"It's Finley," I said, my heart pounding in my ears.

There was a beeping sound, then the gate swung open like the mouth of an alligator.

The British voice told me to turn right at the stop sign, then Tony's house was the third one down on the left.

I pulled into the driveway and parked next to a vintage red Porsche. I'd never seen it at the office, so I figured it had to be his "fun" car. I couldn't imagine being so flush with cash that I'd have a car for work and a car for recreation, but I'm sure I could get used to it.

I tucked my keys into my clutch as I walked past the garage and up a pathway to what was easily a five-thousand-square-foot house. Like all the other homes in the community, the stucco was painted a shade of beige, in this case peachy beige—and the trim was fresh and white.

I went up one tiled step, took a deep calming breath, and then stood in front of etched glass doors as I pressed the doorbell. I mentally reminded myself not to look overly excited. Be cool and collected.

I heard a giggle just as the door swung open. I lowered my gaze and found myself looking into a pair of big chocolate brown eyes. The mini-Tony had to be his daughter, Isabella. She wore shorts and double tank tops. Her long brown hair was pulled up in a ponytail and when she smiled, I saw that she had inherited her father's dimples as well. Lucky little sucker.

"I'm Finley. Your dad is expecting me."

I heard the giggle again and looked past Isabella, expecting to find another child.

Wrong.

Very wrong.

A goddess of a woman dressed in a strapless red Prada gown came around the corner giggling into her champagne flute. Tony was right behind her, looking dapper and handsome in a tux. His eyes met mine. As he scanned me up and down, all the humor drained out of his face.

I took in his uncomfortable expression, the woman dangling from his arm, and then replayed the invitation in my head:

"Are you free Saturday night?"

"What do you need?"

"You."

"E-excuse me?"

"I have tickets to The Magic Flute *tomorrow night. Is there any chance you're free tomorrow night. I know it's short notice but—*"

"Short notice is fine."

"Great. Can you be at my place at about six?"

Ohgod, ohgod, ohgod. He'd never actually asked me out. I wasn't his date. I was the freaking *babysitter.*